THE
RELUCTANT
TRADER

David N Robinson

CROSETS PUBLISHING

Published by Crosets Publishing

THE RELUCTANT TRADER

To one or two special friends.

You know who you are . . .

Prologue

It is a meeting of four Arabs: two Saudis, one Egyptian and one Bahraini. Between the four, there is enough power, money and connections to change the political landscape across more than one continent.

The meeting has been shrouded in secrecy, the Egyptian having been escorted by means of a private elevator to the top floor of the very best suite that Bahrain's most luxurious hotel has to offer.

'We would be honoured if we could find a way to do business together,' one Saudi says to the Egyptian at length, a suitable amount of time having passed since the welcome coffee and dates have been offered and consumed. 'We envy your connections. It is our understanding, for instance, that the British prime minister and you are old friends?'

The Egyptian nods. 'We knew each other at university. In those days, we did a lot together. Some good, some which might best be forgotten.' He gives an apologetic shrug. 'Sadly, I don't have much influence over the man – he's not a client, you understand, just someone I have known for years.'

'Hasn't he recently announced his retirement? How he plans to stand aside once the European referendum is over later in the year?' It is the Bahraini speaking, his words drawing nods of agreement from the other three.

'I am glad you mention influence,' the other Saudi says, turning to look directly at the Egyptian. 'Media reports suggest there are three probable contenders to succeed the prime minister.' The Saudi clears his throat, the Egyptian waiting for the punchline. 'We hear you might have a certain amount of influence over one of them.'

The Egyptian smiles, clearer now about where the conversation might be leading.

'Put it this way, gentlemen. The person viewed by many as the front runner has been a client for many years. Someone, shall we say, with one or two items of dirty linen in his cupboards. A man who chose to entrust his laundry – and a considerable amount of money – into my care.'

The two Saudis exchange a glance.

'In that case, we have a business proposition we'd like to put to you. One that could prove extraordinarily lucrative.'

'Enlighten me.'

'We think it might be beneficial to gain periodic access to this connection of yours. All parties fully aware of the leverage you may hold, obviously, but without any of the details getting in the way.'

'You want to influence who gets into Number 10 Downing Street?'

'Oh no,' the Saudi says with a smile. 'We trust you will already be doing all you can to ensure the right person wins. All that we would like is to be able to offer a little guidance from time to time. Subtle pressure, helping to steer the new British prime minister in certain, arguably more appropriate, directions once in office.'

'In that case,' the Egyptian says, after a suitable period of reflection, 'I think we might be able to find ways of doing business together.'

Chapter 1

Monday 25ᵗʰ January 2016

Courchevel, France

Early afternoon sun streams through the windows of the restaurant at the top of Col de Loze. The sun, still low in the sky, casts long shadows despite the hour: the weak rays strong enough to raise skiers' hopes of a suntan but feeble enough to prevent all but the foolhardy from eating outside. The temperature outside is ten degrees below. Centigrade. Not as cold as the freezer. Certainly colder than the fridge.

Inside, the restaurant is packed. This is a reservations-only venue. A place where skiers turning up on spec without influence or affluence are shown the door. Adam Fraser is sitting alone at an inside table, happy to observe the eye candy that Courchevel freely provides. The in-crowd eat here. The rich, the famous, even royalty. Adam has the potential to look like an A-lister. With his designer skiwear and healthy suntan, there is more than a suggestion of affluence about the man in his early thirties lunching by himself. People-watchers at nearby tables will have been creating their own legends for this solitary diner: the carefully swept-back thick black hair, strong jawline and striking physique hint at an aristocratic bloodline. Perhaps a British peer, the sort with generations of money at his fingertips? In Courchevel, anything is possible.

Of course, the après-ski cocktail circuit might not guess Adam's real-life story. Might they imagine that this smartly kitted-out lunchtime patron is a former soldier? A *disgraced* former soldier, at that. Someone who, in the not too distant past, had been sent packing for certain *unpublicised* misdemeanours in Afghanistan. Would they surmise that this same man, chastened by his failings, had reinvented himself as a businessman, throwing himself headlong into a new career as an oil trader? A man finally making a success of his life, earning real money for a change, thus able to afford to ski in Courchevel, to eat in its swanky restaurants and drink its eye-wateringly expensive bottles of wine.

The plot twist, the explanation of his solitary dining habit, would require inside knowledge, known only to a select few. Several weeks ago, those in the know might whisper conspiratorially, the man had been talent-spotted. By a woman who was primarily after his skills and then, because Adam is such a charmer, his body. Xandra – sometimes Xan, never, ever Alex and rarely her christened name, Alexandra – is a lady of independent means: considerably wealthier than Adam, not that he's the type to keep score. They may yet be very much in love. Whether Adam is the kind to remain faithful to someone that much older remains to be seen. At the moment, he and Xandra are 'an item', as and when it suits. Witness this lunchtime: she is currently ensconced in a private alcove on the far side of the restaurant, attempting to woo a business prospect over a boozy lunch. Not party to this business development initiative, her several-years-younger toy boy has been left to dine alone.

In point of fact, Adam Fraser is perfectly content to be lunching by himself. His table is not the best-positioned, but it does have one redeeming feature: a chessboard, set in the centre. Given the number of Russian and Ukrainian visitors, a chessboard in a Courchevel mountain restaurant is arguably less a novelty, more an essential item. Adam is a big fan of chess. He likes the strategy and forward-thinking and especially the cunning and deviousness needed to win. There is a half-empty bottle of claret on the table in front of him. A plate bearing the remains of recently consumed lamb cutlets, grilled on the restaurant's charcoal fire, rests to one side. On the chessboard, Adam is replaying moves from the latest game between a Norwegian Grand Master and a Ukrainian. Next to the chessboard, an internet-enabled phone allows him to follow each of the moves step by step.

Absorbed in the game, he never sees the woman coming. One moment the chair opposite is vacant, the next it isn't. He feels her presence, knows that he should be lifting his head to look – but doesn't.

Head down, chin resting on upturned palms, elbows on the table, Adam is a chess-wizard in deep concentration.

His visitor is female. He can smell the perfume, see the designer all-in-one ski suit, unzipped at the front with an expensive pale-blue cashmere sweater underneath. Slowly, her hands come into his field of view. Elegant fingers adorned with gold, silver and platinum. Many are bearing rocks, the stones gleaming and sparkling under the LEDs overhead. They look the real deal. In Courchevel, they usually are.

The moment eventually arrives when it would be rude not to sneak a peek. Slowly he raises his head, vaguely aware of the air leaving his lungs. This woman is an apparition. A siren: radiant, perfect even, and if not an A-lister, deserving of a place in their hall of fame. The combined package is mischievous, playful and alluring. Lips soft and sensual, skin the colour of warm peach and curly dark-brown hair that flows freely – not a hint of it having been misshapen by a ski helmet.

She watches Adam with a smile, bright blue eyes hiding behind long eyelashes.

'Do you play chess?' he asks, finally coming up for air, stumbling for the right words.

She doesn't answer straight away, studying the pieces on the table in front of Adam. Picking up the white queen, she turns it over in her hand.

'Better than you might think,' she answers in time. English, Adam is in no doubt. Younger than him. Late twenties at a guess. Where's the catch? She grabs a passing waiter by the arm.

'I'd like a glass of champagne. And for you?'

'I'm well taken care of, thanks,' he says weakly, ruefully raising the wine bottle. 'Care to join me in a glass?'

'I prefer champagne,' she says, and the waiter disappears. She toys with the chess piece once more.

'Enjoying the skiing? Part of a large group? Husband or long-standing boyfriend waiting in the wings about to pounce?'

She laughs, throwing back her head as she does so.

'Absolutely.' She leans forward conspiratorially. 'Watching our every move, recording it on his camera phone just in case we step out of line.'

'Good. I'm always at my photogenic best after a half bottle of red wine.' His laughter is more nervous than he'd intended. He holds out his hand. 'Adam, by the way.'

She takes his hand in hers.

'Emms,' she says, then adds as an afterthought, 'short for Emma. Don't ask me why. It just seems to have stuck.'

'So, Emms, short for Emma, when am I going to meet the cameraman? Jealous lover about to leap across the room and invite me outside, is he?'

'I was joking,' she replies, now biting her bottom lip. For reasons Adam cannot fathom, he finds this gesture distracting in the extreme. Perhaps it is the alcohol? She waves her hand in a general direction across the room.

'I'm here with friends. Sadly, no husband or boyfriend to report, just boring journalists like me passing through on the way back from Davos, taking a mini-break in this mind-numbingly expensive resort first.'

'Courchevel isn't exactly neighbours with Davos, at least not that I'm aware?'

'But it's the place to be, Adam. Besides, it's only a quick hop by private helicopter from Switzerland to the Altiport. For mere mortals, the train from Davos to Geneva takes a bit longer, but it's not impossible.'

The waiter reappears with her champagne. Adam takes it as his cue to pour a final, very large glass of wine, and they clink a toast.

'What sort of day job brings you to Courchevel, Adam? No wife or mistress in tow?'

He glances casually towards the corner where Xandra is preoccupied with her business meeting, then looks back at Emms.

'Free and single, currently only semi-attached.'

Liar, Adam Fraser.

'I work for someone called Ricky Al-Shawabi. An obscenely wealthy philanthropist living in tax exile in Monaco. I'm his new oil trader. At present, taking a well-earned rest, trying to enjoy the ambience.'

Adam starts rearranging the pieces on the chessboard in front of them.

'Fancy a game?'

She puts her glass down and leans forward, head resting on her hands. Their faces come close together above the chessboard. Once more, she is biting that bottom lip.

'That could be interesting,' she purrs. Then, as if a quick decision has been made, she leans back.

'Actually,' she says, pointedly noticing Adam's empty plate as if for the first time, 'since you've already eaten, I have a better idea. Are you a good skier?'

She raises one eyebrow, a gesture that yields a non-committal shrug from Adam.

'Then let's forget chess. It's a glorious day, the slopes are empty, and I feel the need to ski. My party over there,' she says, waving her arm vaguely once more, 'are thinking of settling in here for the afternoon. I'd rather ski. Can I tempt you?'

Adam splays his hands in front of him.

'Is the Pope a Catholic?'

'Great. Give me a couple of minutes to get my things, and I'll meet you out by the ski racks at the front.'

She leaves as quickly as she had arrived. Adam checks his phone for messages. He sends Xandra a quick text, then gathers his jacket and makes his way to the cashier's desk. Presented with an unreasonably large bill courtesy of the extravagant bottle of wine, he peels off several fifty-euro notes from a billfold and makes to leave. It is as he is wriggling his body into his ski jacket that he catches the movement out of the corner of his eye. It came from the far side of the restaurant. A man and a woman are sitting together at a corner table by the window. The man, a muscular African, is nursing a drink, while the woman holds a camera with a telephoto lens. Now, the lens is pointing out of the window: a few seconds earlier, Adam is sure it had been aimed directly at him.

Chapter 2

Saturday 23rd January 2016

Warwickshire, UK

Mohammed Ahmed Hassan Al-Shawabi: Egyptian by birth, British by adoption and English by education. Flamboyant, opinionated, often devious, and generally overly self-confident, Al-Shawabi is not a man who could be described as one of life's shy and retiring.

As a teenager, the young and already bumptious Al-Shawabi had boarded at one of England's finest schools. For reasons best known to his teenage school friends, he had earned himself the nickname 'Tricky' in honour of the then about-to-be-impeached US president, Richard Nixon. Tricky at school morphed into 'Ricky' at Cambridge. From there, for better or worse, the name Ricky had stuck, the less Anglo-Saxon *Mohammed Ahmed Hassan* name swiftly consigned to the bottom drawer along with his Egyptian passport and birth certificate.

Ricky's voracious appetite to be at the centre of everything took on a life of its own during his time at Cambridge. As an undergraduate, he was never far from either the action or the in-crowd: rowing for his college first boat, playing rugby for the Varsity squad and running in the athletics team. Like Ricky, a large number of his contemporaries went on to better and greater things. In the words of the current British prime minister and his one-time college rowing friend, Justin Ingleby, Ricky's propensity to be *'nauseatingly successful whilst at the same time irritatingly difficult to avoid'* is what sets Ricky apart from so many others. Vivacious, over-burdened with opinions and ideas, Ricky was, is, and ever shall be, the party animal. In his twin-room set at Cambridge, Ricky had entertained, his parties legendary. Even in those days, Ricky had splashed the cash. Female companions always existed in Ricky's life. Thirty-five years, two marriages and countless philanderings later, Ricky remains unscarred by much of it and unchanged by any of it. Arrogantly over-confident, never short of company, and ostentatious with money: despite – or arguably because of – all of this, Ricky has always been supremely well-connected.

Ricky's very existence on this planet is about connections. Here was a man able to thrive on *the fruits of his hardly-earned labours*, as Ingleby had once had joshed about him. These days, Ricky sprinkles his brand of magic dust liberally but carefully, instinctively knowing how and where to apply grease to the wheels of a commercial transaction here, or when an exchange of favours might be helpful there. His edge is enhanced by his apparent British-ness, providing him with an aura of trust and respectability. When, on occasions, he is minded to raid his bottom drawer, cross the cultural divide and prove, when it suits, that deep down, he is still an Egyptian at heart, it puts him at an enviable advantage. The Al-Shawabi business empire – *providing tax and risk-managed structuring solutions to clients in the energy and financial sectors* – has a network of connections and contacts that is unrivalled. Better still, Ricky's business is globally accredited, recognised by leading experts as one of only a handful that is fully compliant with the very latest anti-bribery best-practices worldwide. Ricky is thus respectable, gold-plated, and you no longer need to take his word for it. Headquartered in Monaco with a network of offices in various tax havens, this is a global operation of some breadth. In the words of Ricky's website, Al-Shawabi is undeniably *well-placed to help clients achieve their full business potential in some of the most important emerging markets on the planet*. No one ever fully understands what this means, but maybe that's the point.

Ricky's success makes him a flamboyant A-lister: a self-made '*squillionaire*', someone connected to all the 'right people'. Or perhaps the 'wrong people' if, for one moment, that misinformed minority, those with nothing but time on their hands ready to nit-pick and drag down all and any doing better than themselves, had a chance to be heard. *He's a tax-dodging middleman*, a few brave souls might be heard to whisper. *Doing dodgy business deals in equally dodgy parts of the world.* Not that Ricky cares. His knowledge, his contacts, his client base have made him bullet-proof: presidents and prime ministers; politicians and government officials; footballers and rock stars; wealthy Chinese, Arabs, Indians, Latinos and Israelis. People with things to hide come to Ricky for help in the professional art of concealment. Al-Shawabi's clientele range from the Great and the Good to the Desperate and Dodgy. Ricky is not one to be judgemental. In the end, clients pay the bills, and Ricky's knowledge remains his insurance policy. In a world where information has value, Ricky knows where the bodies are buried. That gives him the edge. So do the secret files he lets people believe that he keeps. Files supposedly going back years. Whether real or imaginary, this gives him clout. It also gives him access. Underneath the bluff and the bravado, behind the façade of high energy and exuberance, maybe his boarding school buddies had it right all those years ago: perhaps deep-down Ricky is, after all, just undeniably tricky?

Unlike the American president, British prime minister Justin Ingleby rarely has time for golf. His weekdays are full of meetings, public engagements and speeches given both at home and overseas. On the rare occasion when a weekend day is free, it is usually taken up with constituency or party matters. Either that or dealing with a never-ending stream of Red Boxes: as his wife is fond of reminding him, civil servants seldom put confidential papers in Red Boxes to cut down on red tape.

This Saturday in January is the annual off-site, an informal gathering of the party faithful: elected members, party officials and, for the evening dinner, a few well-chosen major donors. The event is chaired and has been organised by the party chairman, the recently knighted Robin Pemberley. The hotel of choice, set in the Warwickshire countryside, has its own private golf course. Although it is the middle of winter, a short amount of time has been set aside on the Saturday afternoon for private meetings which, in party vernacular, is shorthand for golf. For once, the weather is mild and the sun is shining. T here is a waiting list for tee-times and, not surprisingly, a pecking order. Ingleby, as prime minister, has the dubious privilege of going first. Joining him on the first slot after the lunch break is Pemberley; Stephen Russell, Ingleby's chancellor of the exchequer; and to complete the foursome, Ricky Al-Shawabi. Ricky has flown in specially and needs no introduction. Russell and Ricky have been acquainted for years, from a time when the former was working for a large American investment bank and when Ricky, very quietly, had taken him on as a client. Pemberley, meanwhile, has been wooing Ricky for ages, hoping to persuade Ingleby's one-time friend to make a not inconsiderable donation to party funds. Ricky's presence today, in the very bosom of the party, is an indication that Ricky might finally be amenable to writing a not-insubstantial cheque.

All four tee off with powerful drives. Ricky joins Ingleby in the PM's specially adapted golf cart, a bench seat at the back hastily improvised to allow the plainclothes protection officer to ride along with them.

'How are things with you, Jingo?' Ricky booms when the two are alone together. 'Long time no speaks. Job still what you wanted it to be?'

Ingleby looks across at his old university friend and chuckles.

'I think it best if that Jingo-ism stuff is taken off limits, if it's all the same to you, Ricky? I could have you locked in the Tower for failing to address me as Prime Minister. Isn't that right, Brendan?'

'Undoubtedly, sir,' his protection officer answers from the rear, hanging on for dear life in his makeshift seat. 'You just have to say the word.'

'You okay in the back, by the way? My driving not causing too much grief?'

'No sir, the coccyx has never felt better,' Brendan replies, the buggy bouncing at that moment over a particularly nasty bump.

'Don't worry, *Prime Minister*,' Ricky continues with false exaggeration. 'You won't hear another 'Jingo' out of me all weekend. It can be our little secret.'

'That, Ricky,' Ingleby says, chancing a quick sideways glance, 'is precisely what I am afraid of. Anyway, nice of you to come and visit your old friends. I hear from Robin that a financial contribution might be in the offing.'

'Some of us try to do our bit.'

'Tax exiles in hiding are rather a touchy subject at the moment, Ricky. In case the news hasn't yet made it to Monaco. I don't suppose you've been affected by the Panamanian whistle-blower in any way? It can't have been good for business.'

'Luckily, *Prime Minister*,' Ricky replies, 'the Al-Shawabi businesses are not involved in any of that sort of malarkey. Anyway, more to the point, rumour has it that you're thinking about stepping down in the not too distant future. Is that true? Had enough of the high office and low pay, is that it?'

'Something like that, Ricky. I've decided I need to be spending more time with the family.'

'Oh, don't give me that bollocks. You're having no fun and the pay's crap. What does an ex-prime minister make on the lecture circuit these days? At least fifty if not a hundred grand a pop, especially across the Pond. Who wouldn't be tempted by the chance to earn their annual salary in a couple of one-hour talkie sessions?'

'You may be right, Ricky.'

'Of course I'm bloody right. You need to come and talk to me when you're on the verge of entering the Sunday Times Rich List. I can help you squirrel your money away somewhere safe and sound and out of the public eye. What about the European Referendum? Won't your early-retirement bugger up how people will vote?'

'It's not early-retirement. I simply believe that after the referendum, it'll be time for a change.'

'Win or lose?'

'We're going to win, Ricky!' he says, thumping his hand on the steering wheel for emphasis. 'With support from people such as yourself, we have to win!'

'I think the real reason is that you're fed up with dealing with all those bloody bureaucrats in Brussels. Still, you need to find a successor. It's giving the press a field day!'

'Not just the press. Robin is bricking himself.'

'Quite. Party chairman used to be such a doddle: lots of glad-handing, boozy lunches followed by a long and gentle slide into a reserved seat in the Lords. Now it's full-on fundraising, all that piffling governance guff to contend with, and you've gone and handed Robin a leadership succession nightmare to deal with as well! Hold on driver, that's my ball over there,' he says, pointing to the right. 'Where did yours go?'

'I think over to the left, sir,' Brendan pipes up from the back.

'I love the perks of high office,' Ricky says as Ingleby stops the cart to let him get out and play his ball. 'I mean, having someone to spot errant golf balls is a serious plus.'

'From what I hear, Ricky, you have quite an entourage of your own these days, too.'

They are on the fifth green, all four within a short putting distance from the hole.

'All joshing aside,' Ingleby says, sizing up the lie of the green before taking his putt. 'If you were minded to make a cash donation, the party would be enormously grateful. At a personal level, it would be a huge boost, both to Robin and myself.'

'How much are we talking about?' Russell asks, showing the characteristic bluntness that some argue makes him a poor candidate to be the successor to Ingleby.

'That depends, really,' Ricky answers. 'I don't suppose there's any *quid pro quo* these days. Presumably, a knighthood is out of the question?'

There is collective tut-tutting and shaking of heads.

'Perish the thought, Ricky. You know we don't operate like that, even amongst friends.'

'Quite right too, totally improper.'

He waits for Ingleby to take his shot, watching the ball clip the rim of the hole and swerve off to the right.

'Oh, rotten luck,' he says insincerely. 'No, I had sort of wondered whether a million or so might be in order? Subject to Electoral Commission rules and so on. What do you think? Would that help oil the wheels? Perhaps a little more if you are desperate.'

Robin Pemberley can hardly contain himself.

'My dear Ricky, that really would be extraordinarily generous. Quite above and beyond, actually. Everyone would be forever and totally grateful.'

'What conditions would be attached?' Russell asks, lining up his shot and sinking the ball in the hole with careful precision.

'Nothing much. It would be a purely philanthropic gesture. A number of my clients are keen for me to do something.'

'Amazing Ricky,' Ingleby exclaims in genuine admiration. 'Just on a technicality, are you able to, legally, I mean? You being a non-dom or whatever.'

'Now, now,' Ricky says, lining up his putt and sinking his ball in one go. 'That's a par for me,' he says, writing the score on his card before retrieving the ball from the hole.

'I own properties in the UK, and I pay taxes in the UK; I have a UK business that, unlike many American multinationals, actually pays taxes in the UK; and I am entitled to vote in the UK. Feels conclusive to me, but who am I to judge?'

'Quite so, Ricky. I am sure everything can all be worked out,' Pemberley positively oozes with obsequiousness.

They only play nine holes. Close to the ninth green, Ingleby and Russell play their approach shot from similar positions.

'What do you think about Ricky's offer?' Ingleby asks, using a pitching wedge to heft his ball inelegantly onto the back of the green. It rolls at speed off the other side and into the long grass. 'Damn!'

'Generous,' Russell replies. 'I'm worried about the optics, though. Taking money from someone at the extremes of aggressive tax avoidance at a time the press are calling for us to close down all these tax loopholes would be high risk. For you, especially.'

'I don't think we've heard all the conditions yet either. Knowing Ricky as I do, there'll be something he wants in return; there's bound to be.'

As they speak, Ricky bounds towards them from across the fairway, his ball already on the green and in a good position.

'This looks like the Mothers' Union,' he calls out. 'Why the glum faces?'

'Just chewing the cud about something, Ricky. Where are you at the moment? On the green?'

'Fair and square, just a nudge away from the pin. I saw you roll off a few moments ago. Not your lucky day, is it, *Prime Minister*?' Ricky winks at Ingleby.

'I don't know. It's not every day that one of our most generous donors offers us a million pounds. Any strings likely to be attached, by the way, Ricky?'

'Not really. I thought I might pay in instalments if it's all the same to you? I'd be happy to keep the taps flowing into the party coffers for as long as it made sense, actually. Of course, always providing that there wasn't some unexpected government-led revolution in or around the UK's various offshore dependencies. That might be the only thing that got in the way, forcing the Al-Shawabi cash flows to cease and desist. One wouldn't want to find oneself being unreasonably penalised, the boat one's in taxed and battered by unforeseen stormy weather, if you get my meaning? It'd be bad for my business and bad for your fundraising. With nothing like that on the horizon, I can't see any reason why the money shouldn't keep flowing freely and unencumbered.'

He smiles thinly, fixing his gaze pointedly on Russell.

'Some of us have a lot of skin in that particular game, as I am sure you appreciate, Stephen.'

Chapter 3

Friday 22nd January 2016

London

The day before the mass exodus to the party off-site, the secretary of state for foreign affairs, Geraldine Macauley, is in London with a full workload. Shortly, she is due to begin her weekly meeting with Sir Desmond Wheatley, the current director-general of the Secret Intelligence Service – or MI6 as it is more commonly known. The elected member for Chipping Hadham since 1997, Macauley is one of the most experienced senior female members of parliament. An unashamed euro-sceptic, she has previously held Cabinet posts as secretary of state for education and, until her appointment as foreign secretary, secretary of state for the home department. A qualified barrister before turning to politics, Macauley presents a formidable figure in the debating chamber of the House of Commons. Tough, determined, ambitious and always well-prepared, she rarely gets wrong-footed by an absence of facts and figures.

Macauley's office is one of the perks of her current position: a grand salon full of gilded mirrors, elegant furnishings, floor-to-ceiling drapes and rich wooden panels. In the centre are opulent red leather chairs on an expanse of green carpet. In one corner, adjacent to two windows, is a large mahogany desk with neat piles of papers and buff-coloured folders stacked on top. To one side, its lid open, is a Red Box containing ministerial papers. They once ruled an empire from this room, its visitors frequently over-awed by its pomp and scale. Macauley loves her job and feels enormous affection for the room. On many occasions, she can be found here, late into the night, working her way through her Red Boxes. Recently widowed, her twin children now married and with families of their own, she has made politics her life's work. An ambition to succeed Justin Ingleby as the next prime minister is her unashamed goal.

She is sitting at her desk, reading through a confidential report when there is a knock on the door. A smartly dressed messenger enters the room.

'Excuse me for interrupting, Foreign Secretary. Sir Desmond Wheatley has arrived. Would you like me to show him in?'

'Thank you, Frank. Please do. If you could, we would love some tea.'

'There's some on the way. Just to check, Minister. The permanent secretary has informed me that he is not expecting to join you, is that correct?'

'Quite correct, but thank you for checking, Frank.' Her meetings with Sir Desmond were one of the few she conducted without officials present.

Sir Desmond Wheatley is a tall, thin man of advancing years with distinctive grey locks that have been slicked back over his forehead. He enters the room with familiar confidence and shakes Macauley's offered hand.

'How are you, Desmond? Take a seat. There's tea about to arrives.' She looks up as another messenger arrives bearing a silver tea tray. 'Ah, here it is.' The tray is hurriedly deposited on the low mahogany table between them, and the messenger quickly departs.

Forty minutes later, and the two of them have covered a lot of ground. Their current topic of conversation is recent developments in both Syria and Iraq.

'It seems, Minister, that recent targeted airstrikes, mainly by the Russians, are having a positive impact. ISIS forces on the ground have been severely weakened.'

'It's not what the media are reporting, but what's new?'

'Our latest intelligence suggests that the militants have something of a crisis on their hands. An acute shortage of cash.'

'I thought ISIS had captured all of the oil assets in Syria and Iraq.'

'That is correct. However, the only way for them to get crude oil out of the country is by road, using battered old oil tankers. We estimate that already over one thousand such tankers have been destroyed by Allied and Russian airstrikes. In addition, similar strikes on the oil production facilities mean that even if they had more tankers, they would be unable to ship much crude oil across the border to Turkey.'

'We're sure it's Turkey where they're heading?'

'No doubt about it. It's where so much of ISIS's funding has been coming from. Until recently, there's been a thriving black market in Turkey for sources of cheap crude oil. Almost overnight, that market has dried up. Today, ISIS are getting almost nothing for their oil. US intelligence estimates that they have an operational cash requirement of about two million dollars a day.'

'That's an extraordinary sum. Why so much?'

'To pay wages, munitions, food and so on.'

'Can't they just seize a few banks and steal the cash they need from the vaults?'

'That has been the other part of the recent air campaign. RAF Tornado fighters have been deliberately targeting banks and other places where we know there are large cash depots.'

'So, ISIS are running out of cash? That's very clever. What's their plan B? They are not likely to give up without a fight.'

'Absolutely not. They'll be forced to raise taxes even more and continue extorting from the locals. The Allies' current plan is to maintain the financial squeeze whilst continuing with targeted airstrikes. The hope is that it demoralises sufficient numbers of ISIS supporters in both Syria and Iraq such that it weakens them permanently.'

'Will that work?'

'The biggest risk is that ISIS's financial backers will find other devious ways to get hard currency into the hands of their fighters on the ground.'

'Is that likely?'

'I might have been tempted to say no, but that was before I received a report from one of my team. I'd like to show you something, Minister, if I may?'

'Of course. What is it?'

'We've had a covert operation underway. The sort where we put an asset in place, undercover, to provide us with an intelligence feed. I am not about to give you any operational details, only the barest outline.'

He opens his briefcase. He extracts a single piece of headed paper from a thin plastic folder and passes it across. Silence ensues whilst she dons a pair of reading glasses and scans it, her legal training allowing her to assimilate the information at speed. Once finished, she removes her glasses, holding them by one of the side arms and turning them in slow, deliberate circles.

'That's very interesting. Very, very interesting indeed. You know that Ricky Al-Shawabi coming to our party off-site tomorrow?'

'It's the reason I wanted to speak to you about it today.'

'Can I discuss this with the prime minister?'

'You can't show him that piece of paper, I am afraid, but I am happy for you to mention it to him alone. Unchecked, it could cause a major political embarrassment if any of this -' he says, picking up the piece of paper and waving it before returning it to his case and closing the metal clasps, '- turned out to be true. We're only making informed guesses at this stage. However, it fits a pattern.'

'Innocent until proven guilty is my motto. Though, so is forewarned being forearmed. Thank you, Desmond. That's most helpful. Now, what else should we cover?'

'In a way, it's linked, Minister. As Al-Shawabi is about to arrive in the UK, we would like to place him under surveillance.'

'Isn't that an MI5 matter?'

'Quite so. However, since he will be spending a certain amount of time amongst MPs and Cabinet members, it makes surveillance more sensitive. I am more than prepared to pass the file over to Sir Alan Crabtree at MI5. I just think it needs careful handling. I would respectfully suggest that Sir Alan resists the temptation to brief his minister, the home secretary. The fewer who are aware of our interest in this particular individual, the better it must be for all parties concerned. I can brief Sir Alan as much as is necessary, and he will be very discreet. That is my advice, Minister.'

'Which I am happy to accept, thank you.'

Not least because Macauley doesn't relish the home secretary, Jeremy Seymour, and his sharp elbows trying to muscle in on her patch, lining himself up to take any credit for whatever MI6's investigation may or may not uncover down the line about Al-Shawabi. Something she knows all too well that Seymour is more than capable of doing.

Especially if it furthers his cause in trying to outmanoeuvre her in the race to get to Number 10.

Chapter 4

Monday 25th January 2016

Courchevel, France

They ski hard and they ski fast. Whether because of the wine or not, Adam skis like a demon. She takes the lead, claiming local knowledge from times gone by when she had worked a season as a chalet girl in neighbouring Meribel. They avoid the worst of the queues and ski several kilometres of well-groomed, near-empty slopes. By some margin, she is the more proficient– certainly the more elegant.

'So, tell me about the world of journalism, Emms,' he asks as they sit side by side on a long chair. 'What do you write about?' They pass under a pylon, the rattle of the pulleys dislodging ice and snow stuck to the metal bar above their heads.

'Mainly business things.'

With a gloved hand, she brushes off small lumps of ice that have fallen onto her goggles before reaching across to do the same to Adam's.

'Who's doing what to whom, mergers, take-overs, changes in legislation, that sort of thing. Tax avoidance is a big topic at the moment.'

'I can imagine. Do you work for someone, or are you freelance?'

'Freelance? Good gracious, no. I need a monthly paycheque. How else could I afford to come to a place like this? No, I work for Reuters in London.'

'Is that the same for your friends?'

'Pretty much. We cover similar ground but for different organisations. It's why we've just been to Davos. The World Economic Forum is fertile soil for all journos.'

Approaching the top station, Adam lifts the safety bar. Several skiers mill around near the lift exit, making it necessary to ski a small detour around them. Adam has the better line. Finding himself ahead of her, he is oblivious to how Emms takes her tumble. One moment she is skiing beside him; the next, she's on the ice. The culprit – for there had to be one – is a fast-disappearing snowboarder who had cut across her path.

'Are you all right?'

Adam sidesteps back up the slope so that he can help pull her to her feet.

'Bloody boarder! He veered right in front. I think I've twisted my knee.'

She grabs his offered hand and slowly gets up off the ice.

'Bugger! That hurts,' she says, gradually putting weight on the leg. 'The last thing I need is a knee injury.'

'Do you think you can make it back down to the village?'

'I don't know. I'll give it a try.'

She puts more weight on the knee to test it, wincing a little.

'It should be okay. I'd like to head back, though. I am sorry, Adam.'

'Don't worry about it. I'll take care of you.' *Just try and stop me.* 'Where are you staying?'

'A hotel by the top of the Bellecôte piste. That'd be kind, thanks. We can ski right to the door. I should be fine.'

Ten minutes' gentle skiing later, Adam is stowing her skis in the hotel's basement locker. He waits whilst she hangs her ski boots on the special racks that the hotel provides.

'How's the knee?'

'Nothing too serious, I think – famous last words! Want to come up and have a drink?'

'Sure,' he says, removing his boots and placing them, and the rest of his paraphernalia, in an empty cubbyhole. He walks with her toward the small elevator in the corner of the basement. When the lift arrives, they both squeeze into the tiny space. She presses the button for level four and the doors begin to close. Suddenly she's kissing him, her lips soft, her tongue active. He feels a surge of electricity as their bodies rub against each other.

'Follow me,' she says breathlessly as the doors open. She grabs him by the hand, half-running, her knee no longer an impediment.

'Try and stop me.'

This time he says the words out loud. He caresses her from behind as she fumbles with the electronic door lock. Thus entwined, they drag each other into the room, the door closing behind them. Somehow, they reach the bed, fumbling their way out of ski clothes that seem designed to make undressing as tricky as possible.

'You've got to give me one minute,' she gasps, struggling for air, fighting her way off the bed. 'Otherwise,' she jokes, backing into the bathroom, 'there's going to be an accident. Catch!' She throws something which lands on the bed beside him.

'Standard terms and conditions I'm afraid, lover boy,' she says, closing the door on him. From inside the closed room, she carries on talking. 'I've been presumptuous and assumed you to be a "large".' After which, all that can be heard, as Adam picks up the foil-wrapped condom and breaks it open, is giggling.

Chapter 5

Monday 25th January 2016

Courchevel, France

The needle takes him by surprise. One moment he and Emms are enjoying a post-climactic cuddle, the next, he is losing consciousness, mildly aware of something sharp piercing the muscle on his left thigh. As the lights fade to black, he thinks he can hear voices.

When the house lights come back up, he is in a different room. Still the same floral patterns on the purple carpet, still the same bland grey walls with a drab mountain-scape painting. Someone has had the kindness to clothe him in an undersized white hotel dressing-gown, complete with a gold embroidered motif. Thankfully, without the gratuitous flimsy white slippers. This is how he presents himself to his captors. Slumped in an uncomfortable armchair, cable ties around the ankles and the same around his wrists. Not a high budget stage production, but effective enough in the circumstances.

Looking around the room, he spots the hired muscle first. Standing by the door, facing Adam, is the man he saw as he was leaving the restaurant at lunchtime. The one who would have been tasked with dragging Adam's inert body from Emms' original room into this one. Adam can see the marks on the carpet where his heels have scuffed the pile. He looks back at the man. Two hundred and twenty pounds of muscular prop forward, a resource that seems to have been provided by a co-operative West African nation. Adam Fraser is not going anywhere in a hurry.

Sitting opposite him, about ten feet away and looking concerned, is a middle-aged woman – the one who'd held the camera and the long lens. Up close, she is his school headmistress, Miss Bateson, come to life, a humourless individual given to scowling and sneering at the slightest provocation. Like the real-life Miss Bateson from his personal archives, this one is looking at him with a mixture of disapproval and disappointment, something from which in his school days, Adam had never really recovered. Like his Miss Bateson, this version is also petite, pallid and wears prim-looking glasses.

The real surprise is Emms herself. Now fully dressed, hair up at the back, she is sitting on the bed a few feet away, an ominous rolled-up linen pouch on the duvet cover beside her. Still looking as angelic as ever, she now wears her work face: serious, with less of the come-hither look.

'Emms,' Adam begins. He is suddenly unbelievably thirsty. 'Rather a surprise ending, don't you think? Been out a long time, have I? I couldn't trouble you for a drink of water?'

He winks at her to see if he can get any reaction but hits a brick wall.

'You've only been unconscious a short while.'

It is Miss Bateson speaking, now polishing her spectacle lenses on a cloth that she has taken from a bag by her feet. 'I'm sorry we had to put you through that little rigmarole, but we don't have much time and there's quite a lot of ground to cover.'

She gives a thin, watery smile, turning her head towards the former apple of Adam's eye.

'Fiona, can you fetch our guest a glass of water? Then it will be time for you to complete your procedures. After that, we can undo the restraints.'

The headmistress looks back at Adam once again.

'Just one or two more things to be completed, I'm afraid. Nothing much to concern you.'

Adam watches as the person formerly known as Emms, now Fiona, emerges from the bathroom carrying a glass of water. She holds it to

Adam's lips, and he gulps down its contents gratefully.

'Thank you, Fiona,' he says once he has drained the glass. 'Or perhaps it can still be Emms? I rather liked Emms, to be honest.' In a stage aside, he leans forward and whispers, 'I hope I met the size criteria? Long and lasting pleasure, and all that? Short but sweet. If you fancy round two, you know where to come. Promise? Next time without the needle, if it's all the same to you?'

Emms, now also known as Fiona, has the grace to smile. She returns to the bed and retrieves the pouch, untying the ribbons and then carrying the bundle back nearer to where Adam is sitting. Kneeling on the floor, she extracts a length of rubber tubing. Rolling up Adam's dressing gown sleeve, she ties the tube around his upper forearm.

'I am going to take some blood. You'll have had this done before. We'll use the vein on the back of your hand so that there's less risk of bruising.'

She busies herself with preparing the needle, working in silence. In no time, Adam is watching claret-coloured liquid being extracted from his hand and sucked into one of several large syringes that Emms has taken out of her pouch in readiness.

'Sometimes,' she whispers, leaning forward across his body to check the pulse on his other wrist, 'there are a few perks that go with the job. Let me consider your offer and I'll get back to you.'

She winks at him conspiratorially.

'How's the knee? Better, by any chance?'

'Miraculous recovery, thank you. There,' she says, removing the needle from his wrist and holding a small piece of cotton wool over the puncture wound.

'Job done.'

She covers the swab with a piece of Micropore tape and places the tubes of blood into the linen pouch.

'Got everything you need?' It is Miss Bateson once again.

'Almost. Now Adam, I just need one or two more bits and pieces, I'm afraid.'

With one hand she opens his dressing-gown to expose his nakedness. With the other, she takes a pair of tweezers from the linen pouch.

'Back for second helpings already?' quips Adam. 'I don't usually do this kind of thing in front of an audience . . .' but then the words stop. He winces with pain as several pubic hairs are yanked out by their roots.

'For fuck's sake, Emma, or whatever your name is. Did you have to do that?'

'Man-up, Adam Fraser.'

She smiles at him, placing the hair samples into a small test tube. Next comes a pair of scissors, which she uses to cut several locks of black hair from the back of his head.

'I do believe you might have something of a bald patch developing. I assume it runs in the family?'

'Ha, bloody, ha. What do you plan to do with all this stuff?'

'Stick your tongue out a moment,' she says and, as he does so, she uses a wooden spatula to scrape it clean, placing the small stick into another test tube and screwing the cap tight.

'Finished?'

'Actually, yes. All done.' She now looks directly at Miss Bateson. 'I'll leave him to you and Beef and be on my way if that's okay? I've got everything we need,' she says, patting the cotton pouch that is now rolled up and tied together once more. Miss Bateson – for that is now the stage name that will be in Adam's mind forever – nods in silent assent.

'So,' Emms, or perhaps Fiona, says, turning to Adam one final time. 'Until we meet again. It was fun knowing you.'

She blows him an air kiss before turning to head towards the door.

'Wait. Tell me. Who are you? Really, I'd like to know.'

'Adam, do I look like a journalist?'

'Truth be told, Emms, you look like a princess.'

'There you go then. I am what you believe me to be.'

At which point she smiles, turns on her heels, squeezes past the bodyguard who goes by the name of Beef, and leaves the room.

Chapter 6

Monday 25th January 2016

Courchevel, France

Alexandra Brock – usually Xandra to her friends, sometimes Xan but never, ever Alex – is not having a great afternoon. The once Magic Circle-trained tax lawyer, alumna of one of London's best tax practices, now evasive tax avoider to the hard-to-find rich and the difficult-to-identify guilty with plenty to hide, has a bad headache. Her long and very alcoholic lunch with the elusive Latin American politician had not, at the time of their unsteady parting on the slopes above the village, reached closure. Back in the Hub, as she calls the sprawling chalet situated in the ritzy neighbourhood just above the centre of Courchevel 1850, her head is throbbing.

'Shetty, I need paracetamol!' she cries out, throwing a document folder onto the leather sofa before collapsing onto the same, moments later. 'In fact, make that a double. A strong black coffee would also be a lifesaver. As fast as possible. I have a splitting head.'

Shetty, an Indian by birth, looks after Xandra and her complicated life – and has done so for more years than she cares to remember. That rare combination of loyal retainer, diary secretary and personal butler, Xandra's general factotum is responsible for making everything in her complicated life tick smoothly.

'Certainly, ma'am. Shall I perhaps organise a massage for you? The man you like is in town at present. It might relieve the tensions causing the headache.'

'That would be amazing, thank you.'

The Hub has an enviable location with views directly onto the slopes above the exclusive enclave of Jardin Alpin. A typical Savoie-style chalet, it is of wooden construction set on four floors. A *sous-sol* in the basement for Shetty and other staff members; four en-suite double guest bedrooms on the ground floor; a large living area and kitchen on the first floor; and Xandra's own spacious suite and private rooms on the top. As a partner in Ricky Al-Shawabi's small yet phenomenally lucrative business, Xandra has profited considerably from the financial success story that is Al-Shawabi. After a brief spell in and amongst London's private equity elite, she was headhunted ten years ago to help Ricky set up his new business venture. Since then, she has amassed personal wealth beyond her wildest dreams.

Xandra looks up and sees Oswald Gerhard, another lifelong member of Ricky's inner sanctum, come into the room. An effete Swiss-German tax lawyer who has been part of the Al-Shawabi furniture for almost as long as Xandra, Ozzie, as he prefers to be called, is on his third marriage, having wed his former personal assistant, an English girl, Gemma, fifteen years his junior. Like most of Ricky's core team, Ozzie travels incessantly and has a network of connections and contacts that is legendary. A wizard at offshore structuring, there are few tax havens that Gerhard doesn't know personally. Need a private nominee company established in Panama to anonymise monies earned out of Luxembourg before being remitted via a Jersey subsidiary? Ozzie will know the way to get it done. Like Xandra, Ozzie is part of the inner circle, second tier only to the great man himself. They make a good team. Xandra focuses on implementation whilst relying on Ozzie to design optimum deal structures. He is very Swiss: very particular and very precise, a stickler for details. The way he dresses is no different; knife-edged pleats in laundered chinos and crisply ironed shirts are a trademark on occasions like this when pretending to be on vacation.

'Ozzie, come and take a pew.' Shetty approaches with a tray containing two paracetamol tablets, a large glass of water and a double espresso.

'You are amazing, Shetty,' she says, downing the tablets with the water before taking the tiny china cup and saucer in both hands. 'Thank you.'

'Mr Oswald, would you care for anything?'

'Tea would be welcome, thank you, Shetty – as would some of that wonderful Madeira cake, if there's any left? I confess to being starving. I couldn't face lunch on the mountain today. Gemma thought the steaks looked raw. How did your meeting go, Xan?'

Xandra puts down her cup and massages her temples, her eyes closed.

'Still nothing definitive. I think he wants a sweetener.'

'For God's sakes, that's rich! We have to sweeten the other side as well. Who does he think is going to be paying for all of this sprinkled sugar? It's going to come out of his cut, surely he can see that?'

'I know, I know,' she says, still rubbing her temples. 'Have you seen Adam anywhere? I need my shoulders rubbed. I was hoping he might have been back by now to oblige.'

Ozzie's young wife, Gemma, decides that this is the moment to make an appearance but does a double take when she sees Xandra and Ozzie huddled together. Laden with shopping bags from an afternoon outing in the village, her arrival elicits a groan from her husband.

'Been raiding the retirement funds again, have we darling?'

'I'm sorry, Oz, I didn't realise you were busy. I'll come back another time.'

'Don't worry, take a seat,' Xandra says. 'Come to think of it, I can't seem to locate Adam at the moment. Would you mind giving my neck and shoulders a rub, Gemma darling? I was about to ask Ozzie to do it. I'm in agony at present.'

'I'd be happy to,' Gemma says, walking behind the sofa where Xandra is sitting, in the process giving her husband one of her 'don't *ever* think about putting your hands on Xandra's shoulders' looks. 'I'm not sure I'm very good at it, but I'll give it a try.'

'You haven't seen Adam, have you?' Xandra asks as Gemma gently rubs the muscles below Xandra's shoulder-blades. 'Ooh, down a bit, to the left, yes, just there, where your right thumb is, yes, that's the spot.'

'Adam? No, sorry, I've not seen him since this morning.'

'He sent me a text whilst I was at lunch saying that he was skiing by himself for the afternoon,' Xandra continues. 'I thought he might have been back by now.'

Ozzie's phone buzzes, the vibration accompanied by the faintest of ringtones.

He looks at the unknown number before answering.

'Gerhard,' he says in a neutral voice and listens for a few seconds.

'Ah, Abdul Hamid, good-day to you too! How are you enjoying London?'

He glances at Xandra and they exchange knowing looks.

'Have you found a property you'd like? You were thinking either Mayfair or Kensington as I recall?'

More listening ensues before Ozzie feels compelled to interrupt.

'Since this is an open line, Abdul Hamid, I suggest we only stick to the outline. At that sort of price, I think we will be able to close the deal for you.'

He listens some more before continuing.

'Very good. If you're sure it's what you would like, just email me the particulars, and we can execute the purchase as soon as possible. What's that?'

He rocks his head from side to side impatiently as he listens intently.

'Of course, Abdul Hamid. We can have the option agreement with you to sign before you leave London. Is that in order? Very good. I'll await your email then. Enjoy your evening at the opera. I think you'll find you've got excellent seats. If I remember, you're seated in the centre of the stalls.' More listening. 'Yes, we very much enjoy working with you as well, Abdul Hamid. Goodbye.' He ends the call and looks at Xandra, raising an eyebrow knowingly. 'Another happy customer.'

'Remind me who Abdul Hamid is?'

'Our Bangladeshi friend. Currently very content. He's just found the dream London property he wants us to buy for him.'

'How much?'

'Four-point five mill.'

'That's the man our West Coast engineering client needs on their side to win the generator contract, isn't it?'

'Correct.'

'What's our fee?'

'Five plus another five when all the generators have been commissioned in Dhaka.'

'Not bad. Ricky'll be happy.'

She looks up momentarily as Ricky's head of security steps into the room.

'Ah, Vladek, you don't know where Adam might be?'

Al-Shawabi's head of security is a former professional cage fighter, originally from Croatia. Of mixed Slavic and European parentage, the former-martial arts specialist is a naturally suspicious character. Single, without obvious attachments or complications, Vladek Meštrović is rarely off duty. Seldom touching alcohol, he takes the business of protecting Ricky and his business empire very seriously.

'Probably on the piss.'

He speaks with a deep, rasping voice, the grating rawness suggestive of a man who has been singing his heart out at some local nightclub – which anyone familiar with Vladek would understand was improbable.

'Stuck in a bar somewhere, probably. Or screwing chalet girls. Most likely both.'

Adam Fraser's arrival on the scene has not been sitting comfortably with Vladek.

'You should be more trusting, Vladek,' Xandra says, head down, as

Gemma's fingers work on her neck. 'Tell you what, Gemma, you ought to consider taking this up professionally. You're good.'

'I bought this wonderful ski jacket at Bernard Orcel this afternoon,' Gemma says to her husband. 'Would you like me to show you later?'

Ozzie looks at Vladek and rolls his eyes. Xandra's mobile chooses this moment to start ringing.

'Hi, Fergs. What news?'

The room goes quiet as Xandra listens, face expressionless. Gemma takes the lull in proceedings as her cue to extract a ski jacket from a shopping bag to show Ozzie. It is a white designer number with black stripes and splashes of turquoise. She mouths a silent 'Do you like it?'

Ozzie's curled lip and shaking head say it all.

'Where is Ricky at the moment?' Xandra's question is followed by more silent nodding as she listens to Fergus, the director of their Monaco operation. 'Well, they should love that. The glitz and glamour of Monaco never fail to impress.'

More silence for a moment before she speaks again.

'It's Ricky at his best. We could throw in some time at the Casino, and then Ricky could take them out on the boat. If need be, we could fly Rodriguez over from Panama. Can I leave you to think about the planning, Fergs, there's a darling? We are meant to be back the day after tomorrow.'

Now a longer pause.

'Look, if this is Ricky's show, then there is no budget. You know what he's like – plan ultra-extravagant. Ricky loves ultra-extravagant. See you in a couple of days, thanks, Fergs.' With that, she ends the call. 'Shetty!'

'Yes ma'am, how can I help?' Shetty says, hurrying in from the adjacent kitchen.

'Is the helicopter organised to take us back to Monaco the day after tomorrow?'

'Yes, ma'am. The forecast is looking good. I have a departure slot booked for two in the afternoon.'

'We might need to bring it forward.'

'What news?' Ozzie asks.

'Ricky's in London at the moment. Before that, he was in Bahrain meeting and greeting some new Saudi clients keen to avail themselves of the full Al-Shawabi service. Fergus thinks they might come to Monaco for a meet and greet.'

'I heard you mentioning something about that.'

'If they come, we might need to move fast. Shetty, did you manage to get hold of that masseur?'

'Actually, ma'am, he's not available, but his partner is and she is highly recommended. I took the liberty of booking her. She will be here in forty minutes. I hope that's convenient?'

'It'll have to be. Now, I am going to take a long soak in the bath. If and when Adam arrives, send him up, can you?'

Chapter 7

Monday 25th January 2016

Courchevel, France

The African removes the cable ties and Adam is allowed to get dressed.

'Are there going to be proper introductions at some stage?' he says eventually, sitting back down in the chair and pulling on socks and shoes. 'Let alone an explanation of what that business with the young and beautiful Emms, or Fiona, or whatever she's called was all about?'

He looks across at Beef as if encouraging him to take his side. The African is standing with his back to the door, arms crossed as if shutting out all attempts at communication. The man's glazed eyes are giving out clear 'do not disturb' signals.

'I would have thought that might have been obvious,' the woman says in a quiet but firm voice. 'You have voluntarily given to us, members and representatives of Her Majesty's Government, samples of your DNA. They comprise a critical component of our never-to-be-disclosed insurance policy. It is so easy to become implicated in all the wrong sorts of crimes if you aren't careful about where you leave your DNA these days. Wouldn't you agree, Adam?' She pauses to see if she has his full attention.

'We haven't time or money for lots of legal niceties and paperwork. What you and I are about to discuss is what might best be referred to as an 'off-balance sheet' understanding between friends. An off-the-record conversation which, we hope, makes you feel motivated to help us. By doing something only you can do. Once you've completed that, assuming all's well that ends well, that will be it.' She gives him a cold, dispassionate look.

'Department?'

'Not relevant.'

'British?'

'Mostly.'

'Beef over there looks a shade Nigerian.'

'I think we can safely say that the man referred to as 'Beef' did have his ancestral origins in one of the West African states – Ghana, I think it was, isn't that right, Beef?'

She looks behind her at the man standing by the door. He allows a thin smile to penetrate his defences, nodding silently with pride.

'Very good, so, despite his Ghanaian credentials, he, like the rest of this show, is British to the core.'

'MI6, or something more exotic?'

'More exotic, I feel sure: but we are wasting time.' She examines her watch. 'It is a quarter past four. I would like you to be back at your chalet by six. It doesn't give us long. Are you happy to proceed?'

'I hardly have much choice, unless Beef over there is about to let me go, which I doubt.'

'Good. So, as you've probably surmised, this is a reasonably low-budget production. Very British, very much below the radar, not much in it for either party except national pride and making sure we all do the right thing. All right so far?'

'You mean I am not being paid for what you are about to ask me to do?'

'Good heavens, no. You already have a day-job working for Mr Al-Shawabi. By all accounts, the pay is unbelievably generous. No, this little private arrangement, absent any paperwork but just with your DNA as the bond we share between us; this has to be pro bono. For the love of your country.'

'Who exactly are you? A name might strengthen the bond of friendship between us.'

Miss Bateson shakes her head, smiling.

'No, nice try, but names are best kept out of this.'

'Fine,' he says with weary and confused resignation. 'So, let's get this over with then, shall we? What is it that you want me to do?'

He is studying Miss Bateson's shoes, noticing the brogue pattern on the leather upper.

'What we want, Adam, what we so very desperately and urgently need, is for you to take us on a guided tour inside the Al-Shawabi organisation: nuts, bolts, wiring diagrams, the works. Your new employer is one Mohammed Al-Shawabi. For reasons best known to himself and his English friends, he prefers to call himself Ricky. Ricky is a man with blue-chip provenance: Egyptian parentage, Harrovian schooling followed by a fine university education courtesy of St John's College, Cambridge. In point of fact,' the school headmistress reports in a sombre tone, scowling with disapproval, 'rumour has it that he may have only scraped a second-class degree by the skin of his teeth. Good provenance or not, Ricky has, more recently, developed a darker side. Underneath the radar, we believe he's become involved with some highly unsavoury people. People who are either poorly-behaved or, in all probability, worse.'

She removes her glasses at this stage, as if making a point.

'Much, much worse.' With the announcement of that bad piece of news out of the way, she replaces her glasses before continuing. 'We need to know who these people are. We want to know what they've been doing. Most critically, we're desperate to find out more about what they are planning on doing. Do I make myself clear?'

'Who's the 'we' in all this? Is it just you, Emma and Beef? Or are we talking about the whole might of the British establishment? Or a portion thereof? Or possibly the Americans, maybe the Chinese and perhaps whoever the fuck else might be interested?!'

He stops when he sees the look of horror on Miss Bateson's face. His mother had forever warned him about swearing in front of his teacher. In the short silence that follows, she takes up polishing her glasses once again. It's a gesture that Adam presumes is not a good development.

'The more people know about an operation, Adam, the more room there is for mistakes,' she says eventually. 'Anyway, we are not asking you to do anything inherently risky – simply relay certain snippets of information, from time to time.'

'How am I meant to do that? Pass along these assorted titbits, I mean?'

It is here that Miss Bateson, as she is now forever to be known, has her moment of genius.

'Why, you'll tell them to Fiona, of course.' It's an answer that brings an immediate smile to Adam's face.

'That's much more my kind of language. So, tell me about Ricky Al-Shawabi: the good, the bad and the ugly. If you want me to do something for you, pro bono or otherwise, you'll need to do more to convince me.'

Which, slowly, carefully and very skilfully, she proceeds to do. Within fifteen minutes, Adam feels Miss Bateson has made some good points. Very good points indeed. After thirty minutes, he feels as if he's become a signed up, if not paid-up, member of Miss Bateson's spying fraternity.

An hour later, when all the operational details have been covered and it's all hugs, kisses and handkerchief-waving on the station platform, he has the feeling that he probably ought to have been spying for Miss Bateson all of his life.

Some Months Earlier

Chapter 8

Spring 2015

Dorset, England

The flowerbeds by her window were full of multicoloured tulips. Bright, cheerful, radiant: everything she felt she could never be again. The hospice nurse would have taken her out in a wheelchair if she had but asked. That day, she couldn't be bothered. She had no energy. Not for food, not for sleep, not for anything – save for that afternoon's long-overdue meeting with her son.

He had promised faithfully that he would make the journey, and, to her surprise, he had kept his promise. In return, she had promised herself, finally, to tell him the truth; and she, too, had kept her promise – well, up to a point. The combined mental and physical effort required to utter even these few final words had been significant. The cancer was exacting a heavy toll: life was ebbing from her frail body as she spoke.

Once she had finished, he asked only a few questions. Most required minimal yes or no answers, asked in this way out of consideration for her condition. For the first time in years, she felt at peace. Exhausted but oddly calm. He leaned across to where she lay propped up in her bed and, in a tender moment, wiped a tear from the corner of her eye.

'You are in no doubt?'

'None,' she answered with surprising intensity. 'There had been -,' she continued, her dry voice beginning to crack, '- a gap in the blindfold.'

She paused, trying to replay the tape in her mind one final time.

'The testosterone had been flowing and they were careless. They thought I was high as a kite – away with the fairies. I wish I had been.'

She reached unsteadily for a glass of water, sipping the tepid liquid through a plastic straw. Her hands were shaking. Turning to look up at him, he saw anxiety, her expression urgent.

'I felt so violated: so ashamed and yet so helpless. No one would have believed me. I had no proof.'

'You didn't consider testing?'

'In hindsight. I left it too late. In those days, it wasn't so easy.' Even now, after all this time, she still looked vulnerable, he thought. 'Anyway, I had no money. My family had disowned me. Can you understand how it felt? Please say you can?'

'Of course,' he said, reaching to hold her hand. 'No one could blame you.' He smiled weakly. 'Least of all me.'

They sat like this in silence for a while. Only when he judged the moment to be right did he ask the killer question.

'Are you going to tell me who it was?'

She hesitated, perhaps longer than he might have liked, before relenting. The room fell silent as the sound of her voice faded. In time, he had only one follow-up question.

'What would you like me to do?'

'What I have been unable to do all these years. I have been a coward. Don't let the man get away with it, now that you know. Promise me in the name of God and all things in heaven that you'll confront him, once and for all.' Seized by a sudden tremor, she seemed momentarily overwhelmed by emotion. 'I have lived through too much suffering because of all that happened.'

He brought her hand to his lips, kissing it gently. It was another tender moment, a loving memory for him to cherish.

'I promise. I promise I'll do it.' He looked into her eyes, seeing relief tinged with great sadness. 'For all the pain and anguish you've suffered over the years, this man needs to pay deeply. I give you my word. Who knows, if we're lucky, he might even pay with his life.'

Chapter 9

November 2015

London

Tucked behind the Albert Embankment, close to the main railway line running from Vauxhall into London's Waterloo station, literally a stone's throw from the riverside spook factory that is the headquarters of MI6, Britain's Secret Intelligence Service, lies Citadel Place. Behind iron gates that impede the idle and curious is indeed a citadel, if not a fortress. Several shiny glass-fronted buildings, just visible through numerous railings and turnstiles, make up the home of the National Crime Agency, dubbed by some as Britain's answer to the FBI.

Born into this world only towards the end of 2013, the NCA was a product of one of those government re-organisations that Britain's politicians and civil servants seem adept at making. Through a combination of the chancellor's sleight of hand and the UK civil service's cleverness of touch, overnight the newly formed Agency was magically formed. It appeared with its new logo, acronym, and a shiny mission statement proudly boasting who it was and what it stood for. Best of all, its financial weight at birth was some forty per cent leaner than its various previous incarnations in aggregate, a cost reduction master class in shuffling the deck chairs sufficient to make the electorate proud.

With powers to direct regional police forces as and where thought necessary, and the aspiration to be as co-operative with its European counterparts as it is hoped they would be in return, the NCA director-general was arguably the most powerful police officer in the country.

Malcolm Scott, the current holder, certainly believed so. One day soon, or so he hoped, it was likely to earn him a knighthood.

Having started as a young constable on the beat in Kingston-upon-Thames, Scott rose through the ranks in record time, eventually making chief constable only twenty years later. One gong from Her Majesty, an unblemished record and seven years of service later, Scott had been a shoo-in for the DG slot even as the deck chairs were still in motion.

Besides the early work on the logo, vision and mission, one of Scott's first jobs was working out how best to spend the meagre budget assigned to him. That, and how to structure the new organisation in a way that made sense – and was manageable. It was evident early on that some part of the NCA's resources needed to be allocated to the fight against bribery, corruption and money laundering. Scott had concluded that, rather than setting up a separate directorate with its incumbent bureaucracy and cost, there might be a more straightforward solution: create a stand-alone unit reporting to his newly appointed director in charge of the Economic Crime Command, Caroline Wicks. The team from Civil Service Human Resources – another government department in the throes of its own makeover – had swung into action. After trawling databases and making discreet enquiries, they had a candidate for consideration: Foreign Office trusty Rollo Campion. Hitherto leading the network of international liaison officers within the FCO attempting to make UK and international law enforcement more joined-up, Campion came strongly recommended. He was therefore encouraged to apply, the interviews largely a formality. Promises of accelerated career progression were given by Wicks and, after due consideration, Campion agreed to join.

Once on board, Campion was allocated a thin slice of the much-pared down NCA budget. One of his first actions was to find a subordinate to do much-needed legwork. Without delay, the team from CSHR, as the newly professionalised and reconstituted team from Human Resources had become known, were back in action. Three applicants were short-listed. After a brief round of interviews, a former MI5 field agent, Margaret Milner, found herself at the top of the list.

Petite, with a pale complexion and dressed more like a librarian or schoolteacher than a former spook, Miss Milner had a face and demeanour that was both easily ignored and quickly forgotten – arguably a positive asset for someone who had spent the last few years as an MI5 field operative. Her application arrived on Campion's desk, accompanied by several glowing references.

'Can you explain to me, Margaret, exactly why you are applying for this post?'

Campion had been dressed in his three-piece suit, waistcoat all buttoned up and jacket still on, the Foreign Office man in him having found it hard to adjust to the NCA's shirt-sleeve order. There was quite a lot about the new role he was having difficulty adjusting to, his glass-walled office cubicle being yet another example.

'Certainly, Mr Campion.'

Dressed in a tweed jacket and skirt, a single row of pearls around her neck and hair swept carefully up at the back, she looked as if she had just stepped out of an Agatha Christie novel than been working for MI5.

'Though to begin on the right foot, I would prefer it if you could address me as 'Miss Milner'. If it's all the same with you?'

Whether privately Campion did or did not think it all right, the former Foreign Office man was not about to argue at such an early stage in their workplace courtship.

'If you like. Is there any particular reason?'

'Well, yes! We hardly know each other,' she had said, the matter-of-factness in her tone bringing that particular line of questioning to a quick close.

In a charitable testament to Campion's insightfulness, the subsequent hiring of Miss Milner after the interview, despite the formality of its beginnings, turned out to be a surprising and arguably inspired decision. Once in post, Campion was happy to leave Miss Milner to her own devices – what he euphemistically referred to as his '*macro-management philosophy*'. Miss Milner's week-one rapid assessment was that no battle against bribery, corruption or money laundering was ever going to be won by anyone sitting at their desk. Quoting ministerial advice passed down from *way On High*, as Campion referred to the latest edict he had received from Scott, the department was under *urgent and significant* pressure to get results. Fortunately for Campion – and to give him credit, he must indeed have seen elements of this at the interview – Miss Milner was a canny operator, once referred to by a colleague as a wily middle-aged fox. Instinctively she 'got it', secure in the knowledge that within a new, currently lean but soon to be bureaucratic organisation such as the NCA, it would be successful war stories that shaped and defined winners and losers, not people playing by the book.

Conventional wisdom expected her to go about her job by planning, sharing with her boss, discussing more widely with colleagues, collaborating with outside agencies such as MI5 and MI6 before finally getting approval from all parties – including the lawyers. Especially the lawyers: the people who, in MI5, had driven Miss Milner to distraction over what field operatives could or could not do. *The Action Prevention Squad* was what she called the Government Legal Service. Her conclusion? Convention was not about to win the day. Plan B was needed, if not plan C. The promise of plenty of Plan Bs had primarily been the reason Miss Milner had finally accepted Campion's offer. In the absence of clearly defined organisational boundaries, this new role provided a niche in the newly formed NCA establishment where she could finally escape both the bureaucrats and the Action Prevention Squad by taking a few matters into her own hands. 'Seeking forgiveness rather than permission', as her father would have said. Credit also to Campion and his macro-management philosophy.

Thus it was that Miss Milner, the lady who within weeks of her arrival was to travel to Courchevel and be known to Adam Fraser as Miss Bateson, found herself assigned a small team of researchers from the graduate FAST programme, one of whom was a bright young graduate by the name of Fiona Morris, the person destined in time to adopt the stage name, Emma. From this small nucleus, off the books and under the radar, Miss Margaret Milner prepared to unleash her first assault on the world of bribery, corruption and money laundering.

Chapter 10

December 2015

Monte Carlo, Monaco

It was Adam Fraser's night to get lucky. Dressed in a bespoke dinner suit, his sun-tanned face set radiantly against his starched white dress shirt, he arrived looking as if he has been part of the Monaco rich list for years. Stepping from the limousine and making his way towards the cavernous white marble hotel lobby, he marvelled at the grandeur of the Hermitage, in prime position overlooking the crowded harbour below.

Adam was far from being the only guest arriving for Aldo Bernadi's party. With a string quartet playing Vivaldi in the background, Adam, along with several of Monaco's finest, was ushered towards the *Salle Belle Époque* at the far end of the lobby where the Bernadi party was in full swing. Monte Carlo in December was party town: tonight, hedge fund manager and successful trader, Aldo Bernadi, was throwing a birthday party to end all birthday parties.

'This evening, my friend, you are going to be amazed,' Aldo had told him earlier in the day. 'Just you wait. The rich and the famous from across the Côte d'Azur will be there. So much wealth, it will be obscene!'

Adam had first met Aldo at Durham University. The two young students had instantly become friends, discovering alcohol, women and love together in roughly equal measure. From the outset, it had been evident that Aldo was a playboy in the making: a gregarious party animal, someone destined to rise to the top surrounded by the best of life's trappings. The young Italian had known well before he started at Durham what he would be doing after university: heading to London and making his fortune. In contrast, Adam, *Adz* as Aldo liked to call him, had been less certain. He flip-flopped between, on the one hand, a sense of duty and, on the other, a desire to follow an altogether wilder path: letting the dice roll and *bugger it*, doing whatever came along next.

After they graduated, Aldo did indeed hot-foot it to London, an even bigger party town than Durham, quickly discovering a flair for making – and spending – serious money as an oil trader. Adam, meanwhile, found himself under-employed and drifting. Only late in the day did the sense of duty finally prevail. With money running out and few other ideas presenting themselves, he took the plunge and joined the Army. Thus, whilst Aldo was busy earning his first million and having a ball, Adam went soldiering in dangerous and unsavoury parts of Afghanistan. As Aldo would later say, with hardly a trace of irony, '*It was pretty clear, my friend, who got the better deal*'. Flush with cash, further millions promised in bonus pools that at the time he was unable to access, Aldo was soon easily persuaded to give up his London life and become a tax exile in what he was to later to describe as *the most expensive but most beautiful place in the world.*

The two friends had thus drifted apart until a few months ago when Adam experienced two wake-up calls in quick succession. The first was Adam's rapid - and unplanned - exit from the Army over a little misunderstanding which both parties were keen to hush up and move on from. The second was Adam's mother sudden death. Both had, in Adam's own words, been life-changing moments in his journey of self-discovery. Suddenly without either job or family and burdened by a newly awakened sense of responsibility, Adam felt a need to seek out and reconnect with his oldest friend. Aldo, of course, had been only too thrilled to take Adam under his wing.

Adz, come to Monte Carlo, I insist! I can help you, it will be my pleasure. We will have so much fun, I promise. I will teach you to make money. It will be fantastico!

This time the sense of *bugger it* had prevailed. Adam had indeed rolled the dice and, without a second thought, moved to Monte Carlo. In turn, his Italian friend wasted no time in teaching him the basics of becoming a successful oil trader. It hadn't been a slow process either. Within a few months, Adam showed that he, like his friend, had a natural talent for networking and making money. With his friend's guiding hand never far from the tiller, he quickly began building a reputation and following all of his own.

'Adz, come, I want you to meet one of the most beautiful ladies in Monaco.'

The food had been cleared, and the noise level in the room was on the rise. Somewhere close by, music had begun to play, though not at levels that yet prevented conversation.

'Frankly, I am disappointed that you are not yet acquainted. Alexandra,' Aldo said, exuding charm to the elegantly dressed woman next to him. 'I'd like to introduce my oldest and dearest friend, Adam Fraser: fellow Brit, reprobate, one-time solider, now like me a renowned party animal. He is also an aspiring oil trader and fellow mischief-maker.'

He smiled at his friend and winked before continuing his introductions.

'Adz, this beautiful lady is fellow Brit, Alexandra Brock, possibly the most glamorous lawyer in the whole of the Riviera.'

The two strangers shook hands, eyes dancing, the moment of first contact positive: the vibes were receptive, interested, and playful – definitely lots of potential.

'Why only the 'possibly', Aldo?' Adam asked, lifting Alexandra's hand to his lips, placing a warm kiss of welcome on her wrist. 'It's a pleasure to meet you, Alexandra.'

'Oh please, call me Xandra. Everyone else does. Or even Xan but just not Alex, I can't abide that name. Is it Adam or Adz?'

'Either is fine. You choose.'

'Let's start with Adam and see where we go from there. No, Aldo, I agree with your friend. 'Possibly being the most glamorous' doesn't quite cut it.'

A waitress glided up to them and refilled their champagne glasses. Roederer's Cristal. Only the very classiest of wines for Monaco's swankiest of parties.

'What brings you to Monaco, Adam? Or is it just the money?'

Adam laughed, peering into his champagne glass before turning to look properly at Xandra for the first time. This was a powerful and classy woman. Older than Adam by a few years, she was intelligent, she was confident and the close-fitting black Chanel dress that clung to her body made her look very sexy.

'The bountiful supply of beautiful women, of course. Aldo only ever introduces me to the *most* glamorous ones, I hope you realise.'

Adam received a playful thump from Xandra's clutch bag.

'*Touché.* I think I like you, Adam Fraser. Come and talk to me whilst we lose some money on the roulette wheels over there,' she said, pointing to the far corner of the grand salon. 'Catch up with you later, Aldo. Great party, by the way.'

Adam took Xandra by an offered arm and, giving a discreet thumbs-up to his Italian friend, headed off in the direction of the miniature casino.

She was down ten thousand euros: Adam, in contrast, was ahead fifteen.

'Damn you, Adam Fraser. You're on a winning streak, you seem unstoppable. I need more champagne. Grab me some, will you?'

Adam lifted two full glasses from a tray held by a passing waitress and gave one to Xandra. They were huddled in a small group crowded around the table, hip to hip. Xandra had to lean across Adam to place her one-thousand-euro chips on the board, her warm body pressing against his, her long, black hair wafting near his face. He could smell vanilla and almonds and had a sudden yearning to take this woman to bed. Placing his two chips on red, they watched as the ball was sent spinning around the wheel, both of them huddled in close as it settled on black number eight. This time they were both losers.

'Not my lucky night,' Xandra said shrugging, draining the champagne from her glass in one gulp. As she turned away to pick up her remaining chips, in a characteristic moment of spontaneity, he pressed his body into hers and whispered.

'Shall we dance?'

'I thought you'd never ask,' she said turning towards him and, after a moment's hesitation, kissing him briefly on the lips.

'Did I do something to deserve that?'

'Are you complaining?'

'No, but it might have left me wanting more.'

'Let's dance first.'

'Lead on,' he said. She took his arm in hers and they headed across to where the music was now playing loudly. As they got close to the dance floor, Adam had a sudden smile on his face. Daft Punk's music was blaring at full volume. Perhaps he really would be up all night getting lucky after all!

Chapter 11

December 2015

Monte Carlo, Monaco

At two in the morning, the Hermitage's duty manager agreed to let Adam take the only remaining unsold suite for half the usual room rate. This was partly due to the lateness of the hour and partly considering that Adam had been, indeed still was, a guest attending Signor Bernadi's party. Adam handed over two one-thousand Euro casino chips whilst Xandra, bearing her own ready-made party bag comprising one bottle of champagne and two glasses, waited for him by the elevator lobby.

They woke with sun streaming through their seventh-floor bedroom window, clothes scattered over the floor. In urgent need of caffeine, Xandra went in search of a coffee maker and set to work. Once back in bed, the coffee too hot to drink, the sun warm on their faces, a brief lover's kiss from Adam on the nape of her neck rekindled their passion. They made love for a second – or perhaps third – time, the previous few hours a delicious drunken haze of pleasure. Adam discovered a lust and desire for her that took him by surprise.

'That was some night,' she said later, sitting up in bed.

'Plenty more of that in the tank, if and when required,' Adam replied. 'Possibly the sexiest, most glamorous lawyer that I've been to bed with in the whole of the Riviera.'

She put her coffee mug down, climbed astride him and started hitting him.

'For that, Adam Fraser,' she said as they wrestled each other playfully, 'I might just demand an encore.'

'Any time.'

They both laughed. Rolling away, she took a mouthful of coffee and winced.

'Yuck, it's gone cold.' She looked across at him. 'What are we doing here exactly, Adam? I mean, this is a one-off, right? One single, solitary night of unbridled passion: a see-you-at-the-next-party sort of affair only, correct?'

'I've no idea. I can't think past breakfast.'

'Aldo says you are a rising star,' she said a short while later. 'A few successful deals under your belt is what I hear.'

Adam pretended to be shocked but was secretly excited by this level of due diligence. It was a good omen.

'Have you been checking up on me? I thought we'd only met a few hours ago.'

'Nothing is secret in Monaco. Aldo and I have known each other for a while: we've even done the odd bit of business together. We meet from time to time. He and I happened to have a coffee earlier in the week. He told me about this new wonder boy: a former soldier, not long out of the Army, newly arrived in Monaco and already making pots of money.'

'Nothing in comparison to what he's been making. He's a clever man, Aldo. Come to think of it, we never did get around to discussing what you did for a living last night. Or if we did, the Cristal shampoo rinsed it clean out of my mind. Apart from probably being the most glamorous lawyer on the Riviera, what else occupies your waking hours? Bona fide lawyer, market trader like Signor Bernadi, or something racier?'

'Oh, I don't know. A mixture of all three probably.'

'Come on, don't be obtuse. Spell it out, girl, shout it from the seventh-floor rooftops. Adam Fraser needs to know!'

'I work for a business here in Monaco called Al-Shawabi. Owned and run by an eccentric half-Brit, half-Egyptian who goes by the name of

Ricky Al-Shawabi. Mean anything to you?'

'Never heard of him. Don't forget, I was in the Army until recently. I haven't studied the Who's Who of business lately. What does this Mr Ricky do for a living?'

'He's an entrepreneur who fixes things for people. Connects people who have particular problems to solve in one location with other people in different locations who may be able to help. Want to negotiate a crude oil deal with the Libyans? Come and see Ricky: he knows who to deal with. Heard about the hydro project in Nepal and want to bid for the generator contract? Ricky will know the right people. Need to find a way to keep hard-earned commissions and income away from prying eyes? Al-Shawabi can help you find a way.'

'Sounds quite a business. What's your role?'

'Ricky's the salesman with all the connections. I simply make everything happen. A sort of back-office lady.'

'You run the show, then.'

'More or less. Operations, finance, tax – especially tax – and treasury. Oh, yes, and HR.'

'Sounds glamorous.'

'Tell me about the Army, Adam.'

'Oh, it was the usual stuff. I was in the Parachute Regiment for several years. I did a few tours, fired a few bullets, dodged a few as well, though that was in Afghanistan mainly.'

'But not all the bullets, if what I heard from Aldo was correct?'

'You seem to know a lot about me all of a sudden. Where's all this coming from?'

'Being responsible for HR includes scouting for talent from time to time. Let's just say that we might have been looking for someone like you. And before you ask, it had – and has – absolutely no bearing on why we currently find ourselves in this grand suite sharing a bed. So back to the Army. You were about to tell me.'

Adam looked up at the ceiling and drew a big breath.

'If I were a smoker, which I am not, by the way, I would be lighting up at this point, do you understand?'

'How about some Cristal?'

'Uncharacteristically perhaps, but no thanks, not at the moment. So, the Army.'

He paused, taking a deep breath before beginning.

'I had two tours in Afghanistan, both times based out of Camp Bastion in Helmand province. It's an amazing place. Enormous, like a massive city plonked in the middle of a war zone. Safe as houses once you're inside, lethal on the outside if you're not careful. Landmines, snipers, roadside bombs, the works. Best hospitals on the planet, though. I mean it. If you ever need major surgery, forget the Princesse Grace here in Monaco. Get a Medevac to wing you to Bastion. Doctors there are second to none – and no waiting lists either. Anyway, the Bastion medical unit has so many drugs and medical supplies, it is obscene. Truckloads, literally. Especially considering that on the outside of the perimeter fence, the locals can't get much of anything. Only out on patrol did one ever come face to face with ordinary Afghan families with all their incumbent pain and suffering: it wasn't school pens they were after; this wasn't some third world tourist location like Angkor Wat or the Taj Mahal. It was medical supplies they craved. Food and good clothing too, but the sick and young were dying because they couldn't get the medicines they needed. It struck me on my second tour, when I was a bit older and more worldly-wise, that maybe there was a way we could help each other: a primitive trading opportunity begging to be exploited. What could these wretched people possibly have that we might want? Guess what? Heroin and opium. Did you know that opium poppies are being grown and harvested less than a mile from the Bastion fence? It is unbelievable.'

'I like it. Your first taste of being a real-life trader. Trading medical supplies for drugs of a different kind.'

'More or less. It wasn't on a massive scale. We weren't driving truckloads in and out of Bastion or anything like that. Just small supplies that could be slipped into our Bergens: antibiotics, syringes, bandages, even paracetamol and ibuprofen – basically, anything you could acquire from the Bastion pharmacy without arousing suspicion.'

'How did you offload the heroin?'

'That was easy. There was no shortage of addicts on the base, only too happy to play dealer.'

'Until you were busted.'

'No one was able to prove anything. Someone decided to grass on me, and suddenly I was up before the CO. They had no proof and didn't want it to go to court-martial. In the end, we struck a deal. It's usually the best way. I was repatriated back to the UK, nothing formal on the record, but immediately discharged. I signed a non-disclosure agreement which I guess I've just broken. What the fuck, let them sue me. They shoved me out on my ear and I found myself on Civvy Street and in desperate need of work. I owe Aldo a lot: he picked me up when I was down, encouraged me to come to Monaco, gave me a fresh start. He's been a good friend, a really good friend. How am I doing? I like this kind of job interview, by the way.'

'Passed both the theory and the practical with flying colours,' she said, leaning across the bed and kissing him. 'I like your honesty, Adam. It's refreshing. I'd very much like you to meet Ricky. That's for another day, though. Right now, I feel in need of a shower. Why don't you make us another cup of coffee and I'll go and figure out how to use the shower in the bathroom.'

A while later, Adam put two mugs of steaming black coffee down on the marble top beside the bathroom sink. Xandra was in the walk-in shower, lathered all over. Adam knew he had played his cards well. He may have just got lucky. Very lucky, thank you, Aldo. Something about seeing this woman naked in the shower, soaped in all the right places, was erotic. He stepped in to join her. She felt his arousal close to her skin.

'Hang on, one step at a time. First, you need a good scrubbing, Adam Fraser. Don't get overexcited.'

She applied a generous portion of liquid soap, Adam reacting immediately to her touch. She ran her fingers gently all over him, working the smooth, soapy lather into every crevice, rubbing carefully.

'Next, the rinse cycle.'

She was toying with him, enjoying Adam's reaction as fine needles of warm water now sprayed over his body from the handheld shower unit.

'The final step,' she said eventually, her eyes sparkling with anticipation, 'should be the blow-dry, don't you think?'

Chapter 12

December 2015

Monte Carlo, Monaco

The invitation to Adam's final job interview arrived two days later. It was hidden amongst several text messages that Adam had been exchanging with Xandra. He might have missed it had he not been looking out for it.

Btw, lunch with RAS this Fri 12 noon - yacht club casual ok? xxx

Adam consulted Aldo, who declared his matchmaking efforts an unequivocal success.

'Adz, you smoothie! You didn't waste any time, did you?'

'It must have been something in the Cristal.'

'The Yacht Club suggests you'll be meeting Ricky on his boat. This, my friend, is something else. One massive superyacht. It's very, very classy.'

'That'll be a new experience. I've never been on one of those before.'

'Get used to it, Adz. You haven't lived in Monaco until you've had your first outing on someone's superyacht.'

'I've not seen yours yet.'

'I've been waiting for the right moment. No, I'm joking. You know me, I don't actually like the water anyway. Come, we can find pictures on the internet. This boat truly is amazing.'

'Have you been on it?'

'A few times, yes. It is incredible. Enormous. Fantastico. Polished wood, soft furnishings, marble: the ultimate in luxury.'

'What's he like, this Ricky Al-Shawabi? Is he a monster or a pussycat? Sense of humour or dry as a bone?'

'He's a charmer, just like you. You'll be fine, trust me. He likes to crack jokes, always the perfect host. Just don't be fooled by all the bonhomie: he's as sharp as anyone I know. Shrewd. If he decides that he trusts you, you could become his friend for life.'

When Friday arrived, Adam's version of casual looked straight out of a clothing catalogue. Male model on quayside posing in freshly laundered linen shirt. No tie – naturally. Close-fitting cashmere jumper to emphasise the muscular physique. Smart but not ironed chinos. Boat shoes. Finally, a jacket slung casually over the shoulder.

'How do I look?' Adam asked Xandra when she greeted him at the entrance to the Yacht Club at the appointed hour.

'Ralph Lauren would be proud.'

'You look terrific,' he said with feeling. Her version of boating casual was jacket and trousers, a striped top and a sizeable multicoloured shawl draped around her shoulders. Flat shoes as well.

'Ready to meet the Great Man?'

'I guess.'

She took him by the arm and led him through the Yacht Club entrance. Instantly recognised by the attentive staff, Xandra was warmly greeted like an old friend of the family. They were both escorted through the clubhouse to doors out the back that lead onto the quayside, an enormous wharf jutting out into the Mediterranean. On both sides of the long finger pier were dozens upon dozens of some of the biggest yachts that Adam had ever seen. It was an amazing sight.

'I feel as if I'm in another world. This is unreal.'

'Welcome to the real Monaco, Adam. This is where the money is.'

She stopped, letting go of his arm and moving a short distance away from him. 'For the next few hours, we ought to keep our relationship purely business, if it's all the same to you. It's time to let them meet the true Adam Fraser, not Xandra's latest *beau*.'

'Sure. Whatever works best. Happy just to be invited. It's going to be a hoot. Where are we going?'

'That big beast over there. It's called Rasmatazz. It's Ricky's little joke. The name is deliberately misspelt to position his initials upfront.'

'Bloody hell, Xandra. It's fucking enormous!'

'As they say, if you've got it, flaunt it.'

'On that yardstick, Ricky's certainly got it.'

'Adam? I'm Ricky, it's good to meet you. Welcome aboard. Come on in, follow me, let me show you around.'

Ricky was in his element, the perfect host showing the Al-Shawabi newbie some of his toys.

'Ever been on one of these beauties before?' He didn't wait for Adam to reply. 'They're quite special. Look, here's Jumbo; he can get you a drink. What will you have? Anything you want. Champagne's open if you fancy, or we have beers, wines, you name it.'

'A glass of champagne would be great, thanks.'

'Make that two, Jumbo. I'm sure Xandra will have one.' He looked at Adam and raised his eyebrows. 'She usually does,' he added as an aside. 'I'll have a Campari soda please, easy on the ice. Tell me,' he said, stopping quickly and turning around. 'Have we met before? Your face looks familiar; I can't quite work it out.'

Adam shook his head.

'Don't think so, Ricky. I would have remembered, I'm sure.'

'Must be me then. It's an age thing, memory on the blink, sadly nothing unusual about that. Meanwhile, the guided tour. Oh, thank you, Jumbo, that was quick. Here's your drink Adam. Shout if it's not to your liking,' he said, taking his drink and continuing as if he hadn't been interrupted.

'Right, guest rooms are down these stairs here, all en-suite; on this floor is the dining room, kitchen and living area. Want to head down and see a bedroom?'

Without waiting for an answer, Ricky raced down the beautifully polished wooden staircase and threw open one of the cabin doors.

'What do you think?' he said, stepping inside the large space and beckoning Adam to follow him.

I think you seem a bit of an arsehole, to tell the truth, Ricky.

'Pretty amazing. Better than a five-star hotel.'

'That's what we're aiming to be. I want my guests to feel pampered. Have a good look around.'

There was a knock on the door as Ricky was in mid-flow.

'Excuse me.'

A man of about Adam's height and age, face like a brick wall and muscles bulging in an ill-fitting suit jacket, filled the doorway.

'Ah, Vladek, to what do we owe the pleasure? Have you met Adam Fraser, our guest of honour for the day, by the way? Adam, this is the most important man in my business. Vladek looks after all of our security matters, isn't that right, Vladek?'

Adam stepped forward to offer his hand, but Vladek blanked him, staring fixedly at Ricky instead.

'The captain is asking whether he can cast off?'

'If everyone's onboard that needs to be, let's get underway.'

'Very good.'

As he turned to leave, Ricky called after him.

'Oh, Vladek, one more thing.'

The man's muscular torso again filled the doorframe. 'Be nice to Adam, can you please? I want him to feel welcome and well looked after, if it's all the same to you?'

'Very good,' he said, and this time stepped forward to shake Adam's hand. His grip was vice-like.

'Nice to have you aboard today.'

Without a trace of a smile, he turned, heading out of the room and up the stairs.

'What was that about?' Adam asked, puzzled by Vladek's behaviour.

'Who, Vladek?' Ricky said, all sweetness and sugar. 'Don't worry about him. He's not very good with strangers. Gets all protective about the core team, especially Xandra for some reason. Doesn't like the thought that someone else might be knocking her off, so to speak. None of my – or his – business actually, and good luck to you if you are, Adam. Speaking personally, it's a path well-trodden. As far as I am concerned, she's a wonderful person, don't get me wrong, it's just that Vladek can be a bit over-sensitive about these things. He'll be all right, I promise. Now, why don't we go upstairs and see who else has arrived? I don't want you missing the fun of getting this monster out to sea.'

The entourage had turned out *en masse* – Ozzie, Fergus, Gemma – the Whole Shebang as Ricky called them.

'Think of it as the unofficial Al-Shawabi Christmas outing,' Ricky, master of ceremonies and entertainer-in-chief, was explaining to Adam. Everyone had been on deck to watch the captain and his crew expertly slip Rasmatazz's moorings and steer the massive yacht out of Monte Carlo's harbour and into the gleaming Mediterranean Sea. Today the temperature was a brisk eighteen degrees centigrade in the sun, colder with the moderate breeze that was blowing. Before long, everyone was heading inside to the warmth of the beautifully furnished interior.

'Ever been on anything like this before, Adam?' Ozzie Gerhard was asking, standing with his pretty young wife, Gemma, next to him. Ozzie's version of casual boat wear made Adam feel positively scruffy.

'No, never actually. I am not even sure what kind of vessel this is.'

'Me neither,' giggled Gemma, sipping her champagne and smiling sweetly at the newcomer in their midst.

Adam gave Gemma his most charming smile as Ozzie began a full technical description of Rasmatazz and its history.

'This is a Turkish-made vessel, built by Bilgin shipyards in Istanbul. Every boat has all of its component parts handcrafted on-site in Istanbul, nothing prefabricated or bought in. As a result, each yacht is ultra-exclusive, ultra-luxurious and ultra-expensive. This particular model, the 160 Classic . . . . .'

Adam's attention started to drift. Out of the corner of an eye, he saw Xandra and Ricky deep in conversation. Occasionally, Ricky cast a glance in Adam's direction, apparently prompted by something that Xandra was telling him. Across the room, Fergus, the Monaco office manager was talking with a tall, long-legged blonde woman. This was Tash, Ricky's current female companion and a real eye-catcher, although immune to Adam's mildly flirtatious early attempt at conversation. The same could not be said of Gemma: one glass of bubbly down and her eyes were wide open, giving Adam unmistakeable come-on signals. He smiled at her again and this time winked, causing Gemma to blush and giggle silently into her champagne. Ozzie's technical narration continued unabated.

'. . . at just under fifty metres in length, it has six cabins and a crew of eight. In the power department, twin Kohler engines . . .'

Which just left Vladek, on his own, standing twenty feet away and watching everybody in the room, but mostly Adam. Adam could sense the menace, feeling the man's unwelcoming eyes boring into him.

Ozzie was in full flow when Ricky and Xandra crossed the room to join them. Ricky listened to Ozzie for a short while before deciding to interrupt.

'Fully up to date with Rasmatazz's technical details are we now, Adam? Ozzie has this amazing encyclopaedic memory for anything technical, haven't you, Oz? Multiple choice questions to follow after the lunch service. Our Ozzie is always very smartly turned out, although rather generous on the starch, don't you think? Lovely to see you here today, by the way, Gemma darling. Looking on great form, if I'm allowed to say that and not get into trouble?'

He blew her a flirtatious air kiss which made her giggle. She nervously reciprocated the gesture and blushed.

'Anyway folks, Henri, our very own Master Chef, and his team have been slaving away in the galley all morning. I am told that we will shortly be ready to eat. Five minutes to powder noses and other parts, and then the Montrachet comes off the ice.'

'You are doing amazingly, Adam. They all love you. You could be part of the family already. How are you feeling?'

It was a snatched sound bite *en route* to and from the restrooms.

'Fine. A bit overwhelmed, but otherwise it's just an ordinary day in the office, really, isn't it?'

She hit him playfully.

'Careful,' he murmured. 'Remember, we're meant to be keeping our relationship purely business.'

She stuck her tongue out at him.

'The only thing I don't get is Vladek. He seems to hate me.'

'He hates everybody. Let's chat later. Come on, time to take our places.'

'Adam, would you mind doing the honours with the Montrachet? It's a 2007 and should be 'tip-top', as the French-speaking Swiss say, is that not right, Ozzie?'

'*Vraiment,* Monsieur Ricky.'

'Not bad, Ozzie, considering you're from the German-speaking lot. What do you think of the wine, Adam? Do we need to send it back or is it drinkable?'

God, you are a pretentious prick, Ricky.

Adam swirled the yellow liquid in the prescribed manner, sniffed it, and pronounced it passable.

'Good, pour away. Before we all get too relaxed, let's give our special guest a foretaste of some of the Al-Shawabi magic. Tash, Gemma, my darlings, sorry about this bit. It will only take a few minutes. Can the pair of you grab a glass of wine and skedaddle for the moment? Tash dearest, why not show Gemma those lovely new diamonds of yours? Hurry along now.'

He paused whilst they left the room.

'So, Adam. We'd like to lift the veil a little and give you a small Al-Shawabi taster. A veritable *amuse-bouche,* as it were, of some of the wonderful things that we all get up to. Ozzie, why don't you kick-off? Let's keep it short and sweet, shall we? We don't want to keep the food service waiting.'

'Very good,' Ozzie said, evidently pleased to be asked to go first.

'I've just completed an innovative deal for some Indian investors. Routing funds through a Delaware subsidiary linked to one of our Panamanian vehicles, we've helped the Indians acquire the sole access rights to consumer banking licences in Indonesia and other parts of South-East Asia. The Indians are delighted and, having deployed a modicum of the Al-Shawabi magic dust, the Indonesians have been exceedingly well taken care of and are very content. Best of all, we stand to make a substantial margin.'

'How much do we think, Ozzie?'

'There's currently five million dollars of fees routing through our Manama operation and another five down the road in about six months. Net of expenses, we should make a profit margin of almost sixty per cent.'

Adam smiled appreciatively. 'Impressive.'

'It's a good example of some of the more innovative things we're doing these days. Fergus, what about you?'

'Several multinationals – American, British, German and a few others – have asked us to help them win major contracts in historically challenging and difficult-to-access markets. This last month we closed two big infrastructure deals in Myanmar, with others on the go in China and Turkmenistan, plus a huge one in Zambia. Our fees for the pair we closed recently will amount to about four million, plus expenses.'

'All good grist to the mill. What I like to think of as our bread-and-butter work. Xandra, do you have anything to add?'

'Over and above what's been covered? Mainly what we are doing behind the scenes to help an American bigwig investor acquire certain Pan-Asian sporting rights. It's all rather delicate so I am, by necessity, being oblique. If everything goes to plan, it should earn us about twenty million over five years. Oh, and I have two very senior Latin American political figures that have just signed up as new clients with one or two more in the pipeline.'

'Very good, thank you. Adam, part of what today is all about is to give you a flavour of the Al-Shawabi business. The other part, which may not come as a complete surprise, is that we have a proposition we'd like to put to you. We've done our due diligence, dug around and discovered the good, bad and the ugly about Adam Fraser. The good news is that we've decided that we like you. More to the point, we'd very much like you to come and work with us. We think you'd make an excellent fit. It's now up to all of us to try and persuade you.'

He paused, allowing time for the others to nod enthusiastically.

'Let me be a bit more specific. It's all about oil, Adam, and it plays directly into your sweet spot. With Iran opening up, Syria and Iraq both basket cases and the Saudis playing games by producing too much oil, the Al-Shawabi business finds itself in a dilemma: we have unique and powerful connections across a turbulent and changing Middle East but with not enough people on our team to exploit them all. In the past, we would have resorted to using people like your friend, Aldo Bernadi, to help out on occasion. It wasn't always very satisfactory, and we only ever did it on a strictly 'needs must' basis.

'We think, however, that now may be precisely the right moment to be expanding our operations in different directions. These Middle Eastern 'oily' friends of ours, they would love us to, how should I put this delicately, to feel encouraged to buy their oil at special, below-market, prices. This is where Al-Shawabi, an internationally accredited organisation, is actually in its element. We have the knowledge and skills to structure the type of contracts and side arrangements that these people want in ways that guarantee discretion, sensitivity and anonymity. At the moment, the oil price is at an all-time low. Approaching twenty-five dollars a barrel. It won't last forever.'

He looked at Adam with eyebrows raised.

'I agree,' Adams replied, nodding. 'Most predict that it is unlikely to get back to one hundred dollars a barrel again for some time. Some are even muttering about a new-normal price of around forty to fifty dollars a barrel, perhaps in as little as the next six months or so.'

'Exactly my point! Logic says that now has to be precisely when we should be using our contacts to buy oil and store it in tankers safely offshore for a few months until the price starts to rise. Then, when we trade out this oil on the open market, we stand to make a killing.'

Adam let out a sigh.

'For a very large crude carrying tanker, laden with product worth many tens of millions of US dollars, that's a huge potential profit.'

'Precisely! Which is why, Adam, you need to come and work with us. Think about it. Let's say no more for now – it's time to eat, drink, digest everything and be merry. We can discuss details at a later stage. Vladek?'

Vladek hastened into the room from outside. 'Yes, sir.'

'Ask Tash and Gemma to come back, can you? And then tell the kitchen that we are ready to eat. Let's bring on the food. I'm starving!'

Present Day

Chapter 13

Saturday 23rd January 2016

Northumberland, England

It's the annual outing to Sir Giles Armstrong's pheasant shoot in the wilds of Northumberland. Sir Giles, Jeremy Seymour's permanent secretary at the Home Office, has had the ten-thousand-acre estate in his family for three generations. Usually let on a commercial basis to parties willing to pay handsomely for the privilege, Sir Giles sets aside a few days of the year for himself, his friends and family. One Saturday in January, towards the end of the pheasant shooting season, he invites his two colleagues, Sir Philip Angel, permanent secretary at the Foreign Office and Sir Nigel Goodhew, permanent secretary at the Treasury, for a day's rough shooting. It is a very private and very informal gathering of three very senior people.

They have a ritual all their own. Leaving the office together on a Friday afternoon, they take the early evening train from King's Cross, dining on board before a late arrival at Morpeth Station, north of Newcastle. Sir Giles's gamekeeper, Peter, waits at the station to meet them, driving them in the Range Rover the short distance towards the Cheviot foothills and the stone lodge that forms part of the substantial country estate. A nightcap or two is taken, usually in front of a blazing fire with the dogs at their feet, before everyone heads to bed quite late. In the morning, the housekeeper has a hearty cooked breakfast prepared for them and, by 8.45 am, everyone is dressed and ready to leave. Peter typically outlines plans for the day over a final mug of coffee as the group study several large-scale maps brought. Then, they head off, Peter driving the Range Rover and Sir Giles bringing up the rear in a battered old Land Rover with the dogs in the back. They head to a far corner of the estate where, amongst woodland and open fields, they spend several hours rough-shooting pheasant. Sometime in the early afternoon, having taken only a few short breaks in between, they call it a day and make the return trip to the lodge, full of anticipation for a very late – and protracted – lunch. It is typically a roast of some description, accompanied by fine claret from Sir Giles's cellar.

Dogs and guns having been cleaned and put to bed, Peter leaves the three of them to have lunch by themselves. Places have already been set at a large round table in the dining room. The housekeeper then delivers a roast on a trolley and Sir Giles carves once everyone is ready. Wine glasses are filled from one of two decanters, and that is the cue for everyone to tuck in. It is also the silent signal, as if one were needed, for the first of many long conversations about the workings of government to begin.

'The key question I'd like to know is who is best-placed to succeed Ingleby as PM?'

Sir Nigel is the eldest and most experienced civil servant of the three, having served six different Chancellors since becoming permanent secretary at Treasury fifteen years ago.

'We'd benefit from Philippa being with us if we're having this conversation.'

Dame Philippa Mayhew was the Cabinet Secretary, the highest-ranking female civil servant of all time.

'Sadly, she doesn't shoot. I did ask her,' Sir Giles answers. 'In any event, I doubt she'd be happy to discover the three of us having firm opinions on that particular subject. More wine, anyone?'

'Yes please!' the other two answer enthusiastically in unison.

'Back to Ingleby's successor. Naturally it is a party matter, not in theory any of our business. Hypothetically, though, who would be our choice for the next PM? Is there anyone we think could do with a helping hand?'

'Or, putting it slightly differently,' Sir Nigel says, picking up the thread, 'is there anyone we absolutely do not want to succeed?'

'That's a tough call,' Sir Philip says eventually. 'It depends really on what the result of the EU referendum is going to be. I can't see any other serious contenders besides each of our three ministers, can you?'

He'd had a similar conversation with the foreign secretary recently. Without ruling out an outsider, they had both concluded that the list of serious front-runners was thin.

'Without beating about the bush,' Sir Giles picks up, 'my personal opinion is that it would be disastrous if the home secretary were picked.' The other two nod in silence: if anyone were to have insights about what Jeremy Seymour was really like, it would be Sir Giles, his permanent secretary. 'He's so unbearably pompous and manipulative. He'd drive everyone round the twist. Cabinet meetings would be a nightmare.'

'Absolutely,' says Sir Nigel. 'I overheard the Foreign Secretary privately muttering the same thoughts only the other day after a particularly rumbustious session in Cabinet. That said, I doubt that my chap wouldn't be any better, even though he seems to be the bookies' favourite. There isn't a lot of warmth and charm that goes hand in hand with Stephen Russell. He'd be a gift to the Opposition, given how badly they appear to be trailing in the polls. What do you think, Philip?'

Sir Philip Angel quietly sips some more wine before answering.

'Without sounding partisan, I do think Geraldine Macauley is the best of all three. Ex-barrister, recently widowed, popular in the party, she presents well and has a steely edge. She dealt with the Americans effectively over recent conversations about our involvement in the Middle East. She is popular at the FCO, and most think she has done a reasonable job. She's certainly up for it. Eurosceptic, but able to field whatever curved balls the referendum is likely to bowl us. I think she'd be tough but fair. On balance, a good candidate.'

'I don't warm to her particularly, I confess,' Sir Giles says. 'She and

Seymour are like chalk and cheese. Whilst he can be pompous, she can be prickly. I suppose, though, I tend to agree with you, Philip. Views, Nigel?'

'I am not sure I agree – about her being prickly, that is. I'm a big fan. The fact that she rubs Seymour up the wrong way is a positive, in my view. No, out of our short-list, I think the foreign secretary is the most suitable. Is she likely to win, though?'

The housekeeper chooses this moment to reappear, bearing a tray with a large apple crumble on it along with an over-sized jug of custard. She places the tray on the table and clears away their plates.

'Splendid. Thank you, Mrs Travis. Would anyone like some Riesling with their crumble? I find it goes particularly well with the crumble.'

'Why not? Great lunch, thank you, Giles. Well done, Mrs Travis. One of your very best.'

The housekeeper beams as she finishes clearing, soon leaving them alone once more. Sir Giles pours the wine whilst the others help themselves to dessert.

'I have my suspicions,' Sir Giles says, pouring custard onto his plate, 'that this leadership contest is going to get dirty. Seymour has been making statements about his personal crusade against tax dodgers and corruption. He and the chancellor have been making contrary statements recently over tax avoidance and the treatment of non-doms. There's a battle looming.'

'Tax avoidance is a side issue, a crude attempt by Seymour to divert attention from the one area he wants to bring to the fore during the referendum campaign. Immigration.' It is Sir Nigel, the Treasury mandarin speaking, his remarks drawing thoughtful nods from the other two.

'Seymour's a cunning bastard. He'll always try his level best to unseat his rivals. I think Giles is right. It's going to get dirty.'

'When Seymour first got elected, do you remember those rumours about a smear campaign against the main rival in his constituency? What's he likely to do this time around?'

'I suspect all bets are off, Philip,' says Sir Giles. 'Seymour's a driven man with his eye on the main prize. He has sharp and selfish elbows. I wouldn't put it past him to do almost anything if it helped stir up public opinion against Russell and Macauley.'

'Perhaps bringing him down a peg or two might be helpful? What do you think?'

'It's an idea,' Sir Nigel says, wiping crumbs from the corner of his mouth.

'Doesn't he own a farm in Norfolk?'

'He used to, until recently.'

'Well, there are plenty of migrant workers in that part of the world, many of them illegals. I wonder how clean the Seymour family's hands are?'

'Using illegal, cheap farm labour, you mean?'

'Why not? How two-faced would it look when he uses an anti-immigration platform as part of his leadership bid if the public got to hear about illegal migrants working on the Seymour family farm.'

'Especially if he was paying them in cash as they all do. Some might conclude that Seymour was deliberating trying to avoid paying his taxes.'

'I wonder if we could find an investigative journalist from the Sunday papers willing to have a poke around? It should be right up their street, taking a pop at an ambitious cabinet minister.'

'As long as we aren't implicated, I think it's an excellent idea, Giles. I could have a quiet word with one of the editors who I know well personally.' Sir Philip Angel takes a small notepad from his breast pocket and jots a note to himself.

'We might also consider a little investigatory work into my minister, given what I've heard whispered in the corridors.' The other two stop eating, waiting for Sir Nigel to explain further. 'He may be the front-runner, but he earned a small fortune whilst working for that investment bank a while back. It's just that no one seems to know where any of the money has disappeared. He lives very modestly; there's no hint of anything in the Members' Register of Interests – it's all mysteriously vanished. Some are wondering whether it might be hidden offshore somewhere.'

'That would be embarrassing.'

'If true, it would certainly squash any ambitions he might have to take over from Ingleby. It probably wouldn't take much to spread a few rumours here or there.'

'I suggest we start with Seymour and see what can be unearthed. We can come back to Russell in round two if need be.'

There is a general nodding of agreement from around the table.

'What about Macauley? How bulletproof is she?'

The other two turn to look at Sir Philip.

'I am not aware of any skeletons in her cupboards. She was only a junior barrister, so unlikely to be a serial tax avoider. No criminal records, no known sexual deviances, rarely drinks, doesn't smoke, nothing that we can see in the family history likely to embarrass her. Hasn't committed any major *faux pas* that I'm aware of, either.'

'There'll be something. Either the tabloids will drag it up or they'll invent something, mark my words,' Sir Giles adds.

'Good. Moving on to another subject altogether, I hear that the PM's old university buddy Ricky Al-Shawabi is looking to make a generous donation to party funds.'

'I doubt he'll get that past the Electoral Commission,' Sir Philip pipes up.

'I've never been particularly convinced that Mr Al-Shawabi and his business pass the smell test if you understand my meaning? Far too racy a character for my liking.'

'Knowing Al-Shawabi as I do, he'll be wanting something in return for his generosity. His sort usually does.' Sir Giles looks at their empty plates. 'Cheese, anyone?'

Chapter 14

Sunday 24th January 2016

London

'I don't know about you, Stephen, but I miss not being able to pick up the phone and order a simple takeaway. What wouldn't I give right now for a chicken korma, some naan bread and an ice-cold Cobra?'

Justin Ingleby is sitting at his desk, shirt sleeves rolled up, and chair swivelled around so that he can talk to Stephen Russell who has just walked into his study. It has been a relatively quiet evening for them both. A drinks reception at Number 10 for competing European ice-skating teams finished over an hour ago. Since then, they have been working on their Red Boxes, preparing for the week ahead.

The home of the British prime minister, Number 10 Downing Street, is the location of his private office, the Cabinet rooms and various functions and staterooms. At the top of the house are some private living quarters. In keeping with a practice started under former Prime Minister Tony Blair, the private residence at Number 10 Downing Street is actually where the chancellor of the exchequer resides. The chancellor's primary residence, next door at Number 11 Downing Street, has a more extensive suite of private rooms and is where the current prime minister Justin Ingleby and his family have chosen to live. There is a connecting door between the two, allowing relatively free passage between the two houses in what could, to an outsider, seem like something straight out of a West End farce.

'I'd settle for pizza, any day,' Russell says. 'Something with a crispy base, lashings of cheese and perhaps a few anchovies on the side.'

Ingleby stretches across his desk, picking up a half-eaten bag of crisps and offering them to Russell. 'These are all I have. Help yourself.'

'Thanks,' Russell says, grabbing the bag.

'When are you on the Today programme?'

'Tomorrow morning. The ten past eight slot.' He groans, and they both raise their eyebrows. 'What a great way to start the week!'

'In person or from the radio car?'

'In person.'

'What do they want to cover, do you know?'

'It should be the economy, but this Panama Papers' leak has put tax avoidance back on the agenda.'

'The old chestnut. If you get James Hackett, heaven help you.'

'He might want to ask about the referendum.'

'I doubt it. There'll be plenty of opportunity to do that come April when campaigning begins in earnest. Knowing you, I'm sure you've got the ground covered.'

'More or less.'

'You'll be fine. You're a natural at this kind of thing. You are the most obvious person to succeed me. I could never say that in public, Stephen, you know that. If it were down to me alone, you'd have my vote. You also seem to have public opinion on your side.'

'That's nice of you to say.'

'Changing the subject, Stephen, I'm pleased you dropped by. You remember our little golf course chat with Ricky at the weekend?'

'I'm not likely to forget it in a hurry. What about it? Trouble brewing on the horizon with the Electoral Commission, is there?'

'No,' Ingleby says, his voice dipping gravely. 'Worse.'

'Go on.'

Ingleby chooses his words carefully.

'Strictly *entre nous*, and not for repeating outside this room, I had a private conversation yesterday with the foreign secretary. In one of her regular chats with Sir Desmond Wheatley, she discovered that MI6 have Ricky's business empire firmly in their sights – and not for good reasons, I might add. They've someone on the inside who's been sniffing around for a while. MI6 are worried about some of the things our Ricky's been getting himself into. Especially in the Middle East.'

'Shit! That's going to make it impossible to accept any of his money.'

'Quite.'

'Bloody hell. What happens next?'

'Nothing. There's nothing we can do, certainly not in the short term. If Ricky starts pressing us to take his money, we simply have to stall him. Say the Electoral Commission are dragging their heels, that sort of thing.'

'What if MI6 are right?'

'Then the faster we distance ourselves from Ricky, the better. The fact that the media think he and I are bosom pals from Cambridge is hardly helpful. As you say, shit!'

Chapter 15

Monday 25ᵗʰ January 2016

London

Seven o'clock in the morning and Home Secretary, Jeremy Seymour, is out for his morning run. It's a misty, damp and still dark winter's morning, the temperature hovering a few degrees above freezing. Seymour, prone to putting on weight, is a reluctant runner, all too aware of his doctor's warning that he needs to shed at least ten kilos and do more exercise. Seymour's driver had picked up the MP from his rented home in St John's Wood less than thirty minutes earlier. Dressed in his tracksuit and running shoes, Seymour had his work clothes and Red Boxes on the seat beside him. He could have run to work from his home, his driver collecting his clothes and boxes and bringing them to the Home Office in Marsham Street separately. The truth is that Seymour enjoys the trappings of high office too much, relishing having his government driver waiting on the doorstep each morning to drive him the short distance to work.

Seymour is relatively new to politics, having been a Member of Parliament for only a decade. Before that, he had been a wealthy, land-owning farmer in Norfolk in a village not far from his constituency. Ten years ago, he sold half his farm to his brother; the other half, more recently, had been converted into a solar energy operation. Elected as a local MP on an anti-EU campaign, he had won his first election by a surprisingly large majority and with not a little controversy. Five years later, after rising to prominence as a vocal backbencher, he was awarded his first Cabinet appointment at the Department of Transport. Here, to the surprise of many, he had achieved a great deal, certainly more than his critics had anticipated. So much so that at the last Cabinet reshuffle, Justin Ingleby had decided that Seymour was ready for a more significant challenge – the Home Office. On one point, his critics were in unanimous agreement. The new home secretary certainly had plenty to sink his teeth into.

With his star in the ascendant, political commentators began taking an active interest in Seymour, the man and his methods. The adjective 'bombastic' appeared in one satirical magazine and quickly stuck; 'pompous' or 'at times risking being out of touch with voters' were also commonly used. Other critics were more pointed still, venturing that Seymour was too sharp-elbowed and overly ambitious for Ingleby's job. To his credit, Seymour had also developed a reputation 'for getting stuff done'. Someone who largely ignored what others said or thought and focused instead on achievement. In his short tenure at the Home Office, he had surprised many by delivering several quick wins in high profile areas such as border control and immigration. Because of his anti-EU sentiments, these were both areas about which he claimed to feel passionate. Opting to keep his powder dry on the public debate about immigration until the referendum campaign was underway later in the year, Seymour was biding his time, focusing his energies on another important issue. One that he believed would help him build voter trust and confidence. Namely, tackling corruption and money laundering head-on, especially where the latter could be linked to the funding of terrorism.

Seymour was not, perhaps, the greatest collaborator in the Cabinet. The phrase *'he who travels fastest, travels alone'* might have been written for his unscripted operating philosophy. Off duty, he was a regular at team sporting events: he was a season ticket holder at Stamford Bridge and had been a keen member of the MCC for years. However, closer scrutiny would reveal that whenever he participated in sports, they were usually individual activities such as running, shooting and playing chess. Some might even dare venture to say that such a solitary choice of sporting activities spoke volumes about the way that Seymour most naturally preferred to operate in his working life as well.

Seymour's usual route takes him through the back streets from his office in Marsham Street to Vauxhall Bridge. From here, he crosses the river to the south, slowly circling back in an anticlockwise direction, eventually crossing the Thames again at Westminster Bridge and onto the final leg of this three-and-a-half-mile circuit. It typically takes him twenty-five minutes, sometimes longer, depending on whether he meets anyone on the way.

Such as today.

Crossing Vauxhall Bridge, he spots Malcolm Scott, the director-general of the National Crime Agency and one of Seymour's direct reports, on his way to Citadel Place just around the corner.

'Malcolm,' Seymour cries, coming to a halt, bending over to catch his breath, hands on knees.

'Early start for you too?'

'Good morning, Minister.'

They shake hands.

'I would have been here even earlier if the trains hadn't been up the spout. Is this your usual circuit?'

Seymour nods, sweat dripping off his nose.

'Something like that. Glad to bump into you. We're due to catch up shortly, I believe?'

'I think so. Later this week, if I'm not mistaken.'

'Doubtless with various officials in tow. Fortuitous bumping into you. It's nice to have the occasional quiet word, just you and me.'

He wipes sweat from his face as he stands upright.

'Any progress on that little matter we touched upon last time? The PM has this bee in his bonnet about money laundering and corruption following the Panama Papers leak. The Cabinet have been left in no doubt that it's flavour of the month. There's always too much talk and not enough action in and around Westminster.'

Scott raises and lowers his eyebrows, nodding without saying anything.

'To make matters worse, there's this new cross-departmental anti-corruption task force the PM's setting up. What a palaver! Endless consultations and review panels and all that sort of bollocks. Forget all that. What's needed is something concrete, a success story all our own. Prove to the world that we've gone and done something, not just been sitting in interminable meetings and waffling on about how much better we are about to get at co-operating and shuffling the deckchairs. Something that could provide a morale boost, both for the NCA and the Home Office. Reputation-enhancing too, if you get my drift?'

More raising and lowering of the eyebrows from Scott. There is not a lot of common ground between these two men: they hail from very different backgrounds, both having been thrown together as a result of the lottery that is public duty.

'Message received, Minister. To tell the truth, we are working on a few things. One, in particular, looks highly promising.'

Scott speaks softly, looking to either side of Seymour rather than directly at him.

'It might even tick all the boxes. An investigation into a certain high-profile individual and his businesses, a bit here in the UK but mostly overseas. We know that this person's been involved in aggressive tax avoidance, but it smells as if it might be a lot worse. We haven't been able to prove anything yet, but we're working on it. Ordinarily we'd be consulting with other departments, flagging his file in the system and so on, liaising with overseas police forces, HMRC, perhaps even the Security Services. However, based on our last conversation, we had in mind a more unconventional approach. One that might bear fruit much more quickly. A covert, NCA-only operation, one that might risk treading on a few organisational toes but pragmatic in its approach. In the mould of a 'let's try and get something done, and done rapidly' operation, mindful about, but not being a slave to, inter-departmental boundaries. Does that sound more like what you had in mind?'

'That sounds perfect, Malcolm. Just the job. I like pushing boundaries. People forget: you can't make omelettes without breaking eggs.'

'Pragmatic policing is the term I prefer to use. Respecting the law but not rigidly sticking to due process. I'm glad we bumped into each other and never had this conversation, Minister. Especially so close to the spook factory.'

Behind them, only metres away from where they are standing, is the entrance to MI6's main London office at Vauxhall Cross.

'So am I,' Seymour says, laughing. He is about to start running again when he stops, remembering something.

'Just one more thing, Malcolm. If you ever feel that it might be helpful to have another one of these off-the-record conversations, just ping me a text. We can either meet at my office or, as you can see, I am usually out for a run most mornings.'

'Very good, Minister. I might just do just that.'

Chapter 16

Monday 25th January 2016

London

'Silence, please. Cue in five, four, three, two, one . .'

'The time is just gone ten-past eight. We've heard in the news this morning that a major government crackdown on bribery and corruption is underway in the UK following the leak of thousands of emails by a whistle-blower in a Panamanian law firm, an action which has sent ripples of fear running through the secretive and, some might say, murky world of offshore tax-havens. Many of these special tax jurisdictions are British Overseas Dependencies. Is the British Government doing enough to stop people using loopholes in the tax system to avoid paying what many argue should be their fair share of tax here in the UK? Here with me in the studio to tell us is the UK chancellor of the exchequer and head of the Treasury, Stephen Russell. Good morning, Chancellor, and welcome to the Today programme.'

'Good morning, James.'

'Right up front, could we get one thing clear? These offshore tax havens: they only operate in the way they do primarily to protect tax dodgers, isn't that the bottom line?'

'No, that's not correct. In any system that operates, yes, there will be some who try and bend the rules. However, the legal, tax and operational rule frameworks that these British Overseas Dependencies have adopted are, and always have been, very transparent. They are designed to encourage a huge volume of trade and money-flows into these small economies which in turn helps provide thousands of jobs for local people.'

'Yes, but you say the rules and laws may be transparent. What I am suggesting is that it may be the rules themselves that might be the problem here. These rules may actually be preventing the authorities – the UK taxman, for example – from knowing precisely what is going on. In short, they are protecting tax dodgers, isn't that right?'

'No, we have excellent co-operation agreements in place between HMRC and many of these places.'

'HMRC being the taxman.'

'Correct. These agreements allow the free exchange of information on many people who might otherwise escape the tax net. So, it is not correct to say that people who choose to place their money offshore or in foreign countries will escape paying tax. We have recently put in place information-sharing arrangements with both the Isle of Man and Jersey modelled on the success we had with the Swiss authorities where, for the last few years, we have been making huge strides in sharing information to increase the tax take.'

'That's all very well and good, but it doesn't cover Guernsey or the British Virgin Islands yet, does it? And what about other countries that are not British Dependencies? What about Panama, Manama even, the Marshall Islands, the list goes on and on? We are only touching the tip of the iceberg at the moment, isn't that the truth of it? Come on, we all know it, why not admit it?'

'I simply disagree. We are making a lot of progress in negotiating with many, many authorities around the world, getting to a basis where information sharing is the expected norm. We can't do this on our own, so we are using the G20 summit meetings to push this agenda hard. We expect to announce significant progress at the next summit meeting here in London in ten days' time. We are all trying to tackle this problem together, and I would like to assure your listeners that we are indeed making real progress.'

'Sticking closer to home, Jersey is being co-operative but not Guernsey. Is that right – and if so, what are you doing to change that?'

'We have a great working relationship with the authorities on both islands. The financial services industry is a huge contributor to the economy of each, and so we need to bring about change in a careful, balanced manner: not in a way that causes a sudden outflow of capital – or, indeed, jobs – from.'

'Which some might argue means we're not doing very much.'

'I think that's unfair, James. A great deal is happening, especially behind the scenes. And as I said earlier, the parallel conversations we are having within the G20 make changes in other jurisdictions much easier.'

'All right, moving on: Justin Ingleby has announced publicly that sometime in the next 12 months, perhaps shortly after the referendum, he will stand down as prime minister. A lot of people are speculating that you, as chancellor, are ambitious for the job. Is that correct?'

'I would be happy – no, I would be delighted to take on the role if both voters and my fellow MPs thought I was a suitable candidate.'

'Let me ask you this. Given the stated intention of this government is to clamp down on tax dodgers – those wishing to evade the taxman and not pay what the public might say is their rightful share of tax – if you were prime minister, would you be happy to consider a complete overhaul of the tax system? Once and for all, go back to basics and try and make everything much simpler and fairer for everyone?'

'We have achieved a great deal in terms of simplification, James, and yes, if there are ways to make other changes, ones that don't damage our international competitiveness, then yes, of course, we should be exploring these.'

'You say that, but what about these so-called non-doms, the wealthy elite who spend a fair chunk of their time in the UK with all their numerous houses and cars and suchlike but pay very little, or indeed no tax at all? That doesn't sound very fair and equitable to me. Would you really be happy for them to continue receiving the favourable tax treatment they receive right now – or would you consider changing the tax law? For example, taxing the non-doms in the same way that you, me and ninety-nine per cent of the working population are being taxed?'

'That's a big question, James.'

'I know. That's why I asked it.'

'For the vast majority of these people, those who are deemed not to be domiciled in the UK for tax purposes, it is my belief – and it is a belief supported by many independent professional advisors who have examined the facts in great detail – that the current system is broadly fair and proportionate. We have listened to many of the concerns and have already announced big changes that will mean more people being subjected to an increased UK tax burden, in particular regarding inheritance taxes. Our conclusion is that it would be detrimental to the UK economy – the inward flow of investment and UK jobs – to make further changes at this time.'

'But there's the rub. Won't voters feel that you're only saying that simply to protect the very rich at the expense of the ordinary taxpayer? If you became prime minister, it would be the same old business as usual: one rule for the super-rich; another for the likes of ordinary folk like you and me?'

'Again, I disagree. I think voters understand the huge contribution that some of these people make and that it is extraordinarily complex to make sweeping changes.'

'I suspect your arguments will convince not everyone. One final quick question. Assuming that you do make it to Number 10, what happens if you discover that one of your Cabinet colleagues has been involved in aggressive tax planning, if not worse.'

'That's simple. I would ask them to leave the Cabinet.'

'As black and white as that? No time to mend their ways?'

'No, I believe members of Cabinet have to lead by example. If I were to become prime minister, I would be very clear with my Cabinet colleagues about that.'

'Stephen Russell, Chancellor of the Exchequer, thank you very much indeed for your time this morning.'

'Back to the mother ship, sir?'

'Yes please, George.' It is Russell's little in-joke with his driver. 'Did you listen on the radio?'

'I did, sir. I thought you were very polished.'

'Thank you. James Hackett's relentless as an interviewer – talk about an attack dog.'

'You held your ground, though. It can't be easy, broadcasting live and all that.'

Russell leans back in the leather seat and closes his eyes. He is shaking slightly, little tremors in his arms and hands. Hardly surprising, given everything. Russell remembers his phone, which he'd had to switch off during the live broadcast. Turning it on now, he waits a few seconds for it to come back to life and enters his password. There are several text messages.

Good job, well done. Nicely handled. JI

It was the prime minister. Not many could claim to be the recipient of regular texts from the PM, he supposes. Another three, no four, from fellow MPs. One from his mother.

So proud, well done, Stephen! He sounded aggressive. I thought you handled it superbly, Mum xx

Then his wife.

Heading to Colefax & F to choose

wallpaper for No 10! Nice!! Love you xx

He scrolls through a few more, then closes his eyes again. There were bits about the job that he hated, especially when trying to play the innocent, pretending that he had nothing to hide.

His phone buzzes again. He looks at it and groans.

Remember our game of golf if you want

to have a go at the non-doms. Some of

us know where the bodies are buried!

Let's talk tonight . . .

It is from an unknown caller, but Russell recognises the hand of Ricky Al-Shawabi when he sees it. Ricky Al-Shawabi! The one man who could bring his ambitions for high office crashing down in one fell swoop. Politics was indeed a filthy game. His hands are trembling once more. He had phoned Ricky late the previous evening and suggested they meet for dinner before Ricky headed back to Monaco.

'You all right, sir?'

The driver is watching in the rearview mirror, seeing Russell holding his hands in front of him.

'Fine, thank you, George. Post-adrenalin rush or whatever. How long before we arrive?'

'I should think about ten minutes given the rush hour traffic.'

He closes his eyes and soon falls into a light, troubled sleep. He is on the small island of Tortola in the Caribbean. Money seems to be growing on trees. When he gets close, none of the notes has the Queen's head on them, but they do have his own, together with his name in bold letters. He reaches out to grab one but before he can get hold of it, it disappears. In its place is a picture postcard bearing an all-too-familiar smiling face. Ricky Al-Shawabi.

Chapter 17

Monday 25ᵗʰ January 2016

Courchevel, France

Adam Fraser's career contained many elements of randomness. It has been a potpourri of new beginnings here: an unpredictable, sometimes unfathomable, set of meaningless meanderings there. It was a Jackson Pollock painting come to life: an agreeable picture, amusing, complicated and colourful, spiced – at times liberally – with sprinklings of *bugger it*. Adam's inner driving force, the beacon that in his good friend Signor Bernadi had been visible from an early age, had until now been largely hidden from view. Periodic signals had been visible – and these had tended to have had the appearance of being honed and refined at the *'make it up as you go along'* school of enlightenment. In his own carefully scripted words, *'it has all been a bit random':* spoken by a man who had been living and waiting for the Pollock paintbrush to splatter him to yet another destination on the canvas.

Out of the blue, along came the lead role for which he had seemingly been yearning. All that was necessary was for Adam to develop the character, learn the lines and then give the performance of his life. Trust his dearest and closest friend to have had a hand in it, for it was indeed Aldo whose recent acts of kindness had sent Adam Fraser's acting career into its newfound trajectory. Inadvertently or otherwise, Aldo had handed Adam the keys that had unlocked the sealed stage door that he had been struggling to open for too long. A sense of purpose, finally. The new Adam Fraser, live-in lover of Xandra, trader of all things to be traded, about-to-be maker of pots of money, was on course to enter the very core of Al-Shawabi's inner sanctum – a man, finally, on a mission.

It remained an act. An agreeable act, one that made him feel good about himself – but nonetheless an act. Assuming his bank account continued to swell, and he thrived on the taste of success, he would need to keep remembering this and stay focused. Early reviews from the critics had been overwhelmingly positive. All things otherwise being equal, he had appeared up until now to be on track for a long stint under the footlights. Always supposing that a few moments of recklessness earlier that afternoon with the woman called Emms didn't risk becoming a serious impediment. Fiona's unscripted casting as Emma was the only bad omen, an unexpected banana skin, randomly positioned on the stage of his one-man show, waiting to trip him up. Her very presence threatened to unhinge his newfound order and equilibrium.

The Pollock paintbrush was poised once again in readiness for a fresh splattering.

Why, oh why, had she had to make this unplanned appearance in his life? Emms' unexpected stage presence risked everything, endangering his new, extraordinarily exciting acting career – *bugger it*!

'Something smells good.'

Adam closes the door to the basement boot locker and climbs the stairs to the Hub's living room.

'Ah, the wanderer returns.'

It is Ozzie, suitably well-starched, sitting upright in a leather armchair, his wife in a bathrobe curled up at his feet. Gemma gives Adam a wide-eyed smile. There have been rather a lot of those of late.

'Had a good afternoon, Adam? Been subjecting ourselves to a dose or two of the après-ski, have we?'

'Bloody good claret, actually. Started with a bottle of Bordeaux at lunchtime, then it's been downhill ever since.'

'Very droll.'

'How was your sauna, Gemma?'

'Not had it yet.'

She puts down the magazine she's reading.

'Care to join me? Shetty turned it on half an hour ago. It should almost be ready.'

Adam is briefly subjected to a flash of bare thigh beneath Gemma's silky dressing-gown.

'I'll join you, darling,' Ozzie says, standing up and pulling his wife to her feet. 'Xandra wants Adam upstairs.' Gemma turns her bottom lip down at Adam in mock disappointment, Ozzie taking her by the hand and leading her away down the stairs.

'Ah, Mr Adam!'

It is Shetty, hurrying out of the kitchen and rubbing flour-coated hands on a cloth.

'Miss Xandra requests that you please join her upstairs. She's got a masseuse coming in about five minutes.'

His head wobbles in a figure of eight pattern that can mean so many different things. Today it is saying, *'Please go, you have no option, don't argue with me, I'm only the messenger.'*

'She has a bit of a headache, sir.'

'Very good, thank you, Shetty.'

Adam is turning to head upstairs when Vladek appears out of nowhere.

'Where have you been?' he enquires menacingly.

'What business is it of yours?'

'Everything's my business.' Vladek presses his body in close so that it almost touches Adam's, their faces inches apart. 'Been screwing the chalet girls?'

Adam blanks him, saying nothing.

'For the record, if I ever discover you stepping out of line, messing around behind Xandra's back, for example, I have it on Ricky's authority to break every bone in your body. Trust me; nothing would give me greater pleasure. Do we understand each other, Adam *bloody* Fraser?'

'Bring it on, Vladek. You just might get the surprise of your life.'

'Ooh -,' he says, moving his face closer, spittle flying, '- are you threatening me? I am *so* scared. I really don't trust you, Adam Fraser. I think you're a fake: an imposter. One way or the other, I am going to prove it.'

'Whatever meds you are on, Vladek, double the dose and get a good night's sleep. Now, if you don't mind, piss off will you? Xandra is waiting for me.'

They stare at each other, the menace hanging in the air between them. Adam then starts climbing the stairs leaving Vladek smouldering in his wake.

'Xandra?' he calls out, halfway up.

'I'm in the bath. I thought you'd abandoned us.'

He enters the functional but chic bathroom.

'It wasn't intentional. One bottle down at lunchtime and I met some Army types – the rest, as they say, is history.' He leans over the bath and kisses her forehead. 'Shetty says you have a headache. I'm sorry to hear that.'

'Male Army types or female Army types?'

'Mostly male. Come to think of it, all male bar one.'

God, you are lying for Queen and Country now.

'I've got a masseuse coming shortly. My head's easing a bit, but could you give my neck a rub?'

'Sure,' Adam says and rolls his sleeves up whilst kneeling on the floor beside the bath.

'How did your lunch go?'

'Very boozy, very inconclusive. I think he's on the hook, it's just a matter of getting familiar with us first.'

Adam nods.

'Did you ski after lunch?'

'Just about made it down the mountain. I had pneumatic drills going off in my head that made me feel sick. Just there, where your thumbs are, can you feel the tension?'

'What's Vladek's problem? He seems determined to see me slide down the mountain into oblivion.'

'He's wary of strangers and, for some reason I confess I find a bit creepy, overly protective of me. The new boy, Adam Fraser, is invading a space that he's not happy about. He'll get over it.'

'I hope so, for all our sakes. That man seems to be carrying a lot of baggage. We may yet come to blows.'

Adam's phone starts to ring. He dries his hands, takes the phone from his pocket and looks at the caller ID.

'It's Ricky,' he says, surprise in his voice. Xandra looks up sharply.

'Ricky, it's Adam. How's London? To what do I owe the pleasure?'

He listens for a few seconds, nodding.

'Day after tomorrow is the plan. I think Shetty's booked the helicopter.' Xandra is nodding. 'Tomorrow?' Adam asks, looking at Xandra, shrugging. She gives him a look as if to say, '*If that's what he wants, fine*'.

'Yes, I'm sure that's doable. Do you want Shetty to organise the helicopter?' He listens some more. 'Okay, if you've already done that, we'll be at the Altiport at eleven in the morning. We should be in Monaco around lunchtime. What time are you expecting to get back?' Another pause. 'Okay, enjoy your dinner and we'll see you tomorrow. Anything we need to be working on in the interim?' More pauses. 'Okay then. Bye.'

He puts the phone away and looks at Xandra.

'Ricky wants us all back yesterday. There's some kind of flap on.

Wouldn't go into the details. The chopper is flying in to collect us in the morning. If Ricky wasn't still in London, my guess is that we'd be packing our bags immediately.'

'Why call you? Why not me? He always rings me.'

'Ricky's all-pervading,' he says, kissing her on the forehead. 'He must have known you had a headache. Do you know what the flap's all about?'

'Fergus mentioned that Ricky met some Saudi bigwigs whilst in Bahrain. There's talk of putting on a 'meet and greet' for them in Monaco if they can be tempted to visit. I wonder if that's the reason.'

'Doubtless, all will be revealed tomorrow.'

'How was he?'

'He didn't sound his normal irrepressible self, but what do I know?'

There is a faint voice from the staircase below.

'Miss Xandra? Your masseuse is here. Shall I send her up?'

Xandra is already getting out of the bath.

'Tell her to give me two minutes, Shetty, and then I'll be ready.'

Adam holds out a bath sheet for her and she steps into it. Xandra is twelve, if not more, years older than Emms. The signs are there if he looks carefully. A few more wrinkles, the odd streak or two of grey hair. He rubs her thighs and calves with a hand towel, his mind wandering. Here is a lovely woman, in good shape. She and Adam have had a lot of fun together. He caresses the insides of her thighs, and she sighs beneath his touch. Good fun, great in bed, high marks all round. Just in a different league from Emms.

How insane is that, Adam Fraser?

Chapter 18

Monday 25ᵗʰ January 2016

Courchevel, France

The low-budget production is over, the stage cleared of its props. The cast: Margaret Milner – Miss Bateson in Adam Fraser's imagination; Emma – once Fiona, now Emms to the departing theatregoers; and the irresistibly named 'Beef'. All three are in their cheap rental car heading back to Lyon airport, their low-cost return flight back to London already outbound from Gatwick. Beef is the elected driver, with Emma and Miss Milner happy to be chauffeured in the rear. During the meandering descent from the Alpine resort, one that involves the occasional hairpin bend and not much talking, Emma wordlessly muses on whether Miss Milner had been a 'Miss' all of her life. Perhaps, once upon a time, she had been married? Then, after some incident or mishap, finding herself back on her own once again, she could have reverted to 'Miss', never again to discuss the intimate details of her former love life? It's possible but feels unlikely. The more Emma thinks about it, Miss Milner is most likely a spinster, especially considering the solitary working life that she has endured hitherto.

That issue put to bed, her thoughts drift to Adam Fraser. As the car finishes its alpine descent and joins the dual carriageway, she reflects that surprisingly, she'd enjoyed her brief moment with Adam Fraser that afternoon. Above and beyond was what Miss Milner had said to her a little earlier. On that point, she might have been right.

As if on cue, she finds her hand being patted gently by her fellow passenger in the rear.

'You did well this afternoon, Fiona. Acted like a pro. My old lot would have been proud. I certainly was.'

Her old lot. For over two months, Miss Milner has been an ex-employee of MI5; yet the Millbank training and methods seemingly remained an inextricable part of her DNA.

'Thank you. Team effort and all that.'

'Oh, I think that's hardly fair. The semen sample was a masterstroke. As I said earlier, above and beyond.'

'I didn't do anything I wasn't prepared to do,' is all she could think to say.

I rather enjoyed it, to tell the truth.

'What next?'

'Since our fish appears to be on the hook, we wait and see whether he swallows the bait. If so, it'll be interesting to see where it leads us.' She glances at Emma. 'Do you have much else on at the moment, workwise?'

'Nothing that can't be moved or put on hold.'

'How about you, Beef?'

'At your beck and call, Miss Milner.' He gives a broad grin in the rear-view mirror.

'Well then, I suggest we try and find you a not-too-expensive apartment near to, if not in, Monaco and get you settled there so that you can wait for first contact. Beef, you don't mind playing babysitter, do you? I am not expecting anything to get nasty. I simply don't want to cast Fiona to the wolves, real or imaginary.'

They both nod to show their acceptance. If Emma needed protection, Beef would give it his best shot, she felt confident.

'Now, my dear, just one other thing. I am happy to say this in Beef's hearing since, both metaphorically and for real, he's the one who'll be watching your back. Take a tip from a former field agent. No emotional entanglements. Keep this totally professional, one hundred per cent business. I am sorry to be so blunt, but entanglements always spell trouble. Do we understand each other?'

The very statement, of course, makes Emma wonder. Is this a partial confession? As near to an admission of a past fling in the middle of an operation as Miss Milner is ever likely to own up to? It's an interesting thought, but only of passing relevance.

'Totally. I completely understand. You needn't worry; Adam Fraser is not my type.'

Or not a type that I'm prepared to admit to liking right at this moment.

Chapter 19

Monday 25ᵗʰ January 2016

En route to London

Planes provide good thinking space, assuming that one's neighbours are peaceful, and the younger generation are not testing vocal cords or lung capacities nearby. Miss Milner prefers the emergency exit rows. Although her five-foot-one frame does not need the legroom, the reclining angle of the seat in front is restricted. Her personal space, therefore, is less under threat of invasion. With a constitution honed by years in the field, she has a well-behaved bladder that needs infrequent attention. As a result, her seat of choice is by a window, where she is content to have time and privacy by herself, lost in her thoughts, watching the world outside go by. In her view, silently is the best way to travel.

With Fiona and Beef seated in random seat locations in other parts of the plane, there is no reason to speak to anyone on the seventy-five-minute homeward leg. Adam Fraser's afternoon's stage performance, though generally positive, still warranted some more reflection time. Specifically, how much, if at all, should she be telling people back at the office – and to whom?

In the *seeking forgiveness not permission* school of philosophy of which she was a disciple, she instinctively favoured radio silence over any muted broadcast. At MI5, the bureaucrats would have been consulted in advance. Planning any type of operation would typically have taken days, if not weeks. That she'd pulled this particular show off in a matter of man-hours rather than man-years was a remarkable feather in her cap – an achievement that regrettably few would get to know about or thus be able to congratulate her on. If the Courchevel performance proved anything, it was that by travelling alone, one could often travel faster. The minister wanted results and quickly? Then he shall have them – and *pronto* – but only if he was content for this little operation not to become a full-blown, let's consult and tell the world type of affair – in particular, kept hidden from the lawyer-types in the Action Prevention Squad.

Forgiveness not permission.

More critical was the question of how much she needed to tell her immediate boss, Rollo Campion. Campion had already been given the barest outline of an early draft of the script. At the time, he had been *über content*, to use one of his irritating expressions, doubtless part of *the whole gamut* of custom phraseology honed and refined by too many years spent at the FCO.

'Give it a whirl, for heaven's sake. Why not? What have we got to lose? Don't forget: having you lead the odd 'below the radar sortie' from time to time is precisely the reason why I recruited you, Margaret.'

She had finally relented about the use of 'Margaret'; now that she was on board and working directly for him, it had seemed futile to object. In his mind, he had won a small but important victory, proving for the avoidance of doubt who was the boss and who was working for whom. She didn't think she had forgotten. Had he recruited her just so that she could run certain *below the radar sorties*? Of the kind that deliberately tested the organisational boundaries akin to Russian fighter jets probing the UK's air defences. She hadn't believed so at the time. More to the point, it had indeed been the other way around. She had only decided to accept his offer precisely because she had believed that with someone like Campion as her boss, she might be able to get away with murder. Not literally, of course, but then again, one never knew exactly what one was going to be confronted with in a real-life operation. That plus the fact that Campion, with his *macro-management* philosophy, would be too much in the helicopter to notice or care about the odd infringement here or there.

Talking of telling people, would Scott, the DG himself, want to be "kept in the loop"? Keen for a quick win, wouldn't he be proud of this opening afternoon preview? More than likely, is her thirty-five-thousand-foot assessment, although it was hardly her place to tell him. Let him read about the accolades as and when Fraser started producing the goods – unless, of course, he had already heard scant outlines of the plot during one of his cosy one-on-ones with Campion. So, back to Campion. What to say to him about this afternoon's *sortie,* if anything? Nothing feels the best answer; nothing feels the safest. Nothing feels the most comfortable so early in the play's touring circuit.

Forgiveness not permission.

There was, of course, the issue of jurisdiction. More particularly, had any toes been trodden on by any of today's cast and crew? If at some later stage the whole production – *from soup to nuts* as Campion, using one of his ghastly Americanisms, might perhaps call it – were to be put under the spotlight, might there be the risk of an 'aha!' moment from any of the critics? The Action Prevention Squad shouting '*ultra vires, completely out of order',* for example? Unlikely from her old lot since they, like the NCA itself, were purely domestic paid-up members of the actors' union: UK theatres only. What about the NCA's next-door neighbours at Vauxhall Cross? MI6 took their actors on overseas' tours – in fact, that's all they did, productions in foreign parts usually of very different genres from Miss Milner's current stage show, typically with terrorism or foreign government-related twists to the plot. Which this wasn't, was it? It was indeed just a bit of private enterprise, a minor show on the regional touring circuit; some under-employed actors doing something frivolous and fun, hoping to gain a bit of recognition and a few ministerial brownie points along the way.

Which only left the French– and perhaps Monaco – authorities. '*You 'ad zis operation in our country and you did not inform us? Zut alors! You British are the very worst!'* The more of the thirty-five-thousand-foot conditioned air that she breathes, the more she is convinced that the best course of action is to do nothing, tell no one.

Forgiveness not permission.

Milner's eyes begin to droop as the plane starts its descent. With options reviewed and all angles considered, she relaxes for the first time since boarding the plane. Her interim assessment? That all remained on track with no additional action or amendment to the script required. No backside covering emails or file notes; no quick telephone calls or voicemails; no meetings to be organised or inter-departmental consultations to be set up. Assuming that the fish had, indeed, swallowed the bait, the current order of business remained to see where it would lead them.

Something niggles though, keeping her awake. For many years her father, a police inspector, had a sixth sense, an ability to sniff out things that didn't quite feel right. She had inherited the same intuition. With the lights of the Medway coastal towns winking at her through clouds below, she finally gets it: Adam Fraser's motives. As her father would have said, if you don't understand motives, you don't solve real crimes.

Had Fraser's ready agreement to become their stage actor been too superficial? Possibly agreed to in haste purely out of some patriotic sense of duty. The disgraced former solider finally able to put some of his demons to bed by performing a fresh act of public service – was that it? It felt tenuous, however good the theory.

Or was it merely because he had been coerced? On the face of it, much more plausible – Adam wasn't presented with much choice after all. What niggles, however, is whether there might have been another motive. Either for a reason of which she is completely unaware – in itself problematic, but hopefully containable in whole or in part by the DNA leverage – or, and this is what has so far failed the smell test: perhaps he agreed to act partly out of his feelings, misplaced or otherwise, for Fiona?

As the undercarriage wheels descend into their landing positions, she considers another plot twist. What if she happened to enjoy similar feelings, misplaced or otherwise, for Fraser? That would be problematic, completely changing the dynamics of the field operation. Having seen the young actress giving the stage performance of her life earlier that same afternoon, going beyond the script of a family show and into the darkened auditoria usually restricted to adult audiences, it had to be a possibility.

Certainly, reason-enough to send Beef to keep an eye on the pair of them.

Chapter 20

Monday 25th January 2016

London

When Ricky Al-Shawabi is in London, he is fussy about where he eats. A luxury hotel such as the Savoy or Claridges is his preference for a power breakfast. When it comes to dinner, Ricky likes to dine with the rich, powerful and famous: usually at one of the small handful of private members' dining clubs dotted around the capital. It is as much about recognition as belonging. He has nothing against restaurants such as Wiltons, where private equity portfolio directors sit cheek by jowl with their investors. He actually enjoys the fish at Scott's, where actresses and film stars come to see and be seen. Occasionally, he might head to Cecconi's if he is craving for somewhere with more of a buzz. However, when the UK Chancellor of the Exchequer Stephen Russell calls late on a Sunday evening and asks whether Ricky is free for an urgent private dinner the following night, there is only one place to take him: Harry's Bar.

Part of the same group as a well-known nightclub in Berkeley Square and several other top-end restaurants in and around Mayfair, Harry's Bar in London is very different from its Venetian or Parisian cousins under the same name. Here the Italian food and service are at the very pinnacle of the London experience, with prices that some might think make Monte Carlo look cheap. Only members can book one of their tables, ensuring that the guest list is exclusive and the dining experience discreet. The moment Ricky sees the doorman in his thick winter cape, standing in the cold to greet guests outside the non-descript looking white front door, and the telltale green and white awning hanging over the property's windows, he feels he is returning home.

'Good evening, Mr Al-Shawabi, it's nice to see you again, sir. Let me get the door,' the doorman says, ringing the buzzer, alerting the next tier of the meet and greet team to get prepared for yet another arrival.

'Good evening, Mr Al-Shawabi, it's so nice to have you back with us.' It's the turn of the lady at reception. 'Let me take your coat.'

'Mr Al-Shawabi, good evening. Welcome back.'

Now it is the maître d', dressed in a dinner suit and clutching menus and a wine list under his left arm.

'How have you been keeping? Are you in London for long? Your guest has arrived. May I show you to your table?'

Then a volley of familiar greetings and handshakes *en route* to where Stephen Russell is sitting at the back of the restaurant, close to a window and nursing a glass of Prosecco. With the curtains drawn, from the outside no one can ever tell who is dining at Harry's Bar. Inside, an unwritten code dictates behaviour: acknowledge fellow diners if you know them, just don't interrupt whilst they are either eating or talking. The use of mobile phones and the taking of photographs are strictly unacceptable.

'Stephen, sorry to keep you,' Ricky says, sitting down and ordering a glass of Prosecco for himself. 'I hope you didn't mind my suggesting we meet here? It's so much more private than a restaurant.'

'Not at all. You must feel at home! Most of the patrons here are probably clients of yours anyway, isn't that right?'

Russell is nearer the mark than he might realise. Ricky looks around and spots a Spanish lawyer and his wife in the corner – they make eye contact and Ricky gives a polite wave. Then there is a party of six: the host, his back to them, a wealthy Italian racehorse owner and long-term client. Finally, two American men, also both clients, are in conversation on the far side of the room, one a senator from Illinois and the other an oil billionaire, neither of whom have yet spotted Ricky. A waiter arrives bearing a cut-glass flute of Prosecco on a small silver tray. After raising a silent toast, Ricky takes a much-anticipated sip from the delicate crystal.

'Party off-site at the weekend a success?'

'Who knows, Ricky. The PM seems to think so. When are you back to Monaco?'

'In the morning. First thing.'

The maître d' interrupts them to take their order. No appetisers, just two entrées and a bottle of dry white wine.

'So, what's bugging you, Stephen? That little pile of hidden gold burning a hole in your conscience all of a sudden, is it?'

'Partly, I won't lie. I've been wondering what to do about it all, to be honest, Ricky.'

'You need to relax a bit more! Your secrets are completely safe, Stephen. Remember, secrecy and discretion are the Al-Shawabi watchwords. You don't have to do anything until you feel the time is right.'

'I've been racking my brains. Short of giving it away, I don't think there is an easy way to make everything squeaky clean and above board.'

'Not without a lot of questions being asked, probably not. Why not wait until you're prime minister? Complete your stint at Number 10, then go out and legitimately earn your zillions once you leave office. No one will notice a little undeclared income by that stage, trust me.'

'What worries me is waking up one morning and learning that the great Ricky Al-Shawabi has a whistle-blower in his business hell-bent on spilling the beans. Someone who's been sniffing around and has the dirt on all of your clients. After what happened in Panama, it has to be a possibility.'

'Is that what this is all about, Stephen?' Ricky laughs, and it is at this point that the wine arrives. Ricky checks the bottle, tastes it and pronounces it delicious, the waiter filling both their glasses before disappearing.

'I think you should relax a bit, my friend. I want to remind you about the Al-Shawabi business model.' They clink glasses and try their wine. 'Not bad, eh? No, when clients ask us to keep things off the books, that's what we do. Off the books. Compartmentalised and non-attributable. Some of the details I keep in my head. Quite a lot, actually. Your option to purchase forty million dollars of our assets for one pound, for example: that agreement doesn't sit on a computer hard drive in Panama or some fancy electronic filing cabinet up in the Cloud for anyone to hack into. You, Stephen Russell, gave us your twenty million to keep safe, out of sight from the prying eyes of the authorities. We invested the money in assets held offshore in our name, not yours. Today those same assets are worth forty million, not twenty. As part of the deal, you have a piece of paper hidden away – somewhere very secret and very safe, I imagine – that we both have had signed, witnessed and sealed: we also have a copy similarly locked away. End of story. You sleep easy at night. We, meanwhile, happily keep managing your forty million, held in our name in trust for an unspecified beneficiary, each year taking our very reasonable management fee. You have a unique client number and passcode. None of our employees know to whom it belongs. Identified solely by this unique client number, we give you electronic access to periodic statements showing the underlying performance and latest asset values. You can exercise your option to buy at any time you choose. Does Stephen Russell's name appear anywhere? Of course not. Is there some top-secret client list that some whistle-blower can reveal in shock and awe to the world? Not for the special kind of deals that we do for folks like you. We'd be dead in the water as a business if there were.'

'There must be some paper record somewhere? At the very least, a little black book of some description. A record of all your clients' dark secrets, tucked away in some safe, hopefully out range of prying eyes?'

'I encourage people to think so, I admit. Hypothetically, it's always been my insurance policy, keeping everyone well-behaved and me able to sleep at night. The fact is, and kindly keep this *entre nous*: it is mostly a figment of my – and their – imagination. The Al-Shawabi way is to keep things simple and very confidential. The day you turn up with your copy of our agreement, we allow you to exercise your option: you pay us one pound, we pay you back the value of your accumulated wealth. After that, the slate is wiped clean – until the next time of course. So, you just need to relax a little, drink your lovely wine and cease being so concerned. Life is good. What do you make of your chances in succeeding Ingleby, by the way?'

Their food arrives. It is presented with panache and looks elegant, a side order of freshly cooked *zucchini fritti* appearing at the same time.

'*Buon appetito*,' their young waitress says, withdrawing to leave them in peace.

'Of making it to Number 10?' Russell says, eyeing his food whilst Ricky tucks into his risotto. 'Fair. The economy is more or less on track, which is the biggest boost to my candidacy. Better than Jeremy Seymour, perhaps neck and neck with Geraldine Macauley.' He takes a mouthful of fish and thinks some more. 'I should be able to beat Seymour. He comes across as a pompous ass, not that well-liked by many people.'

'I shouldn't be telling you this, but neither Seymour nor Macauley is a client – certainly not at the moment.'

'Ricky, is it true that you have connections with just about everybody on the planet?'

Ricky laughs and sips a little more wine.

'Only those that are useful. That's the name of the game, though, isn't it? To be brutally frank, I sense it's what you feel least comfortable doing. Networking, making and using contacts to your advantage. Despite what you say, by the way, Seymour seems good at getting things done. He, too, is not the world's best networker from what I can gather, but he does have one advantage. He's undeniably shrewd. Very canny. What about Macauley?'

'Geraldine's the one I've got to watch out for. She has shades of Maggie T about her that I suspect might appeal to a certain group of voters.'

'I wouldn't be so sure. Anyway, it's none of my business, but in your shoes, I would be putting as many of the resources I had at my disposal to try and work things in my favour.'

'For instance?'

'Aren't the tax men and women of Her Majesty's Revenue & Customs part of your portfolio responsibility as chancellor? I mean, they report to you, don't they?'

Stephen nods as he takes a mouthful of fish.

'So why not ask for them to do a trawl through all current Cabinet ministers' tax affairs? You could position it as your attempt to maximise transparency, requiring all government ministers to lead by example and all that baloney. You said as much on the radio this morning!'

'With any particular objective here, Ricky? Apart from pissing off everyone big time.'

'Well, you never know what you might unearth about your fellow MPs, in particular those who might be jostling with you for the keys to Number 10. Especially if one of them – and I am not talking about yourself, you understand – was found to have been less than transparent about their tax affairs. Perhaps Seymour or Macauley, for example: it would be massively unhelpful to their campaign if they were found to be tax dodgers, don't you think?' Ricky finishes the last of his risotto and puts his fork down. 'That was delicious. Yours all right?'

'Great, thanks. Actually, Ricky, Geraldine Macauley was partly why I suggested we have this little private get together. I want to tell you something, but first you need to promise me something.'

'That depends on what it is.'

'You can't repeat what I am about to tell you, not to anybody. You never heard this from me either, is that clear? It's not even for discussion with your chum, the prime minister. Especially not with him, do I make myself clear?'

'Perfectly,' Ricky replies, elbows on the table and holding his wine glass in both hands. 'Loud and clear. Fire away, I'm all ears.'

'You have an informant in your business,' Russell says, his voice lowered, the words barely a whisper.

'Someone working for the British authorities, I can't tell you who. For some time, it would seem, this person – he or she, I don't know who – has been passing information about you directly back to London.'

'Bloody hell, Stephen! That's preposterous. How can you be sure?'

Ricky puts down his wineglass, wiping his brow with the back of a hand.

'Because the PM was told directly. Justin is worried, not least about what it means if you were to become a major donor. I'm much more worried for other reasons. If there's an insider in your operation spilling the beans, I've got a career to lose if the shit starts hitting the fan.'

'I'm stunned. How long's this been going on?'

'At a guess, for quite some time. Months at least, maybe longer – who can say?'

Ricky's mind is spinning, working through the angles and possibilities. Who could it be? Xandra, Ozzie or Fergus? Not Vladek, of that he's confident. What about Gemma or Tash – Shetty even? Adam Fraser, the new boy? No, Fraser had to be ruled out; he'd only just come on board. In point of fact, if what Russell is saying is true, then of them all, Adam Fraser and Vladek were probably the only ones who could be trusted.

'I don't know what to say. I'm in shock. What am I expected to do with this information?'

'There is nothing you can do, Ricky, other than be aware of it. To reflect that I have gone out on a limb in speaking with you. Way above and beyond what I should have done as a Cabinet minister for sure. You never heard it from me, you have to promise?'

Ricky nods but is hardly listening. A red line had been crossed. No one did this kind of thing to Ricky Al-Shawabi and got away with it. He can feel the inner demons stirring, an anger building. One of his team a traitor, spilling the beans to the authorities? Spying on him and his business? It was outrageous. Totally and utterly preposterous. What conniving, duplicitous son of a bitch would do such a thing?

A short time later, saying their goodbyes on the South Audley Street pavement, Ricky's mind is already elsewhere, his demons playing havoc with his normal sense of proportion.

Whoever had done this deserved to be beaten to a pulp and left to rot in hell. How dare they? Given the years of hard work, sweat and time that he, personally, had invested? If people wanted to play these sorts of stupid, high-stakes games, Ricky would show them how much of an evil cunning bastard he could be. See how they liked that. Ricky would find this person. Oh yes, he was going to hunt him or her down, tie them in chains and beat the living crap out of them. He might even enjoy this foreplay. Because once he had their confession, heard their pitiful pleas for mercy and forgiveness, seen them beg for their life, then a slow and painful death would be the least they would deserve.

Chapter 21

Monday 25th January 2016

London

There is a dark side to Ricky. Ricky the *bon vivant*, Ricky the networker, the Dr Jekyll character, happy to party and rub shoulders with the very best of them. Ricky, the ever-charming entrepreneur, the epitome of capitalism at its best and most successful. Yet on black and stormy days, when boxed tight in a corner, anger stoked and raging, frustrations near boiling point: this is when the dark side shows its face, Ricky's inner demons feeling brazen and energised enough to make an appearance. Climbing lustfully from a locked hiding place several layers down, their mood is wildly unpredictable, often violent, usually sadistic. Anger is the most common villain of the piece. On other occasions, neat testosterone pumping through the system can also do the trick. Either or both seem able to unlock the restraints, becoming both firelighter and fuel. Deep down, Ricky is proud of his demons, though he likes to pretend that they don't exist.

Vladek, of course, understands this all too well. In the mists of time, too long ago to recall, Vladek had been recommended to Ricky by one of his darker connections. A man with a history of professional violence, Vladek has needs similar to Ricky's. At the peak of his fighting career, Vladek had been spoiled. Women had thrown themselves at him: young, submissive, often drug-infused, they had led Vladek on a dangerous path, allowing violent moves learned inside the professional cage to be transferred into the privacy of the bedroom.

When Vladek had been forced to retire, after being nearly kicked to death by a half-crazy Latvian fighter, Ricky took Vladek under his wing, helping him find a new niche as Ricky's protector and occasional master of the demons. For all of Vladek's alcoholic abstinence and shortage of words, it is he who enjoys helping Ricky to vent his anger and find pleasure in the dark ways they have both got to know and love. The former cage fighter knows how and where to find the girls, particularly enjoying the rougher elements of Ricky's shows. Ricky likes them young, Ricky likes them defenceless, and so does Vladek. Ricky likes them drugged, and Ricky likes them tied up, often two or three at a time: so does Vladek. Once Ricky's demons have vented their anger at these poor helpless creatures, once he is descending from his climactic frenzy, ritual allows Vladek to take over. As Ricky leaves the ring, Vladek is left to his own devices, the only rules of engagement being that at the end, it is Vladek who is responsible for restoring order and calm, leaving no trail or trace. The recent flood of migrants has been a boon. Plenty of opportunities, very few questions to be asked, especially when a scattering of used banknotes is left as a token of their perverted gratitude.

When Vladek is not at hand, Ricky is more vulnerable. Tonight, Vladek is in Courchevel as an enraged Ricky stumbles out of Harry's Bar. The Cabinet member's assigned driver has been waiting patiently all evening, ready to whisk his charge back to Downing Street. Ricky is happier walking: anger raging, the demons are now on the prowl and in need of feeding before returning to their lair. For the moment, Dr Jekyll is in hiding. The demons have a plan. They always have a plan. On the way to his private residence a few blocks away in the heart of Mayfair, Ricky is going to walk through the back streets. Strutting between the occasional Latvian and several hailing from the Balkans, he will find one who is young and vulnerable. Preferably blonde, the demons tell Ricky, but he is not overly fussy. She will probably be from Romania and will likely find the large bundle of notes that Ricky keeps in his pocket just for this purpose irresistible.

Two hours later, the girl leaves, and the demons have receded once more into their locked vaults. The young Albanian can hardly walk. Her ankles are bruised, and she has suffered multiple traumas to both face and body. Drugged to the eyeballs, she has no idea which way is up, let alone out, so Ricky has to help her get dressed and then shuts and locks the door on her as she staggers away. Blonde, vulnerable, most likely under-age, almost definitely illegal, Ricky knows that she will have nowhere to go to complain. For her troubles, she is five hundred pounds the richer. The bruises to her face and body will mean that she will struggle to work for days.

Life's a bitch, Ricky reflects as he gets ready for bed. The last things he does before turning out the light is set his alarm for the morning when a car will collect him and take him to Northolt airfield where his jet will be waiting. Let it be a lesson, Ricky thinks as he rolls onto his side and closes his eyes. If people want to fuck around with Ricky Al-Shawabi, then just let them find out how much of a vile evil bastard he can be.

Chapter 22

Monday 25ᵗʰ January 2016

Norfolk and London

The Nesbitts had worked for the Seymour family for generations. Nancy Nesbitt had been cook and housekeeper at the property all her working life. For the last ten years, she had worked for Jeremy's brother, Thomas, who had bought half the farm from his brother when Jeremy had given up farming and entered politics. Hubert, Nancy's husband, still works as a farmhand and had done so for as long as anyone could remember, as had his father before him. Hubert and Nancy's only son, Len, is now continuing the family tradition. Len Nesbitt is as loyal to the Seymours as they come. However, to use Jeremy's own words: 'despite his undoubted loyalty, Len was one of life's chancers.' Meaning that the younger Nesbitt is a commercial animal, always on the lookout for opportunities to earn a little extra tax-free cash on the side.

No questions asked. No answers given.

So it was that when Mister Jeremy, as Len always called his local Member of Parliament, happened to run into Len on a flying visit to the farm recently, Len had been delighted when Jeremy had slipped him a generous handful of large denomination notes and had asked him to perform a small errand.

The errand proved not particularly taxing either, which for Len made the whole experience that much more enjoyable. First off, he was required to make a phone call to a mobile phone number that Mister Jeremy had given him, asking for someone who went by the name of

Murphy to call him back. Within thirty minutes, he was speaking to the man in question, reading out over the phone verbatim the instructions that Mister Jeremy had provided. Murphy had then asked whether Len had a package for him. When Len had replied in the affirmative, they had agreed on a time, place and method for meeting and the call had ended.

On the appointed day, Len had driven his battered old Vauxhall Astra down to Chelmsford. His rendezvous had not been until two in the afternoon, giving Len enough time to visit a local pub and enjoy a couple of pints of IPA over a sandwich and a large packet of crisps. At just after one-thirty, he had set off in the Astra again, this time bound for the superstore in Princes Road where he had found a suitable parking place and waited. At five minutes to two, he had climbed out of the car and walked to the front entrance, standing just beside the cash dispensers that were positioned adjacent to the glass sliding doors.

At precisely two o'clock, a man wearing a dark green Barbour jacket and waterproof hat had approached Len.

'Excuse me,' the man had asked. 'Are you waiting for Simon Turnberry?'

'No, sorry. I was expecting to meet his brother, Adam.'

'I think he's gone to Ipswich.'

Which had been the agreed-upon set of signals for Len to hand over the small parcel that Mister Jeremy had given him – a package that had been nestling in the poacher's pocket of his own, considerably tattier, Barbour jacket – and then leave, which he duly had done.

No questions asked. No answers given.

During the Troubles, Murphy O'Connor's father had been killed by a terrorist bomb intended for their next-door neighbour in East Belfast, a Unionist with radical leanings. His mother had decided there and then to up sticks and move with Murphy to the relative safety of London. Murphy's mother had previously been a teacher and had easily found work. She knew even at that stage that her sixteen-year-old son was destined to become a casualty of the education system.

Ever practical, Murphy never let his lack of academic prowess get in the way of finding his feet and making a success of his new life. A naturally street-savvy young man, Murphy quickly built new friends and a wide network of contacts in and around the East End of London. Proving himself adept at hustling for work, he ran errands for people, buying and selling things, collecting debts. Especially collecting debts. Murphy found that he had a talent for tracking down all and any who owed money but thought they could get away with it. At first, he had relied on his networks and the grapevine; then he discovered the power of the internet. It had transformed his life.

Murphy's transition to full-blown private investigator was arguably inevitable but didn't occur overnight. Instead, more and more people began asking him to do other things besides helping to recover money that was owed: finding those who had gone missing; discovering what certain others were up to; and, a popular request, learning whether husbands, wives or lovers were being unfaithful. Ten years ago, one of those requests had come from an unusual source, a man called Nesbitt. Nesbitt had commissioned Murphy to start a piece of work digging around in the dirt about a particular individual hoping to become a Member of Parliament. This was when Facebook had been in existence for only a couple of years, and Twitter hadn't yet been born. Without much information on the Web about the man in question, Murphy had decided a more practical approach was required. He had thus made the trip to Norfolk to begin ferreting around. In no time at all, old school and family connections were whispering to him in the local bars and pubs about the man's previous heroin addiction, some suggesting that he remained an occasional drug user. When the information became public, including one incriminating photograph that Murphy unearthed putting most of the allegations and whisperings beyond doubt, Nesbitt had paid handsomely.

Murphy had wondered at the time whether Nesbitt had any links to Jeremy Seymour, the man who had eventually won the local election by a landslide. His suspicions had finally been confirmed by the landlord of the local pub just before he had left Norfolk: Hubert Nesbitt was a farmhand on the Seymour family farm. With the Nesbitt assignment completed and payment received, Murphy had forgotten all about it – until very recently when out of the blue, a different man, another Nesbitt, had requested an urgent conversation. Too much of a coincidence. It took less than ten minutes searching on the Internet for Murphy to verify that Len Nesbitt was, in fact, Hubert's son.

Finding a suitable lay-by on the A12 and bringing his BMW to a temporary halt, Murphy broke open the package. In it, in amongst bundles of twenty and fifty pounds notes, he found the written instructions that had something of a déjà-vu feel about them. Reading them, Murphy was in no doubt that Jeremy Seymour's hand was once more pulling the younger Nesbitt's strings.

Murphy had never been a man of many scruples, and he felt something of a buzz about the prospect of working for this particular returning client. With the retainer fully paid in advance, Murphy had confidence that Seymour, assuming that he was indeed the real client once more, would prove more than capable of paying any success fees due, if and when requested. The client instructions were indeed clear: more digging in the dirt was required, this time on a much higher profile target - the Foreign Secretary. The assignment seemed feasible and well within Murphy's capabilities. The principal problem for Murphy was where to begin.

Sometime later, back in his rented flat in Barking to the east of London, Murphy was ready to set to work. On the table in front of him were two carefully chosen bits of dirt-digging equipment. One was high-tech, a top-of-the-range laptop computer; the other was somewhat more down to earth, a simple pen and a large pad of A3 sized plain white paper. On the broad expanse of white paper, he drew several columns representing Geraldine Macauley's friendship groups: her parents and immediate family; school friends; university friends; Bar School friends; barristers' chambers colleagues; constituency party members; Houses of Parliament colleagues; Foreign Office officials; and finally, a catch-all 'others' category. His next task was to research the names of one or two key people in each category who were likely to know most about Geraldine Macauley at each period in time. These wouldn't necessarily be her closest friends or family members: more probably, they would be people who would have known most about her from the position they had held. For example, a former school housemistress, Macauley's college tutor, or one of the secretaries in the barristers' chambers where she had worked. What Murphy ideally wanted was a handful of people still alive today who might be able to divulge information about aspects of Macauley's life that may thus far not have hit the public domain.

It proved quite a job. After two days of researching, Murphy had whittled his list down to ten names: he had in reserve another thirty or so to fall back on if these first few didn't bear fruit. This wasn't an exact science, the process akin to throwing darts at a board whilst blindfolded with only limited knowledge about where the dartboard might be hanging.

The picture that emerged was of a hard-working woman with a strong academic background. Geraldine Macauley, née Finlay, had achieved three grade A's at A levels at Cheltenham Ladies' College, where her chosen subjects had been History, Politics and Economics. She had also been Head of House and Deputy Head Girl. Her non-identical twin sister, Emily, had been less academic and had gone to a different school. Unlike her twin, Geraldine had shown little interest or prowess at sport but had been a talented pianist, achieving her Grade 8 exam with distinction by the age of sixteen. At King's College London, studying law, she had emerged with a first-class degree. Her fellow students described her as well-liked and studious, showing little interest in social events other than those revolving around the law, music, or politics. Her friendship groups had fallen broadly into one of these three categories. She had shared a house in Balham for two years with four other law students before meeting and falling in love with another aspiring lawyer, Mark Macauley, with whom she had shared a small flat in their final year at university.

Whilst Geraldine had gone to the Bar, Mark had joined a large law firm, and they had both seen their careers take off. Within two years of leaving university, they were engaged. A short time later, as a now quite accomplished junior barrister, she had become pregnant with twins. After their birth, Geraldine had returned to work and stayed for another three years, juggling parenthood and life at the bar. Finally, with the twins in a day nursery, Geraldine had concluded that if she was ever going to enter politics, this was her moment, especially with her husband Mark about to become a partner in his law firm. She had stood for, and easily won, her first parliamentary election in the constituency of Chipping Hadham. From that moment, her life and career had changed forever. Her private life, what little she now had of one, was ever more to be in the media spotlight.

Chapter 23

Tuesday 26th January 2016

Surrey

The care home felt a sad and strange place. God's waiting room, the residents call it. The atmosphere was sterile, and the place felt eerily deserted despite the muted cacophony of electronic beeps and over-loud televisions blaring from several of the bedrooms. This was a place where disposable latex gloves were put through their paces: dressing and undressing, hoisting and manoeuvring, wiping surfaces and liberal spraying of antibacterial fluid in all directions.

For Eileen Burroughs, a visitor was a rare and exciting event. A spinster who throughout her life devoted much of her energy to her work, Eileen now had few friends – and no family – left alive. Eighty-nine, increasingly frail, she felt vulnerable and frightened, spending most of her waking hours alone in her room, either watching daytime television or attempting to complete the crossword. She craved conversation with people other than her fellow residents, who only seem minded to discuss ailments or the quality of the food.

The arrival of the well-dressed young man at her bedroom door is the highlight of her week. He introduces himself as a researcher working on a new political biography about the life and times of Geraldine Macauley, and Eileen is thrilled to have his company, indicating for the man to take a seat in her one and only visitor chair. She presses the button that brings her reclining chair into more of an upright position, using the time to begin composing her thoughts, struggling to hold back a tear as she remembers with fondness her time working for Geraldine.

She begins by explaining about the barristers' chambers where Geraldine had worked and Eileen's role as lead secretary to several barristers. She had been working at the chambers for several years by the time Geraldine arrived. The two of them had worked on and off for over five years, enough for Eileen to realise that this tough, tenacious young lady was intelligent, fair-minded and driven. Had she been surprised when Geraldine had decided to go into politics? At the time, yes, but with hindsight, it had probably been inevitable, perhaps the perfect calling.

The man takes notes diligently, writing in ink in a small blue notebook as she describes in glowing terms what Geraldine had been like to work for. At one stage, a Filipino nurse in uniform brings Eileen a hot chocolate drink: when asked, the man requests a coffee for himself. As the nurse leaves the room, Eileen continues with her story.

She describes working with Geraldine as if it had only been yesterday, the distant memories clear in her mind. Her visitor's coffee arrives, along with a small plate of biscuits, and Eileen relates how she had had to support Geraldine at work throughout her first pregnancy and how well Geraldine had coped with the arrival of twins.

'Did she take much time off work?'

'She never stopped, is what I remember. She would ring me up and dictate over the telephone. I would type everything up and then send it around to her house the next day. Sometimes, if it were urgent, we'd send things by fax. There weren't mobile phones in those days, and word processors were still a novelty. Of course, everything's so different now. Back then, we had to work hard to support our barristers when they were out of chambers. Maternity leave and, heaven forbid, part-time working were both frowned upon. My, how times have changed! Though I have to say, at the time, Geraldine was wonderful. She never let having babies interfere with her work in any way. How she ever found the time to read through her briefs whilst feeding the twins and doing nappies and everything, I simply do not know. Anyway, she came back to the office full-time after about three months, I seem to recall, but, as I say, she never really stopped any of her client work. Not that time at least.'

The man looks puzzled.

'Was she pregnant a second time?'

'Oh yes,' Eileen says, holding her mug of hot chocolate with both hands and sipping it gently. 'Let me think; it must have been about two years later. She had a baby girl.' She puts the mug down, spilling a little on the table in the process. 'Clumsy old me,' she says, mopping it up with a tissue.

'Now, where was I? Oh yes, anyway, after this second birth, Geraldine was off for much longer. It was about the same time that she must have been thinking about going into politics since she never really came back to work after the second pregnancy. It was all a bit of a shock, to be honest.'

'What was?' the man asks, pen and notebook poised.

'Losing Geraldine to politics as well as her losing the baby.'

'Oh dear,' the man says, a look of sympathy across his face now. 'What happened?'

'None of us knew. Cot death, apparently. It was so distressing for her and everyone. I mean, who wouldn't have been upset, poor thing?'

They talk some more. Did she drink, smoke or have affairs with anyone? Eileen looks shocked.

'Have an affair? What can you be thinking? I never met anyone so devoted both to her work and her marriage. You know that he's now dead, the husband?'

The man nods as he continues writing.

'Lost to cancer, just a few months ago. I read it in the paper. I meant to write, but -,' she gives the man an apologetic smile, '- it's difficult these days. Poor Geraldine, she will have been so sad.'

'Do you still keep in touch?'

'Sadly, no. She's far too busy. I liked her, one of the best people I ever worked for. Do you think she'll ever be prime minister?'

'Who knows?' the man answers, closing his notebook, the signal that his visit is almost at an end.

'Will you come back and see me again?' Eileen asks, her eyes full of hope. 'It is so nice to have a visitor.'

The man smiles. 'I'd like to,' he proffers gently, not wanting to disappoint. 'Let's see how the biography goes. If I need to ask you a few more questions, would it be all right if I called again?'

'Of course. I should like that.'

At which point, the man gets to his feet, shakes Eileen's hand gently, and leaves, the older woman's eyes already tearful at his departure.

Chapter 24

Tuesday 26th January 2016

London

The news of Macauley's second pregnancy – and subsequent infant death – is a development. Murphy feels like a bloodhound, sniffing the air and trying to pick up the scent. The first order of business had to be to find a copy of the birth and death certificates.

Back home and on his laptop, Murphy begins hunting for the formal record. Every birth, marriage and death in the UK is recorded by one of many local registrar's offices located all around the country. Each entry in the local register has its unique reference number. Centrally, all registrations are managed by the UK Home Office's General Records Office or, to use its acronym, the GRO. It is to the GRO that details of all certificates issued are sent. Annoyingly for Murphy, members of the public cannot search through the GRO's records, either over the internet or in person. They can, however – if they wish – order copies of certificates by making an online application, the speed of response depending on how much someone is prepared to pay and whether they have first been able to track down the relevant reference numbers. Various website developers have created tools to make this search easier to help genealogists and others compile family trees. For a fee, Murphy can access extracts taken from the birth, marriage and death registers, including the all-important reference numbers.

After a few false starts, he finally tracks down the birth record of one Amelia Jane Macauley, born to Geraldine Macauley, née Finlay, on 3 June 1985. The extract is not a full replica of the birth certificate, nor is all the information provided. It does show, though, the GRO reference that Murphy now needs to request a copy of the certificate, the reference indicating: the year and the quarter in which the birth was registered; the geographic district in which registration took place; and the record number. Murphy prints this out and begins another search, this time for the death record. Eileen Burroughs had indicated that the child had died aged at about six months. Search as he might, Murphy is unable to find a record of the death anywhere. He tries a new search with a broader range of date options but again draws a blank. Knowing that no birth, marriage, and death databases are ever one hundred per cent accurate, he navigates to a different website but again, after yet more searching, finds nothing.

Now in unfamiliar territory, he begins a different line of investigation, this time trying to understand why a death registration might be missing. One reason, he discovers, is if the young baby had died outside the UK. Deaths of UK citizens abroad need first and foremost to be registered in the country in which they die: there is no obligation to report the death additionally in the UK. Is this what happened with young Amelia Jane? If so, trying to locate her death certificate was going to be like searching for a needle in a haystack. Apart from talking to Macauley herself about what had happened, it was likely to be the end of the road for this particular line of enquiry.

Unless.

Tempted to throw in the towel, Murphy has an idea. How about a quick game of *what if?*

What if he couldn't find the death record because the baby girl hadn't died? *What if* she had been, for example, a love child? Could Macauley have decided simply to hand custody of the baby girl back to the natural birth father? Or *what if* Macauley's pregnancy had been an accident? Could she and her husband have simply agreed to have the child handed over for adoption? Murphy feels a need to see a copy of the birth certificate. There might be some nugget or other hidden in amongst all of this, after all. Perhaps a golden one. In particular, whose name would be on the birth certificate as the father of the child? The father's name didn't need to be recorded on a UK birth registration. Usually, the name would be there, but for an unwanted pregnancy or a host of other reasons, it did not have to be. *What if* the name of the father was not given? This wouldn't tell Murphy anything more than he already knew, except it would make him suspicious because it might suggest that Macauley's husband had not been the baby's father. Even more interesting, *what if* the named father was someone other than Geraldine Macauley's husband? That would suggest that Macauley had indeed had a love child who she had then subsequently abandoned.

The gossip columns would love that!

He navigates to the GRO's website to order a copy of the certificate. It takes just a few clicks of his mouse and a small number of keystrokes to enter the relevant details and reference numbers and finally, his credit card details. He decides that this is worth paying the necessary supplement to ensure that he receives it in the post within forty-eight hours.

Now all he needs to do is wait and see what comes back.

Chapter 25

Tuesday 26th January 2016

Monte Carlo, Monaco

The Bell 429 helicopter has a capacity for seven passengers; today, excluding Shetty, who is driving back later with the mountain of luggage, there are just the five of them. The flight from Courchevel's Altiport has been nothing short of stunning. The bright sunshine was glistening off the frosty white snowy mountains. Then there was the dramatic drop-off from the Alps down to the rolling plains beyond the Rhône valley. Finally, the Mediterranean Sea itself: azure blue, inviting, the small wave peaks reflecting the sun. As the pilot brings the aircraft through its final banked turn, flaring at the last moment in readiness for landing, even the high-rise, over-populated principality of Monaco looks uncharacteristically beautiful in the winter sunshine. Not far from the individually marked landing pads that comprise Monaco's heliport, a small minivan and driver are waiting. Minutes later, after wriggling through the narrow streets and underground tunnels, all five are deposited by the entrance of an unremarkable high-rise block that is the nerve centre of the Al-Shawabi global operation.

Little has been said on the journey from Courchevel. Heads have been hunched over mobile phones, fingers and thumbs scrolling through emails. All except Vladek, who has been sitting motionless, observing. Keeping the peace, as Xandra calls it: threatening with menace as Adam prefers to think of it. In the cramped space of the lift taking them to the fifth-floor reception, there is no avoiding a moment of brief physical contact. Finding Vladek uncomfortably close, Adam distracts himself by remembering another confined lift ride the previous afternoon.

There is a reception committee of one by the glass-fronted Al-Shawabi front desk, a pretty young woman responsible for meeting and greeting and answering the telephones.

'Bonjour!' she says, standing in welcome as her visitors emerge one by one from the lift.

Ozzie, despite his wife's ever-watchful eye, can't resist giving her his warmest, most flirtatious smile.

'*Bonjour, Natalia. Ça va?*'

'*Oui, Monsieur Gerhard, ça va, ça va!* Monsieur Fraser, Monsieur Al-Shawabi asks please that you go directly to his office. He is expecting you.'

Xandra, Ozzie and Adam exchange looks.

'Have fun,' Xandra says to him.

Ricky's office is predictably vast. An expanse of floor to ceiling windows provides panoramic views over Port Hercules and the Mediterranean Sea beyond. Ricky sits at a modernistic glass desk, positioned at an angle to afford him both the external view and a clear line of sight over all who enter his domain. His personal assistant, a fierce-looking woman in her fifties, allows Adam to venture in only after first checking with Ricky to see whether he is ready.

The Great Man is staring at his computer as Adam enters, his face partially obscured from view. The clock on the wall behind him indicates the time: just after twelve-thirty in the afternoon.

'Come in,' Ricky booms when he sees Adam, bounding to his feet and swiftly moving around the desk to the seating area in the middle of the room. Bright red leather sofas and armchairs are positioned around a glass coffee table allowing first-time visitors to wallow in the soft leather and be not a little intimidated by the view.

'You made good time. How was the snow?'

'Excellent, thanks. Skiing not your bag, or did you simply run out of time?'

'Oh, the latter. I love to ski, but I was just too busy. I had to go to Bahrain to meet some important new contacts. People who, if we all play our cards right, Adam, are going to make us an obscene amount of money.'

'Presumably the same ones we're going to be bringing to Monaco sometime soon?'

'Ah, change of plan on that front. The Saudis now want to meet in Dubai. Hence the call to bring everyone back sharpish. I need Xandra to go to Panama to sort some things out for me whilst you and I head off to the Gulf. Anyway, I stopped off in London for the weekend on the way back. I had to meet some friends, catch up on the gossip, do a spot of networking at the highest levels, that sort of thing.'

He smiles, the self-effacing Ricky Al-Shawabi trying to be only a trifle modest in front of the new boy. Despite the bonhomie, Adam senses underlying anger, something that hadn't surfaced in his dealings with Ricky thus far.

'I learnt something in London.' Ricky is back on his feet, pretending to admire the view, whilst in reality, pacing back and forth. 'It's got me rattled, actually.'

He turns to face Adam now, his hands on the back of one of the red leather chairs as if to steady himself.

'What I'd like is some advice. You're one of the very few I feel able to trust with what I am about to tell you.'

Adam's stomach begins to churn. A washing machine within has come to life: the power switched on, the revolutions slow, but the stress-activated motor nonetheless operational.

'You've only been with us a short while, but I guess you know a little of what we get up to by now. It's time to take Adam Fraser deeper into Ricky's confidence.'

He turns mid-pace and gives Adam one of his schoolboy '*not guilty, m'lud*' smiles.

'I want you to become a fully paid-up member of the Ricky Al-Shawabi inner sanctum. Before we embark on that particular voyage of no return, I need to feel reassured about your commitment. Fair dos?'

He is leaning forward over the back of the chair once more, bent at the waist, eyes probing. Adam nods his head and says that it is fair, the cue for Ricky to continue.

'Because whilst the Al-Shawabi journey is most definitely paved with gold, the substantial rewards that will undoubtedly come your way do not materialise without a modicum of risk. When we start together on this adventure, I would like you to have your eyes wide open, not blindly following, perhaps somewhat lustfully, in Xandra's wake. Am I making myself clear?'

'Perfectly, Ricky.' Adam has finally found his voice, which arrives in time to drown out the sounds of washing machine noises from his stomach. 'Just for the record and to put your mind at rest, I am thrilled to be here, to be working with you and the team. It's daunting but exhilarating. If anything, I'm just a tad anxious about whether I'll be able to make a big enough contribution for you to want to keep me on the team permanently.'

'I wouldn't worry about that, Adam. I have the perfect role for you. However, thank you. I am pleased you want to be here. You see, the thing is, Al-Shawabi has many strands to its business, but they all have one thing in common: they all make money. A lot of money. Success brings its rewards and, as you can see, touch and feel,' he says, waving his arm around the room, 'we have, over the years, been pretty successful – and for two reasons. Firstly, we go out of our way to help people who want us to help solve their problems. Secondly, and most critically, we try not to be judgemental about who these people are or what the nature of any underlying problems they are dealing with might be. Bureaucrats, business leaders, world and political leaders: they all have their populist mantras, but these are often at odds with their private personal aims and ambitions. So what we do so well at Al-Shawabi is to allow these people to fulfil their private aims and ambitions whilst providing a cloak of invisibility and anonymity for their more public positioning in life. These people find our methods, our solutions, our discretion and the trust we engender beyond valuable. Which is why they pay us so generously. Some hate paying taxes and choose us to help find ways to avoid doing so; others may have acquired wealth in ways they'd rather not have discussed – and want to keep it that way; and there are those eager to use their position of power to enrich their short time on this planet. We have written the book about how best to help people manage their wealth, however acquired: discreetly, professionally and anonymously.'

'That sounds like skating perilously close to what some might label tax evasion and bribery. Possibly even money laundering.'

'Adam, Adam, Adam,' Ricky says, shaking his head, once again on the move, this time towards a small corner bar at the far side of the room. 'How can you think like that? Al-Shawabi is a globally accredited business.' He looks across at his guest. 'Water, coffee, tea, that sort of thing?'

'Water would be fine. Sparkling if you've got it.'

It might short-circuit the electric motor currently grinding inside my stomach.

'Several less successful organisations,' he says, returning with a large bottle and two glasses, 'are weighed down with armies of tax planners hiding behind complex structures and a veritable maze of compliance protocols and 'know your client' procedures. Many of them do indeed fly too close to the wind, becoming targets of law enforcement officials. These second-rate competitors tie themselves in knots trying to duck and dive out of the clutches of various authorities. What a hell of a way to run a business! We run Al-Shawabi differently. Our client acceptance criteria are very straightforward. We only ever take on clients who are recommended to us through our network of well-established personal connections and contacts. Some like to pay extra to remain anonymous. That's fine by us. So, they give us their assets: we look after them, put them in our name and allow these clients to re-acquire them at any point in time in the future that suits them. No computer records, no tiresome audit trails, no vulnerability to whistle-blowers.

'So, let's take the case of a Pakistani government minister. One day this hapless individual discovers that he is the key decision-maker in a tendering process for a multi-billion-dollar contract that a German multinational is desperate to win. As part of their efforts to win the contract, the Germans wisely employ Al-Shawabi as their internationally accredited intermediary. Our expertise and connections allow us to position the German business to be the favoured bidder. We soothe and nurture the Pakistani; he feels favourably disposed to the Germans. Everyone is happy. The Germans win a contract worth billions; they pay us a substantial multimillion-dollar sum as a consultancy fee; and out of that money, we use a nominee company in a well-chosen location to invest part of that fee in assets such as real estate or tradable securities. Then when we next meet this Pakistani government minister, we might say to him, by way of a discreet conversation: 'We would like to present you with a gift: why not allow us to grant you an option to buy this property or these securities at a time of your choosing – and at a ludicrously discounted price of course? For argument's sake, one dollar.' We make it all legally binding, execute a simple memorandum that is signed and witnessed, and we each keep a copy locked away somewhere. Nothing is recorded in any ledgers or computer systems. Our clients are thrilled. The Pakistani minister is delighted. Everybody else is none the wiser.'

'Okay, Ricky,' Adam says, taking a swig of water in the hope that it will drown out the growling in his stomach. 'I think I get the picture. Where exactly do I fit in?'

Ricky stares at Adam. Neither says a word. An unspoken line is about to be crossed, a disclosure soon to be made that cannot be retracted. It is decision time, and Ricky needs to decide.

Heads he's in; tails he's out.

Adam's insides are churning: the washing machine is on its rinse cycle.

Thank you, Miss Bateson, for being so kind as to make my life so complicated.

'The thing is, Adam, I have a small but urgent matter that I need your help in resolving.'

The coin seems to be landing on heads.

'How I can help?'

'Despite everything, despite all the money I pay people, all the trust I put in my team and all the accumulated riches that my Al-Shawabi colleagues now have at their disposal. . . Despite all of that, I have learned in the last twenty-four hours from the most impeccable source that someone in my inner circle has been revealing some or all of my state secrets to the British authorities.'

Adam's face remains a picture of composure even though he feels a sudden icy blast of freezing water rapidly pumping in and around his bowels.

Bloody hell, Emms, that was quick! I've only been a signed up and trusted member of the Miss Bateson spying fraternity less than eighteen hours, and here we are, already seeing our duplicitous acts laid bare.

'Who is it?' Adam asks with more composure than he would generally credit himself with.

'That's the problem,' says Ricky slowly, his tone chilling. 'I simply don't know. I'm told that he or she has been at it for some time. Exactly how long is anyone's guess. Which is precisely why, Adam dear boy, you are one of only two people I can trust to help me.'

'The other being?'

'The other being Vladek. He and I go back a long, long way. I would trust him with my life. He may not be everyone's cup of tea, but he owes me for everything he now has, and he wouldn't betray me, of that I'm confident.'

Ricky looks at Adam and smiles thinly.

'I need your help to find this duplicitous bastard, Adam. Whoever it is has got to be found. I promise you, when I know who it is, things are going to get very, very ugly.'

Adam's bowels are turning to liquid.

'Any ideas?' Adam finds his first steps as a duplicitous bastard quite difficult.

How did they find out so soon, Emms?

'I've been racking my brains. It could be anyone. I doubt that it's Xandra. I hope it's not Ozzie; he frankly knows too much. As does Fergus, for that matter. It could be Gemma. I can't believe it would be Shetty, but who knows?'

'What about someone in Fergus's team?'

'All possible, but remember, this is a lean business. We're talking less than a handful of employees. What little they know is not going to be of much help to anyone: they can't be ruled out, but it's unlikely.'

'How about Tash? Or Natalia on reception?'

'Both possible. I am glad you mentioned Tash. I've been wondering about her all the way back from London. I found her rummaging around inside the safe in our bedroom the other day. Said she had lost one of her earrings. Didn't think anything of it at the time, but in light of this, it raises question marks.'

Adam feels emboldened.

'To the extent you have secrets to hide, things you wouldn't want competitors – or the British for that matter – to learn, where exactly might you be keeping those, Ricky?'

Miss Bateson, wherever you are, I hope you are proud of the way I deliver my Oscar-winning lines?

'Other than in my head, you mean? Every 'option to purchase' agreement has to be signed by me. Once it has been witnessed, I retain one copy, the client takes away the other. Mine is kept in a special safe here in my office.'

'Are they scanned or photocopied at all?'

'Never.'

Steely eyes are penetrating Adam's inner soul as Ricky speaks his lines.

Adam takes courage in his hands and ploughs on. 'And if anyone were interested in either stealing from you or finding out things you didn't want them to know, it would be those documents they would be after, is that right?'

'Most definitely, yes.'

'So, the million-dollar question, Ricky, is who else besides you can access the safe?'

'No one.'

'I thought you said Tash had been looking inside it?'

'That was the safe in our bedroom. Not the one here in my office.'

He points to a cabinet in one corner of the room. It doesn't look out of the ordinary, but perhaps that is the point.

'Only I can get into that one. It's special and cost me a fortune. When I'm dead and gone, my lawyer has instructions. Until then, its secrets are for my eyes only.'

'So, what are you worried about? If there's either a mole or a whistle-blower on the prowl, what damage can be done?'

'Because we can't run our business like a leaky sieve. If clients knew that the things they were telling us in confidence were at risk of being disclosed to the authorities or the wider world, they would run a mile. I certainly would.'

He looks at Adam, sipping water from his glass, his eyes cold and penetrating.

'I'd like to hear your views. How should we catch this person? As the new boy on the block, you are the one person who can't have been spying on me. How are we going to flush out this double-crossing traitor, do you think?'

Confusion in the brain department. Just checking we are not at cross purposes: are you wanting to flush out Adam Fraser or A N Other British mole? The possibility that there might be more than one, you see Ricky, is now genuinely scary.

'Stealth and vigilance is my immediate reaction. Unless you want to create an unhealthy cloud of suspicion ever more to hang over the business. Maybe limit the people who have access to certain things, be it work or information? Possibly lay a few false trails, though I'd need to think about that.'

The washing machine is no longer spinning. It does, though, continue to make random flushing noises.

Ricky smiles.

'I like that last idea, Adam. I'm not sure how it would work but let me think about it some more and we'll talk again. I agree, by the way, with your other two points. It is why I want you alone to work with me on this new Saudi project. Adam Fraser, the new rising star of the latest and most lucrative Al-Shawabi production of all time.'

'What sort of show are we talking about exactly, Ricky?'

Ricky, once more back on his feet, is pacing. This time he stops by the windows and stares out whilst continuing to talk.

'Let's just say that sometimes the way we are obliged to work is necessarily complicated. Our Saudi friends have, for reasons it would be imprudent to enquire too much about, a burning need for a lot of physical cash. We know them as friends of friends: they know us – are we able to help? Of course, we can, but it will be expensive. Our terms? We require a ten per cent mark-up – and we are happy, by the way, to take some of this money as crude oil instead of cash. Enter Adam Fraser, our oil trading supremo, the man who will eventually trade out the physical crude and, in the process, make us a generous profit. Meanwhile, Ricky just happens to have a Latin American client keen to offload a ton of used notes in bulk. Our terms? This time, Ricky requires a thirty-three per cent profit margin for his time and trouble in dry cleaning their dirty money. We take the Latino cash and deliver it to the Saudis in a location of their choosing. Bottom line, we earn a profit from the Saudis, yet more profit from the Latinos and yet further profit still from the turn you will be making from trading out the light Arabian crude at a substantial mark-up. As a gesture of goodwill, you will earn ten per cent of that particular trading profit as a personal thank you from your kind Uncle Ricky. How does that sound?'

'Pretty damned amazing, Ricky. Un-bloody-believable actually.'

'This arrangement is strictly between the two of us. Not a word to Xandra or anybody – or else the whole profit-sharing arrangement's off? Do we have a deal?'

'We have a deal.'

The two of them shake hands.

'Go and pack some clothes. We'll take the chopper to Nice airport as soon as you're ready. The jet is fuelled and ready to go.'

'Who's coming beside you and me?'

'Vladek. I was going to ask Tash, but now I'm having second thoughts.'

'Why not invite her and Gemma together? That way, we can keep them both under observation, see if they do anything strange or unusual?'

'That's an excellent idea. I am sure Ozzie won't mind a few days without his wife. He usually seems more than capable of coping on his own.' Ricky gives Adam a knowing look.

'Fine, then I'll go and tell the others and get packed.'

'If you see Xandra, send her in, will you?'

Adam turns to leave, but Ricky interrupts him.

'One other thing, Adam. Just for the record, I am so pleased you decided to join us. I will make you rich beyond your wildest dreams, you know that don't you?'

'I'm pleased to be here too, Ricky.'

Chapter 26

Tuesday 26th January 2016

Monte Carlo, Monaco

It is just after six-thirty in the evening. With everyone *en route* to the Gulf or, in Xandra's case, Panama, Ozzie Gerhard finds himself unexpectedly a free agent. Freshly showered and making ready to leave, Ozzie plans to make the most of his unexpected evening in Monaco without any risk of his super-vigilant wife casting restraining glances in his direction. The decision about what to do has been easy. Tonight, he is going to meet with Céline.

Céline is a local girl. Very pretty, very vivacious and very much Ozzie's idea of a pleasant evening's distraction. Although Monaco is small, Ozzie has only recently discovered Céline. Like a hungry salmon seeing a delicious fly, having pondered the dangled bait for sufficient time, Ozzie feels in the mood. Now looking at his most charming – brand new lemon shirt, tan chinos, chestnut brogues and a freshly pressed jacket – there is a spring in his step as he applies the finishing touch: a liberal application of cologne.

They had met by accident, sitting at adjacent tables on the terrace at Ozzie's favourite coffee shop on the Place du Casino. The sun was out, the awnings up, the gas heaters providing additional warmth against occasional gusts of wintery wind. They were both sipping espressos. Ozzie was reading the paper, and she was checking emails on her phone. A young African, most likely Moroccan they'd concluded later, was dodging waiters and cruising the tables, hawking an array of handbags that were bunched together on an upper arm. Ozzie dismissed the man with a cursory wave of the hand. His hawker fly swat, as Gemma liked to call it.

Approaching Céline's table and seeing a single woman on her own, the man concluded that the risk of another fly swat remained high and that the phone itself was a prize altogether greater than any handbag sale he might otherwise make. He thus chose to grab it. With the phone in hand, he had spun on his heels, hastily moving for the exit. Sadly, as Ozzie had recounted numerous times subsequently to all and any unable to escape the tale of his derring-do, the escape route took *le voleur* directly past Ozzie's table.

Not one usually to pick a fight, Ozzie, for reasons he now still struggles to fully comprehend, on a whim stuck out a leg. The unexpected manoeuvre sent the poor unfortunate sprawling to the deck, hitting numerous empty chairs and tables and sending crockery and linen flying in the process. Not to mention Céline's phone, which by this stage had fallen from the man's hand and begun a graceful slide across the terrace. Realising when it was prudent to call time, the man had leapt to his feet, hot legging it as fast as he could, handbags flailing in his wake, as he sped into the surrounding neighbourhood and quickly was lost from view.

Ozzie's public version of his bravery ends at this point. It makes no further mention of the woman. Not even an offhand remark about how pretty the young journalist with the short dark hair was. Or how beguiling he found her retroussé nose that wrinkled whenever she smiled. Or, for that matter, how grateful she appeared to be to Ozzie for his moment of gallantry. Witness her desire in some way to repay him with an invitation to sit at her table and share their life stories.

The only person who sees through Ozzie's foreshortening of events is Gemma. Ozzie's former personal assistant might not be a tax planning wizard, but on affairs of the heart she has a first-class degree with honours. Ozzie's dismissive comments do not fool her. A defenceless young woman, caught up in the heat of the moment by a strange man's chivalrous act, and the man in question pretends he doesn't have either the time or inclination to learn her name or anything about her? This man couldn't be her husband. She knows the man she married, the man well into his third marriage. The man she tries to keep in check but knows it to be an uphill battle; the man, she keeps telling herself, she is almost certain to divorce the moment she can prove beyond doubt his infidelity. Only then, once the substantial financial settlement that she will be entitled to is safely deposited in the bank, will she go out and find herself a better offer.

As dinner progresses and the wine flows, Ozzie's initial impressions that Céline might have been working for a magazine such as Vogue or Tatler begin to evaporate. Belated attempts to retract early braggings about what he does and how well he does it are in vain. Céline's eyes are, it would seem, set on the Pulitzer Prize. The alcohol brings its own sense of realisation. Ozzie Gerhard, he slowly concludes, is becoming central to the, as yet unpublished Céline exposé – the one that is going to propel her towards journalistic glory. The Sauternes with the foie gras and the expensively aged Burgundy with the *carré d'agneau*: they all help cushion the blow. Too late to go off-limits, Ozzie takes solace in a fine twenty-year-old Bas-Armagnac. There are, he reflects whilst sipping the mellow liqueur, a few compensations in life worth having. The woman is sexy, her smile alluring, and her laughter appealing. She is seducing Ozzie with her flirtatiousness. The promise of forbidden treasure nags as a blouse button inadvertently comes loose.

They finish their meal and Ozzie pays the outrageously expensive bill, gallant in his role of unnamed source. He remains hopeful but no longer sure that he has not crossed too many lines that might have the potential to enrage Ricky. Her refusal to join him for a nightcap either at his place or hers puts a dampener on an otherwise enjoyable evening, what little he is later able to recall of it. What does stay with him, as he stands on the pavement saying his goodbyes in the light rain, is the way she kisses him goodnight. A full mouth-to-mouth clinch, her nose rubbing his, an electric current stirring life beneath the waistband of his trousers. Perhaps another time, he deludes himself as they eventually go their ways, ever grateful that Gemma is not there to see the simmering passion of their parting embrace.

It never even crosses his mind that there might be a cameraman. Someone waiting in the shadows, taking several high-clarity, close-up images with a sophisticated night scope, the noise of its motor drive unit lost amidst the night-time bustle of Monte Carlo's traffic.

Chapter 27

Tuesday 26ᵗʰ January 2016

En route to the Middle East

The plane is somewhere high over the Aegean. To the rear, languishing amongst the cream calfskin leather, the girls are still awake plotting how many of Dubai's shopping paradises can be visited on this short trip. A lone male steward has served and cleared dinner. Ricky is asleep in the seat to Adam's left, and Vladek is doing whatever Vladek normally does in the chair immediately behind Adam. Adam could easily swivel his seat through one hundred and eighty degrees to find out, but he rules against doing so, concluding instead that the man is best left to his own devices.

Over a light dinner, the chairman and chief executive of Al-Shawabi Enterprises has given Adam and Vladek an outline of the planned Arabian experience. Suites have been reserved at the Burj Al Arab. Adam will be accompanying Ricky on an off-road trip with a difference, meeting with the Saudis somewhere in an as-yet-unspecified remote corner of the desert sands. Tash and Gemma will fend for themselves but under the watchful gaze of Vladek. Assuming that all goes to plan, everyone will be back in Monaco by the following evening.

Adam's eyes are closed, but the discs in the hard drive of his mind are spinning furiously.

Where are you when I need you, Emms?

He had tried to make contact before leaving his apartment in a rush earlier, the procedure agreed by Miss Bateson simple yet effective.

Adam sends an innocent-looking text to Fiona, a supposed maiden aunt; in parallel, he sends a different message from his Twitter account. On their own, each is innocent enough. When combined, they are more revealing.

We need to speak urgently!

Adam has, of course, said nothing to Xandra. Nothing about his meeting with Emma. Nor anything about Ricky's spy in the camp theory. The two have hardly spoken since arriving back in Monaco that morning. Could Xandra be working for the British? Did that explain why she had been so happy to bring Adam on board a few weeks ago? To deflect attention away from her, to prepare the ground to be able to accuse him when the chips were down? He hopes not, and it feels unlikely. She doesn't stand to gain from selling Ricky *down the Swanee*, especially considering the small fortune she has amassed personally from Ricky's enterprise over the years.

What about Ozzie? The same logic applies. He might know where the bodies are buried, but his fingerprints are all over the spades and shovels, not to mention the looted treasure stuffed into his swollen bank accounts courtesy of Ricky. Fergus would be unlikely for similar reasons, although he is harder to read. Unlike the rest, each of whom has been tempted on account of their employer's generosity – not to mention the eye-watering cost of Monaco accommodation – to live in close proximity in and around Ricky's magnificent villa above Cap d'Ail, Fergus has chosen a path of independence. Together with his long-term partner, Giorgio, Fergus has his own small place near *Le Nouveau Musée Nationale*. Thus able to operate outside Vladek's immediate radar, avoiding too much scrutiny. If that so happened to be the reason for his choice.

Talking of Vladek, why not him? It is hard for Adam to conceive why Ricky puts so much faith and trust in the former professional fighter. Here is a man with a permanent grudge against so many people, especially Adam. Why would Vladek go blabbing secrets to the British? Al Qaeda, maybe, but the British? As much as Adam would like it to be so, he can find no convincing motive that would give any credence to the notion of Vladek in the role of informant.

Ricky had been quick to finger Tash. Gemma might be much more likely. As Ozzie's one-time personal assistant, she would have a lot of knowledge about the Al-Shawabi business. Her new husband's womanising might provide a motive – the jealous wife, happy to spill the beans about the Al-Shawabi operation as a form of retribution. Tash is a different kettle of fish, much less probable in Adam's view. In her early twenties, an otherwise innocent young woman, stunningly good-looking but worldly unwise, in debt and about to fail an art degree. Enter stage left Ricky, the ultimate sugar daddy, a man willing to shower the confused and grateful young lady with gifts and trinkets beyond her dreams, not to mention access to the substances she craves – but that is pure speculation on Adam's part. Tash's debt of gratitude is likely to cast long shadows of obligation over her relationship with Ricky. There is not much scope for Tash in the role of Judas.

Which – barring Shetty, the office receptionist, a few local hangers-on and any others working for Fergus that Adam hasn't yet met – leaves Adam himself. Only very recently cast as lead actor in Miss Bateson's latest low-budget production, Adam finds himself in an uncomfortable if not awkward position: supposedly incapable of being the mole that Ricky believes he has; whilst still culpable of being the mole that Ricky doesn't yet know that he's got.

The good news, if indeed there is any, is that regardless of how hard anyone might be tempted to dig, Adam is confident that no one will have yet worked out this ham actor's true motivations. They might hazard a guess, but they wouldn't get it. Miss Bateson thinks she knows, but even she has been duped by the professional actor inadvertently cast in an am-dram production. Emms could probably point at Cupid's arrows in mid-flight and have an 'aha!' moment: but even she would be wide of the mark. The truth is that no one has yet got close. It is this knowledge that keeps him awake on a long flight to Dubai. It causes internal washing machines to churn back into life at the slightest provocation. Adam Fraser, a man on an undisclosed mission. Signed up for a journey that sees him bringing Emms and Miss Bateson along as co-directors of a show they ill-advisedly believe they control.

As the washing machine keeps reminding him, life is not that simple.

Each person's journey is driven by desires and motives, often beyond many the understanding of many.

Adam senses a change of plan when he hears the alteration in engine pitch. A few minutes later, the pilot enters the main cabin. Spotting Ricky asleep, he asks the male steward to wake him.

'Sorry to disturb you, sir,' he says deferentially, once Ricky is awake and functioning. 'We've been asked by Saudi air traffic controllers to divert and put down at Al-Ahsa airport. It's about fifteen minutes' flying time from here.'

'Where the fuck is Al-Ahsa?' Ricky asks grumpily.

'It's south-west of Bahrain, sir. Not too far off our route.'

'Can't we simply ignore them? How long otherwise until we get to Dubai?'

'Ordinarily a little over an hour's flying time. However, I don't think we can ignore the request. Not unless we want a pair of armed F-15 Eagles on our wing, prepared to shoot us down.'

'I don't suppose we have many options then.' Ricky checks his watch. 'What's the local time?'

'One o'clock in the morning, sir.'

'Very good. Let's see what these people want.'

What the Saudis want soon becomes clear the moment the Gulfstream G650 rolls off the runway at Al-Ahsa International Airport and is met by a chase vehicle with the words 'Follow Me' in English illuminated on a signboard on the back. The jet is led to a small hangar at the edge of the airstrip and brought to a halt by a ground controller armed with fluorescent yellow wands. The plane's engines shut down, and the pilot comes back into the cabin.

'A boarding party is ready and waiting on the tarmac, sir. Are you happy if we open the doors?'

Ricky peers out of the window but sees nothing but pitch black.

'I guess we have no choice,' he says absentmindedly.

The night air is surprisingly chilly, the cold soon felt inside the cabin once the doors are opened and the stairs lowered. Moments later, a man in military uniform with three gold stars and a single gold crown on his epaulette comes into the cabin. Adam knows about Saudi military ranks from his time in the Middle Eastern theatre. This is a high-up: more senior than a colonel; the man is a Saudi soldier known as an 'Amid', someone of considerable influence and authority.

'Good evening, Mr Al-Shawabi. My apologies for interrupting your flight. My name is Amid Abdulraheem al-Dosari. You have been invited, please, to join me for a short trip into the desert. Your pilot and crew are to remain on board. We will service your aircraft for you with our compliments.'

He looks at Gemma and Tash.

'Please,' he adds, removing two cellophane-wrapped packages from under his arm and handing one to each of them. 'It would be appreciated if you could wear these and cover yourself before leaving the aircraft.'

Two black Mercedes SUVs are waiting outside. The men climb into one, and both women, now dressed in black abayas and matching black woollen headscarves, are directed into the other. The two cars begin moving away from the aircraft and hangar, passing out of a well-guarded checkpoint into the inky blackness of the Saudi Arabian desert. In the darkness, the car's headlights show the perfect condition of the black road surface. A short while later, in what appears to Adam to be the middle of nowhere, the cars slow almost to a halt and turn off the road onto the desert sand. The drivers of both vehicles get out and, with the aid of flashlights taken from jacket pockets, begin the process of letting some air out of the tyres. The small convoy is about to head into the desert.

With only the stars and a very occasional white triangular marker to guide them, they set off across the Arabian sands. Adam is more bemused than scared. He imagines Gemma and Tash being anxious, especially as both vehicles periodically mount crested ridges of sand before wallowing in a controlled slide down the other side. Adam loses track of time, gazing out of his window at the three-hundred-and-sixty-degree star-scape in the sky above. Then, just beyond one particular dune top, a small encampment appears up ahead. A few lights, a scattering of tents both large and small and several immaculate, very expensive-looking cars lie clustered in a group together.

No sooner have they come to a halt than Ricky is out of the car. He has recognised the people emerging from the largest tent to greet them.

'Ibrahim, how wonderful to see you!' The two men embrace warmly.

'Ricky,' the Bahraini says warmly. 'I am so very sorry to have disrupted your plans. However, it is better this way. You remember my two very special Saudi friends who we met briefly in Bahrain?'

Ricky turns to greet the other two who, similar to the Bahraini, are both dressed from head to toe in white.

'Of course! This is an unexpected pleasure, gentlemen.'

'It is so nice to meet you again, Ricky,' they say warmly.

'Believe me, the pleasure is all mine. Can I introduce my colleague, Adam Fraser?'

Adam steps forward to shake everyone's hand. Vladek waits quietly by the car along with the driver.

'Come, let us go inside,' one of the two Saudis says and lifts the flap on the side of the big tent. Vladek, realising he is not required to come with Ricky and Adam, gets back in the car, the cue for both vehicles to move off towards a second tent some distance away.

The inside of the big tent is both spacious and comfortable, the floor covered in rugs and cushions. Adam and Ricky are shown where to sit, coffee and dates are served, boxes of paper tissues thoughtfully placed by their side, along with pastries and cold drinks. The long Arabian dance of ritual pleasantries is about to begin. Adam loses track of time – here it is an irrelevance. This meeting will last until it is finished: only then will it be over, as he was once warned was the Middle Eastern custom. They discuss everything and anything – the health of their families, the price of oil, even the next UK prime minister. At one stage,

Adam is asked what it is that he does. When he replies that he is an oil trader, this statement is received with much enthusiasm and admiration from the three Arabs.

'Then we should do business together, Adam, you and I,' one of the Saudis says.

'I should like that very much,' Adam replies.

His answer is the cue for Ricky to begin steering the conversation around to matters of business. The ensuing discussion is short on details and precision, long on sage nodding of heads. The words are chosen with care to hover, as Ricky later says to Adam, ambiguously at twenty thousand feet or higher. But the direction of travel is clear, as is the amount of physical cash that their Saudi hosts seem eager to procure. Three hundred million US dollars. Cost to the Saudis being three hundred and thirty million. Paid for partly in cash up front and the remainder in crude oil at a discount below the current Brent spot price. Adam can do the maths. The upfront cash is sufficient to cover Ricky's costs for dry cleaning the Latin Americans' used US dollar bills. The oil represents the profit, the icing on Ricky's cake. On this transaction alone, the profit will be at least one hundred million. If and when the oil price moves off its current floor, possibly back to forty or fifty dollars a barrel, the profit could almost double. Nice business if you can get it. No names, no audit trail, the only paperwork being the in and out entries in one of Ricky's untraceable offshore bank accounts and the Saudis' gifted oil. The contents of two very large crude carrying tankers, each fully laden with over two million barrels of light Arabian crude, currently at rest just off the Malaccan Straits.

The slight distraction is the delivery destination for the physical cash. It is dropped innocently into the conversation as harmlessly as if it were Esher in Surrey or Beverly Hills in Los Angeles. The Saudis want it airlifted into Iraq. Then transferred into the bellies of two armoured personnel carriers, the ultimate location to be disclosed upon arrival. Adam knows the country from bitter experience. It is one hell of a dangerous place to be doing business. If Ricky is fazed by this low-flying bombshell, he takes it in his stride. Finally, once any lingering concerns have been put to flight, hands are shaken to signal high altitude agreement by all parties, and drinks once more offered and declined. The deal is struck; business in the desert has been concluded.

Almost, that is. But not quite.

Everyone is back on their feet. One of the Saudis is addressing his guests.

'Ricky, Adam, please come. We would like to give a little demonstration.'

All of them step out of the back of the tent and onto the desert sand, facing what appears, in the pitch dark, to be the vast emptiness of the desert. They stare into the void for a few moments before one of the Saudis gives three claps of his hand and the area is immediately lit by floodlights.

About thirty metres away directly in front of them is a robust looking long wooden stake that has been driven securely into the ground.

A short while later, screams fill the air. The sound is piercing, almost primaeval: positively chilling, the noise traceable to two men being dragged out of an adjacent tent, their hands and feet lashed together. Both are roughly manhandled by several men in Army fatigues, the men pulling the pair towards the spot where the stake is impaled in the ground. One of the prisoners is beaten with a nightstick to quieten him. The other is told to kneel in silence, a single captor to his rear ready to pounce if another sound is made.

One of Ricky and Adam's two Saudi hosts then steps forward and reads something out loud in Arabic from a scroll of paper that he has taken from inside his robes. At one point, he stops, and the kneeling prisoner nods his head. Something further is then spoken, at which point the guard behind the kneeling man removes a large knife from a sheath on his belt, grabs the prisoner's hair with his left hand and yanks the head backwards, slitting the man's throat from behind in one grisly manoeuvre.

The second prisoner, eyes wide with terror, realises that it will be his turn next and begins wailing and shaking uncontrollably. He is pulled to his feet and dragged so that his back is to the pole, the corpse of his now dead and twitching fellow-prisoner immediately in front of him at his feet. The man's hands are temporarily unbound before being tied once more so that his arms encircle the pole behind him. Having checked that the rope's bonds are secure, the men in Army fatigues now leave the scene. The Saudi with the Arabic scroll steps forward and again reads something aloud. This time, once the Saudi has finished reading, instead of waiting for any response from the prisoner, the Saudi puts away the scroll and claps his hands loudly, again three times. Then, as in a performance of the theatre of the absurd, the floodlights go out.

The demonstration is at an end.

The only sounds audible are the frantic pleadings of the now-abandoned prisoner, about to face a slow and agonising death in the bleak emptiness of the desert.

It is the cue for all five to head back inside the tent.

One of the Saudis gently leads Ricky and Adam back through the rear tent flap towards the front entrance once more, his gestures and mannerisms, indicating that it is time for everyone to leave.

'We Saudis value trust and respect in our friendships and business associations. For those we consider to be our true friends, we treat them like family. We welcome them as our special guests, bestowing hospitality and friendship: lavishly and honourably. For those ever breaking that trust, we make it clear at the outset that there can be no tolerance. As people of the desert, we find that the simple ways are usually the best. Those two thought they could steal from us. We tracked them down and they will have paid for their crimes with their lives. Our sincere hope, Ricky, is that as our relationship blossoms, we will have cause only to celebrate our mutual success. I trust we make ourselves clear?'

Ricky looks shocked, or so it seems to Adam. However, his words do not betray any such emotion.

'Perfectly clear, thank you. I feel the same way myself to be candid, although it's harder for me to exact the same sort of punishment that you have just demonstrated when I don't live in a desert.' The remark draws polite laughter. 'Where do we go from here, gentlemen?'

'We will have the oil contracts for you to sign in the next couple of days, *Insha'Allah*. When will the cash be available?'

'By now, that should have been sorted. As soon as the paperwork is signed, we can make the delivery.'

'Excellent. There is plenty of incentive all round. Look, your cars are here.'

The two black SUVs pull up close to where their small group is standing.

'Until we meet again,' Ibrahim says to them both, and hands are shaken warmly once more.

'May our friendship be long, and our businesses prosper as a result.'

'Indeed.' Ricky and Adam climb back into the rear of their car under the watchful, scowling eyes of Vladek seated in the front next to the driver. Ricky buzzes his window down.

'Thank you for your hospitality.'

'Thank you, Ricky, for your forbearance with the unexpected change of plan. Your plane will have been refuelled and a new flight plan filed. You will have been cleared through Saudi airspace for your journey home.'

As the small convoy starts to pull away, Ricky closes his window. Not fast enough, however, to prevent the plaintive whimpers of the prisoner tied to the stake from being audible.

Chapter 28

Wednesday 27th January 2016

En route to Nice

Back onboard the plane, doors closed, and permission granted to taxi to the active runway, Ricky gets into a celebratory mood.

'Crack open the Bollinger, can we?' he says to the steward who, soon after, emerges with a tray of glasses brimming with champagne.

'To the most lucrative business deal we've ever done, Adam,' he says, raising his glass as the engines begin to roar. The plane is soon accelerating down the runway and into the air.

Ricky is once more full of his usual good humour and bounce. As soon as the plane is set in the cruise, he grabs a half-empty champagne bottle from the steward and heads towards the rear where Gemma and Tash are sitting.

'Sorry about the abortive shopping trip, ladies. We'll have to do it another time. What's up, Tash? You look awfully glum at the moment? We should be celebrating! Big deal in the bag, lots of diamonds and pearls all round when this goes through. Why the sour faces?'

'What happened out there in the desert, Ricky? It was ghastly. First, we heard screams, then this terrible blood-curdling sound. It sounded like someone was dying.'

'Yes, well, I would wipe that from your memory if I were you. I wouldn't have brought you on this trip if I'd known you'd be subjected to anything like that.'

He puts his hand reassuringly on Tash's and squeezes it.

'I'm sorry. You too, Gemma. Please accept my apologies.'

He smiles at her and she responds with a watery smile of her own.

'It was simply a touch of Saudi Arabian justice, executed according to local rules. A couple of rapists or worse getting their just desserts if you'll forgive the pun? Just forget about it. The ways of the Arab world and all that. Have some more Bolly!'

He refills their empty glasses and waves the empty bottle at the steward.

'Think we need another one here pronto, steward!' he says, getting to his feet and walking back to his seat.

'Can you see that the ladies' glasses are kept topped up, there's a good sport?' He hands the empty bottle back to the steward before slumping down in his chair, swivelling his seat to look directly at Adam.

'So, my oil trading partner. How does it feel to be on track to becoming a multi-millionaire?' Ricky sees Vladek looking at him, scowling. 'Don't look so bloody miserable, Vladek. I always share the spoils of war, you know that. Go and sit with the girls for a moment, can you?'

Vladek takes his can of diet cola and heads to the back of the plane without a sound.

'How can you be confident it's not him?' Adam asks once he's out of earshot.

'What's not him?'

'The informant. It doesn't feel likely, I have to admit, but you seem to have ruled him out without a moment's hesitation.'

'I know, but you have to believe me on this. Vladek and I have been through a lot together, good and bad. He can be a miserable shit, and he probably hates you for joining the party but he's one hundred per cent loyal. You've got to trust me on that, Adam.'

'If you insist. However, if either Gemma or Tash are the guilty party, in hindsight it might have been unwise to bring them on this trip.'

'Oh, I don't know. What are they going to say to any supposed spymaster? We met these evil people in the desert. *What are their names?* We don't know. *What are they planning to do?* We don't know. *Where did they take you in the desert?* We don't know. *Name of the nearest airport?* We don't fucking know! None of that is going to help anyone, is it?'

'I guess not.'

'If anything, that public execution scene in the desert might make whomever the bastard is think twice before sneaking on me ever again, wouldn't you agree?'

Adam raises a glass in a silent toast. 'Let's hope so. It sounds like the deal is in the bag, though, Ricky. Are you sure you can lay your hand on enough cash?'

Ricky looks at Adam with eyebrows raised.

'Are you kidding? There are thousands of drug-producing Latinos desperate to legitimise their dirty money. Xandra will be sorting all that out as we speak. She's very resourceful. Worth taking care of would be my advice. Doesn't she have a birthday coming up soon?'

'In a couple of days, I think.'

'We should have a party in the villa. I'll get Shetty to organise it.'

'That'd be great. I'm sure she'd appreciate it.'

Ricky swirls the remnants of his champagne in his glass and then drains it in one gulp.

'I suppose the rough stuff didn't particularly faze you this evening. Given your military background, I mean.'

Adam hesitates before replying.

'Faze me? No, it didn't faze me. It was meant to be barbaric, I guess. Sort of did the trick too, though I thought it a bit over the top.'

'It's not all champagne and private jets in our line of business, Adam. We have to learn to take the rough with the smooth.'

'I guess. Taking three hundred million of cash into Iraq is not exactly going to be a bowl of cherries either.'

'You're right. Especially,' he adds with a sardonic smile, 'with Vladek and you being my duly-appointed designated drivers for the next phase of that particular Arabian adventure.'

Chapter 29

Wednesday 27ᵗʰ January 2016

Monte Carlo, Monaco

Adam slips out of the villa at just after six in the evening, dressed in running clothes and trainers for his regular eight-kilometre circuit. The early evening air is chilly, the skies clear, the wintry sun already below the horizon. Monaco is not large. His habitual route is a long, thin loop that takes him to the northeast corner of the Principality, then back into Monaco-Ville itself and around Port Hercule before heading home. There are a few ups and downs along the route to give it variety, but Adam usually achieves a sub-thirty-minute workout, a degree of stress on the system that gets his heart pumping and allows a sweat to form.

He is about a third of the way around when he discovers he has company. Just past the Casino's famous gardens on the same stretch of road that Formula One drivers use to slow themselves down before the switchback linking to the tunnel section, he finds that he is not alone. Two others are trying to keep pace on the opposite pavement. In time he recognises both, although Beef, the larger than life Ghanaian, is easier to spot: Emms, with her hair up and sweatband in place, is a veritable mistress of disguise. The cavalry has answered his call to arms.

She crosses to his side of the street and he slows his stride to allow her to catch up.

'Can we ease the pace a little, Adam?' she says when they are close. 'If we keep this up, Beef is likely to have a coronary.'

Adam slows to a jog, grinning at his new running companion.

'Nice to see you too, Emms. Do we have time for a passionate embrace?'

'Not whilst we're are out for a run, Adam.' Her tone is almost schoolmistress-like: shades of Miss Bateson.

'Knee looks better.'

She nods, a bead of sweat dripping from her nose.

'Miraculous what exercise can do.' She bites her bottom lip once again and Adam remembers why he became a lost man so readily.

'Do you want to grab a coffee?'

She shakes her head.

'Maybe head back to your hotel room for a quickie? No needles this time.'

Again she shakes her head, but this time she is smiling.

'How about a slap-up dinner for two, candlelight, string orchestra in the background, that sort of thing?'

'Is this the real reason for the panic call, or is there something else?'

'I really would like us to spend more time together, Emms. A quick jog around the streets of Monaco is hardly enough, panic or no panic.'

He glances at her and sees that she's still smiling.

'Better for us all if we keep moving. Tell me about the crisis. What's happened?'

Adam tells her. He tells her about Ricky's mole theory, and he tells her about his recent trip to Saudi. He also explains Ricky's option to purchase agreements. The ones locked away from view in Ricky's safe.

'They sound interesting,' she says as they come to the point in the run where Adam typically turns back.

They pause briefly and wait for Beef to catch up. He is trailing about a minute in their wake.

'They're the only written proof about the true Al-Shawabi business model. Ricky keeps no electronic client records, apparently.'

'There must be an address book?'

'Of course there is an address book! Ricky's address book is legendary. Just nothing in it that might incriminate him or anybody else.'

'Have you seen any of these agreements?' she asks.

Merely standing in her presence feels exhilarating. She is practically perfect. She looks at him in the half-light provided by the streetlights and smiles once again, her nose wrinkling at him as if having a conversation of its own. *'It's all right,'* it seems to be saying. *'Once all this business crap is out of the way, we can sort things out.'*

'No, not yet. He keeps them locked in his safe. The only person with access rights is The Maestro himself.'

'I'm sure we can find a safe-cracker.'

'Ricky assures me it's top of the range.'

'Our boys and girls are quite good.'

Beef finally makes his appearance.

'Nice to see you again, Beef. Sorry about the running. I did offer to stop for a coffee but -,' he says, pointing at Emms, '-the boss wasn't so keen.'

He is out of breath, but not as much as his size might suggest.

'That's no problem, Mr Adam.' He smiles thinly as the sweat pours down his cheeks. 'It's good for me. Apparently.'

They move on once more, heading back on themselves, this time in a wide, sweeping arc that will bring them around to the port area.

'How do you think they found out about you so soon, Adam?'

'You tell me. Several things suggest themselves. One is that you, Beef and Miss Bateson have sprung a leak somewhere in the midst of your little operation.'

She looks at Adam, surprised.

'It's just a thought.'

'Who's Miss Bateson?'

'I have no idea what her real name is. Miss Bateson was my former primary school head-teacher. The lady who seemed in charge in Courchevel looks the spitting image. Since no formal introductions were made, in my mind she's become Miss Bateson.'

Emms laughs.

'I get it. It's not her real name but let's stick with Miss Bateson. I rather like it. Anyway, you wonder if we have a leak, is that it?'

'Has to be a possibility. Either that or there's someone else in or around Ricky's operation who's also working for you lot. Point of fact, Ricky is convinced it can't be me since he thinks that whoever it is has been in place for ages.'

'Bloody hell!'

'Ricky still trusts me enough to want to send me to Iraq with over three hundred million dollars of his money, I'll have you know.'

Emma stops in her tracks. A frown appears as if she is registering the scale of the problem for the first time.

'We have to get you out of there, Adam. You can't be doing stuff like this. Come back to London with me. We can leave tonight.'

'It's so tempting, Emms. I'd be saying yes but for one thing. I'd like to get my hands on Ricky's files first. I want copies of those option agreements.'

'Why? We can send in the professionals to do that kind of stuff, Adam. Don't risk getting mixed up with Ricky's crazy adventures in Iraq, for God's sake!'

Beef catches up with them once again. They are standing right by the quayside, close to where all the private yachts are moored.

'What's up?' he asks. His over-washed burgundy t-shirt is drenched with sweat, the dark stains showing up clearly under the light from the streetlamps.

'Nothing,' Emms says and starts running to catch up with Adam, who has gone on ahead.

'If you hadn't turned up and made me an unwitting member of your spying fraternity, Emms,' Adam says once she has caught up with him, 'I would, in any event, have been traipsing around the world in Ricky's wake to whichever location he so chose to take me: Iraq, Afghanistan, Mogadishu or wherever. Iraq's no big deal. I've been to worse places. Don't look so alarmed.'

'I think you should quit.'

Spend the night with me and I might consider it.

'Soon but not just yet. I want to try and unearth some gold first.'

They are running around the perimeter of the port. Ricky's villa above Cap d'Ail is almost in sight.

'Have dinner with me, Emms. I am on my own tonight. Let's go wild, blow the budget, create some memories. We almost started something in Courchevel, you and I.'

He laughs as he says this but then looks at her in all seriousness to gauge her reaction.

'I can't. I'm sorry, Adam. I promised 'Miss Bateson',' she says wrinkling her nose at him, 'that I'd be on the last flight out of Nice to London tonight to brief her personally.'

Adam is quite certain she is aware of the effect that her gestures have on him.

'I'll try and get back tomorrow. When are you off to Iraq?'

'I've no idea. As soon as we've agreed the oil contracts and have all the money ready. Not for a day or so yet, is my guess.'

'Let's meet again when I'm back.'

She touches his arm briefly. Lustful electric currents tingle within him at the gesture.

'By then, you may have got your hands on those documents.'

She stops, and they wait once more for Beef to catch up.

'In any event, Adam, so that you know: I appreciate the offer. About tonight, that is. It's definitely tempting. However, business before pleasure. Ah, Beef! Time to say our goodbyes. I need to grab a shower and head to the airport. Let's speak again when I get back.'

'Sure,' Adam says with a heavy heart. 'Ricky's holding a party for Xandra in a couple of days. Monaco is a small place. See if you can get yourself invited.'

She blows him an air kiss.

'I'll see what I can do. Just stay out of trouble. Shout if you need help.'

With that they disappear off into the night, leaving Adam to run the remaining distance back to the villa. He stops to cross a busy road and chances a backward glance. There is no sign of either Emms or her Ghanaian minder. What he does see, though, sends a chill down his spine. About fifty metres away is the unmistakeable form of Vladek. Also out for an early evening run, seemingly heading in the same direction as the other two. For one brief second, their eyes make contact.

A gap appears in the traffic, Adam's cue to run across the road. Is this a random event or had Vladek been following them? If the latter, how long had he been on their tail and how much might he have seen?

Chapter 30

Wednesday 27th January 2016

Monte Carlo, Monaco

Every morning in winter, usually before sunrise, Vladek liked to run. Typically, he would exercise for thirty minutes, often longer. Afterwards, he headed to the gym for an intensive workout, a well-honed routine that involved weights and repeated attacks with hands, feet, arms and legs on the large punchbag that Ricky had installed especially for him. The oblong bag hung suspended from the ceiling like a heavy pendulum. If time and opportunity permitted, he would repeat some or all of the same routine in the evening: if not the gym, then certainly another run.

Vladek often followed Adam Fraser whenever the former soldier took his daily run. It had been Vladek's little game of cat and mouse around the streets of Monaco. There was something about Fraser that wasn't right. He sensed it but couldn't put his finger on it. When Ricky explained on the plane yesterday that there was a British mole in his operation, Vladek instantly zeroed in on Fraser even though Ricky said it was impossible. Everything about the former soldier was just a little too artificial. Unauthentic. Vladek was determined to prove it. Which was why he'd taken to following Fraser. The soldier might be fast, but the former cage fighter was confident that he could outrun the Brit. Vladek was practised at being stealthy, careful to ensure that he kept clear distance between them both to prevent Fraser realising that he was being followed. Thus far, Vladek was confident that he had got away with it.

Vladek is caught off guard as Fraser slips out of the villa at a different time to normal. Rapidly changing and putting on his running shoes, Vladek heads after him, hoping that he has left sufficient time to pick up the other man's tail. Most routes from the villa begin the same way. Fraser is mostly a man of routine. Tonight, Vladek thinks it is likely to be the eight-kilometre clockwise loop. Catching sight of his quarry in the distance up ahead after only three minutes of fast running, Vladek knows that he is right.

With leg muscles feeling sluggish from the recent trip to the Middle East, Vladek is grateful for the chance to stretch them out. The run also provides good thinking time. Ricky has informed him about an intended party in a couple of days' time. Vladek will be expected to find suitable entertainment on the night. There is one question that needs his attention at short notice: which girls and from where? Vladek has already starting to mull several ideas.

Up ahead is the Casino. Vladek slows his pace, watching two new joggers who have started to keep pace with Fraser. One was a woman, and the other appears to be a heavily built West African. Vladek slows as well, the woman crossing the road to run alongside Fraser. A burst of speed allows him to narrow the gap momentarily, Vladek now able to see more clearly what is happening. Fraser and the woman are talking! They seem to know each other. Vladek had been suspicious of Adam Fraser and his motives from the beginning, but this looks bad – a clandestine liaison on the streets of Monaco? Possibly a love interest or perhaps evidence that Fraser might be the mole that Ricky is so worried about? Either was bad news, the latter fatal for Fraser if only Vladek were able to prove it. Who was the man? Some kind of minder for the woman?

Vladek is forced to reduce his speed to a jog, the African unable to keep pace with the other two. This pattern continues for a couple of kilometres: Fraser and the woman in front, the African in their wake, and Vladek at the rear trying to remain inconspicuous. Suddenly Fraser and his new companion come to a halt. Vladek ducks into a doorway and watches. The conversation between Fraser and the woman is full of intensity. Both seem oblivious that anyone might be observing them. The West African finally arrives. More words are exchanged before all three move off once again, this time heading back towards the centre of Monte Carlo.

The pattern continues until they near the quayside at Port Hercule when all three stop once more. Fraser and his two running companions are about to separate. It gives Vladek an immediate – but easy – decision to make: follow the woman and her minder to see where they go? Or stay on Fraser's tail. The woman and her minder win. It is here that Vladek makes his only mistake. Breaking cover, he happens to glance in Fraser's direction, noticing the Brit waiting for a pause in the traffic before crossing a busy road. Unfortunately for Vladek, it is the moment that Fraser chooses to look behind him. For a millisecond, their eyes make contact: then, Fraser is gone.

Vladek, concerned that in the moment's distraction he might have lost the other two, quickly finds that he needn't have worried. They have slowed their pace to a walk, making their way purposefully toward Rue Grimaldi, a street leading away from the port area. The pair make no attempt to cover their tracks. Sometime later, they stop by the glass-fronted door of an apartment block. Using a key card taken from a rear zipped pocket of her shorts, the woman unlocks the door and the pair head inside towards a bank of elevators. Vladek can see everything from his position on the opposite side of the street. A lift arrives, the pair get in, and the doors close behind them. Crossing the road and pressing his nose against the windowpane, Vladek squints at the floor indicator: the car has stopped on the fourth floor. He checks his watch and curses. He'd promised Ricky that he would be back, ready to escort him and Tash to an evening function in less than thirty minutes. No matter. Now that Vladek knows where these two associates of Fraser are based, whoever they might be, he will be able to come back and snoop around another time.

Chapter 31

Wednesday 27th January 2016

Monte Carlo, Monaco

Adam Fraser may not be as fast on his feet as Ricky's former cage fighting security guard. However, his military service did teach him how to operate behind enemy lines, making him reasonably confident about his ability to tail someone without the risk of being detected. Especially in the dark.

Following their brief moment of eye contact, Adam is happy to let Vladek believe that he is continuing on his way back to the villa. He finds a gap in the traffic and sprints across the busy road before heading around a corner by a supermarket and into a side street. Now out of direct line of sight of anyone who might have been behind him, Adam hurriedly makes a wide loop back on himself, sprinting through narrow alleyways before picking up Vladek's trail a few minutes later. What has helped is that both Emms and Beef are no longer running, a change that causes the Slav to slow his own pace to follow at a safe distance in their wake. Adam shadows all three to a nondescript apartment building sandwiched between a pharmacy and a patisserie. Hiding in a darkened storefront several metres from Vladek, he watches as Emms and Beef enter the apartment building. Vladek waits for the pair to take the lift then rushes across the street, pressing his nose against the glass window.

When Vladek takes off soon after, presumably on his way back to the villa, Adam decides that he urgently needs to warn Emma. There is a procedure they have agreed, for use in dire emergencies only. He takes out his phone and texts '999' to his maiden Aunt Fiona. Twenty seconds later, the phone buzzes, an incoming call from a number he doesn't recognise.

'Emms?'

'No.' The Ghanaian's voice is instantly recognisable. 'What's up?'

Adam explains about Vladek having followed the pair of them to the apartment on Rue Grimaldi. This receives a simple grunt from Beef. Before Adam can say anything further, he finds himself speaking to Emma.

'Are you all right?' she asks, urgency in her tone. 'I was in the shower.'

'Can I come up?'

'No, you can't. Where are you? Back at the villa?'

'No,' Adam replies and explains about Vladek following them back to their apartment.

'Shit!'

'I love it when you talk dirty. Can I come up?'

'No, you can't! I'm heading to the airport. I'm cutting it fine as it is.'

'You're no longer safe where you are, now that Vladek knows the location.'

'Great!'

'You should have been more careful.'

'I was worrying too much about you, to be honest.'

'Me you too. Why do you think I circled back to make sure you were safe? Just as well I did. Can Beef stay behind and clear the apartment?'

'Looks as if he's going to have to.'

'When are you back?'

'Tomorrow late morning. I am planning on meeting Miss Bateson, as you call her, later this evening. Then I'm back out here on the first flight tomorrow morning.'

'Haven't you heard of telephones? Why not simply give her a call? That would be much easier, surely? Cheaper too.'

'I know, I know, I completely agree. However, she's paranoid about not using telephones to discuss operational details. This is all meant to be below the radar. You and I definitely shouldn't be talking like this either.'

'So call me. Please? The moment you land tomorrow morning. Xandra's not back until the evening at the earliest. We can head off somewhere. Just the two of us. Call it operational planning or whatever makes Miss Bateson happy. Leave Beef and it can be just you and I. What do you say?'

There is a moment's hesitation. He imagines her taking this call wrapped in an undersized bath sheet, the towel only just held together at the front. One tug, that is all it would take.

'I've got to run. Let me think about it. For now, just stay out of trouble, promise? No sudden trips to Baghdad. Is that a deal?'

'Only if you call me as soon as you're back. On this number. I'll be waiting.'

Then, to his surprise, she lowers her guard. Just momentarily. It is sufficient to send his hopes soaring.

'Me too. *À demain!*' and the line goes dead.

.

Chapter 32

Wednesday 27ᵗʰ January 2016

Monte Carlo, Monaco

Ricky is generous to those in the inner sanctum. As part of Adam's employment arrangements, he's been provided with a two-roomed apartment with a view of the garden. It is basic but comfortable, located in a separate block about twenty metres from the main house. Xandra is in an altogether more spacious, some might say palatial, apartment next door, complete with panoramic views of the Principality and the Mediterranean beyond. She has several oversized rooms to his two standard-sized ones. It doesn't bother Adam. He has a small bathroom, a large bedroom, and somewhere to sit and eat. What else does a man need?

Returning to his apartment following his run-in with Emma and Beef, Adam completes his workout routine on the living room floor: press-ups, sit-ups and several intense manoeuvres with weights. Drenched with sweat, he takes a long soak in the shower, allowing the fine needles of water to run over him, firstly hot then, at the end, switching to ice cold. He thinks about Emms and wonders whether she'll call in the morning. He dries his hair on the towel, wrapping it around his waist before padding barefoot towards the small kitchenette set to one side of his living room. He grabs a beer from the fridge, twisting off the metal cap and taking a long, steady drink of the cold liquid.

There is a quiet knocking at his door. Adam is up and on his feet in an instant. Leaving the bottle on the table, he moves closer to the door.

'Who is it?' he asks, checking to ensure that his towel is tied securely around his waist.

'It's only me,' a woman's voice answers softly.

Adam opens the door to find Gemma standing there. It has started to rain outside, and she is already wet.

'Can I come in?'

Adam stands aside to let her in and closes the door.

'I'm sorry, I've just stepped out of the shower.'

They move into the sitting room. Adam can see that in addition to her wet clothes, Gemma has been crying.

'What's up?'

'I needed someone to talk to, I'm sorry. Ricky and Tash are off at some function with Vlad the Impaler and Xandra's away. Meanwhile, my fucking husband is off with yet another floozy, having given me some cock and bull story about a work meeting. He thinks I don't know he's screwing this latest in a long line of stupid bitches, probably in some Monaco bedroom. I need a shoulder to cry on, Adam, and you're the lucky volunteer.'

She wraps her arms around Adam's naked shoulders and hugs him close, sobbing gently. He gives her a reassuring hug, aware of his state of undress, smelling the perfume in her curly blonde hair, aware of the connotations of them being together like this, feeling her tears as they run off his shoulder and trickle down his front.

'Can I get you a drink?' Adam asks a short while later.

She moves away from him a little and wipes the tears from her eyes with the back of her hand. She is pretty. Younger than him, vivacious. Adam has been increasingly aware of Gemma's flirtatious advances in his direction. Now, with her body pressed close to his, with only a thin towel to separate fiction from reality, he knows he needs to be careful, already feeling himself stir. His state of undress is hardly helpful.

'Do you have any wine?'

'Sure. Red or white?'

'A large glass of white would be lovely. As would a tissue. If you have any?'

'In the bedroom. I'll get the box.'

He heads off into the room next door, slipping on a fresh pair of sweatpants and a t-shirt before carrying the box of tissues back into the living room.

'You didn't need to get dressed on my account,' she says with a weak attempt at humour, grabbing several tissues and wiping her eyes.

Adam takes a bottle of wine from the fridge, two glasses from the shelf next to it, and comes and sits on the small sofa next to Gemma.

'There was a need on my account.'

'I hope I'm not intruding?'

'Not at all. Xandra's away and I was going to have an early night. Talk to me about Ozzie. What's going on, Gemma? You're obviously upset.'

He twists the screwcap on the bottle of wine and pours two large glasses for them both.

'You'd be bloody upset if you were married to Oswald Gerhard. Cheers, by the way, Adam. This is kind of you.' They clink glasses. 'Thank you,' she says and gives a watery smile.

'Tell me more.'

'Ozzie believes I'm oblivious to his philanderings. Even though we're married, he thinks he can still go off and screw anything in a skirt he fancies. That's what's so wrong about Ozzie. He can't seem to get it into his thick head that he might actually be hurting my feelings by shagging all these other women left, right and centre.'

'Can you be sure, Gemma?'

'Of course I'm bloody sure. The stupid idiot can't keep secrets to save his life. He leaves his phone around the house. I can read his text messages as well as the next person. He'd be useless as a spy, absolutely hopeless. He talks in his sleep, the silly idiot. His latest fancy is someone called Céline.'

She takes another gulp of wine and holds her glass out for Adam for a refill. She is dressed in a simple t-shirt and skirt. The shirt is damp from the rain outside and leaves not a lot to the imagination. As Adam pours the wine, she tucks her legs up under herself to face Adam on the sofa.

'I've got a few tortilla chips if you'd like some? I might even have some nuts and olives somewhere.'

'Olives if you've got some.'

Adam gets up and roots around in a cupboard. Finding a new can, he opens it, drains the brine, and tips the contents into a bowl before bringing it, together with a half-eaten packet of tortilla chips, back to the sofa.

'Do you love him?'

'Blimey, Adam. That's a big question. I fancied him, he lusted after me. The rest, as they say, is history.'

'You're a poet but didn't know it.'

She giggles again.

'Do you fancy me, Adam?'

Adam is beginning to wonder whether Gemma's visit this evening might have been premeditated.

'From the moment I saw you, Gemma.'

Gemma, like Emma: pretty, sexy even, but hardly in the same league.

Gemma's "come-hither" look is creeping back into her dry eyes. He hadn't noticed before, but her skirt is a wrap-around. With legs tucked beneath her body, an expanse of thigh is showing.

'Ozzie is out with Céline tonight. I read her text. The lying bastard told me that he was going away to Milan. That leaves me home alone. So, what with your Xandra away, I thought we might keep each other company.' She gives an unambiguously flirtatious smile. 'You know, hang out together, cheer each other up.'

'Good plan. How are we doing at the moment?'

'If you took your clothes off again, that would make me happier,' she says, giggling. 'I thought we might have had some fun in the sauna earlier in the week. That was until Ozzie decided to invite himself.' She takes another large mouthful of wine.

Adam smiles and decides to change the subject.

'What did you make of our little excursion to Saudi?'

'I'm still trying to get over it, to tell the truth.' She gives a slight shudder. 'What were those barbarians doing to those poor people?' Gemma's mood has changed.

'Didn't you see anything?'

'No, we only heard the screams. What happened when you and Ricky went off together? Tash and I were terrified, all alone with Vlad the Impaler and some Arab women who didn't speak any English.'

'The Saudi elders were welcoming us as friends, demonstrating what would happen if we ever double-crossed them. It was crude but effective.'

'Was anyone killed? It certainly sounded like it.'

'One man was beheaded. Another was tied to a stake and being left to die in the desert sands.'

'My God, Adam – that's horrific. What on earth was Ricky doing with those dreadful people?'

At which point Adam's ears begin to twitch.

'I've no idea,' Adam says in all innocence. According to Ricky, the notion of a second British mole remains a genuine possibility.

'But you must have heard them talking. You were there, listening to all the conversations. What could be so important to cause two innocent people to be killed?'

'Look, Gemma, I don't know. Why not ask Ricky if you're that interested?'

'He's not going to tell me, don't be a fool. No, I asked because you raised the subject of our Saudi trip. I think that's half the reason I feel so jumpy this evening. Whatever the pair of you were up to, it must have been something important, surely?'

'I think you're right. Ricky seemed to think so.'

'So why all the secrecy, Adam. What did the Saudis want so desperately that they had to kill two innocent men to convince you?'

'I suggest we forget about it. We're both tired. It's been a busy few hours.'

'I have a better idea.' She leans forward, her face close to his, both thighs now exposed by the split in the skirt. 'Let's go to bed.' She reaches behind and draws him to her in a long, hard kiss, her tongue quick to find his.

'God, it's tempting,' Adam says, coming up for air seconds later. 'Right this moment, I think not, I'm sorry. Another time, maybe, just not tonight.'

She puts down her wine glass and climbs onto his lap, one of her hands in his groin as she tries to kiss him again.

'Come on, Adam,' she implores. 'I want you! I want you to take me to your bed and make me very, very happy. Please?' She kisses him again, her tongue wrapping around his before he can stop her. Adam somehow stands up, Gemma's legs curled around his torso, the balance of her weight carried by her arms which remain locked around his neck. Slowly she drops her legs to the floor, Adam feeling her nakedness beneath the rucked-up skirt close against him.

'I thought you fancied me,' she says, a hurt look in her eye, rejection written in her face. 'It's the perfect night for it, Adam. We could have such fun, you and I, you know that don't you?'

'Of that, I have no doubt. Just not right this moment. I don't want to be taking advantage of your unhappiness about Ozzie. I'm sorry. It just wouldn't be right.'

'He'd never need to know!'

'Another time. I'm flattered to have been asked.'

'That's charming,' she says, a flare of anger replacing lust. 'If that's how you feel, I'm going.'

She moves unsteadily in the direction of the door.

'That may be best,' Adam says, a hint of regret in his voice as he follows in her wake. As Adam reaches for the latch, she makes a last ditched attempt to change Adam's mind, swivelling around and grabbing his head with one hand, the other tugging at his sweatpants.

'Let's do it, Adam. I want you,' she says. 'I can feel you want me too.'

As she sinks to her knees, Adam already has the door open, the cold night air bringing her up short.

'Damn you, Adam Fraser. What the fuck's wrong with you?'

'It's just not the right moment, Gemma,' he says, hastily adjusting his trousers. 'For the moment, I'd rather just stay friends, okay? Anything more is too complicated.'

'I hate you,' she flares angrily. 'Do you know that? I think you're a selfish prick. What harm would it have done?'

'Goodnight, Gemma,' he replies. 'See you in the morning. Just forget this ever happened,' he says, closing the door. He leans on the wall next to the front door and listens to make sure she has indeed gone away. Her and Ozzie's apartment is only around the corner.

What had all that really been about?

Chapter 33

Wednesday 27th January 2016

Norfolk, England

Sunita Richards worked freelance principally because it suited her circumstances. Her husband was away from home a lot, often working abroad, leaving her with two small children to look after. In amidst the constant juggle of parenting, Sunita's busy life only permitted her limited, short bursts of time to devote to her former career as an investigative journalist.

More often than not, she picked her own topics – subjects she found interesting and considered likely to have broad appeal. After some initial desk-based research, she typically pulled together a few strands of a story likely to appeal to a feature's editor of a prominent Sunday newspaper. Only then did she hawk it around, seeing whether any of her contacts would commission her to write the completed article. Over the years, she had established a solid reputation for investigative scoops, rarely finding that a strong story was not snapped up. On rare occasions, an editor even contacted her directly and gave her a specific commission. Exactly as had happened two days earlier.

The Sunday Journal was a tabloid newspaper with an edgy reputation. Typically, its readership enjoyed exposés that delved into the private lives of politicians and A-list celebrities. Thus, when Sunita had received a call late on Monday asking her to trawl through the background and life of one Jeremy Seymour, she had been neither surprised nor fazed by the request. The paper was running a feature article at the weekend on those most likely to succeed Justin Ingleby. They had lots of material on

Seymour the MP, but less so dating back to his time as a farmer before that. Might any skeletons be lurking in the cupboard? Perhaps Sunita could oblige?

As Sunita knew, any well-intentioned school leaver could sit in front of a computer and use a search engine to glean rudimentary background information. However, to get the real story required a greater level of skill. It needed someone with the experience and aptitude to sift and to sort. It required shoe leather and human interaction: getting out and talking to people, teasing and cajoling, eking out snippets that others rarely found. Even if, as on this occasion, it required going back several years.

If only they but knew one another, she and Murphy would have made a great team: polar opposites in character and background; very similar in terms of getting results, albeit using different approaches. In contrast to Murphy, Sunita's method was typically gentle. She usually gave the appearance of someone timid, innocent and quietly approachable.

The previous day, having dropped the children at school, Sunita had headed home to begin work on the back-story of Jeremy Seymour the farmer. The Seymour family, she learned, had farmed in Norfolk for the last five generations. Jeremy inherited the three-thousand-acre farm from his father in the early nineteen-eighties; by that stage, the business had been split between a cereal farm and a soft fruit and vegetable operation. A substantial business in its own right, it had employed a small contingent of dedicated local farmworkers. In common with most farms, the workforce had been supplemented throughout the year by seasonal workers assisting mainly with fruit and vegetable picking. Ten years ago, Jeremy had sold the fruit and vegetable farm to his brother, retaining the less-workforce-intensive cereal farmlands, sub-contracting the day-to-day farming to another farmer at the time when Jeremy became a full-time Member of Parliament. Five years later, Jeremy had ceased farming the land altogether, instead investing his money to create one of the biggest solar energy concerns in Norfolk. There was a different story waiting to be told about taxpayer-funded solar energy subsidies from which one J Seymour MP had personally benefited, but that was not part of Sunita's current brief. She would flag it for the Journal's political editor to pick up on – in case it wasn't yet on the paper's radar.

The rest of Tuesday had been spent planning a trip the following day to Norfolk. Needing a convincing cover story, she decided to be a historian writing about the history of farming in East Anglia and the Norfolk Broads. After making a few calls to prepare the ground, she was finally ready.

Sunita sits in seventy-three-year-old Nancy Nesbitt's kitchen. It is late morning, and Nancy has had a fresh brew stewing nicely. Her husband, Hubert, is out on the farm somewhere and there is little going on in the house at present, Thomas Seymour and his wife currently being away on holiday. No sooner had she answered the doorbell than she was taking pity on the pretty young Indian woman she finds on her doorstep, quickly inviting her inside away from the brisk, cold January wind. In no time at all, the two of them are sitting down with strong cups of tea 'for a bit of a natter'.

Nancy is happy to reminisce about the old Seymour farm, excited that someone might be interested in knowing what had happened all those years ago – especially if they were writing a book about it. Sunita asks a few questions to get the ball rolling. Before long, the Seymour family history is being described in great detail. Sunita takes notes in her reporter's notepad in her tiny, neat handwriting.

'What about the seasonal workers? Permanent farmworkers presumably had farm cottages like this one, but where did the seasonals live?'

'Oh, that was simple. Mister Jeremy converted two of the large field shelters. The ones down by the ford at the back of the farmhouse. He made them into accommodation blocks. They were smart. They had dormitories, washrooms and a large living area. Very grand, they were. Mister Thomas still uses them today during peak berry-picking season.'

'Are they mostly migrant workers?'

'Almost all of them. By the busload sometimes. Poles, Romanians,

Bulgarians and a few others who miraculously appear from nowhere looking for work. At first, Mister Jeremy thought they were good news. They worked hard and he didn't need to pay them much, either. Always in cash, mark you, that was why everyone kept coming. No questions asked, they just turned up for work and the Seymours paid in notes and coins. It wasn't popular with the village folk mind, there was a lot of resentment. Too many foreigners, many of the locals used to say, sometimes not that quietly either. Then, it got ugly, one summer. Very ugly, in fact. No one put it this way, but I think it was what eventually tipped Mister Jeremy over the edge, with him wanting to sell out to his brother Thomas.'

'What happened?'

'It began with my daughter Hilary. She's a lovely girl. A bit simple, mind, but very kind and gentle in a loving way. She'd been brought up nice. A bit too trusting, I have to say, but she'd never say boo to a goose, certainly not to anyone who was nice back to her. Anyway, she had a thing for one of the migrants, we never did find out which one. Hilary refused point-blank to speak about it, not to her brother, Len, or me. To this day, it's a sealed door, poor darling. She'd had a bit of tumble in the hay with this lad and got herself pregnant. When her father found out, he got so cross. As for Mister Jeremy, none of us had seen him like it before ever: much angrier than my husband Hubert, and that's saying something. He went shouting and swearing at them all, wanting the man in question to confess. When no one did, he sent them all packing. The villagers were delighted. The whole community rallied around to try and help. Even so, a lot of that year's harvest simply never got picked. Mister Jeremy swore then and there that he wouldn't have any more of them on the farm. Next thing he's gone and sold the business to his brother Thomas. Now he's a Member of Parliament, can you believe?'

'What happened to the baby?'

'She lost it, poor little lamb. About eighteen weeks pregnant, she must have been. Went off to see some specialist in London, but they couldn't do nothing to save the wretched thing. Mister Jeremy was marvellous. He paid all the bills, allowing Hilary to see this doctor privately and everything. In the end, it was perhaps for the best, though still a trauma for her, poor love.'

'I can imagine. Tell me. The farm today – does Thomas still use migrant workers, or have they now disappeared for good?'

'Of course they haven't disappeared. No one can run a farm like this without them. They are ever so polite and trust me, they do work hard. No, Mister Thomas soon realised that he needed them more than ever. He went out of his way to encourage them all to come back, to make them feel valued and appreciated once again. Today, everyone's happy once again. It's all by the book these days, though – none of that cash in hand nonsense. Even the villagers aren't grumpy anymore. Don't tell Mister Jeremy, though!'

Hilary Nesbitt works the morning shift as a shop assistant in the village bakery. By the time Sunita tracks her down, it is just after one-thirty in the afternoon and Hilary is preparing to finish and head home for a late lunch. In her early forties, with long silvery hair tied up at the back, she has a happy face and a welcoming smile.

'Sunita. That's a lovely name,' she says once they have shaken hands. 'Are you Indian?'

'My parents were. I was born in the UK. I was wondering, Hilary, whether you had a little time that you could spare me?'

She explains the history she is researching, also mentioning that she'd spent the morning sharing a pot of tea with her mother.

'Of course I can. Tell you what: why don't we sit over there?'

Hilary points to a small area reserved for customers buying teas, coffees, cakes and sandwiches to eat in rather than take away.

'If you've been with Mum, you'll be awash with tea. I bet she didn't feed you. I can get you a sandwich if you've not had any lunch? Some fizzy water, perhaps?'

'That would be lovely, thank you. Here, let me give you some money.'

A short while later and they are chattering away like old friends. They pick over a small plastic tray of assorted sandwiches, Hilary revisiting much of the ground that Sunita had covered with Nancy earlier that morning.

'Your mother was telling me about Jeremy selling the farm to his brother.'

Hilary smiles wistfully smile. 'Oh, that Mister Jeremy – what a lovely man. I do miss him, now that he's in London most of the time. Such a warm and kind-hearted soul. His brother Thomas's nice too, but I always keep a candle burning for Jeremy.'

She sees Sunita looking at her and she giggles, her cheeks flushed.

'Oops! That's got to be our little secret, not for the book you're writing, please? No, I've always had a soft spot for Jeremy. I've had this crush on him ever since I was a little girl. He's been ever so kind to me over the years.'

'Your mother mentioned he was helpful during your pregnancy.'

Hilary puts her sandwich down, suddenly angry.

'What right did she have to go blabbering to you about all that? She had no reason to bring any of that stuff up, she really didn't. What did she say exactly?'

'That you had become pregnant by one of the farmworkers and both your father and Jeremy had been furious. Jeremy had kicked all the migrant workers out and had then helped you see a private obstetrician. Sadly, you'd lost the baby at about eighteen weeks. That was the sum total of all she said, honestly, Hilary.'

'Well,' she says, the reddening in her cheeks diminishing, 'that's all right then.'

'You have nothing to be ashamed of, least of all with me, Hilary. It sounds as if you had a horrid time.'

'It's my private business. I just don't like anyone knowing about it. You are not going to put that in your book either, are you, Sunita?'

'Not if you don't want me to, no. Why all the secrecy?'

'I just don't want to talk about it. Mister Jeremy and I came to an agreement. He's kept his side of the bargain, and I don't need it raked up again, thank you very much. Perhaps if that's all, we should end this conversation if you don't mind, Sunita?'

'Certainly,' she says, wiping her mouth with a small paper napkin and draining the water in her glass. 'Though – what agreement, Hilary?'

'Never you mind! It was our little secret. Just between him and me. If I ever spoke about any of it, then he would stop the money.'

She looks up, alarmed.

'Oh, my Lord! Forget I said that. Please don't ask me any more questions.' She is standing up, hastily clearing the plates away. Sunita is no hurry, however.

'What money, Hilary?'

'I never said nothing. We never had this conversation,' she says, her hands laden with empty plates and glasses, her eyes brimming with tears. 'I'd be most grateful if you never came around here ever again, do I make myself clear? I have nothing else to say. Good day to you.'

With that, she turns and hurriedly heads out towards the back of the bakery.

Chapter 34

Thursday 28ᵗʰ January 2016

London

Margaret Milner is surprised and not a little irritated: her weekly catch-up with Rollo Campion has morphed into an unscheduled four-way exchange. Today the extras include the NCA's director-general, Malcolm Scott and Campion's immediate superior, Caroline Wicks. That Campion has not seen fit to warn her is troubling. Contrary to conclusions reached on her plane ride back from France, Miss Milner had today been minded to divulge certain additional information to Campion for him to do with as he saw fit – especially after hearing the latest report from her field agent on her flying visit back to London from Monaco late the previous evening. That was before arriving at this meeting to be faced with both the director-general and Wicks in attendance. Now she is no longer so certain.

Dressed in a grey knitted suit, jacket buttoned-up and horn-rimmed glasses hanging by a gold chain around her neck, Miss Milner's composed, diminutive frame exudes control and authority, even if at this particular moment she doesn't feel it. 'Miss Bateson to life', as Adam Fraser might have said. 'A powerful force to be reckoned with' is what Campion says in a pre-briefing conversation with Wicks and Scott, moments after they have unexpectedly invited themselves to Campion's weekly update with Milner.

Introductions made, Scott sits next to Miss Milner at the circular meeting room table. One day, assuming he doesn't blot his copybook, he hopes to become 'Sir Malcolm'. For now, he is simply 'the DG'.

Sometimes 'Scotty' to those who want to take his name in vain. Wicks, looking harried, takes the seat immediately opposite Milner, depositing with a thud a large pile of papers on the table in front of her before sitting down.

'So, Margaret.'

The DG immediately walks into the first name minefield that Campion had been forced to navigate his way around. However, while Campion at that first meeting had received a rebuke, on this occasion Miss Milner is content to let the use of her first name pass unnoticed.

'I hear from Rollo that you've been something of a busy bee.'

The room has walls made up entirely of frosted glass, a soulless cube that feels harsh and impersonal. It is more of an interrogation room than a meeting room, a reflection that, in the circumstances, might have seemed apposite.

'No more than anyone else, I feel sure,' Miss Milner replies.

'Like it or not, your section finds itself centre stage. Tax avoidance and its less well-liked cousin, tax evasion is the Cabinet's hot potato at the moment.'

'I can imagine.'

'Perhaps you can. If I were to tell you that the home secretary himself is showing a keen personal interest in the subject, that might explain why Caroline and I wanted to join this meeting with you today.'

'Is there something specific you wanted to discuss?'

'Come, come, Margaret, we're amongst friends here. No need to be oblique,' Campion intervenes.

'I was telling the DG and Caroline earlier about our little off-balance-sheet stage show.'

He pauses for effect, but she knows what's coming.

'Starring Ricky Al-Shawabi and his business empire. They were keen for an update. I told them all that I could but said that you might be able to add a little more colour.'

She couldn't help noting that *Operation Ricky* had miraculously morphed from being her sole responsibility, operating under Campion's macro-management rules of engagement, into something of a joint production.

'Very good,' she says testily, fixing her eyes on Rollo, who inexplicably was busy doing everything possible to avoid making eye contact. 'Sadly for our visitors, at this early stage there is little of substance to report, I'm afraid.'

She says this whilst staring at Campion pointedly, trying but failing to communicate her irritation.

'Not a regular sort of operation, though, is it Margaret?' It is Wicks who says this, reading a report taken from amidst her pile of papers and making annotations in the margin as she speaks. She looks up, smiling thinly at Miss Milner across the table. 'Not exactly through normal channels, is it?'

Her statement is delivered in a flat, calm voice but feels like a rebuke. Before Miss Milner can say anything, Campion dives in with both feet.

'That's right, Caroline. Since it's not, on the face of it, a UK-based operation, we felt the risk of treading on toes minimal. We considered bouncing it around with my old lot, the foot sloggers at FCO liaison.' The use of the plural is again not lost on those around the table. 'However, Margaret here is such an experienced operator, she felt...' He briefly makes eye contact with Miss Milner and pauses.

Her icy stare is sufficient of a warning to force him to change tack mid-sentence.

'I mean to say, we both felt that by travelling alone, as it were, we might all get to the results quicker. Allowing us to cut to the chase. To be more efficient, you know, that sort of thing.'

Campion beams in all directions. Judging by the blank expressions on his superiors' faces, his words fail to make an impression.

'If I've done anything irregular, please accept my apologies,' Miss Milner says disarmingly. She is looking directly at Wicks.

Seeking forgiveness and not permission.

'Not at all, Margaret,' the DG answers before Wicks can respond. 'Quite the opposite. We might have one or two jurisdictional issues to own up to if any of this blows up in our faces. Speaking as an ex-policeman myself, someone who has seen more than his fair share of red tape and bureaucracy, I am – and I'm speaking off the record here, I hope you understand – delighted to see the occasional piece of private enterprise in the cause of getting something done. As long as no laws are broken, providing that we don't damage the reputation of the department and assuming that we keep this operation low-key and off everyone's radar, I am not about to lose any sleep over it, wouldn't you agree, Caroline?'

Wicks purses her lips, nodding her head in a figure of eight pattern. As a gesture of affirmation, it is unconvincing, but she is not about to disagree with the DG in front of Campion and his underling.

'As long as there are no screw-ups,' is all she says eventually, the choice of phrase making Miss Milner wince.

'This Ricky Al-Shawabi. He's a character by all accounts.' The DG is quick to pick up the thread once more. 'Closely connected to the PM, he's rumoured to be considering making a substantial party donation. Are we convinced that a low-budget operation, below the radar as it's been described, is the right way to go?'

'That depends, I suppose,' Miss Milner replies, making a point of looking at her watch.

'On?'

'On whether speed is of the essence,' she says, pausing to remove her spectacles and frowning at their poor state of cleanliness. She rubs each lens assiduously, using a small piece of cloth taken from the handbag at her feet. 'You see, although we're only a few days into the operation, we've discovered quite a lot already. Certainly, a lot more than envisaged.'

'Such as?'

Which is the cue for Miss Milner to make an important decision: stick to the plot outline, stay at ten thousand feet and hope that it will be sufficient; or take them on a low-flying sortie, give them something more granular such as a scene-by-scene exposé direct from the theatre floor. On the spur of the moment, she opts for a carefully worded middle ground: selectively revealing to her captive audience snippets about Al-Shawabi's 'option to purchase' agreements and how they operate; consciously omitting any details about her cast, crew and the methods deployed in their recruitment – and especially keeping dry-powder concerning Ricky's recent foray into Saudi Arabia.

'Have we enough yet to send in the Monaco police?'

'No,' she replies calmly.

'Can any of this be proven?'

'Not currently, no.'

'Will you be able to get this proof?'

'We don't know. We believe so.'

'News of these option agreements will be music to the home secretary's ears. It won't do the NCA's reputation any harm either.' The DG smiles at everyone, the rest of the room quick to realise that any such organisational reflected glory will shine on the DG as well.

'There is one matter.' Miss Milner looks directly at Campion. 'Forgive me, Rollo: I was going to mention it to you first, but since we're now all here together, it may be best if I aired it with everyone present.'

Full of sudden magnanimity, Campion waves his arm in the air theatrically, his cue for her to continue.

'Get it out in the open, Margaret! Spill the beans! I'm sure we'd all like to hear, it's no skin off my nose.'

She straightens the edges of the notepad on the table in front of her. Out of the corner of one eye, she notes with satisfaction that Caroline Wicks has stopped reading the report she has been wading through and seemed to be waiting for Miss Milner to continue.

'Very good. It has been brought to my attention,' she says slowly and deliberately, looking at each of them in the eye, 'that we may not be the only UK agency who has someone on the inside of Ricky's operation.'

The DG and Wicks glance at each other: eyebrows are raised, and shoulders are shrugged. This is a piece of intelligence that they have not heard before.

'The indications are that whoever it is, they may have been interested in our friend Ricky for quite a while.'

'Wow!' The DG exhales. 'What do you make of that, Caroline?'

'Unlikely to be MI5 – it's not their patch. Wouldn't be the FCO either, would it, Rollo?'

'Definitely not. Not their *modus operandi*.' Miss Milner keeps her head down whilst listening to this, resisting the urge to smile. 'The FCO doesn't have people undercover. That's the Security Services' job. It has to be MI6. Why don't we make discreet enquiries?'

'Now hold your horses, we don't need to be in such a hurry.' It is the DG again. 'We haven't had this confirmed, it's only a rumour. Meanwhile, the NCA finds itself with an informant in situ who, in only a matter of days, is unearthing what has the potential to be a gold seam. It could be our first big coup. Why rock the boat?'

'Let both assets run, you mean?' Campion asks.

'Why not?' Wicks interjects. 'This operation of ours is hardly going to tarnish the NCA's brand, is it? What's the worst that could happen?'

'How's this for an idea?' The DG is smiling. 'Why don't I have a private word with the home secretary? Make it his decision as to whether to widen the net or not. MI6 is part of the foreign secretary's remit, not Seymour's. Let's leave it to Seymour to decide what he wants to do.'

'He's a politician, with his own political agenda,' Wicks says. 'He won't want to talk to MI6. That's Macauley's patch.'

'Precisely. So why not let him decide rather than try to second-guess him?'

There is a polite cough from Miss Milner, and all three turn their heads.

'Was there something else, Margaret?'

'Well, yes, actually, there is.'

'Spit it out,' the DG says impatiently.

'We only began our field operation a few days ago. No one but the very small team working for me, as well as all of us in this room, knows anything about it. Less than forty-eight hours later, Ricky learns about a British mole in his camp from one of his sources. He's led to believe that he has an informant in his midst who has been in place for some time, but there is no way this can be corroborated. I am left with one of two obvious conclusions. There is another British source working inside Ricky's operation, feeding information back to a different agency other than our own. Or, and this is what could be troubling: one of us, inadvertently or otherwise, might have let slip information about our operation to a third party who then tipped Ricky off, this third party covering their tracks by suggesting that the asset in question had been in post for a while.'

As she reflects after the meeting has ended, it is the moment when she feels certain that she could have heard a pin drop.

Chapter 35

Thursday 28ᵗʰ January 2016

London

It was a left-hand-not-knowing-what-the-right-was-doing kind of problem.

In theory, liaison between various governmental bodies should be straightforward. In reality, life was never quite that simple.

The key was whether the culture of the body in question was able to foster a willingness to collaborate or not. Given that MI5 and MI6 were created out of a political desire to spy on others and keep secrets, it was not hard to see why collaboration and inter-departmental liaison might be challenging. Regardless of the oversight committees and liaison groups that the politicians and civil servants kept dreaming up, if Miss Milner's experience in MI5 told her anything, it was this: people paid to keep secrets were unlikely to relish the prospect of collaborating with others unless it was in their self-interest.

In theory, liaison between the Security Services and the UK police authorities should have been simplified with the National Crime Agency's formation, the UK's umbrella policing body. In practice, as many insiders had predicted all along, the NCA's birth in many ways added another layer of complexity: liaison was now an industry in its own right. Executive Liaison Groups – comprising members of regional police forces, the NCA, and the Security Services – were formed whenever targets of mutual self-interest were identified and thought to warrant a coordinated approach. Since these consumed time and resources, such liaison groups tended to focus either on high priority terrorist suspects or those considered to be involved in espionage or acts likely to be against the national interest. The groups in practice were supported by lawyers and the judiciary so that, if or when anything was brought to trial, no one could accuse interested parties of not following due process. What Margaret Milner referred to as the 'Action Prevention Squad'.

The magic phrase in this industrial-scale liaison was, of course, self-interest. As a UK-focused body, the NCA's self-interest made itself naturally pre-disposed to liaise with MI5 more than with MI6 since the latter Security Service was primarily concerned with activities outside the UK.

Sometimes it was difficult to pinpoint precisely what the self-interest of each and every party might in reality be. Ricky Al-Shawabi was a case in point.

For example, MI6 might have had him on their radar because of concerns about his activities in the Middle East. When Ricky visited the UK, MI6 liaised with MI5 to ask them to put Ricky under limited surveillance. However, since Ricky's file had not been flagged by either MI5 or MI6 as a high priority target, he escaped some of the mandatory NCA liaison protocols attached to terrorists and foreign intelligence assets. There was thus limited need or self-interest in either MI5 or MI6 liaising with the Metropolitan Police – or, indeed, the NCA – about Ricky since MI6's concerns related to matters outside the UK. Likewise, since no one in the NCA had flagged his file, the UK police authorities had better things to be worrying about than MI6's concerns about Ricky Al-Shawabi. At the very highest levels, this MI6 operation was ultimately the responsibility of, and of potential interest to, the foreign secretary alone: not the home secretary.

Meanwhile, by an unfortunate coincidence in this particular case, Ricky just so happened to be on the NCA's radar in connection with possible tax evasion and money laundering activities. Most if not all of these appeared to be occurring outside the UK. Therefore, there was limited self-interest in the NCA liaising with MI5 about Ricky; nor was there any apparent need for liaison with MI6 since what concerned the

NCA about Ricky was not a matter that, on the face of it, either risked the UK's national security or was linked to terrorism – and thus likely to warrant MI6's attention. Unless Ricky's case file had been flagged explicitly by MI6 – which again in this case it hadn't – then they, MI6, wouldn't be expected to have any interest in the NCA's operation against Ricky. At the very highest levels, this NCA case was ultimately the responsibility of, and of potential interest to, the home secretary only: not the foreign secretary.

A left-hand-not-knowing-what-the-right-was-doing kind of problem.

Which went some way to explain why Margaret Milner left the meeting with Campion, Wicks and the DG feeling ill at ease, in need of fresh air to clear the tangled cobwebs in her mind.

Silently cursing Rollo Campion for not keeping this undercover operation off everyone's radar, she collects her hat and coat, a thick woollen tweed affair, and heads out into the cold January air to walk towards Westminster Bridge. She has a new walking circuit that she's become fond of. If she only but knew it, the route is not dissimilar to that frequented by Jeremy Seymour. Along the embankment path adjacent to St Thomas's Hospital and over Westminster Bridge to her favourite – and perhaps aptly named – meditation spot: St Margaret's Church, Westminster. As the cobwebs begin to be swept away, her immediate conclusion is that it was her fault for telling Campion about Operation Ricky in the first place. She had made naïve assumptions about how macro Campion's macro-management philosophy truly was.

Lesson learned for next time: seek forgiveness and not permission, especially from one's immediate superiors.

Wandering the River Thames' path directly opposite the Houses of Parliament, one question continues to nag: should she have flagged Ricky's file from the outset? It is, of course, a rhetorical question. Her rationale had been simple: *she who travels fastest avoids the Action Prevention Squad.* Had she endangered lives? Hopefully not. By going it alone, is she likely to achieve results quicker than anyone else? Only time would tell, but she remains optimistic. She has a good feeling about Adam Fraser. Besides, it still wasn't too late to raise a flag on the file if it helped cover a few backsides, hers included.

The Saudi piece was the most concerning, however. This new plot twist has indeed more than a whiff of MI6 about it. Was the smell strong enough, though, to compel her to lay her operation bare, warts and all, on the table in front of the spooks at Vauxhall Cross? Expose her cast of actors to different directors and critics? Perhaps, but not yet, is what her gut tells her as she climbs the steps leading from the riverbank to the main road by the entrance to Westminster Bridge.

As she arrives at the church, an organist is rehearsing. It is a piece she doesn't recognise, the music stopping and starting as errors are picked up and corrected. Miss Milner takes her place in one of the pews at the back. The melodic sounds are soothing and help the cogs in her mind to spin more freely.

The DG's plan made no sense at all. What was his game, allowing politicians to decide on who to liaise with or not? As she listens to the music, she has a sudden light bulb moment. Perhaps the DG had already let slip to the minister about the NCA's operation against Ricky? Yes, that seemed logical - there would likely have been a lot of whispering going on. Campion whispering to Wicks, who might have privately told the DG who, in a low breath during an interval at Covent Garden or wherever they held their little tête-à-têtes, might have whispered the little nugget to the Home Secretary. Then what? Does Seymour tell Ricky? It was starting to get complicated, the light bulb's momentary brightness fading rapidly.

The organist moves to a different piece. Bach's Toccata and Fugue. This time, there seem fewer mistakes. Miss Milner listens with her eyes closed as the familiar notes echo all around. Eight absorbing minutes later, the music ends, and the church reverberates with the final chord's lingering sound. Opening her eyes, she finds herself taken by surprise. Two people are sitting in the row in front, and she never heard them arrive. One, a woman of about her age. The other, a man of Indian extraction a few years younger. One of whom she recognises. As if feeling Miss Milner's eyes boring into the backs of their heads, they both choose the exact moment to swivel around to face her.

'Hello, Margaret,' the man says. 'Long time no see. Do you mind if we take a little walk?'

His name is Pratab. Pratab and Miss Milner are known to one another.

From a different life.

Together, they have spent many, many hours in each other's company. Walking the streets of London. Drinking teas and coffees in numerous cafés. Eating fast food, slow food, any kind of food – sometimes alone, sometimes together, always in close proximity. Bus stations, railway stations, airport arrival halls and football grounds. Always with their hidden hearing-aid earpieces, talking to each other in short, sometimes terse, soundbites.

'Subject is paying his bill, making ready to leave.'

'He's discarded the newspaper in the bin by platform 3.'

'Now he's speaking with an unknown woman. Both have boarded the number 9 bus heading to the Aldwych.'

Some say the past catches up with you. Others that it never leaves you. Either way, Miss Milner feels both surprised and comforted to see Pratab once again. It feels like only yesterday since they had been working together.

'Pratab, what a surprise! How are you? How is Misha?'

'Exceptionally fine, thank you. How about you?

'Very satisfactory, thank you. Who is your companion today?'

Pratab weaves his head in a strange, circular motion.

'This is my new boss, Nicola. Come please, let us walk.' He is now standing, and so is Nicola. It is unlikely to be her real name, but Miss Milner is hardly bothered.

They head out of the church, Pratab leading the way in the direction of Westminster Abbey.

'We'd like to borrow just a few minutes of your time if we may, Miss Milner?' It is Nicola who says this, and her words bring a smile to Miss Milner's face. The team at MI5 may be a bit old-fashioned but they are a proper and professional bunch.

'By all means,' Miss Milner says, intrigued.

They pass the Abbey and turn left into Great Smith Street. A short distance beyond the cathedral choir school, they come to a halt in front of a four-storey block with a locked gate and railings designed to deter unwanted access. It is not a property that Miss Milner recognises. Still, she reassures herself, the facilities team at MI5 have access to numerous strange and wonderful places. Pratab keys in a six-digit combination and the gate opens. They take a lift in silence to the third floor and Pratab uses a key taken from his coat pocket to open the door to an apartment with no discernible number or identification markings on the outside.

Nicola gets straight to business. They sit around a circular table whilst Pratab brings in a small laptop and plays with the keyboard for a few moments.

'What you are about to hear is extremely confidential, I am sure you don't need reminding. However, I think it's always better to be clear at the outset.'

'Is this an official exchange of information, or are we simply talking off the record, as old friends?'

'A bit of both, but mainly the latter. Nothing is being put in writing and we'd prefer it that way.'

'Has this conversation been cleared?'

The two women stare at each other, Nicola eventually nodding, ever so slightly. Weirdly, the gesture crystallises and concludes the train of thought that had been spinning around Miss Milner's mind since leaving the meeting with Campion and the others earlier. The best way to ensure departmental liaison was less about process and working groups and more about having like-minded people who trusted each other. Enough to feel safe in sharing each other's secrets.

'It is a recording. Audio only but the sound quality is good. You will hear two voices. One belongs to Stephen Russell, the chancellor of the exchequer. The other is someone you may also recognise.' She nods at Pratab and male voices begin filling the room.

'So, what's bugging you, Stephen? That little pile of hidden gold burning a hole in your conscience all of a sudden, is it?'

'Partly, I won't lie. I've been wondering what to do about it all, to be honest, Ricky.'

'You need to relax a bit more! Your secrets are completely safe, Stephen. Remember, secrecy and discretion is the Al-Shawabi promise. You don't have to do anything until you feel the time is right.'

They sit in silence and listen to the entire conversation without speaking. Miss Milner has a scowl on her face for much of it. Once it had finished, Pratab closes the lid on his laptop and quietly leaves the room.

'We thought you might find that helpful.'

'Very,' Miss Milner says after some thought. 'Thank you.'

She polishes the lenses on her glasses once more, wiping one of the lenses in a circular pattern whilst thinking through all that she's just heard.

'Are you able to tell me why you were recording this conversation?'

The other woman shakes her head.

'It doesn't sound beneficial to one man's aspirations to become the next Prime Minister, does it?'

'I have nothing to say, I'm sorry.'

'I quite understand. Well, Nicola, thank you. Thank you very much indeed. That was very helpful. Do you need anything from me? Apart from a vow of silence?'

'Nothing. Thank you for taking the time, Miss Milner. It is a shame this meeting never happened, wouldn't you agree?'

Chapter 36

Thursday 28th January 2016

London

In keeping with their promise of expedited delivery, the Government Record Office's envelope arrives in the morning's post. Murphy opens it carefully and extracts the copy of the birth certificate. The words leap at him off the page.

Date of birth: 3 June 1985. **Name:** Amelia Jane. **Sex:** Girl. **Father's name:** Patrick John Williams. **Name and Maiden name of mother:** Geraldine Alice Macauley formerly Finlay.

Murphy can hardly contain his excitement. In 1985, Macauley had had a child by a man who was not her husband. This was indeed a bombshell! Who was or is this man? A few minutes spent trawling the internet, and he has what he's confident is the answer.

Patrick John Williams, QC.

Another barrister! His age: a year older than Macauley.

This was a scoop like he'd never imagined.

It wasn't difficult to speculate what might have happened. Williams and Macauley meet on a case. Perhaps they knew each other from Bar School? It's not relevant. One night they go for a drink, maybe to celebrate an outcome in court: one thing leads to another, they hit the sack, and she gets pregnant. In 1985 an illegitimate child would have had the potential to ruin any political career ambitions Macauley might have had if the scandal had broken: certainly scuppering her chances of passing the local party selection process.

Murphy's creative mind starts working overtime: perhaps he couldn't find the death record because the little girl hadn't died. Instead, Macauley, her husband and this Patrick Williams must have agreed to give the child up for adoption.

That means that the woman who today was a contender to become the next UK Prime Minister was in fact, the same woman who, over thirty years ago, had wantonly abandoned one of her children in the interest of saving her career!

The press would have a field day.

Quod Erat Demonstrandum!

Murphy feels light-headed. He now has to contact Nesbitt urgently. He can't speak to any journalist until he's had the green light – presumably from Seymour himself – and he needs Nesbitt to sort that. He's also now due a hefty success fee, something he would very much like to have in his hand before speaking to anyone from the press.

Chapter 37

Thursday 28th January 2016

London

Jeremy Seymour steps out of the meeting, dragging his permanent secretary, Sir Giles Armstrong, with him. They have been listening to a presentation about border control procedures with a cast of many, sufficient in number to allow the meeting to continue uninterrupted in their absence. Thursday was usually the weekly Cabinet meeting. However, the PM had been in Paris overnight and was not due back until later in the day. It had given Seymour an unexpectedly free morning. The meeting with Border Agency officials had been a last-minute addition. Seymour feels few qualms about letting his subordinates continue without him.

'What have I got on later this afternoon?'

'You're due in the House at two for a private member's bill reading. Other than that, not a lot. Why?'

'I've just received a text. My brother is in town, and I wondered if I had time to meet him for lunch.'

Seymour wonders how many other Ministers told fibs to their permanent secretaries. Quite a few, he supposes.

'Then I shall clear your diary. Do you want me to book somewhere? Will you need a car?'

Seymour shakes his head.

'No thanks. I'll walk and then head straight to the House straight afterwards. Can you meet me there later, say at four o'clock, so that we can run through my diary and any urgent paperwork?'

'Certainly, Minister. Shall I give your apologies to the meeting you've just left?'

'Yes please, thank you, Giles. That would be most helpful.'

A light rain falls as Seymour crosses Vauxhall Bridge. Despite all the running he's been doing, he wasn't as fit as he ought to be, especially when, like now, he was in a hurry. The time is just after twelve-thirty. The MI6 building looms large on the southern riverbank ahead of him, standing like a sentry on the south bank in the gloomy January light. Beyond is the railway bridge that marks the entrance to Vauxhall station. There, as agreed, is Malcolm Scott, wrapped up warmly in a winter raincoat with a dripping umbrella in hand.

'Good to see you, Malcolm,' Seymour puffs, struggling to catch his breath. The two men shake hands. 'I got your text. What's up?'

'Shall we walk?'

Scott has to raise his voice to make himself heard, the rumble of a passing train overhead making conversation difficult. He opens his umbrella and the two venture into the drizzling rain. Once clear of the bridge, they turn left down a quiet side street beside the railway tracks and into Vauxhall Pleasure Gardens, an expanse of wintry parkland.

'You remember our last conversation?' Scott asks as they walk together under his umbrella.

'Of course. You had some kind of operation underway.'

'What if I were to tell you, in strictest confidence, that the subject we were pursuing was Ricky Al-Shawabi?'

Seymour stops in his tracks.

'Bloody hell, Malcolm. Ricky's an old university friend of the PM, I suppose you know that?' Scott nods but says nothing. 'He's about to become a major party donor, so we're led to believe. He even came and spoke to us at the off-site last weekend.'

Which is the cue for Scott to relay the same ten-thousand-foot summary that Margaret Milner had given earlier.

'Oh, what a tangled web!' Seymour says once he has heard it all. 'This could prove deeply embarrassing, especially if the allegations were to stick. It could hurt the PM acutely. Depending on where this all ends up, it could even force him to resign.' Seymour's eyes stare into the middle distance. 'I'm so glad you told me, Malcolm. How long before we'll know more?'

'That depends on how quickly you want to push.'

'This operation's got to be your top priority. I never liked Al-Shawabi. Too big for his boots. Never trust a man who has made too much money without working for it, that's always been my litmus test.'

'Ordinarily, we ought quietly to be consulting with a few other government agencies. With Ricky living and mostly operating outside the UK, our first port of call would, in theory, be MI6, just to check that he's not on their radar. His file's not flagged, but you never know.'

'Do we have to?' Seymour asks, scrunching his nose in an involuntary sneer. 'For the moment, couldn't we keep this purely a Home Office matter? Better still, just between the NCA top brass and myself?'

'It is your call, Minister. We have information suggesting that another agency may be interested in Ricky besides ourselves. We think it could well be MI6 but we're not certain. Are you sure we shouldn't be quietly sounding each other out?'

'I suggest we leave it for a few days and see what emerges. We can always go and talk to them a little later, don't you think? Right now, I'd rather keep this in-house. This is going to provide a much-needed PR boost, I hope you realise? It might even change the political landscape. I don't think we need Geraldine Macauley basking in our shared glory if you and I can get away with wallowing in the reflected glow of success by ourselves, do you?'

'As I say, it's your call, Minister.'

'Please keep me posted on how this develops, Malcolm. This is very exciting, well done!' He turns to go, then has another thought. 'By the way, let's not mention this at the meeting tomorrow. Sir Giles Armstrong would only go and tell all the other permanent secretaries and then everyone in Whitehall would know. Very good, Malcolm, excellent work. Please congratulate the team from me. I'll see you tomorrow, then.'

They shake hands and go their separate ways: Seymour heading towards Westminster Bridge and his parliamentary office and Scott back to his. The director-general wants to make a confidential file note of everything that has been discussed and agreed, not least to cover his backside. As he knows all too well, private meetings are all very well: however, in the absence of officials there are seldom minutes – and without a written record, recollections about what was either said or not said, agreed or not agreed, between a politician and their direct reports, were often subject to misinterpretation, if not outright rebuttal.

Jeremy Seymour is crossing Westminster Bridge when his private mobile begins to ring.

'Seymour,' he says curtly, not recognising the number.

'Mister Jeremy, it's Len Nesbitt.'

Nesbitt calls Murphy straight back after speaking with Seymour. They agree to meet at the same Chelmsford superstore, this time in two hours, meaning that Nesbitt needs to set off immediately he finishes his call. He has just enough time to raid a substantial cash reserve that he keeps for unforeseen emergencies such as this, Mister Jeremy having just promised to repay him that coming weekend. Based on experience, he does not doubt that his local Member of Parliament will keep his word.

At the appointed hour, Nesbitt hands over another, slightly thicker parcel to Murphy O'Connor and, as instructed, passes on one other important piece of information.

'We're happy for you to speak to the tabloids. The sooner the better.'

Murphy notes the plural 'we': not the singular 'I'.

Sometime later, his car parked up in the same lay-by as before, Murphy finishes counting all the money, satisfied he's been paid in full. It's time to call Michael Myers from the Daily Post, a contact he's used on several occasions and with whom he has a good relationship. Five minutes later, and the deed is done. Michael asks Murphy to send through a copy of the birth certificate. With the picture finally emailed, Murphy leans back in the driver's seat and closes his eyes.

Another very satisfied client.

Chapter 38

Thursday 28th January 2016

London

'What else is there, Philip?'

The foreign secretary looks weary. It has been a long day. Although only four-thirty in the afternoon, her schedule is still far from over. An evening reception at the Singapore Embassy is scheduled for later in the evening.

Sir Philip Angel ticks off another item from his list. Removing his reading spectacles, he turns to look directly at Geraldine Macauley.

'You've had a couple of calls this afternoon from a journalist from the Daily Post. He's been unusually persistent. Apparently, he feels that he needs to speak with you urgently.'

'Who is it?'

'Michael Myers. He does those special investigations for the Post from time to time.'

'Wasn't he one of the ones making a noise around the time of the Panama Papers fallout?'

'That's him. He was busy stirring the waters and partly to blame for the PM feeling that he had little option but to publish his tax returns if you recall.'

'I do. What does Myers want?'

'He wouldn't say, other than he's about to publish something and needs to speak with you today.'

'Should I call him?'

'It's your decision, but it's probably best.'

'Do you have his number?'

Sir Philip passes the foreign secretary a piece of paper. Rising from her chair, she heads to the phone on the corner of her desk and dials the number.

'Would you like me to leave?' Sir Philip asks.

'Not at all. Let's both listen, shall we?'

She routes the call through to a small speakerphone on the table in front of where Sir Philip and she have been sitting. A few seconds later, the phone can be heard ringing at the other end of the line. On the third ring, it is answered.

'Michael Myers.'

'Michael, it is Geraldine Macauley returning your call,' she says, winking at Sir Philip. 'How can I help?'

'Thank you for calling back, Foreign Secretary. We are about to run a piece in the morning, and I wanted to give you a chance to comment on it first, is that fair?'

'That depends, Michael, on exactly what the piece is and what you want me to comment on. Why don't you tell me?'

'Very good. It's about your daughter, Amelia Jane. Born on the third of June 1985. According to a copy of the birth certificate that we've seen, Amelia Jane's father is a Patrick John Williams and not your husband, would that be correct?'

Sir Philip looks aghast at Macauley's now ashen face. He is poised to hit the button to end the call but the foreign secretary shakes her head.

'What about it?'

'Can you confirm that she is your child?'

'Yes.'

'And the father is not your husband, is that also correct?'

Macauley looks as if all colour has drained from her face.

'Yes.'

'And the child did not grow up with you, is that also correct?'

'Correct.'

'Do you have any regrets?'

'Plenty.'

'Is there any comment you'd like to add?'

'None whatsoever. You should respect people's private lives, Myers, and be very careful what you print. That is all I wish to say, good day.'

She hits the 'end call' button and sits back in her chair. Her hands are trembling.

'I'm sorry about that, Minister. I shouldn't have let you talk to him.'

'It's not your fault, Philip. It was inevitable that one day it might surface.'

'Is there anything we can do? Do you want me to talk to the editor? See if we can delay for a few days?'

'No, I'd rather see what they are going to say first. I suspect they'll get the facts wrong; they usually do.'

'What about damage limitation?'

'Concerning what? Me or the government?'

'Both.'

'The facts are the facts. This is something that I've had to live with. People will be able to make their own minds up.'

'Even if it damages your career in the process?'

'Even if, Sir Philip. Though I am not sure that it will. It may yet be a blessing. Are we otherwise done, for now?'

'More or less, Minister. Nothing that can't wait.' He pauses briefly.

'Should I be alerting the Cabinet secretary?'

'That's entirely your call. Depending on what they eventually print, I can speak to the PM in the morning if need be. If you feel that it would be helpful to let Philippa Mayhew be aware of the conversation we've just had first, I am not going to try and stop you.'

'Very good, Minister. Thank you. I think I probably should. If that's it for the moment, I shall leave you to it.'

'Oh, one more thing. Could you see if you can track down my sister Emily? I need to speak to her on the phone urgently.'

Sir Philip gathers his papers together and makes to leave.

'I'll get on to it right away. I've kept the rest of the afternoon free until the reception this evening. You wanted time to work on your Red Boxes.'

Chapter 39

Thursday 28ᵗʰ January 2016

Monte Carlo, Monaco

Adam has slept fitfully, his brain active, the internal disk drives thinking about all the women suddenly in his life: Xandra; Emms; Mrs Bateson; and now Gemma. There was also the looming trip to Iraq and beyond that he's got to work his way through. It was enough to keep anyone awake at night. At five-thirty, he finally gives up on the idea of getting more sleep. He slips out of bed to put the coffee on and to do some stretching.

Two espressos and a large glass of water later, and Adam decides to go for a swim. In the winter months, Ricky's outdoor pool, positioned on the lower terrace away from the main villa, is kept heated and insulated from the elements by an electrically operated cover. Adam makes his way down some stone steps leading to the pool, guided by the feeble light of several solar-powered lamps.

To his surprise, despite the hour, the cover is open, and someone is in the water, quietly swimming laps. It is Tash. In the pre-dawn half-light, he can't but fail to notice that she's completely naked. She looks up when she hears him approaching and starts treading water.

'Sorry, Tash,' Adam says, about to retrace his steps. 'I didn't think anyone would be here. I'll come back another time.'

'Don't leave, Adam,' she calls out plaintively. 'The water's lovely. I really don't mind.'

Adam turns around and slowly comes back down to the water's edge.

'Are you sure?'

'Quite sure.' He can hardly see her in the dark. 'I'm not prudish.'

Adam throws his towel on the back of a pool lounger and heads to the deeper end of the pool, ready to dive in. Tash's slender body swims elegantly away, her long blonde hair flowing in her wake as she performs a lazy breaststroke.

Adam dives and swims two short lengths, catching up with Tash back at the deep end and stopping to catch his breath. Then, up close, he sees her face.

'What happened?' he asks, holding on to the poolside.

The area around her left eye and cheek is puffy and badly swollen.

'It's nothing,' Tash says, already beginning another length of breaststroke. Adam follows, in no time swimming alongside her.

'What do you mean it's nothing?'

They are side by side, each performing a slow breaststroke.

'What happened?'

Tash swims a few more strokes.

'I slipped.'

At the moment she reaches the shallow end, she turns and switches to front crawl. Adam follows and they meet once more back at the deep end.

'Did Vladek do that to you?' he asks, both of them treading water to keep stationary.

She doesn't answer, instead shaking her head. Adam grabs hold of the side of the pool to steady himself. With his other hand, he reaches across to touch her face, gently feeling the swelling and bruising around her cheek. She is young: beautiful and vulnerable and her bruised face makes Adam feel a wave of sudden anger.

'Was it Ricky?'

She thinks about this, biting her lip and closing her eyes, nodding her head ever so slightly before swimming away, once more reverting to breaststroke. Adam catches up with her and they stop in the middle of the pool, a place where they are both just able to stand. There is a glimmer of light in the east, the dawn soon to arrive, the light sufficient to allow Adam to see the tears in her eyes.

'Anything broken?' he asks.

'No,' she says feebly.

'Why did he do it?'

She wades into shallower water until able to stand and turns to look at Adam.

'He thinks I'm spying on him. I'm not, Adam, I promise. But he seems to think that I am.'

'Why? What have you done, or are you meant to have done?'

'I don't know, and that's the honest tr

More tears. They start swimming again.

'So, he slaps you around, is that it? Knocks you about and thinks it's okay. That's hideous, Tash. You should walk away. Forget about Ricky, go and start a new life with someone else.'

Someone your own age who treats you properly, not some sugar daddy who treats you like shit and turns your face into pulp.

'It's not as simple as that, Adam. We're both needy people. He gives me access to certain things. Stuff I couldn't get anywhere else.' She looks at him with a weak, embarrassed smile.

'Such as?'

'Can't you guess?' They are at the deep end once again. 'Plus, loads of other stuff. Money, clothes, jewels: anything a girl could want.'

'And in return?'

'In return, I let him do what he wants with me.'

'Sounds like you've got the raw end of the deal. Why does Ricky think you've been spying?'

At this point, Tash hauls herself out of the pool and onto the side before standing up. If she is self-conscious about her nakedness, she doesn't show it. Which is how Adam sees several welt marks on her torso and lower back. He climbs out after her.

'Did Ricky give you those too?'

He points to the abrasions on her back. Before he can look any closer, she slips on a dressing-gown and covers herself up.

'Him and Vladek,' she mumbles.

'Vladek?'

'I don't need to burden you with this, I'm sorry. Just forget you saw me this morning. It's my fault.'

'No it's not. Tell me, why Vladek as well as Ricky?'

He reaches for his towel and sits next to her on the edge of a lounger, the two of them huddled together to keep warm in the cold dawn air.

'It's complicated. You mustn't get involved.'

'You let two grown men who should know better beating the shit out of you? Why, for God's sake? Just walk away.' She shrugs, head down, leaning against Adam for warmth. 'What is it that Ricky thinks you've done?'

She looks at him, all hunched-over, her eyes flickering from side to side. Her demeanour is suddenly pathetic and vulnerable.

'Ricky has these files in a safe in his office. Contracts with various clients.'

'He mentioned them.'

'Did he? I'm surprised? He told me he never discussed them with anyone. His assistant types them, prints two copies then deletes the electronic file once the papers have been signed. Clients keep one copy and Ricky puts the other in his office safe. That way, there's never any electronic record anywhere. Nothing that can be hacked.'

She looks up at him again.

'A few weeks ago, Ricky asked me to help him with something. It was so ultra-secret, he made me swear on my life never to talk about it with anyone.' She snorts and looks at Adam. 'I guess I'm about to break that vow.' She rubs her nose with the back of her hand before continuing. 'So much for my life expectancy.

'Ricky's crap at anything to do with computers. For my sins, I'm pretty good. He told me he'd met some Russian bigwig who'd persuaded Ricky that he needed to move into the digital age. As part of some deal Ricky, it seemed, was becoming amenable to sharing a few secrets. Whatever, for this ultra-secret project, he needed someone – me – to make digital copies of all his files. No one else knew, not even his secretary. He wanted everything uploaded onto the computer in his study, here at the villa. It's a machine with all the latest security. So, one Sunday morning, not long ago, I was dragged along to Ricky's office where he presented me with two thick lever-arch files taken from a safe in the corner. There were hundreds of contracts, all individually stapled, each with two or three pages per agreement. Everything was to be scanned onto one of those USB smart drives. It took much longer than expected, the whole time Ricky never letting me out of his sight. Later, back at the villa, I used the memory stick to upload the files onto his computer, as Ricky and I had agreed. After I'd finished, I erased everything from the USB stick and handed the empty drive back to him.'

'So what's his problem?'

'Ricky is convinced that I made a duplicate of the memory stick and gave a copy to the British.'

'What? Why the British?'

'He's suddenly obsessed with the idea that someone from Britain is spying on him. He's convinced himself that it's me.'

'On what basis?'

'How the fuck should I know? Because Judge Ricky has convened his jury of one and I've been found guilty of treason for whatever reason. He's never previously needed any excuse to treat me like a whore, using and abusing me to his heart's content. As far as he's concerned, I'm just this useless piece of trash that he and Vladek can do what the fuck they want with anyway. If I'm lucky, one day soon they might even kill me.'

'I hope you're joking? Because if you're not, I meant what I said earlier. Just get out of here – today, this morning, now would best of all. Take all the diamonds and gold and Armani dresses that Ricky has bestowed on you and walk out the door before it's too late. Don't ever think of coming back either.'

She smiles weakly at him, her expression almost quizzical.

'I can't. I'm too invested and Ricky knows that. You're a decent man, Adam. I like you. You look after people. More than Ricky ever does. Not to mention that creep, Vladek. Nothing's ever that simple. If I walked away, they'd come after me. Especially Vladek. He's evil. He's worse than Ricky.'

'Why? You haven't given a memory stick to the British, have you?'

'No,' she answers a bit too quickly.

'What's Ricky's problem?'

She pauses, her eyes searching Adam's for a hint of understanding.

'He's convinced I made a second copy.'

'How, exactly, were you have supposed to have done that? You just said he never left you alone the whole time. You couldn't have made a copy; he would have seen you doing it. Then, at the end, you handed back the deleted drive to Ricky. What's the problem?'

'You're right, I couldn't have made a copy. However, I never said that I hadn't still got the original.'

Now it is Adam's turn to look surprised.

'You mean you did keep a copy after all?'

'Not a copy: the original. After I'd uploaded the files to Ricky's computer, I told him that I had erased the smart drive.'

'But you didn't?'

'Not exactly.'

'How so?'

'The memory sticks come in a pack of three. I told him that I had erased the original drive but handed him back one of the two unused ones instead. I kept the original.'

'That was high risk.'

She shrugs.

'Why?'

'I felt that I needed a form of insurance policy. Against Ricky.'

'Smart idea badly thought through. Do you think Ricky knows?'

'I'm not sure. I doubt it. I think he got cross because it dawned on him that I'd maybe seen too much. I thought I was just being clever.'

'He beat you up as a warning, is that what you think?'

'Something like that. Welcome to my world. Not looking too clever now, am I?'

'Where is it, Tash? The memory stick? Do you still have it?'

She shakes her head defiantly.

'No. And he won't find it on me.'

'How can you be sure?'

She has a triumphant glint in her eye.

'Because -,' she says emphatically, '- I don't have it any more.'

'Where is it?'

'Somewhere secret. I thought about giving it to you but after what we all went through in Saudi, I was in two minds.'

'In what way?'

'To tell the truth, Gemma and I were trying to work out whether you could be trusted.'

'But now you think I can be, is that it?'

'Adam, I just don't know. All I do know is that Ricky got mad with me and I'll now be wearing a lot of make-up at Xandra's birthday party tomorrow night.'

'It's not going to stop there though, is it? What's Gemma's role in all this?'

'She's the only person I trust. About the only true friend I've got at present.' She smiles weakly. 'Maybe apart from you.'

She looks directly into Adam's eyes.

'If anything happens to me, go and see her. She'll know where to look.' She attempts another smile, but it fools neither of them. 'I need to go.'

She stands and Adam also gets to his feet. It is nearly light, the bruising around her eye much more visible.

'Just forget about all this, please, Adam. Promise me you won't say anything, either to Ricky or Vladek? It'll only get me into trouble.'

'It goes against my better judgement. If you get me the memory stick, I promise I can get you out of this mess. I'll make sure you're properly taken care of, in a place where no one will ever find you.'

She touches his cheek with her palm of her hand.

'It's a kind offer. I'll think about it. I want to believe in you, I just need time to get my mind around it all. Perhaps tomorrow, Adam. Before the party. That feels a good time to be making an exit, don't you think?'

'Why not right now? I can wait here while you go and get everything. We can both be out of here, safe as houses, by lunchtime.'

'I told you, I don't have it. I can get it, but not immediately. Let's talk later. I need to get back. Ricky will be wondering where the hell I've got to.'

She kisses Adam briefly on the cheek and turns to leave, Adam's eyes following her as she makes her way up the stone steps back towards the villa.

Chapter 40

Thursday 28th January 2016

Monte Carlo, Monaco

Adam's acting career has seen him play a multiplicity of roles. Adam Fraser the former soldier: name, rank and number withheld, disgraced and booted out for minor drug infringements, a waster throwing away a promising career for no apparent reason. Adam Fraser the reluctant trader: under-employed, saved from the dole queue by his one true friend, Aldo Bernadi, the man who taught him everything about wheeling and dealing and the art of pretending to trade oil. More recently, Adam Fraser the ladies' man: seduced by Xandra, beguiled by Emma, lusted after by Gemma and now a damp shoulder to cry on for Tash.

There is one role he's unable to play: Adam Fraser the timid spectator, the man who sits by and does nothing when innocent women and children are abused on his watch. It's a line in the sand thing. Hearing Tash's story, seeing her scars, Adam knows that a line has been crossed. Time to toss the coin. Is it to be Ricky or Vladek? It's an easy decision. Ricky can be the second wave for all sorts of reasons. For now, it has to be Vladek.

Back in his room, Adam dries off from the swim and gets dressed. Proper footwear with a solid sole and stout uppers, loose-fitting trousers, and a simple shirt with no collar. Vladek is a former cage fighter who will want to fight dirty. All hands and feet. He will hop around on the balls of his toes, bobbing left and right, ducking and weaving, jabbing with bare fists and legs when he thinks he has a shot. Adam knows what

Vladek's biggest mistake is likely to be. He will underestimate Adam. What Vladek doesn't know is that Adam is no rookie fighter. A college boxing and judo champion, he had never been beaten in hand-to-hand combat whilst in the Paras. Fraser's MO is to think as he fights. It's similar to chess – working out an opponent's tactics, thinking ahead, and waiting patiently for the right moment to pounce. It's by now seven-fifteen in the morning. Vladek will be in the gym.

Vladek is hard at work, punching a large sandbag suspended from the ceiling. He stops and sneers at Adam when he clocks that he has a visitor, then continues as if there was no one there at all. It allows Adam to watch, to seem in awe of the man's dance routine. He takes it all in. The way Vladek improvises a roundhouse to shoulder height here, an elbow to the face there, all the time neither missing a beat nor in any way breathless. It looks impressive, even if Adam spots one weakness. Which is good, since Adam is here for one reason and one reason alone. He wants to teach Vladek a lesson, a hitherto unseen side of the Adam Fraser character. Too bad – the die has been cast, and Vladek is going to suffer.

What Adam sees is that whenever Vladek executes a snap kick to what would be an opponent's upper body, he always follows through with a triple right-left-right punch to the face. Kick, pause: jab, jab, jab. It is a pattern that's repeated over and over. Kick, pause: jab, jab jab. In the ring, he would doubtless keep going like this until the referee felt it was time to jump on the Croatian to pull him away. Cage fighting, after all, was about kill or be killed.

'You come for a fight, Adam Fraser? Finished screwing the girls behind Xandra's back, have we?'

'You're a pile of shit, Vladek.' The rebuke causes Vladek to stop his workout and turn to face the visitor. Vladek is dressed as he would have been in the ring: shorts and bare feet, fingerless gloves limited protection for his knuckles.

'You speak to me like that and you're going to pay with your life.'

'If you beat up young, innocent girls, Vladek, then you're the one who's going to be suffering, trust me.'

'What are you implying, you piece of shit?' Vladek advances, eyes blazing, the distance between the two men closing fast.

'I saw what you and Ricky did to Tash,' Adam answers, standing rock-still as the Croatian bears down on him.

'And I think you need to be taught a lesson.' He comes in close, the two men's faces eventually no more than a foot apart, Vladek's forehead sweating and eyes blazing. Adam is ready, knowing that all hell is about to break loose.

'That bitch deserved all she got. As for you, you fucking interfering...'

Adam's headbutt to Vladek's nose, executed at speed, takes his opponent by surprise. There is a loud crunch as cartilage and bone are crushed, the force sending Vladek reeling backwards, struggling to regain composure, blood spraying. The training and experience of live bouts in the ring soon kick in, though. Broken nose or not, the cage fighter is now one hundred per cent focused on his opponent: reactions on autopilot, dancing left and right on the balls of his feet, looking for an opportunity to strike back. It's kill or be killed. To his surprise, his opponent moves with unexpected agility. Momentarily, Vladek's face registers incomprehension.

'That was for what you did to Tash's back and abdomen,' Adam says, ducking out of the way as an attempted kick to the face by Vladek goes astray.

'You'll be fine with a broken nose. They mend pretty quick.' This time, no jab, jab, jab. Thirty-love to Adam.

A feint left from Adam comes moments before another roundhouse kick in the direction of Adam's face, the snap kick missing his cheek by a whisper. Vladek is fast and Adam needs to be careful. One slip, and he'll be toast. He sees but doesn't feel the follow-through: jab, jab, jab – all three off-target. Luck is still on Adam's side.

'Why the fuck do you care about Tash? Get real, she's a whore. Ricky and I do what the fuck we want with whores.' Without warning, he lunges. Whilst Adam avoids the high-speed kick to the groin, this time he doesn't escape the follow-through completely – it's the third jab that gets him, Vladek's fist connecting with Adam's left shoulder-blade. It sends him spinning, a searing pain shooting across his shoulder and down into his arm.

Thirty-fifteen.

They dance and feint around one another, each circling the other, both sweating hard. Adam's left shoulder feels as if he has run into a concrete wall at speed. Concentrate, he tells himself, deciding it's the moment to taunt his opponent further.

'Is beating the shit out of Tash the only way you get it up these days?'

His remarks only serve to enrage his opponent. Another powerful kick misses, as do the follow-through punches. Kick, pause: jab, jab, jab.

'Did you think I didn't know you were following me the other day? As a head of security, you're completely useless...'

It is the final straw, the remark that sends Vladek ballistic. Eyes wild, he comes in for a death kick. Adam has been waiting for this. Out of one eye, he sees the foot incoming: Vladek's leg bent at the knee, rotating towards his throat, snapping upwards at the last moment. Adam ducks, feeling air move near his left ear in the process.

Pause.

A brief opportunity to offer Vladek a target for the jab, jab, jab follow-through. Instead, at the last moment, Adam performs an unexpected backward swerving manoeuvre, his hips and upper body moving in different directions. He narrowly avoids the incoming volley of fists aimed at where his head ought to have been – jab, jab, jab. However, in the split second before the third and final jab, Adam's body, now hunched low, over his knees, he snaps his legs straight. The rapid upthrust allows him to deliver a knockout punch of his own, one that begins at the waist and ends up connecting his fist with Vladek's eye socket. The Slav pauses in slow-mo for an instant then sinks heavily to the floor.

'For what you did to Tash,' Adam sneers with some satisfaction.

First round to Adam Fraser.

Chapter 41

Thursday 28th January 2016

En route to Nice

Fiona Morris has paid the premium to sit in the front row and gets rewarded on the plane with extra legroom and no one in the seat beside her. No longer wearing the expensive cashmere jumper and sparkly rings and bangles so beloved of Adam Fraser, the young field-officer-in-training is today in down-to-earth jeans and a cheap, fleecy top. She is in a quandary –not a little anxious and quite a lot confused. Miss Milner's words of instruction, delivered in the form of a casual, almost parental piece of advice, are still going around and around inside her head.

'Take a tip from a former field agent. No emotional entanglements.'

Initially, she had been a FAST-stream graduate, rotating off the civil service programme early because a talent scout at MI5 had thought she had been bright enough to warrant a quick transition to a permanent position. Her first line manager had been Miss Milner. To this day, Fiona has never yet progressed beyond the 'Miss' stage, not even when her boss had announced, four months after joining, her intention to move to the NCA. When Milner had invited the young field agent to come across with her, Fiona had readily accepted.

Field agent. It is, she reflects as the plane reaches its cruising altitude and the engine pitch changes, a strange title.

What do you do?

I'm a field agent.

It sounded like a marginal step up from buying and selling properties.

I work for the NCA. As a field operative.

Agent, operative, who could care less? Not Fiona, it would seem, or indeed her stage name lookalike, Emma.

Do you work undercover?

What kind of question is that? Of course she works undercover, she's an actress, working for the Miss Milner school of low-budget actors. Previous credits include ski-loving journalist, person executing honey trap on unsuspecting man, and nurse. She had looked up the name of her supposed specialisation whilst waiting at the airport.

Phlebotomist: specialist clinical support worker who takes blood samples from patients.

More interesting than being an accountant, not as much fun as a winemaker, but might still turn heads at a party.

What do you do?

I'm a phlebotomist. No, actually I work undercover for the Security Services.

She likes that last bit – the Security Services. Capital letters too, all very mysterious.

Are you a spy?

I'm sorry, I'm not allowed to talk about that.

Certainly more exciting than saying that she works for the civil service. Or indeed the police, which is what she's meant to say.

I work for the police.

So what exactly do you do?

Without going through the whole rigmarole again, she wonders what the correct response would be to that question.

I'm meant to be a case officer for an agent in the field.

Now, that is starting to sound like an important job suddenly, despite her not being sure what, precisely, a case officer is meant to do.

Explain the 'meant to be' comment? Are you a case officer or not?

Which brings her full circle to the reason she is currently confused, if not anxious.

Because I might – inadvertently, you have to understand, Miss Milner – find myself unexpectedly in something of an emotional entanglement.

It wasn't meant to be this way. She was meant to be in a steady relationship, forget any workplace entanglements. Yes, possibly it had all been a bit too steady for too long: and yes, maybe some of her female friends had been suggesting that she dump the boyfriend and move on. But to become entangled with someone else behind the poor man's back? It wasn't the way she was planning to end the relationship, was it?

Or perhaps in going 'above and beyond', in the words of Miss Bateson née Milner, of what might have been expected in reeling Adam Fraser into the bosom of the NCA's low budget operation, she had known exactly what she was doing all along?

Never having run an agent of her own in the field before, she finds herself having to rely solely on her improvisation skills. For her, there had been no training courses, no rehearsals, nor scripted lines.

I've even been given an agent of my own to look after.

The implication being that her agent doesn't belong to anyone else: not strictly true given that he appears, like herself, to be in a relationship already. Perhaps that was the nub of her quandary? With possession nine-tenths of the law, maybe it explained why, as an inexperienced agent handler, she felt so possessive about Adam, her desire to continue going "above and beyond" in the relationship still very much alive?

There is one other matter bothering her. She had held something else back in her debriefing. The fact that she and Beef had been followed back to their rented apartment by Ricky's head of security. Why hadn't she confided this little operational snippet to Miss Milner? The truth was obvious, now she thought of it: she hadn't wanted to risk being taken off the case, potentially losing contact with her agent forever. *Her agent –* there it was again. Well, too bad, Miss Milner: the deed, as the record will show, was done.

More's the pity.

'Hi, it's me.'

'Emms?'

'I guess.'

'Where are you?'

'Gatwick. About to board my flight. How about you?'

'Same old place. Waiting for your call.'

'Can we meet?'

'Are you serious? Of course we can meet.'

'Can you come to the airport when I arrive? I'd like that.'

'What about Beef?'

'I'll say I've been delayed.'

There is a pause, neither knowing quite what to say.

'I am looking forward to seeing you.'

'I know, I can't wait.'

'I'm a bit scared, to be honest.'

'I'll look after you, I promise. What time do you arrive?'

'Ten-twenty your time.'

'I'll be there.'

Chapter 42

Thursday 28ᵗʰ January 2016

Monte Carlo, Monaco

It is shortly before Adam is due to leave for the airport. There has been no sign or trace of Vladek since Adam's run-in with him in the gym earlier. Just as he's leaving his room, Adam almost collides with Ricky on the staircase.

'Adam. Just the man. I've got Alphonse upstairs in my study. Have you met Alphonse yet? My lawyer, who's just flown in from Geneva this morning. He's got the oil contracts for us to sign. Everything is in order, just needing our signatures. Can you spare ten minutes?'

'Sure,' Adam says, following in Ricky's wake up two flights of stairs to a part of the villa complex that he has yet to breach.

'Did you and Vladek have a falling out or something?' Ricky asks, taking the stairs two at a time.

'A minor disagreement. Why do you ask?'

Ricky comes to an abrupt halt and spins around, the move happening so fast that Adam almost runs into him.

'I don't need the two of you at each other's throats. Kindly desist, Adam. I know he's been winding you up, and I've told him to grow up as well. I can't afford to have one or other of you out of action because of some stupid pettiness. Am I making myself clear?'

'Perfectly.'.

'Good. I suggest you kiss and make up later in the day and forget all about it. We're going to be heading to Iraq shortly. I need you both fit and healthy. Do we understand each other?'

Adam nods, the rebuke given and received if not acknowledged.

'Perfectly.'

'Good. Then let's say no more about it.'

Ricky continues up the stairs and opens a couple of doors before stepping into an enormous room overlooking the Mediterranean.

'Adam, I'd like you to meet Alphonse Trombert. Alphonse has looked after Al-Shawabi's business interests for as long as I can remember. Alphonse, this is my new oil trader, Adam Fraser.'

The two men shake hands. Trombert is about Ricky's age: mid-fifties, tall and thin with thick grey-black hair and glasses. He is dressed in a dark three-piece suit. He looks the part: sombre, pallid and not especially memorable.

'So Alphonse, where would you like us to sign?'

Alphonse has several documents laid out across the large table set to one side of the room.

'Firstly,' the lawyer says, addressing Ricky directly, 'we need to appoint Adam and yourself as sole directors of the new Monaco-based oil trading company as well its sister Guernsey-based trading subsidiary. You need to sign these three documents first, then Adam signs each of them in the space below,' he says, pointing to each document in turn. 'I will witness everything separately later.'

In swift succession, he points out various bank mandates, more company registration forms, and finally the oil contracts themselves. These latter documents run to many pages.

'I have checked everything, Ricky. They seem in order. They transfer to Al-Shawabi the ownership of four million two hundred thousand barrels of crude oil, currently on board two tankers lying at rest near Singapore. The current market value of the combined cargo is over one hundred and five million US dollars.'

'Is the transfer unconditional?' Ricky asks.

'Not yet. These contracts will be held in escrow by the vendor's lawyers until they have confirmation that the three hundred million in cash has arrived in Iraq.'

'I suppose that makes sense. They won't renege on this deal, there's too much at stake. Their upfront cash payment should, in any event, cover all our costs. The oil is just our profit. Have we received the two hundred and twenty-five million yet?'

'I checked on the way in from the airport. It arrived in Panama this morning.'

'Excellent! Adam, grab a pen and let's get this lot sorted.'

The signing process takes a few minutes, Adam mindful of the time.

'Whilst we are on the legalities,' Adam asks, his pen poised over one of the oil contracts, 'what about the arrangements for my profit share, along the lines you and I talked about, Ricky?'

'Alphonse, do we have that other agreement?'

'Indeed I do,' Trombert says, pulling two further documents from out of his case. 'There are two copies: one for our files and one for you, Adam. Do you want to have a read-through first to check that I have all the details correct?'

Adam scans the two pages briefly, spotting the all-important wording he is looking for:

'*Commission to accrue to the benefit of Adam Fraser at the rate of ten per cent of the net profits arising from the sale of the crude, for the purposes of this agreement, profit arising being by reference to an assumed buying cost of twenty-five dollars a barrel.*' He smiles.

'That looks perfect, thank you, Ricky.'

He and Ricky proceed to sign both documents, Ricky handing a copy to Adam.

'There you go, Adam. Welcome to Al-Shawabi. Over the coming months, you are going to become a very wealthy man.'

'Thank you, Ricky. Very nice to meet you too, Alphonse. If we're done, Ricky, I'll leave you both to it.' Adam folds the document in two and chooses this moment to shake the lawyer's hand.

'By the way, Adam, I meant to say. Now we have the money and the paperwork is sorted, we'll be flying to the Middle East later tonight. I'll let you know exactly when nearer the time. We'll save Xandra's birthday celebration for another day once we're all back. She won't mind. Just remember what I said to you on the stairs earlier. I need both you and Vladek in one piece over the next few days.'

'I hear you. When are you expecting the shipment of banknotes to arrive?'

'The plane with all the cash is due to land in Nice airport later this afternoon. Once it's refuelled, the three of us – you, Vladek and me – will then board the same plane for the final leg into Iraq. By all accounts, it's going to be quite an adventure.'

Chapter 43

Thursday 28th January 2016

Monte Carlo, Monaco

Vladek dabs his face carefully with the towel, eyeing himself closely in the mirror. He had been lucky. The damage looked – and felt – worse than it was. A snapped nose cartilage, but no bones were broken. His eye socket was puffy and swollen, already discoloured, the eye red and angry, the upper cheekbone tender. Painful, but he'd had worse. Despite the warning he had just received from Ricky, Adam Fraser was going to suffer, of that there was now no doubt.

Ricky had found him as he was leaving the gym.

'What on earth happened?' was all he'd asked.

So Vladek told him.

'You have to stop all this nonsense immediately, do you understand?' he snapped angrily. 'You've been needling the man for days. Kindly cease and desist, and that's an order. Over the next forty-eight hours, I need you both fit and able and not at each other's throats.'

Vladek simply nodded.

'How did Adam come to know about Tash's injuries?'

'They met by the pool earlier this morning.'

'That woman's a bloody liability.' He paused, staring directly into Vladek's bloodshot eyes. 'She's the one who's been spying on me.

Stealing my secrets, I'm sure it's her. Maybe it's time I found someone else. Can you take care of it for me?'

Vladek smiled. He liked this kind of work.

'Of course. What do you want me to do with her?'

'I want her gone by nightfall.' Ricky narrowed his eyes until they felt like laser beams penetrating Vladek's soul. 'Tash tells me she wants to rest on the boat today. The Mediterranean's a big place. The ideal location for someone with needs like hers to drift away happily. Just don't leave any traces.'

With that, he turned on his heels, humming a tune to himself as he went back to his private apartment.

Chapter 44

Thursday 28ᵗʰ January 2016

Monte Carlo, Monaco

Tash toys with the USB drive, turning it first in one direction and then the other. The moment Ricky had asked her to scan those damned documents, she knew that the beginning of the end was approaching. She'd seen some of the names, her eyes flitting through the contracts and realising all too clearly what had been going on. That knowledge was a death sentence – her sugar daddy, Uncle Ricky, bad news. A powerful man who had found ludicrously profitable ways of doing bad, if not evil, things.

It was going to end in tears.

Adam Fraser might have thought she had a way out but, deep down, she knew she hadn't. She's too invested, already sliding down the slippery slope and well beyond the ability of kindly souls like Adam to rescue her. Up to her neck in too many addictions, out of her depth in dangerous knowledge, what unsettles her is whether, despite everything, she might secretly have become addicted to Ricky and all his unpleasant foibles.

It was time to bring matters to their natural conclusion.

She looks at the USB stick and smiles to herself. They had come in packs of three. One she had given to Ricky, telling him it was the original which had subsequently been wiped clean, just as he'd asked her to do. He still thought that she'd made a duplicate, the fucking idiot. How on earth could she have done, with him standing over her the whole time? No, it had been much simpler to swap the real one for a blank and palm the wrong one off on her gullible lover. This one, the third and final stick twirling between her fingers: it too is empty, just like the one she'd already given him. Sorry, Ricky. Only one other person on the planet knows where the real one is, the smart drive with all those secret files on it. Ricky can rant and rave, search high and low all he likes – he'll never find it.

She touches her swollen cheek with a finger, thinking about her conversation at the poolside that morning, Sorry, Adam Fraser. It was a gallant try but wasn't going to work. Tash was beyond salvation. The time had come. All that remained was to find a way to make it quick and painless.

Craving a line of coke, she reaches for the designer clutch by her feet, locating one of several bags of white powder in an inside pocket. She pours a long, thin line onto the tabletop, neatening the edges in a practised manner with her little finger. Then, taking a well-used plastic straw from her bag, she inhales, first one nostril then the other. She sniffs hard until all the powder has disappeared. The rush is instant, her dark mood lightening, the mind clearing and a plan forming.

First, she'll hand this third USB stick to Shetty so that he can pass it to Ricky later, once he's back from whatever he's going: once it's too late. Let Shetty try and convince the great man that there are no more copies in existence! She giggles at her ruse, knowing it to be a childish and petty gesture unlikely to fool anyone. It still amuses her, though, and because of that, she wants to do it.

Next, she'll head to Ricky's boat. It's her favourite place to escape, somewhere she knows she can be all by herself, the perfect place to enjoy one final bender to beat all benders. She'll begin with a few more lines of coke and then see where the mood takes her.

It was indeed time. Time to bring matters to their natural conclusion, once and for all.

Chapter 45

Thursday 28th January 2016

Monte Carlo, Monaco

From the back of the bathroom cabinet, Vladek removes a bottle of baby powder. Unscrewing the cap, he carefully removes the perforated cover that restricts the flow of talc. Inside the bottle, nestling amongst the white powder, are several small sachets that Vladek now teases out with tweezers. Each contains different pills of various sizes, shapes and colours. Blowing away any residual talc, Vladek selects one particular sachet and tips three white tablets into the palm of his hand.

Leaving the bathroom, he heads to his desk and selects a cheap, brown envelope, placing the three pills inside before tucking the envelope flap in on itself. Finally, he folds the envelope in half and secures it safely in a rear trouser pocket.

The crew have all been stood down for the day bar one – Ricky's most senior and most-trusted skipper is more than capable of steering the yacht in and out of Monaco's crowded harbour with Vladek's help. Once well out to sea, he and Vladek have a quiet word, a generous wad of banknotes exchanging hands before Vladek slips away to find Tash. He finds her sheltering on the sun deck, eyes glazed, legs curled beneath her, lounging on a cushioned deck chair. It is her favourite space, giving her an unrestricted view of the ocean. She looks up from pretending to read a magazine and, if surprised to see Vladek, doesn't show it. She raises her sunglasses and watches Vladek approach, her demeanour cool and disinterested, in sharp contrast to how she usually feels in Vladek's presence.

'What is it?' she snaps at him.

'That depends on what's on offer.'

'Fuck off, I'm not interested,' she says, pretending to skim through her magazine.

Vladek squats down beside her, positioning his face now close to hers. Her eyes are bloodshot and the pupils dilated wide.

'Have you been fighting?' She stares at his puffy eye and swollen cheek. 'Now you know what it feels like.' She touches her cheek and winces. 'We're a matching pair.' She giggles. 'Who did that to you?'

He doesn't respond, instead tracing his fingers lazily along the insides of her folded legs, the palm of his hand brushing her thigh. She tries pushing him away, but he fends her off and continues stroking.

'Stop it. I hate you! Leave me alone. You and Ricky are both fucking perverts, the pair of you. Just go, get the fuck away from me!'

To her surprise, Vladek obeys her command, reaching into the back pocket of his jeans to retrieve a small, brown envelope. He waves it in front of her before dropping it in her lap.

'A present from Uncle Ricky. To say sorry for your pain. It's something special that he asked me to get for you.'

She takes the envelope and opens the flap.

'What are they?' she asks, her eyes wide, full of curiosity.

She has become used to unexpected gifts like these.

'Have I tried them before?'

Vladek shakes his head.

'They are Ricky's very special happy pills.'

'How many should I take?'

'One for joy, two for ecstasy or three for oblivion.'

'How long do they last?'

Vladek shrugs. Instead, he reaches across for a bottle of mineral water and pours some into a glass for her.

'Would you like one?' She laughs at him as he shakes his head. Then, a snap decision made, she snatches the proffered glass of water and puts all three tablets in her mouth before swallowing them down with a big mouthful of water.

'Let's give oblivion a go, shall we?'

Chapter 46

Thursday 28th January 2016

Monte Carlo, Monaco

Just after eleven in the morning, Vladek leaves the yacht with a spring in his step. He has a lot to do, aware that Ricky expects him to be ready to leave for the Middle East later the same day. Despite Ricky's warning, getting his own back on Fraser feels a high priority. First, he wants to check out the people in the apartment block in Rue Grimaldi. Two people who may yet provide the opportunity to prove his case against Fraser.

To begin with, he waits patiently on the pavement outside the block in question. He thought about pressing a few entry-phone call buttons hoping that someone might buzz him through the security door. Instead, he decides to wait to see if he gets lucky first. Sure enough, an older woman soon emerges from the block's main lift, crossing the lobby on her way out of the building. She presses the button to release the door, and Vladek rushes forward to hold it open for her. She gives him barely a nod as he darts inside, running to catch the lift before its doors closed.

There are four apartments on the fourth floor, and he begins by knocking on the first door, number 41. There is no answer. He does the same thing with the next apartment, number 42, and a smartly dressed young man in a jacket and tie and carrying a clipboard answers the door.

'Hello. I'm looking for a large African and a white English woman. Is this their apartment?'

The man with the clipboard smiles and opens the door wider.

'*Mais bien sûr.* Please come in.' he says, extending his hand. 'Guy François.'

Vladek accepts the offered hand and finds himself inside a tiny, sparsely furnished apartment with poor light and limited external view.

'They were here,' the man says, 'but decided to move on. The place wasn't to their liking. It's too bad. They were only here for one day, and we always ask for a month's rent in advance. Their loss!'

'I need to find the African,' Vladek says gruffly. 'He owes me money. Do you have a contact number?'

The agent consults his clipboard.

'I have a UK number.' He reads it out and Vladek keys it into his phone.

'Is that the number he called you from last night?'

The man looks puzzled.

'I don't know. Let me check.' He takes out his mobile and flicks through the 'recent calls' list.

'No, good thought. He used a French mobile. Do you want that number?'

Vladek nods and keys in this number as before.

'Do you know where they've gone?' Vladek asks.

'I have no idea. I doubt that I'll be hearing from either of them again.' Vladek puts his phone away and turns to leave. 'If he calls, do you want me to mention your name?'

But by then, Vladek is already on his way out of the door.

Chapter 47

Thursday 28th January 2016

Monte Carlo, Monaco

Her flight had been early, Adam only just making it in time. Eager to avoid public displays of affection, they had greeted each other in the arrivals hall like the acquaintances they were supposed to be. In the taxi to Aldo's grace and favour apartment, the electricity between them both had been palpable. Their destination was where Aldo had let Adam use when he'd first arrived in Monaco.

'Keep the keys, my friend. In this town, you never know when a bolt hole comes in handy!' Aldo had winked furiously. Despite Adam's protestations, his friend had insisted. It wasn't the Ritz. Simply furnished, it had a bed, a shower and a small living space with no view. It did, however, come serviced: once a week, someone changed the sheets and kept the place clean.

Thigh-to-thigh in the back of the taxi, they were like teenagers on a first date, hands occasionally touching, squeezing, speaking inconsequential trivia to hide their nerves. By the time Adam was closing and locking the door to the apartment and turning to face Emms, the fleecy top had already been abandoned and her jeans were dropping to the floor.

'Returning guest privileges,' she muttered in answer to a hastily asked question about the absence of foil-wrapped packages on his pillow. Madly and deeply they thus tumbled: once, twice, and then again for good measure. Not a thigh-needle in sight, not a word about risks or complications, hardly a care in the world but for each other. They showered, Adam went out to find food for lunch before returning. They then began all over again.

'Did I tell you that are beautiful, Princess Emma?'

'You are blind, Adam Fraser?'

She twirls a short strand of his hair around her fingers.

'What did Miss Bateson say?'

'You are officially her star actor. Potentially, an Oscar nominee!'

'What about Ricky's spy in the camp theory?'

'She listened but didn't comment.'

'Did you mention that Vladek had been following you?'

His question is not answered immediately. Instead, she bites her bottom lip and looks sheepish.

'Not in so many words,' is what she says, not convincingly. 'What about you? Has much happened since I've been away?'

So, he tells her about Gemma and he tells her about Tash. He tells her about meeting Alphonse the lawyer and, feeling that he can avoid it no longer, he tells her about his confrontation with Vladek.

'Adam, that was mental. He could have killed you!' she says, with surprising vehemence.

'Only if I'd lost. Luckily, I have always been good at giving people what they deserve.'

'Now you've bust his nose or whatever, he won't rest until he's got his own back. Which means beating you to a pulp! You're bonkers, Adam,'

'I disagree. Ricky has already intervened and put Vladek on a short rein. He needs us both too much to let Vladek go off the rails.'

'Why?'

'Because he's volunteered us to be his designated drivers for the two cars driving Ricky's laundered money deep into Iraq.'

'No, Adam, I forbid this!' She is bolt upright in bed, eyes blazing. 'I mean it. You can't go risking your life doing such a foolish thing. Come back to London today. We can catch a flight this afternoon.'

'We need that USB drive, Emms. I am this close to getting it,' he says, pinching a thumb and forefinger together. 'Maybe Tash will hand it over later today? In which case, job done, and we can go and elope somewhere together!'

'Do you mean that?' Her eyes are smiling at him.

'I find it very sexy when you do that, I hope you realise?'

'Do what?' she asks.

'That thing with your bottom lip. It makes me want to do wicked things to you, every time.'

'What are you waiting for?'

'What are you going to say to Beef?'

'I'll say my flight was delayed.'

'He won't believe you.'

'You're right. Not to worry, he'll have been tracking my phone. He'll know where I am.'

'Will he be waiting downstairs?'

'Ninety per cent probability, yes. He's good, is Beef.'

'Any risk of him blabbing to Miss Bateson?'

'I doubt it. I told him that you and I would be spending some time together soon after I got back.'

'When did you tell him that?'

'Before I got my flight this morning. He's smart enough to work things out.'

'You could always use this place as your temporary base if you and Beef wanted.'

She is lying on her stomach, leaning on her elbows, looking at him.

'That's not a bad idea, Adam. I might need to throw open the windows to clear the air first.'

'Whatever. I need to head back to the villa to see if I can find Tash. Xandra's due back this evening.'

'What's going to happen, Adam? Between you and her, I mean?'

'Who knows? I seem to have competing priorities all of a sudden. Let's take each day as it comes.'

He kisses her on her forehead and runs his finger down her spine.

'I wasn't expecting you in my life, to tell the truth. Now you're here, I'm a bit taken by surprise.'

'In a nice way, I hope?'

'Absolutely,' he says, kissing her gently. 'No complaints whatsoever.'

Chapter 48

Thursday 28ᵗʰ January 2016

Monte Carlo, Monaco

The villa is deserted. No sign of Ricky, but that is typical for the middle of the afternoon. No sign of Tash though, and that is more concerning. He checks the pool, shouting her name a few times around the villa to no avail. Nothing. No sign of Vladek either and that is a positive development as far as Adam is concerned.

Ozzie is at work and Xandra is still abroad. He hesitates before knocking on Gemma's door but when he does, there is no sign or response from her either. About to give up, he sees Shetty heading across the courtyard, carrying a large pile of laundry.

'Shetty!' he says, running across to meet him. 'I was beginning to think there was no one here.'

Shetty looks upset.

'Oh, Mister Adam! I'm so very pleased to have found you. Have you heard the terrible news?'

Adam looks at him, bewildered.

'What news, Shetty?'

'About Miss Xandra, sir? She's been taken in for questioning by the Americans.'

'How so? I thought she was in Panama.'

They have reached Xandra's apartment and Adam opens the door to

246

let them both in. Shetty places the laundry on a table and turns to face Adam.

'Her plane back from Panama had to route via Miami. She was stopped by US Immigration. They said they needed to question her about something.'

'When did you hear?'

'She phoned about half an hour ago. I've tried calling Mister Ricky, sir, but he's not been available. I am so very glad to have found you.'

'Does Xandra have a lawyer she can use?'

'Most definitely, yes. One of Mister Ricky's very best. He's based in Miami. She's already spoken and he is on his way out to the airport to get everything sorted.'

'That's a bummer,' Adam says more to himself than Shetty. 'Does Ricky's man in Panama, Rodriguez or whatever he's called, know about this?'

'Yes, sir. I called him myself. Xandra asked me to. Mister Rodriguez said that he, too, will try and pull some strings from his end.' Adam doubts that this will be a cast-iron guaranteed way to get Xandra sent on her way back home but says nothing.

'It doesn't sound as if there's much we can do from this end. Poor Xandra. She's unlikely to be back for her birthday.'

'It seems unlikely, Mister Adam.'

'When's Ricky due back? We're meant to be flying to the Middle East tonight. I don't yet know what time.'

'No sir, I'm sorry, sir.'

'What about Tash? Have you seen her? She was in a bad way this morning. I've just searched around the place but can't seem to find her.'

'She's on the yacht, sir. She came by this morning and wanted me to take something to give to Mister Ricky. She was most insistent about it.'

'When was that?'

'About ten this morning, sir.'

'If you want, you can give it to me. I'll be seeing Ricky in the next couple of hours.'

'Very good, Mister Adam.' Shetty reaches into his tunic pocket and removes a small USB stick. He hands it to Adam who studies it carefully.

'How did she seem to you, Shetty?'

'Well, sir...' He starts shuffling nervously, 'She didn't look in the peakiest of form if you understand my meaning.'

'Yes, I know what you mean. I saw her by the pool earlier. Her face was a mess. How was she when she came to see you?'

'I'm not sure I completely understand the question, sir. She seemed her normal self, more or less, but at the same time serious. That's all I can say.'

'Thank you, Shetty. Will she come back to the villa this evening?'

'I don't know. With Mister Ricky away, perhaps she'll stay on the yacht. She often does. Do you want me to find out?'

Adam hesitates, then shakes his head.

'No, we've all got more enough on our plates. I can talk to her once we're back from the Middle East. Let me know if you hear any news about Xandra, can you? I don't think I ought to be ringing her, do you?'

'No, sir. Not if she's busy with the interrogations. If I hear anything, I'll call you on your mobile, if that is in order, sir?'

'Thank you, Shetty. Now, if you'll excuse me, I need to dash.'

Chapter 49

Thursday 28ᵗʰ January 2016

Monte Carlo, Monaco

Adam is suddenly worried. He has tried texting his maiden aunt, Aunt Fiona, with the magic numbers '999'. Thirty minutes have passed, and he's still had no call. He's also tried the mobile number that Emms had rung him from when she was at Gatwick Airport earlier in the day. The number rings but is unanswered. The washing machine in the pit of his stomach has sprung back into life.

Emms, where the bloody hell are you?

The starting point for his search had to be Aldo's apartment. Adam sets off at a brisk run. What if they are not there? What if Beef had rented another apartment? What if Adam can't find them? What if something has happened to them? What if, what if?

Cross each bridge as you come to it, soldier.

By the time he approaches Aldo's apartment block, his heart is thumping loudly, both from the exertion and nervous anticipation.

I have the USB stick, Emms. It's what you, Miss Bateson and I have been looking for.

Entering the building, he takes the stairs three at a time, tugging open the fire door on the first-floor landing and coming to a halt by his apartment front door.

The door is ajar, splintered wood on the inner door-frame visible. Most likely caused by a shoulder barge or a heavy boot. He presses his body against the outside wall close to the door hinge and slowly pushes the door inwards. It swings open without a sound, inch by inch, the gap widening. When about halfway open, he peers cautiously through the gap to see if he can see anything.

Nothing.

With his back to the wall, he edges cautiously inside. Reflected in a mirror on the far side of the narrow hallway, he can just make out a body on the floor around the corner. Hearing nothing, Adam peers around the corner into the living room. The African is lying on his side with one leg bent under him. Scuffed bloodstains mark the carpet. It is Beef.

He checks the bathroom and the bedroom to make sure no one is hiding, waiting to ambush. Whoever did this had not hung around. Adam kneels beside Beef and checks for a pulse. At first, he cannot feel anything. However, the skin on his thick neck is warm and he locates a faint rhythm. He calls out Beef's name, giving the man a gentle shake. The Ghanaian groans faintly but otherwise doesn't move.

Several thoughts fly around Adam's head at once. Who to call for help? Who did this to Beef? What's happened to Emms? Adam thinks he knows the answers to all three. He takes out his phone and thumbs through his directory to find the number he's looking for and hits dial. Four rings later and the line at the other end is answered.

'Aldo, It's Adam. I've a crisis on my hands. I need your help urgently.'

Chapter 50

Thursday 28th January 2016

Monte Carlo, Monaco

Aldo is nothing if not resourceful. Within ten minutes, two paramedics are kneeling beside Beef's inert body. They seem professional and very thorough. Beef, they conclude, has several fractured ribs and, more critically, a punctured lung. He remains unconscious throughout, undoubtedly assisted by a large injection of pain-relieving morphine that one of the paramedics administers whilst his colleague races to get a stretcher.

With Beef being carefully lifted onto the stretcher – no mean feat given the man's weight – Aldo arrives. He greets Adam like a long-lost friend, both watching in silence as Beef is wheeled away.

'Will you be taking him to Princesse Grace?' Aldo calls after them.

'Yes. He'll need to be in theatre as soon as possible,' one of the paramedics replies, manoeuvring the stretcher into the waiting elevator.

'Thanks,' Aldo says, stepping back inside the apartment and closing the door as far as it will go.

'I'd better get that fixed,' he says, looking at the damaged frame and lock. He finds his mobile phone and dials a number.

'Bonjour, Céline, ça va? Are you busy? How are you getting on with the man from Oz?' he asks cryptically. He listens, explains that he needs some help with a minor crisis in the apartment that Adam is renting. They talk for a short while and then he rings off. 'Have you met Céline?'

he asks Adam.

Adam shakes his head. 'I don't think so.'

'Talented lady. She's acquainted with your friend, Ozzy, it would seem.' He gives Adam a knowing wink. 'Enough of that, for the moment. Let's sit over here for a moment – ' he points to a small table with two chairs ' – and you can tell me precisely what's been going on?'

'Back up a minute, Adz. Are you saying that you're working for the British? Bloody hell, you are a wily old fox! When did all this come about?'

So, Adam tells him. He tells him about his trip to Courchevel and he tells him about Emms, Beef, and Miss Bateson. He explains about his trip to Saudi and the proposed oil for cash operation. He also explains Ricky's mole-in-the-Al-Shawabi-camp theory and about both Vladek and Tash.

'I always knew Ricky was a devious bastard,' Aldo says at one point. Once Adam has finished, he starts firing more questions.

'Where do you think Emma is?'

'I think Vladek was following the African, Beef. I went to the airport to meet Emms. She and I spent a bit of time together here before I had to leave.'

Aldo raises his eyebrows, giving his friend a knowing look.

'When are you meant to be leaving for Iraq?'

'In the next couple of hours.'

Aldo's face registers surprise.

'There's a plane inbound to Nice this afternoon stuffed with used US dollar bills. We are meant to be flying it to the Middle East tonight.'

'Into Baghdad? Ricky's mad. He'll never get away with it.'

'He has a plan. The money's to be loaded onto two trucks and Vladek and I are playing delivery driver.'

'Are you nuts? You can't do this.'

'He's paying shed-loads of money for the privilege.'

Adam tells his friend about his profit share arrangement, Aldo whistling in amazement.

'Adz, look at this logically. You think Vladek is holding your woman captive?'

Adam nods.

'Until now, Ricky believed that there was no way you could be working for the British. He trusted you. He still trusts you. He's asked you to be his partner in this Iraqi deal. You've just signed all the papers, for goodness' sake. So, let's now assume that Emma, under duress, will suggest that you have been working for the British after all. Ricky will be in a quandary. Does he believe her or does he trust his instincts about you? If he believes her, he will go berserk. The question is, how essential are you to him in Iraq?'

'Fairly key. Without me, he's got no one to drive one of the trucks full of cash.'

'Wrong. Drivers are two a penny. No, you are essential to him for two reasons. Firstly, you know too much. You have the inside knowledge of this cash-for-oil trade in Iraq. You've even met with the two Saudis. They, the Saudis, will have the rightful expectation that you are going to be an integral part of the next phase. In Iraq. For that reason alone, Ricky needs you, regardless of whether he believes what this woman, Emma, may or may not have told him. Secondly, and perhaps just as critically, you have one piece of leverage that Ricky is desperate to get his hands on: a certain USB stick he feels could ruin him if it ever got into the wrong hands. It sounds to me as if you are holding many of the chips in your hand, my friend. All except one. Admittedly, one rather crucial one.'

'Emma,' Adam says, and it is Aldo's turn to nod in silence.

'Do you have the device on you?'

Adam delves into his jacket pocket and brings out the USB stick.

'Let's take a look.' Aldo reaches for his briefcase and removes a small notebook computer. He powers it on, takes the device from Adam and slots it into the side of the machine.

'Here it is,' Aldo says and double-clicks on an icon on the desktop. 'Bugger! There's nothing here. The drive is blank.'

'It can't be.' Adam looks shocked.

'See for yourself,' he says, swivelling the computer around and showing him the empty file structure.

'Shit! That means that Tash must still have the original hidden somewhere after all.'

'This device is not going to be much use to man or beast.'

'But Ricky doesn't yet know that, does he?' Adam says.

Which is the moment Adam's mobile phone starts to ring. He looks at the caller ID and then looks at Aldo.

'Guess who? It's Ricky.'

'Then you'd better take it.'

Adam slides his finger across the keypad to accept the call.

'Ricky. How are we doing? What's up?'

Adam thumbs the button that allows the call to be heard on loudspeaker.

'Adam. The time has finally come -,' says a rather flat and tired-sounding Ricky, '- for us to be on our way to the Middle East. Our plane is leaving as soon as you get here. I am not sure where you are currently hiding. Mindful of the well-being of a very attractive-looking young lady who Vladek has just brought to my attention, could you kindly make yourself present at the aircraft door, alone and unarmed and in possession of the USB stick that Shetty has given you to pass to me, sometime within the next forty-five minutes? Otherwise, Adam, there might be unfortunate consequences. Do we understand each other?'

Before Adam has any chance to say anything, Ricky ends the call.

Chapter 51

Thursday 28ᵗʰ January 2016

London

By the time Justin Ingleby steps from his car, Brendan, his private security officer, is out of the front passenger seat waiting to follow the prime minister back into Number 10 Downing Street. Also emerging from the black Jaguar saloon is Iain Goodall, Ingleby's private secretary. All three have just returned from an overnight visit to Paris. As the door to Number 10 opens to let them in, the chimes of Big Ben strike three o'clock. The noise echoes around the small Downing Street courtyard.

'What time is Sir Alan Crabtree due?' Ingleby asks.

'In about ten minutes, sir. The meeting is in the library.'

'Perfect. Who's coming?'

'Sir Alan suggested the Cabinet secretary attend. I've taken the liberty of also inviting Dominic Hall, given the subject matter.'

'Very good. In that case, could you ask the pair of them to step into my office as soon as they arrive? I'd like a quick word with them first before the meeting starts.'

Dame Philippa Mayhew is Ingleby's Cabinet secretary and has responsibility for helping the cogwheels and inner workings of the Cabinet machinery run smoothly, a job she has managed with ruthless efficiency for the last five years. Dominic Hall is Ingleby's head of communications and plays an unofficial role as Ingleby's Cabinet enforcer. If government ministers need bringing into line, it is Hall who gives them a bollocking rather than the prime minister directly. A tough, no-nonsense operator, he and Dame Philippa work closely together, advising Ingleby on the best way to get things done. In this regard, they are thought to be two of the most important and influential people in Westminster.

At three-fifteen precisely, Justin Ingleby strides confidently into the Number 10 library with Dame Philippa in his wake bearing several manila files and a large notebook. Bringing up the rear is Dominic Hall, who closes the door to ensure they have complete privacy. Seated at the rectangular table is the director-general of MI5, Sir Alan Crabtree and another female member of his team. They both stand when Ingleby enters the room.

'Good afternoon, Prime Minister,' the director general says. 'May I introduce Angela Stevens, a section head working in my department?' Introductions are made and everyone follows Ingleby's lead and sits.

'Now, Alan. I understand you have called this meeting. What is it you wanted to discuss?'

Sir Alan Crabtree clears his throat and takes a deep breath before launching into his well-rehearsed lines.

'Prime Minister. Something has come to our attention of a highly sensitive nature. Having given the matter due consideration, I concluded that it was essential that you be aware of it. It's extremely confidential, to be confined to those within this room only. Do I make myself clear?'

'Absolutely,' Ingleby says, glancing at Dominic Hall and making a facial expression that doesn't escape the Cabinet secretary's notice.

'I am going to ask Angela to play a recording that was made earlier this week. Please do not ask me for the operational details and background: I am not at liberty to divulge those. At this stage, it is not particularly relevant. It was made at a private members' club in Mayfair over a dinner between the Chancellor of the Exchequer and a known acquaintance of yours, Ricky Al-Shawabi. Angela, over to you.'

Several minutes pass as they sit in silence, listening to the same recording that Margaret Milner had heard earlier in the day.

'So what's bugging you, Stephen? That little pile of hidden gold burning a hole in your conscience all of a sudden, is it?'

'Partly, I won't lie. I've been wondering what to do about it all, to be honest, Ricky.'

'You need to relax a bit more! Your secrets are completely safe, Stephen. Remember, secrecy and discretion is the Al-Shawabi promise. You don't have to do anything until you feel the time is right.'

'I've been racking my brains. Short of giving it away, I don't think there is an easy way to make everything squeaky clean and above board.'

The words draw everyone in, as if listening to a live radio dramatisation. After a while, the conversation moves around to the subject of who is most likely to succeed Ingleby as prime minister.

'Geraldine's the one I've got to watch out for. She has shades of Maggie T about her that I suspect might appeal to a certain group of voters.'

'I wouldn't be so sure. Anyway, it's none of my business but in your shoes, I would be putting as many of the resources I had at my disposal to try and work things in my favour.'

'For instance?'

'Aren't the tax men and women of her Majesty's Revenue & Customs part of your portfolio of responsibility as chancellor? I mean, they report to you, don't they? So why not ask them to do a trawl through all current Cabinet ministers' tax affairs?'

Dominic Hall notices that the prime minister has placed his head in his hands, shaking his head slowly from side to side. A few minutes later, they hear Chancellor Russell taking the discussion into altogether darker waters.

'You can't repeat what I am about to tell you, not to anybody. You never heard this from me or anybody else, is that clear? It's not even for

discussing with your chum, the prime minister. Especially not with him, do I make myself clear?'

'Perfectly. Loud and clear. Fire away, I'm all ears.'

'You have an informant in your business. Someone working for the British authorities, I can't tell you who. For some time, it would seem, this person – he or she, I don't even know who it is – has been passing information about you directly back to London.'

Angela lets the recording run to the end and then closes the laptop in the same manner as she did with Margaret Milner earlier in the day.

'Over and above the other stuff, that last exchange, the bit where Russell talks about the informant in Ricky's business: that is a clear security breach – and, for a government minister, a breach of confidentiality.' It is Sir Alan speaking.

'The other matters are also problematical, not least because there is more than an inference that Russell has been salting money away from the eyes of the UK tax authorities for some time. I appreciate this is tricky for you, prime minister. Not only is Russell your chancellor and one of your most senior Cabinet colleagues, but also Ricky Al-Shawabi is known to you personally, isn't that right?'

Ingleby is too stunned to speak. Instead, he looks dejectedly at Dominic Hall.

'What do you think?' he asks eventually, his voice sad and despondent.

'It's clear Russell's position is untenable. It has to be with that kind of conversation on the record.'

'Can we keep the lid on it for just a few days? We've got the G20 meeting next week. I'd rather not be rocking the boat until that's behind us. What's your view, Sir Alan?'

'There is no rush,' Sir Alan says. 'However, there is a parallel MI6 operation quietly investigating Ricky. We have to assume that some or all of this might have compromised the operation. What I don't understand is how Russell knew.'

'Oh, that's simple,' Ingleby says. 'Sir Desmond Wheatley gave the foreign secretary a confidential briefing last Friday. Geraldine spoke to me about it over the weekend. I mentioned it to Russell during a private discussion in my office here on Sunday night. I told him categorically that it was not for repeating to anyone.'

He looks up, seeking sympathy from the stern faces all around the table.

'He's going to have to go, isn't he?' he says, looking directly at Dame Philippa.

'It seems inevitable, Prime Minister.'

'The end of a political career and his ambition to be prime minister. What a foolish man. The stupid thing is,' he says almost wistfully, 'he'd been doing so well. I thought he stood a real chance of succeeding me. Oh, bugger!' He pinches the bridge of his nose with his thumb and forefinger, his eyes scrunched tightly shut.

'Thank you, Alan. Also, thank you to you, Angela. All right, here's what we are going to do. Philippa, Dominic and I need to set aside some time urgently to discuss all this and agree on a plan. For the moment, nothing gets said to anyone outside this room, is that clear? In particular, Alan, please do not mention any of this business either about the chancellor or about Ricky to Jeremy Seymour? The last thing I need is the home secretary starting to foam at the mouth with excitement about his accelerated prospects of getting to Number 10 now that one of the three top favourites is about to bow out.'

'What shall I say to Sir Desmond?'

'Tell him that I've been briefed but have asked you, and through you, MI6, to keep the focus as originally intended and to maintain total silence on the Stephen Russell angle. Is that clear?'

'Perfectly. Sorry to be the bearer of such bad news, Prime Minister.'

'It had to be done. Some parts of this job I love. Others I can most definitely do without. This is one of the latter, no question.'

Chapter 52

Thursday 28th January 2016

London

Deep within the MI6 building at Vauxhall Cross in London, an operational crisis is unfolding within the core project team involved with Operation Contango. Contango is the code name assigned by Rory Beaumont, the current head of MI6's Middle Eastern Section, to the periodic surveillance of the overseas business activities of one Mohammed Ahmed Hassan Al-Shawabi, the man more commonly known as Ricky. Having just ended an urgent, encrypted call from his deep-cover field agent based in Monaco, Beaumont feels the information he has received warrants a crash meeting with the deputy head of operations, Annie Maclean. Maclean's secretary is shrewd enough to spot an emergent crisis and tells Beaumont that he can have five minutes with the DHO as soon as she is free. To that end, Beaumont is now pacing in the small anteroom immediately outside Maclean's office, waiting for her to finish a transatlantic teleconference call.

'You can go in now,' the secretary says to Beaumont, seeing that Maclean's call has come to an end.

Maclean's office has a sterile, functional feel to it. Devoid of all unnecessary papers and files, it is a cold and featureless room complete with utilitarian furniture: its only redeeming feature is the magnificent, angled view northwards across the River Thames towards Tate Britain and, in the distance beyond, the Houses of Parliament.

'Rory. What's the problem?' Maclean says, winking at Beaumont.

When Beaumont first began working for Maclean, he thought he was being singled out for special treatment by this unusual habit. Over time he noticed Maclean winking at most people. It was occasionally off-putting, but maybe that was the point? It no longer bothered him, and he usually ignored it. Maclean is a tough cookie in her mid-forties and not one to waste time with superfluous flirtatiousness.

'We have a situation unfolding rapidly in the Middle East. Are you up to speed with Operation Contango?'

They are standing either side of Maclean's desk, Maclean holding a pair of reading glasses in one hand, twirling them slowly as she eyes Beaumont carefully.'

'Al-Shawabi. Trading oil in return for financing ISIS with cash in Iraq, is that the one?'

'Correct. We thought the cash delivery was likely sometime in the coming weeks. We now know from a source in Monaco that it is imminent. A plane stuffed with US dollar bills is apparently in the air as we speak, heading via Nice and on to the Middle East overnight tonight.'

'Going where exactly?'

'Flight plan says Dubai.'

'Doesn't sound likely. What's the aircraft?'

'It's a Cayman-registered Boeing 737-800. It's new. Longer range than the older versions. We think it's Saudi-owned ultimately but it's hard to be certain.'

'You think it might put down in Saudi rather than Dubai?'

'It's got to be possible. The Iraq border crossing with Saudi is just north of a city called Arar.'

'I know Arar. We've had one or two operations in and around there over the years. Usually at around the time of the Haj.'

'There's a complication.'

'What?'

'It appears that one or two protagonists on Ricky's team claim to be working for the British. If they are, they are not ours.'

'I don't understand.'

So Beaumont explains what his agent in Monaco has just told him.

'What the fuck's going on? This is outrageous!'

'It can't be '5', we've been collaborating with them over Al-Shawabi this last week when he came to London. I wondered if it might be the new boys and girls at the NCA.'

'The NCA? Are you kidding me? They shouldn't be getting themselves involved in overseas operational matters. If it's true, it's outrageous. Do you want me to contact the DG?'

'I wouldn't burden Sir Desmond just yet. We could go straight to Malcolm Scott. He's the NCA's top man. Why not confront him and see what he says?'

'Right, I'll call him in just a moment. Meanwhile, what are we going to do about Contango?'

'Let me see if we can get a Reaper drone in theatre in about four hours from now. That way, we stand a chance at least of staying on the front foot.'

'Follow the cash to its final destination, you mean? I like it.'

'I'll need you to authorise it from our side first, then I can get on to the Ministry of Defence immediately.'

'Approved,' she says. 'It is totally congruent with current Allied mission objectives against ISIS in both Syria and Iraq. Even the Russians should be supportive. How much cash are we talking about, by the way?'

'About three hundred million dollars, so we're told.'

'That's a shitload of money. Right, go and talk to the MOD, get this cleared at the highest levels. Any problems, they can call me directly. Let me know when we have this all green-lighted, and we can both go and watch the action in the war room. We haven't had an all-nighter for a few days.'

The war room was the special operations control centre deep within the bowels of the building, where live satellite and drone camera feeds allowed field operations to be watched live.

'Meanwhile, I'll talk to Scott at the NCA. If they've really got assets in Al-Shawabi's operation and haven't checked in with us first, then there's going to be hell to pay, mark my words. Good work, Rory,' she says, reaching for her phone.

Chapter 53

Thursday 28th January 2016

London

Having accompanied the home secretary back from the House of Commons to Marsham Street in his official car, Sir Giles Armstrong is now sitting opposite Jeremy Seymour, going over a few diary issues over the coming week.

'Do I need to go to Belfast on Monday, Giles?'

'It has been over a year since your last visit, Minister. The Northern Ireland police have gone to a lot of trouble to prepare for this visit. Malcolm Scott is also meant to be going.'

'I suppose if I have to. Will you be coming?'

'I had planned to, yes.'

'Good. The next few days look jammed solid. There's so much going on.' He stops and looks up. A messenger has knocked and is entering the room.

'Yes. What is it?'

The messenger clears his throat.

'Excuse me for interrupting, Minister, Sir Giles. I have Malcolm Scott on the phone for you, Minister, and he says it is extremely urgent.'

Seymour looks at Sir Giles and raises his eyebrows.

'I wonder what that's all about. Do you mind if I take it, Giles?'

'Not at all, Minister. Shall I leave?'

'No need. Please put him through,' he says to the messenger, checking his watch as the man leaves the room. The time is just after six-thirty in the evening.

'Malcolm,' he booms, taking the call from the phone on his desk. 'What is it?'

He is standing as Malcolm Scott starts speaking but rapidly sits down when he hears what Scott has to tell him.

'Bloody hell, Malcolm, when did this happen?'

He listens in silence, his eyes closed and his face looking ashen.

'We are bidden when?' He listens some more. 'Just a moment.' He looks across at Sir Giles and covers the mouthpiece.

'Giles, what time is my dinner tonight?'

'In about an hour, Minister.'

'I'm going to be late. You may need to send my apologies.'

'What's happened?'

Seymour shakes his head angrily.

'Summoned to a meeting at Number 10.'

'This is the first I've heard anything about it, Minister. Shall I make a few enquiries first?'

'No,' Seymour says distractedly.

Removing his hand from the phone's mouthpiece, he continues his conversation with Scott.

'We'll be there in half an hour. Thanks, Malcolm.'

He puts the phone down heavily. Sir Giles notices that Seymour is sweating.

'Shit! Politics!' is all he says at first.

'What's happened?'

'It's a long story,' he sighs. 'The NCA has been running a small operation against a high-profile individual and inadvertently didn't check with MI5 or MI6 first to see if there had been any interest in the man.'

'Inadvertently or deliberately, Minister?'

Sir Giles is all too aware of some of the departmental boundary infractions that can sometimes flare at ministerial level.

Seymour exhales heavily and looks directly at Sir Giles.

'A bit of both, I suppose. The bottom line is that the shit has hit the fan. The foreign secretary and Sir Desmond Wheatley are going apoplectic. We've been summoned to a meeting at Number 10 in thirty minutes. We are more than likely about to get a caning.'

'But if you didn't know about it, why are you so concerned?' Sir Giles asks, then sees the look on his Minister's face. 'Ah! Do I take it that you did know about it?'

Seymour nods slowly but says nothing.

'And who might be the high-profile individual that we are be talking about?'

Seymour fiddles with a pencil, pushing it first one way through his fingers, then the other.

'Ricky Al-Shawabi,' he says finally.

'Oh,' Sir Giles says, now comprehending. 'In that case, Minister, I suggest you might need quite a lot of padding in those trousers.'

Chapter 54

Thursday 28th January 2016

London

The meeting is held in the Number 10 library. It is the second appearance in the same room that afternoon for Sir Desmond Wheatley, Dame Philippa Mayhew and Dominic Hall: for everyone else, most notably the home secretary, the foreign secretary, Sir Giles Armstrong and Sir Philip Angel, and both Malcolm Scott and Caroline Wicks, it is their first. By design, the most prominent absentee is the PM himself. It is for this reason that the meeting is chaired by Dame Philippa, although the presence of Dominic Hall, Ingleby's enforcer, leaves no one in any doubt about the subtext. The mood is frosty, the tone of the preliminary discussions muted and clipped.

Dame Philippa begins by stating that she feels that it might be helpful to conduct what she refers to as a 'drains-up review' of what has happened, a blow by painful blow accounting of the left and right hand's actions that have led to the current state of each party not knowing what the other has been doing.

First to speak is Sir Desmond. He carefully skirts around some of the operational details of Operation Contango but not before making it clear that MI6 has had a deep-cover asset in place for some time. In answer to a direct challenge from Caroline Wicks as to why Ricky's file had not been flagged in the system, Sir Desmond explains that on occasions when MI6 and MI5 work closely together on a case, as had happened with Operation Contango, and when the subject is an individual of such public prominence as Ricky Al-Shawabi, it is common practice to leave that individual unflagged in the system, especially when he or she is operating substantially outside the UK's domestic jurisdiction.

Malcolm Scott then presents the NCA's side of the story. He tries to put the case against Ricky into context: the NCA's operation had been deliberately low-key, there had been a Cabinet three-line whip to make the fight against tax evasion and corruption a priority, and in the absence of any flagging of Ricky's file – and believing this operation against Ricky was not in any way about matters that were against the national interest – it had been Malcolm's view, with the full support of his minister, that no consultation with other agencies was required.

There is a sharp exchange of looks between Jeremy Seymour and Scott at this stage, something that is not lost on either Dame Philippa or Geraldine Macauley.

'We now come to some of the operational considerations,' Dame Philippa intervenes. 'As I understand it, Malcolm, you have one member of staff badly injured and two field operatives missing. Is that right?'

'Yes, that is correct.'

'Sir Desmond, do you have any further information that might shed light on their plight?'

Sir Desmond purses his lips, looks briefly at the foreign secretary, then chooses his words carefully.

'We have good reason to believe that both operatives are at this moment on an aircraft bound for the Middle East. We believe the plane's destination is Iraq, but we cannot be certain. I cannot vouch for their safety. The matter is now broadly out of our hands.'

'Why only broadly?' Wicks asks, suddenly on the offensive.

'Because Caroline,' Sir Desmond says smoothly and calmly, 'Operation Contango involves our allies in the Middle East and not just ourselves.'

'What will likely happen to them?' It is Malcolm Scott's turn to ask about the two missing members of his team.

In silence, Sir Desmond opens his hands wide, palms upwards.

Dame Philippa has not yet finished asking questions.

'Sir Philip and Sir Giles, did either of you know anything about any of this?'

Both shake their heads in unison.

'Nothing at all,' says Sir Giles.

'Nor me,' says Sir Philip. 'Meetings between the foreign secretary and Sir Desmond are usually private matters for the minister alone.'

'But you knew, didn't you, Home Secretary?' Dominic Hall interjects.

Jeremy Seymour pretends to shuffle papers but eventually mutters quietly that he did. He takes a linen handkerchief from his pocket and mops sweat from his forehead.

'How did you hear, Jeremy?' Hall continues.

'From Malcolm Scott directly,' Seymour says eventually.

'But doesn't Sir Giles attend your regular meetings with the NCA?' Dame Philippa takes up the thread once more.

'Not when I bump into Malcolm on the street.' He looks apologetically at Sir Giles and then looks down at his papers, assiduously avoiding the foreign secretary's eyes.

'All right, everybody, thank you for your time. I think we have all the facts that are available at the moment. Malcolm, Caroline, I suggest for now that your investigation into Ricky Al-Shawabi is put on hold pending the safe reappearance of your team members and until Operation Contango has come to its natural conclusion. Sir Desmond, I trust that you will do everything in your power to try to safeguard the lives of our two missing people?'

'As long as it doesn't compromise our national interests, Dame Philippa, yes of course.'

'Very good. Meeting adjourned. Dominic, is there anything you wanted to add?

'Only that I'd like the home secretary and the foreign secretary to stay behind for a few minutes.'

'In the prime minister's absence, I am going to tell you both what I think.'

Dominic Hall has taken off his glasses and is fiddling with them, opening and closing the side arms randomly. The foreign secretary is on his immediate right, the home secretary on his left.

'I think one or more of you have been playing games, trying to score points. As a direct consequence, one British subject lies badly injured in hospital in Monaco, and two others are missing, assumed endangered, by hostile parties. All of us have to live with that. Geraldine, I think that at times MI6's ways are archaic and deliberately designed to be non-collaborative. Sir Desmond's people should have flagged Ricky's file, don't you agree?'

'Yes. Now that I know the facts – which let me assure you, Dominic, until this afternoon I did not – I agree. MI6 would have been better advised to flag Ricky's file.'

Hall now turns to Seymour.

'As for you, Jeremy, I think keeping this matter wholly within the Home Office suited your own particular purposes and ambitions. Keeping it from your officials just compounded the problem. This does not feel at all collaborative from where I am sitting. If the PM were here, he'd be extremely disappointed with your behaviour. Damn it, you are two of the most senior Cabinet members in government. You have to do better than this, the pair of you. End of sermon but recognise that this is a mark against you both – Jeremy, you in particular.'

'How did it go?'

Justin Ingleby is dressed in white tie and tails, hastily reviewing a speech he is shortly to make at the Mansion House. Dominic Hall and

Dame Philippa have this brief opportunity to update Ingleby on the conversation just finished in the library.

'It's been a rough day,' Hall begins. 'First, the Stephen Russell bombshell. Now we have Jeremy Seymour playing silly buggers trying to point-score against Geraldine in connection with an operation that he knew he should have consulted with her about in advance. I have just given them a bollocking on your behalf, especially Seymour. That man is an arse. Heaven help us if he ends up being your successor.'

'It would be impossible to do this job without someone like you, thank you, Dominic.'

'Unfortunately, there's something else,' Dame Philippa says. 'It never rains but it pours. I'm sorry, Dominic, I haven't even had the chance to brief you yet either.'

'Go on. What is it?'

She explains about the phone call that Geraldine Macauley had received from Michael Myers, the Daily Post reporter, earlier in the afternoon.

'Oh, God, no!' Ingleby says when he hears the news. 'That's all I need. I am about to fire the chancellor of the exchequer for both a breach of trust and a looming personal financial scandal. Now you're telling me that the foreign secretary is likely to have to resign over some issue that hitherto she helpfully had forgotten to tell anyone anything about. It's an absolute disaster! Not least since it leaves Jeremy Seymour with an open door to succeed me. What a bloody nightmare! This is terrible, terrible news. We are going to have to spend some time on this tomorrow – and urgently. When does the Myers story break?'

'In the morning, we think.'

'The sky is falling in. All I need now is for Ricky Al-Shawabi to be arrested for money laundering, and my nightmare will be complete.'

Chapter 55

Thursday 28ᵗʰ January 2016

En route to the Middle East

The plane is white and has no markings. Adam is driven out to the waiting aircraft by one of the ground crew at Nice's business aviation private terminal and deposited on the apron at the foot of the stairs leading up to the plane. Darkness has long since set in and a chill wind is blowing.

He begins climbing the stairs. His legs feel like lead weights, the washing machine in his stomach now going at full tilt. He steps inside the aircraft and a man dressed in a smart, black uniform welcomes him on board, escorting him along a narrow corridor that partitions off the owner's suite at the front from the main cabin at the rear. In the back, everything looks and smells brand new: premium calfskin leather and opulent furnishings in abundance.

Sitting at a large, square table, a glass of champagne by his side is Ricky. A few rows behind is Vladek, the Slav's left eye and cheek still swollen. In the seat next to Vladek is Emms, her face a mess, eyes red and puffy. She barely seems to acknowledge Adam's arrival.

'Adam,' Ricky says in greeting, gesturing with his hand for Adam to take the seat opposite. The pilot appears and asks Ricky whether he is ready for them to get going.

'Ready when you are. Time to get this little show on the road!'

The two men sit staring at each other. From the front of the aircraft, they hear sounds of the external stairs being removed and the cabin door being secured. Shortly after, the engines start firing up: first one side and then the other.

'Thank you for being prompt, Adam. Sorry about the shenanigans with your friend back there.' He jerks his head towards the rear. 'Vladek wanted to bring her along to keep us company. I hope that was all right? Fiona, isn't it?' He shrugs as if trying to coax a response from Adam. Adam says nothing. 'Lovely girl. I see why you like her. Especially now that Xandra's been temporarily detained in the US. I mean, what man doesn't need a few extra home comforts from time to time?'

They begin to taxi, and the steward arrives to offer Adam a drink.

'Please don't spoil him, he's got to work later. Water and limited rations only, I'm afraid. Isn't that right, Adam?'

Adam shrugs indifferently and the steward scurries off, soon to return with a tall glass of sparkling mineral water. He places this and a small bowl of nuts on the table beside him.

'I said not to spoil him!' barks Ricky at the steward.

The plane is approaching the end of the active runway. Three muted chimes sound in the cabin to indicate that take-off is imminent. Seconds later, the engine throttles open to the maximum and the plane begins to accelerate.

'She works for the British police. I suppose you knew that?'

Still no reaction from Adam. 'Yes, Vladek is skilled at coaxing useful snippets out of people. Admittedly his methods can be a bit rough on occasion, but they save a lot of time and effort in the long run. Sorry about that.'

He smiles thinly, still getting no response from Adam. 'As I understand things, not only are you and she on intimate terms but also, so I am led to believe, you may be part of her little operation as well. Can you believe that?'

'That's bollocks. You're losing the plot, Ricky. She's a lovely lady but give me a break! Vladek has more than enough reasons of his own to start fabricating stories against me.'

'Yes, that thought had crossed my mind. However, to be safe, I thought she should come along for the ride, just for insurance purposes. No harm done. Nothing that a bit of make-up won't solve over the next few days.'

'Very amusing. Is that what you said to Tash, Ricky?'

He looks at Adam coldly.

'Be very careful, Adam Fraser.'

'You're a sick man, Ricky. Iraq is a dangerous place for anybody, let alone a western woman.'

With surprising vehemence, Ricky's mood changes. He leans forward, eyes flaring.

'Don't you fucking lecture me about what's sick and what isn't. I've had Tash plotting against me, Xandra detained by the authorities in the US and now some fucking crumpet of yours admitting that she's working for the British and suggesting that you've been spying on me on their behalf. I call that pretty damned fucking sick, if you ask me.'

'It's her word against mine. Who do you trust, Ricky?'

They stare at each other in silence for several minutes, the dark mood simmering between them.

'I think you've got something of mine. Something that Shetty asked you to give to me.' Ricky holds out his hand, expectantly.

Adam looks at the hand. One sharp yank combined with a rapid corkscrew twist and Ricky's shoulder would be dislocated. A follow-through uppercut to the lower jaw, just above the neckline, and Ricky's lights would go out. Then it would be Adam against Vladek. Adam fancies his chances. However, within the confines of an aircraft cabin, it was always going to be tricky, especially with the crew to deal with. On balance, although it was tempting, Adam's instincts tell him to wait his turn.

Trust me, Ricky – the right moment will come and not a moment too soon.

Instead, Adam reaches into his jacket and places the USB stick in

Ricky's palm.

'What's on it?'

'I'm surprised Tash didn't tell you. You and she seemed to be on such intimate terms down by the pool earlier this morning.'

'She was nursing her wounds.'

'Thieving little bitch. She only got what she deserved.'

'That's more or less what I said to Vladek in the gym this morning. I repeat, what's on the USB stick, Ricky?'

'Haven't you looked?'

'As if I had the time, Ricky.'

He leans forward once more. 'Oh, yes, Adam, you had the time. The question is, did you feel so inclined?'

'I guess for the moment you won't know, will you?'

They stare at each other as the plane continues its climb.

'Adam, you and I both need each other on this trip. There's a lot at stake. I suggest we both try to calm down and get the job done, shall we?'

Adam is tempted to remind Ricky that he'd started this mood change in their relationship by choosing to take Emms captive but decides not to.

'I'd like to go and see her,' is what he actually says.

'It won't do you any good. She'll be sleeping for the next few hours. Vladek gave her something to calm her down.'

Which explained the blank expression on her face when Adam was boarding the aircraft.

'One of your happy pills, was that it, Ricky? The same sort you give to Tash to keep her quiet?'

'If I were you, Adam,' he says slowly and deliberately, 'I would find yourself a comfy chair, kick back and get some sleep. You are going to need to conserve your energy for what's coming tomorrow.'

With that, Ricky hits the recline button. Turning out the reading light above his head, he dons a pair of eyeshades and, once the seat has moved to the horizontal position, he simply rolls onto his side and turns his back on Adam.

Chapter 56

Friday 29ᵗʰ January 2016

Saudi Arabia

Twenty-five minutes from landing, the lights come on and the steward brings each of them hot towels. All four stir, stretching in their seats, each stifling yawns.

'Last chance to use the facilities, team,' Ricky booms loudly, standing up and opening an overhead locker. To a somewhat bewildered Emma he throws a plastic-wrapped black abaya and matching headscarf. To both Vladek and Adam, he lobs desert khaki jackets and matching trousers.

'Got to look the part, the pair of you. You are now Iraqi soldiers like me. It'll be cold out there. It's the desert at night, and it's January.'

Emma spots Adam and they smile weakly across the cabin at each other. She mouths a single word. '*Sorry.*' Adam shakes his head and goes in search of the bathroom to change.

Twenty minutes later, they hear the undercarriage descending.

'Where are we?' Adam asks Ricky in time.

'Saudi. Close to the Iraqi border. About two hundred kilometres from where we were before. A city called Arar. About forty kilometres from the border.'

Minutes later, they land with a heavy 'thud'. Exactly as on the last trip, the plane is met by an airport truck with the words 'follow me' illuminated in yellow on its roof. The captain announces over the intercom that the local time is two-thirty in the morning and the outside temperature is down to just one degree Celsius. The plane is led to a remote corner of the airfield, close to a private hangar where the doors have been opened wide, but the hangar itself remains in darkness. Adam can see vehicles parked on the apron near to where they have come to a halt. Climbing out of one of them is a man Adam thinks he recognises. Sure enough, once the steps are in position and the main door opened, Adam is not surprised to see the familiar face of Amid Abdulraheem al-Dosari entering the cabin.

'Good evening, Mister Al-Shawabi,' he says, bowing gently. 'Nice to have you back with us once again.'

Then with a brief nod to all three other guests, he continues.

'Welcome all of you to the Kingdom of Saudi Arabia. If you are ready to go, we have everything prepared that has been requested. Please follow me.'

He leads them down the stairs and onto the apron. Waiting on the tarmac to greet them is Ricky's Bahraini intermediary, Ibrahim. Ricky and Ibrahim greet each other like old friends and head off together in a huddle. Parked close by are two ex-US Marine Mine Resistant Ambush Protected vehicles painted in desert khaki, along with two armoured Jeeps in the same colour. Adam knows all about MRAPs, recalling with some envy that the US military had gifted a number to the Iraqi Army at the end of the US's military presence in Afghanistan. It had been a sore point with soldiers in an under-resourced British Army. They had had to make do with the woefully inadequate modified Snatch Land Rovers that gave little or no protection against mines and IEDs whilst the Americans were handing out top of the range freebies to the locals. The MRAPs had a long wheelbase and could carry up to ten troops in the back. Two of them would be more than capable of carrying large volumes of cash securely.

Ricky and Ibrahim return, and Ricky directs Vladek to take Emma and sit with her in the back of one of the Jeeps. Meanwhile, he, Ibrahim and Adam follow al-Dosari in a wide sweep around the aircraft's engines to the 737's rear cargo door. Al-Dosari pushes the locking lever inward to extend it and then activates the hydraulic opening mechanism. The large cargo door opens slowly upward. Adam can see the cargo for himself: hundreds of olive-green Army kitbags, each supposedly stuffed with used US dollars.

'Go and grab one, Adam,' Ricky has to shout. Although the plane's engines are shut down, the auxiliary power unit that powers all the aircraft's electrics is still active and very noisy. Adam climbs inside the hold area, releases the cargo netting securing the payload and selects a bag at random. He brings it to the open cargo door so that Ricky can examine it. Ricky unclips the locking device on the kit bag and asks Ibrahim to reach within. Rummaging around with his hand, the Bahraini eventually pulls out a neat bundle, all tied together with string. This is a stash of fifty-dollar bills. Ibrahim tosses it back and picks out another one. Same again, only this time it is a one-hundred-dollar bill bundle. Again, Ibrahim tosses it back and delves deeper, collecting yet another sample: another one-hundred-dollar-bill bundle. Satisfied, he puts the bundle back and closes the kit bag. He and Ricky smile, they shake hands and Ricky gestures to Adam to come closer.

'Now go and collect one of the two armoured vehicles and reverse it up close to the cargo door,' he shouts. 'There should be three hundred kit bags in total, each bag containing one million dollars. I want one hundred and fifty bags stashed in each vehicle. Is that clear? While you get the first vehicle, I am going back to the Jeep to get Vladek so that he can help you load up. I shall babysit the girl whilst you all do the work. Ibrahim here will be making random checks on various bags as they come off the plane.'

Adam nods, climbing down from the hold and walking to the first MRAP. It has a simple push-button ignition. The vehicles are a bit clunky, but Adam has driven them before and knows how they handle. He manoeuvres the vehicle carefully, slowing reversing towards the cargo bay door. There isn't a lot of visibility, and it needs two attempts before getting the vehicle close enough. Vladek has, by this stage, joined him at the cargo door. It is the first time the two of them have been together, alone, since the gym incident less than twenty-four hours previously. It is a fact that is not lost on either of them.

'Very, very soon, Fraser, and guess what, you little shit? I am going to kill you. Yours will be a prolonged and painful death. Trust me, I can't wait to get started.'

'Fuck off back into your hole, Vladek. I punched your lights out with almost no effort a few hours ago. I'd be more than happy to do it a second time. This time, you might even die if you're lucky.'

'Pity, then, that I have the girl and you don't.'

They stare at each other menacingly, then turn away. For the moment, there is work to be done. Adam opens the rear doors of the MRAP before climbing into the aircraft hold. Soon he is tossing bags towards the cargo door for Vladek to load onto the first vehicle. He counts each bag as he goes. When he reaches one hundred and fifty bags, he climbs down to help Vladek load the sorted bags onto the vehicle.

Meanwhile, Ibrahim has selected four bags at random. One of them he empties completely, counting each and every bundle to make sure it tallies to the one-million-dollar total. From the other three bags, he takes out random wads of cash. One such bundle he unties and counts the whole pile of notes in its entirety to make sure the totals again tally. The rest he seems satisfied by merely seeing that the money looks and feels real. Once all the testing is finished, these final four bags are loaded. With the first MRAP's rear door closed, Adam drives the vehicle away, parks it, then brings the second vehicle around, once more reversing it carefully. The loading process is repeated with this second vehicle, Adam finding that there are indeed one hundred and fifty bags remaining on the aircraft, ready to be offloaded. Again, Ibrahim pulls four bags at random and repeats the same tests he did previously. Finally, the unloading, sampling and reloading complete, the second vehicle's rear door is closed. All three then walk over to where Ricky and al-Dosari are talking. At this distance from the aircraft, the noise is much reduced and there is no longer any need for anyone to shout to make themselves heard.

'Is everything in order?'

Ibrahim nods his head and smiles.

'Thank you, Ricky. All the money appears to be there. There are indeed three hundred bags: three hundred million dollars in total.'

'So, you will now contact your lawyers and have the oil contracts released unconditionally?'

'I will do it this instant.' He takes out a mobile phone and selects a number from the memory and presses dial. A few seconds later, he begins speaking rapidly in Arabic. After a brief wait, he ends the call.

'There, it is done. Your lawyers in Geneva will have the documents in their hands as soon as they open for business in the morning.'

'Very good. It's been a delight doing business with you, Ibrahim.' They shake hands, clasping each other warmly.

'The pleasure is all ours, Ricky.'

'Okay, listen up everybody, here's the plan. Amid Abdulraheem al-Dosari and Ibrahim will lead our little convoy in their Jeep and escort us to the border. Adam will go second, Vladek third, and me and the girl fourth in the other Jeep. We keep to a maximum speed limit of eighty kilometres an hour and no more. When we reach the border, al-Dosari will deal with the Saudi border guards. It has all been arranged and there should be no problems. He and Ibrahim will then drive off, leaving the rest of us to proceed through No-Man's Land to the Iraqi border. Once we are through the Saudi side, I will become the lead vehicle and thus be the first to arrive at the Iraqi border checkpoint. I am assured by Ibrahim that there should be no problems with our entry into Iraq. Certain palms have been well-greased: I have more available to sweeten the way if needed. Once inside Iraq, you will both follow wherever I go: Adam immediately behind me and Vladek at the rear. Is that clear? No one stops unless I stop first. Unless there are questions, we should get going.'

The time is just after four o'clock in the morning. Everyone heads to their respective vehicles, Adam managing to pass close by Emms on his way. He gives a brief smile and a reassuring wink as he does so.

Chapter 57

Friday 29ᵗʰ January 2016

Iraq

The border crossings go like clockwork. The Saudi guards spend less than a minute talking with Amid Abdulraheem al-Dosari: the man's rank most likely outweighs anyone else's for many kilometres around. Before any time at all, the small convoy of vehicles is being ushered through. As he waves goodbye to the departing Saudis, Ricky's Jeep moves to the front as agreed and both Adam and Vladek follow through No-Man's Land until they get to the Iraqi border post. At four-thirty in the morning, the Iraqi soldiers on duty on this side hardly give the three vehicles a second glance, the convoy continuing across the border without needing to stop.

They drive along Iraqi Highway 22 for almost an hour in the dark without seeing a single other vehicle or, indeed, without passing any checkpoints. At a tiny settlement called Al-Nukhib, so small that one could blink and miss it, the road divides and they bear north on Highway 21. Forty minutes later and Ricky's Jeep begins to slow. To the east, the sky is just starting to lighten, the first signs of the approaching dawn. A small sign to the side of the road indicates that they are approaching another small settlement, Al-Kasrah.

Adam and Vladek both brake to match Ricky's reducing speed, all three vehicles pulling off the blacktop onto a small dirt road to the right immediately beyond the settlement. They continue along this track for a few hundred metres before Ricky turns to the left, driving carefully into what appears, in the vehicle's headlights, to be a disused factory compound. The main structure is large, with a chimney at one end that is half-collapsed, the first indication that the factory hasn't been in use for some time. The small convoy snakes its way around the far corner of the building towards the back, a large opening that once would have had doors on rollers. Today the doors are missing, allowing all three to drive into the empty, cavernous space. It is pitch black inside, the only light coming from the west-facing doorway. The first rays of wintery sunlight from the approaching dawn are still some way away.

Ricky brings his Jeep to a halt, turning off the engine and killing the lights. Adam and Vladek in their vehicles do the same.

Ricky gets out of his Jeep and stretches. Adam and Vladek again do the same.

When Ricky unexpectedly yanks opens the rear door of the Jeep, grabs Emma's arm and roughly pulls her, screaming and yelling, from the back, Vladek starts to smile, just as Ricky is smiling. Somewhat belatedly, they turn their heads in unison to see if Adam, too, is smiling.

Which is when they realise that Adam is no longer there.

Chapter 58

Friday 29ᵗʰ January 2016

Iraq

For a brief moment, Ricky's head of security impresses Adam.

'Give me the girl,' Vladek cries to Ricky. 'Then get in the Jeep and drive around with your headlights on. We'll find the bastard.'

The former cage fighter's reactions are quick, the plan he articulates clever. For a second, Adam wonders whether the Slav might be a chess player. Then he thinks about it and rapidly downgrades his assessment – draughts, not chess. Vladek is thinking only a couple of moves ahead. A chess player would be at least five moves further along in the planning.

Adam should know.

It is almost comical. Emms' screaming and yelling tells Adam all he needs to know about her and Vladek's whereabouts.

Adam had deliberately parked some distance away from Ricky. He had judged the exact moment when the other two were likely to be distracted, choosing that moment to take off in the dark at a fast sprint towards a pair of disused oil drums that he had seen in the MRAP's headlights. The drums are twenty metres away, at a spot roughly equidistant from where he had been and where the other two now are. In the dark, he nearly misses them but as he comes to a halt and crouches low, he feels one with his hand and shuffles behind them both accordingly.

Vladek has one hand clamped roughly over Emma's mouth to mute her screams. His other hand is doubtless twisting her arm forcibly behind her back. Adam knows from experience that it will be painful. Emma will also be struggling to breathe. With Ricky now in the Jeep about to start the engine, if there were ever a moment when it would be good for Adam to strike, it would be now. As soon as Ricky gets in the Jeep and turns on the headlights, it will provide yet another distraction in Adam's favour. Regardless of whatever logic Vladek's brain might tell him to the contrary, the moment the Jeep's headlights come on, Vladek will feel compelled to look in the direction that the light beams are playing. Which is why Adam is approaching Vladek from behind in a crouching run, from out of the shadows, with the Slav's head about to turn in the wrong direction.

Swiftly, silently and stealthily.

A crowbar might have been useful. Any sort of weapon would have done. Right here, right now, Adam only has the tools God gave him. With one exception. The former Para is wearing a pair of very sturdy boots. Approaching an enemy unarmed from behind, they teach all sorts of theory in the Army about how to defeat an opponent. Adam favours the blunt, direct approach. Besides, he still hasn't finished paying Vladek back properly for what he did to Tash. With Emma at risk, a hefty kick between Vladek's legs from behind, powerful enough to crush both testicles and coccyx, seems a good place to start. Certainly better than attempting to strangle him or deliver a karate chop to an exposed neck.

The moment the headlights from Ricky's Jeep come on, Adam delivers the kick with maximum force, the manoeuvre taking his opponent entirely by surprise. Vladek screams, letting go of Emma and collapsing to the floor. He doubles up, howling in pain. Adam wastes no time delivering a vicious follow-through kick directly to Vladek's momentarily exposed neck and jaw. There is a sickening sound of broken bone and cartilage, the split-second between life and death passing in an instant. Vladek is no longer a threat. The real danger is Ricky, who has by now caught both Adam and Emms in the Jeep's headlights. Quick as a flash, he's out of the Jeep and pointing a SIG-

Sauer handgun in their direction.

'Don't move, either of you.' He edges forward, the Jeep's engine still running. 'Both of you, put your hands on your heads. Do it now!' Emma does as she's told, but Adam takes his time. Ricky fires a shot deliberately wide of the mark; it's enough to make Adam comply. Emms screams.

'Oh shut up, woman,' Ricky says as he draws nearer. He is about ten feet away from them both, the gun held firmly in his right hand. Adam is impressed: Ricky's hand is rock-steady, no sign of nerves at all.

It's nearly time, Ricky.

'You're a bastard, Adam Fraser. If you've killed Vladek, be under no illusions whatsoever. I am going to kill you too. Very slowly and very painfully. That's a promise.' He flicks his gun hand at Emma briefly. 'Move away from him unless you want to die too.'

The distance between Adam and Ricky is now down to six feet. Still lethal, assuming Ricky is good with a gun and not easily distracted.

It's very nearly time, Ricky.

'Tell me one good reason why I shouldn't pull this trigger, Adam?'

'That depends, Ricky.'

'Depends on what, Adam?' The gun hand is rock-steady. The SIG-Sauer is being held at chest height, Ricky's right arm slightly extended, the P226's muzzle aimed directly at Adam's heart. Adam watches Ricky's eyes. They seem uncharacteristically focused. Too bad.

Any moment now, Ricky.

'On whether you've got what it takes.'

'To do what, exactly?'

'To kill your only son, Ricky.'

At which point Emma, who has had her eyes scrunched tight with fear, only hears the sound of a gun exploding.

Chapter 59

Friday 29ᵗʰ January 2016

Iraq

Adam can almost see Ricky's brain trying to process what he's just heard. Again and again, the words loop around and around, not quite computing. *Warning, brain malfunction.* Momentarily, it causes him to freeze. It takes about half a second for the computer system to crash and then reboot.

The real problem Ricky has is that he's been watching too many gangster movies. Single-handed gunmen are the stuff moviegoers love to see. The hero pulls out a gun and shoots the baddies with the weapon in one hand, usually the right. It looks a piece of cake. Except in real life, a pro will always use a two-handed grip. One to hold the gun, the other to steady the firing hand, ensuring that a quick-witted opponent cannot deflect the gun hand out of the way. A two-handed grip is rock-steady. The one-handed grip is for amateurs on a fun day out. Too bad for Ricky, Adam spots the weakness a mile away. Six feet of separation is all he needs. It helps when the gunman has a brain malfunction,

Adam springs forward with enormous energy. He catches hold of Ricky's gun hand with his left hand and pushes it to the right, causing the gun to deflect across Ricky's body. The gun's momentum is paused by the action of Adam's right hand, which is simultaneously trying to wrestle the weapon out of Ricky's grip. With Ricky's body unguarded, Adam performs a similar move to the one that had just floored Vladek. He uses energy from his forward momentum to bring his knee up hard into Ricky's groin. The gun explodes at the exact moment that Adam makes contact. Ricky falls to the floor, and Adam takes possession of the P226.

Interim evaluation from the field? Ricky was just about okay with a gun; the bad news was, he was too easily distracted.

'Emms, be a love and turn off the Jeep's engine, can you? While you're there, grab a few bundles of notes from out of one of those kitbags and put them in the Jeep's cubby box. We might need some cash later.'

Badly shaken, somehow she complies. As the engine noise dies, the only sound is that of Ricky, doubled up in agony and writhing around on the floor.

'Sit up, Ricky. We've got some talking to do, you and I.'

He is holding the SIG-Sauer in both hands. His arms are locked straight, his legs comfortably wide apart.

'You bastard, Adam. Go on, kill me. See if I care. You'll never get out of this place in one piece.'

'Maybe. But tell me. You keep calling me a bastard. Been working things through, have you?'

Despite Ricky's obvious pain, Adam watches with amusement as Ricky shakes his head, trying to think straight but failing. *Computer still malfunctioning. Still does not compute.*

'Worked what out?'

Adam laughs loudly, a reaction that seems to irritate Ricky.

'Why are you laughing? What are you talking about?'

'Emms,' he calls out loudly. 'While you are in that MRAP, I think I saw some cable ties in amongst all the crap on the floor in the passenger footwell. When you're finished what you're doing, I'd like you to tie up Ricky's hands and ankles for me so that I can put this wretched gun away.'

A short while later, Adam places the P226 in the back of his trouser waistband. He bends to check the cable tie fastenings, yanking both nylon straps an extra couple of notches so that they cut deep into Ricky's wrists and ankles.

'Did you get the money?' he asks her. She nods. 'Good, thanks.'

'Right. So, Ricky, perhaps we need to travel back in time to your days at Cambridge. How many years ago was that now? Thirty-three or so, wasn't it?' Ricky stares blankly. 'From what I gather, your taste for a rough night out with defenceless young girls isn't something that you and Vladek have only recently been cultivating, isn't that so? You were pretty active in your Cambridge days too. Wild parties in those rooms of yours at St John's College, lots of illegal substances flying left, right and centre. Ring any bells?'

Ricky stares at Adam blankly, the pain in his groin throbbing acutely.

'Do you remember a particular girl called Rachel? She was in the year below you. St. Catharine's College, read History, probably meek and mild-mannered in those days. Just how you like your women, isn't that right, Ricky? Good-looking, submissive, too timid to complain much. She fell under your spell, so I believe. Once was more than enough. As with all the defenceless women you like to prey on, you drugged her, at least you thought you had. She was smarter than you. Without your knowledge, she had spat out the pills and simply pretended to be out of her mind. You blindfolded her, and then you and your sidekick in that perverted little clique of yours tied her up, raped her and abused her hideously. Sounding a bit more familiar, Ricky?'

'You're making this up, Adam. This is some stupid, fabricated cock and bull story you've contrived just to try and humiliate me.'

'Is it, Ricky? What if I told you that that particular woman, Rachel, became pregnant because of what happened that night? That she was too afraid and too ashamed about what had happened to have an abortion. That she had dropped out of university to become a single mother and to rear her little bastard son, as I think you called me earlier correctly, Ricky. Yes, now you understand, don't you? Her name was Rachel Fraser. I'm her only son. Sadly, for the two of us, and I regret very much having to mention it, but there seems no way to escape the truth: the fact is you appear to be my father.'

Chapter 60

Friday 29ᵗʰ January 2016

Iraq

'On Rasmatazz that first time, you asked me whether we had met before. My face had looked familiar, do you remember?'

Ricky looks in shock. His mouth has started twitching as if trying to frame words to speak but is unable to do so.

At last, feebly, he manages to speak. 'You can't prove any of this.'

'Actually, Ricky, I can. My proof is in two parts. Firstly, for reasons I don't need to bore you with, this lady here,' he says, pointing at Emms, 'is a dab hand at collecting samples of people's DNA. Isn't that right, Emms?'

Despite everything, Emms manages a smile. Even in a black abaya and scarf, her face bruised from Vladek's earlier rough stuff, she still looks beautiful.

'It'll take no time at all to collect samples to take back to England for testing in due course.'

'You mentioned two parts.'

'Ah, yes. When my mother was close to death, she finally plucked up the courage to tell me everything. In particular, that one of her rapists that night had this unusual birthmark. She said that she could see it beneath the blindfold that you put on her rather too clumsily. I know the birthmark well. On the lower abdomen, a blotchy affair that looks like a tiny map of Wales. I have one in more or less the same place. Uncanny, isn't it? I saw yours the other day when you were getting out of the pool. Want me to remind you?'

'I don't think that will be necessary.'

'I'll take that as an admission of guilt. She also recognised your voice. You were careless, Ricky. Your lustful perversion that night fucked up both her life and mine.'

'Did you plan all this?' Ricky asks. 'To get your own back? We could come to an arrangement, you and I. We could kiss and make up. Start all over. I could arrange a financial settlement.'

'Don't make me laugh! A financial settlement? You really are sick, Ricky. I promised my mother that I would make you pay for your sins. All my life, I've grown up believing that my father had died years ago. As soon as I heard what had actually happened, I was appalled. This is payback. I thought the best way was to get close to you without you realising. Tear you apart from within, piece by piece. Not just your money but your reputation. With luck, your life.'

He stops suddenly. The faint sound of a diesel engine can be heard. Something powerful. They are about to have visitors.

'Emms, get in the Jeep and lie as low as you can on the floor.' He turns to look at Ricky.

'Your friends from ISIS about to arrive?'

Ricky shrugs.

'Perhaps.'

'I haven't got it in me to kill you, Ricky. The good news, though, is that I feel certain that you are going to die. Regrettably, I feel no sadness at the prospect whatsoever.'

'For what it's worth – and I know this may sound pathetic, Adam – I applaud you for what you've done. I don't think I could have done the same in your shoes. Your mother must have given you better DNA than I ever did. Just get out of here before it's too late.'

'Let me ask you one final thing before it's too late.'

A misty, pale desert dawn is now visible through the open doors of the deserted warehouse. With the opening facing almost due west, the light inside is still limited. To Adam's adjusted eyes, it looks almost like daylight. When whoever drives in, there will only be a short window when Adam has the element of surprise.

'Stay in the Jeep, Emms. Whatever happens, don't run off anywhere,' he shouts. With the sound of the approaching engine getting nearer, Adam runs over to one of the MRAPs, the one he had driven, which is parked some distance from where Ricky is lying on the floor with his hands and legs tied. He winds down the window and checks that he can operate the headlights without the ignition on. He can.

Now all he can do is wait. He takes out the P226 pistol and checks the magazine. Fully loaded, this one holds ten 9mm Parabellum rounds. Two shots already fired, Adam counts seven bullets in the magazine with another in the chamber. Eight in total. Only time will tell if eight is too many or too few. How many will there be? At a minimum, there will be three. A driver and one to drive each of the MRAPs. What would Adam do it? He'd be throwing in a couple of extra people, one for each MRAP. Driving around the Iraqi countryside with three hundred million dollars in the back, he'd want additional protection. He cocks his head and listens. The engine noise now sounds very close. Deep and powerful. A military vehicle, no doubt. It sounds heavy enough to be an MTVR, the American abbreviation for their Medium Tactical Vehicle Replacements, a form of a twenty-first-century upgrade to the old Bedford truck. Probably with a machine gun mounted just above the driver's cabin. The memories of Afghanistan quickly flood back. Adam knows his vehicles all too well.

Then he hears something else: a second engine, coming fast up the rear. Two of them. That was bad news. Two drivers, two to man the machine guns, two spare drivers for the MRAPs and another couple of spares, one for each vehicle carrying the cash. That made at least eight in total.

Eight bullets for eight people.

This was going to be challenging.

Chapter 61

Friday 29ᵗʰ January 2016

London

Once the MQ-9 Reaper is airborne, the Middle East ground controller at the Ali Al Salem airbase in the Gulf of Kuwait hands over the flight controls of the unmanned aircraft to RAF controllers based at 13 Squadron RAF Waddington in Lincolnshire. Operating out of a small, unmarked shed to one side of the airfield, this unlikely nerve centre of UK Gulf theatre operations sees a small team of three remotely pilot each and every drone: one to fly the aircraft; one to operate the sensors and cameras; and the third to analyse all the various pieces of intelligence data gathered by the drone's surveillance equipment. Armed with Hellfire missiles, the MQ-9 has a highly sophisticated array of sensors and cameras, all sensitive enough to allow the Reaper to operate at high altitude and thus minimise the risk of detection.

It is just after three o'clock in the morning. In the war room, deep in the basement of the MI6 building at Vauxhall Cross in London, Annie Maclean and Rory Beaumont stare at the bank of video monitors showing the live video feeds from the Reaper positioned high above the south-western corner of Iraq. Until the small convoy of three had passed across the border into Iraq, they had needed to rely on satellite images rather than the RAF's Unmanned Aerial Vehicle or UAV, as the Ministry of Defence preferred to call its drones. The satellite had been necessary to avoid the Reaper infringing Saudi airspace, something that Saudis were extremely sensitive about.

What had been clear, even in the satellite images, had been the significant number of what appeared to be bags that had been offloaded from the 737-800 aircraft and placed in the back of both MRAPs by two people.

'Must be the ISIS cash. It has to be.' It was just after one o'clock in the morning, Beaumont stifling a yawn.

'How much do we think?' Maclean asked.

'Sarah,' he said, pointing to a young analyst glued to her screen since the plane arrived, 'estimates approximately three hundred, maybe more, bags have come off the plane. Assuming each hold roughly a million dollars, that's a lot of cash about to wend its way into the open arms of the Caliphate.'

'Shit!' Maclean ponders. 'It's exactly as we thought. We've got to take it out, haven't we?'

'It's all been pre-cleared with Langley. They've taken it all the way up to US Central Command. The Americans are right behind us. If we don't launch our Hellfire missiles in the next few hours, they'll be stepping in to finish the job. They've got ground attack aircraft ready and waiting on a carrier in the Gulf.'

Two hours later and the Reaper has followed the small convoy to the disused factory off Highway 21. The MQ-9's infrared cameras have picked up the heat signatures of three warm engine blocks and four people inside the abandoned building.

'Has to be the drop-off location,' Maclean mutters.

'Looks that way. What do you reckon? Will they dump the bags and leave? Or are we expecting some kind of handover?'

'What would you do?'

'Given who we're dealing with, I'd be happier simply dumping the money and scarpering. I wouldn't want the crazies from Daesh to come along and decide they'd like to kill a few Westerners just for the hell of it.'

'Three hundred million is a lot of cash just to leave lying around unguarded in an abandoned building in the middle of the desert.'

Maclean rubs her eyes. There was a time when she had once thought these all-nighters were fun. Now they were a chore.

'Who do we think we've got down there? Our friend Ricky? One of his sidekicks? Perhaps the missing pair from the NCA's bungled operation?'

'That's our best guess.'

'Do we know anything about those two?'

'One's a young woman, an ex-graduate trainee called Fiona Morris.'

'Yee Gods.'

'I know, what an introduction to fieldwork she's having! The other is more interesting. Ex-Para, name of Adam Fraser. He has been working in Ricky's operation for a couple of months. A close university friend of our man on the ground in Monaco. In fact, he helped orchestrate Fraser's hiring by Ricky. Fraser's more than capable of looking after himself, so it would seem.'

'If he can get out of this mess alive and in one piece, his training won't have been for nothing. We might even take a look at him ourselves,' Maclean says with a wink.

'Assuming our Hellfire missile doesn't take him and the girl out of the equation first.'

'How soon before we can begin firing our missiles?'

'I think we should wait a bit longer, on the assumption they're about to have visitors – the bad guys arriving to collect the cash, I mean. Once they reach the warehouse, that's when we strike. Shame about the collateral damage, but it can't be helped. If Ricky and his entourage bug-out first, I suggest we simply blow the building with the two MRAPs – and all the money – sky-high. As long as they leave in the Jeep and not one of the MRAPs.'

'You don't think we should strike now while we know the money is a sitting target?'

'I vote that we wait a bit and see who turns up.'

'Okay, you've convinced me. Can you talk to the controllers at 13 Squadron? Explain the battle plan and ensure that all the necessary approvals are in place? I'd also like you to confirm our approach with USCENTCOM. No point pissing off the Americans unnecessarily, is there?'

Chapter 62

Friday 29ᵗʰ January 2016

Monte Carlo, Monaco

At precisely five minutes to five in the morning, Beef utters his first words since the end of his three-hour operation. Margaret Milner knows this for a fact because she had checked her watch only moments before.

The African had emerged from theatre shortly after eleven o'clock the previous evening. Miss Milner had been sitting by his bedside the whole time, having taken one of the last flights out from London and commandeered a taxi to take her directly to the hospital. The doctors tried to make a fuss but soon discovered that this particular Englishwoman in her smart tweed skirt was not one to take no for an answer. The nurses allowed her to remain in the chair by his bedside whilst they bustled in and out of the room every twenty minutes or so, checking the Ghanaian's pulse and blood pressure.

'Miss Milner,' is what he actually says, and his words catch her by surprise. They come out as a dry croak.

'No more speaking, Beef,' she says, patting his hand. 'Welcome back to the land of the living. There's no one more pleased to hear your voice than me, and that's the truth. Let me go and find a doctor and tell them that you're awake.'

Miss Milner wanders off, relieved. She has been dreadfully worried these last few hours. What would the Action Prevention Squad make of it all?

Margaret, you didn't do a risk assessment, did you? Highly irresponsible. No wonder one of your team nearly died.

It was not merely to assuage her guilt that she'd turned up in Monaco to be by Beef's bedside. Fiona had called her in a panic mid-afternoon the previous day, already back in Monaco after her flying visit to London the night before. She had even broken their agreed protocol by making a call directly from her mobile. Now that Miss Milner thinks of it, it must have been very close to the time when Fiona had disappeared, and Beef had got injured.

'There's been a development. Adam's meant to be heading to Iraq tonight. I've tried to persuade him not to go, but he won't listen. I think Beef and I are being followed. By Ricky's head of security, a Croatian called Vladek.'

'In that case, listen. You and Beef are to come home immediately. That's an order. Pack up and come back this very afternoon, do you understand?'

'I said the same thing to Adam, but he wouldn't listen. There's this memory stick that Ricky's girlfriend Tash has created. It contains details of Ricky's most secret transactions.'

'Where is it?'

'We're not sure. Either Tash still has it, or Adam thought she might have given it to another woman, Gemma.'

'We can sort this out when you're back in England. Just take Beef and head to the airport right away. If Adam gets the memory stick, that'll be a bonus. Your safety is of much greater concern to me right now, do you understand?'

Later that same afternoon, Miss Milner had spoken to Caroline Wicks, fresh back from their dressing down at the hands of the MI6 team. From what little information Miss Milner had been able to glean, it now looked as if Fiona was being held in custody by either Ricky or his head of security. She'd also learnt that Fiona and Adam were both on Ricky's jet bound for Iraq. It didn't yet make a lot of sense, another reason for her coming to take a look at the Monaco operation for herself. Privately, she had to concede, the outlook both for Fiona and Adam seemed rather precarious.

The surgeon who had operated on Beef arrives to give his patient a thorough examination.

'It's good news,' he says to Beef in Miss Milner's hearing. 'I'm hopeful that you will make a full recovery. Your left lung had collapsed, and a few of your ribs had been broken and were splintered. I think we've managed to patch everything up. In time, you should be good as new. For now, just try and get some rest. With luck, we might get you out of bed later today.' He turns to Miss Milner.

'Are you a friend or a work colleague?' he asks.

'A bit of both,' she answers. 'More of a business colleague, I suppose.'

'He's going to be fine. A bit bruised, certainly sore, but nothing much else to worry about. Are you able to let any friends or relatives of his know?'

'Of course. Thank you, doctor.'

'Very good. Try not to let him talk too much.' He turns and points to Beef. 'In particular, as you will find out for yourself, you need to go easy on the laughing!'

Which, when Beef hears this, causes him to grin broadly.

Chapter 63

Friday 29ᵗʰ January 2016

Monte Carlo, Monaco

Miss Milner finds the villa without difficulty. In the practised way that only a former MI5 pavement artist can make look so easy, she wanders in through the front entrance with her small carry-on bag in her left hand. Her manner is suggestive of someone totally at ease with staying in places like this all her life. Her casual arrival trips no silent alarms nor causes security gates to come crashing down. Instead, she moves with the confidence of someone who knows exactly what they are about and, indeed, where they are going.

'You must be Shetty,' she says to the surprised Indian housekeeper. 'I've heard all about you from Adam. I am so delighted to make your acquaintance.' She holds out her hand, which gingerly he shakes. 'Now I gather Xandra's not here at the moment. Is that right?'

'Yes, ma'am. She's still travelling.'

'Oh, that is such a pity. I'd been so looking forward to meeting her. Adam speaks so very highly of her, you understand. Oh, silly me, I should have introduced myself. I'm Miss Celia Bateson. Adam's aunt on his mother's side. Is Adam around at the moment?'

'No, ma'am,' Shetty answers, his face alarmed. 'I'm sorry to tell you, Mister Adam is away travelling as well.'

'Oh, my goodness. Do you mean I've come all this way and he's not here! That really won't do. When are you expecting him back?'

'I don't know, ma'am. Perhaps tonight, perhaps tomorrow. I'm so very sorry.'

'This is very awkward. He had agreed that I could stay in his room during my visit. I don't suppose he told you any of this?'

Shetty shakes his head. As an intended negative answer, it is an imprecise movement.

'No, ma'am. I'm very sorry. Would you like me to show you to his apartment?'

'Well, yes, I suppose I would, yes, please. That would be most kind.'

'This way,' he says, pointing and letting her go in front of him. 'Allow me please to carry your bag, Miss Bateson.'

Arriving shortly after that at Adam's apartment, he opens the door and ushers her inside ahead of him.

'If you'll be permitting me, ma'am, perhaps I could bring you a fresh pot of tea?'

She sits on the sofa, nursing Shetty's teacup and saucer in both hands, casting a professional eye over Adam's apartment as she contemplates her next move.

Slow down. Deep breaths now. You always get there much more quickly if you are not in such a rush.

She follows her advice and performs a few breathing exercises, letting her eyes absorb whatever information she can. Adam hasn't really moved in, that is evident. There are no keepsakes or photos anywhere. Not a book, not even a newspaper. She eventually gets up and wanders around, finding a few clothes in drawers and on hangers but not a lot else. Even the fridge is bare apart from a small carton of milk, a packet of ham and several half-eaten blocks of cheese.

She is in the kitchenette when she hears the front door being opened and closed. It takes a tremendous amount of self-discipline not to shout

out at the unexpected visitor. Instead, teacup and saucer still in hand, she casually drifts around the corner of the kitchenette to find another woman in the apartment doing something, she can't quite see what, with Adam's sofa.

'Oh, hello,' Miss Milner says in a casual, unruffled manner.

The other woman jumps, startled.

'My God, you frightened me. Who are you?'

'I'm Miss Celia Bateson. Adam's aunt on his mother's side.' The legend is sounding almost familiar after two try-outs. 'And who might you be?'

'Oh, yes. I'm sorry, I'm Gemma. Gemma Gerhard. I live here. At least, in the apartment next door but one.' She reaches forward and they shake hands. Her palm is hot and sweaty, the handshake a little clammy. She is nervous and Miss Milner finds this interesting.

'Have you lost something, dear? It's just that you seemed to be searching for something just a moment ago.'

'Oh no, just an earring. I was around the other night, having a drink with Adam. I realised later that I'd lost an earring. I wondered if it had slipped down the sofa.'

'Shall we take a look?' Miss Milner asks.

'No, no, don't bother. I just had a quick look. It's nothing. I'm sure it will turn up another time.'

'Adam has mentioned your name. You're married to Oswald, is that right?'

'Yes,' she says, pushing a stray blonde lock back behind an ear. 'That's right, well remembered. Ozzie's mine, for better or worse.'

'Would you like some tea? Shetty has kindly just made me a pot. I could do with a bit of company. I was meant to be meeting my nephew, Adam. Shetty's just informed me that he's unexpectedly gone off on his travels. I feel a bit of a lost soul.'

'Welcome to my world. Ozzie's always going away and leaving me alone. I would love some tea. I'll get a mug from the kitchen.'

'Adam told me. You're a good friend of Tash, I think it is? Ricky's girlfriend.'

Gemma looks surprised.

'You seem to know an awful lot about everybody.'

'Oh, you have to excuse me. I'm a bit like that. Adam tells me snippets, and they all get filed away.' She taps the side of her head. 'I've always loved the name Natasha. One of my best friends from school was called Tash. That's the reason. Have you known her long?'

'Tash? She's been around a few months. Ricky has these passing fancies. To be honest, he treats women like dirt. Poor Tash.'

'In what way?'

Gemma looks pensive and sad.

'We're quite similar. Both of us have men in our lives who mistreat us. In my case, my charming husband can't seem to keep his hands off other women. For Tash, well, let's just leave it at that.'

'Leave what at that, Gemma?'

'Do you really want to know?'

'Try me. A problem shared is usually a problem halved.'

'You like Adam, don't you, Gemma?'

It is a while later, and they have covered a lot of ground.

'Is it that obvious?' She smiles. 'He's about the only decent human being around here. All the rest are following Mammon, obsequiously dancing to Ricky's tune. No, sadly for me he's otherwise spoken for. Too bad. How about you? Is there a man in your life at the moment?'

Miss Bateson née Milner shakes her head wistfully.

'No, sadly not. There's always too much going on. Now tell me, what were you really doing earlier? It wasn't an earring you'd lost, was it?'

Gemma looks sheepish, almost guilty.

'You're good, whoever you are. Are you really Adam's aunt?'

'Let's stick with the earring story for the moment, Gemma. I'm not here to judge. I could even help. I'd just like to know.'

Which is the cue for the walls to start crumbling.

You always get there much more quickly if you are not in such a rush.

'I've known about Ricky's secret files. I was Ozzie's secretary, for goodness' sake. We all knew about them. No one apart from Ricky was ever allowed to see them. Not Xandra, not Ozzie, no one. So when Tash told me that Ricky had asked her to scan them all into his private computer, I couldn't believe it. We talked about it, and I suggested she copy them onto a USB drive. They are the small memory devices that you can plug into the side of a computer to transfer and store files.'

'Yes, I am familiar with USB drives, Gemma.'

'Why doesn't that surprise me? Anyway, to cut a long story short, Tash scanned all the documents and did indeed copy them onto such a drive. She then took the device to Ricky's private computer and uploaded everything, pretending to wipe the drive clean before handing the empty stick back to Ricky.'

'Only pretended? You mean, she kept the original and gave Ricky a spare, a brand-new blank stick, isn't that what happened?'

'Who are you really, Miss Bateson? You don't miss a trick, do you?'

'What's happened to the original, Gemma?'

'Tash was petrified that Ricky would find it on her. Either him or his pet Rottweiler, his head of security, Vladek. I call him Vlad the Impaler.

Horrible man. Anyway, Tash asked me to keep it for her. We swithered about where to hide it. Then I had the brainwave of hiding it here, in Adam's flat. Adam was Ricky's new golden boy. Tash and I were convinced that no one would ever think to look here. I just needed to put it somewhere where he wouldn't discover it. So when I came around the other night, I sat right here on the sofa and tucked in down the side.'

'Well then, we probably ought to see if it's still there, don't you think?'

Moments later, Gemma has in her hand what she'd been looking for earlier: the small USB stick.

'You're not really Adam's aunt, are you, Miss Bateson?'

'No, Gemma, I'm afraid I'm not. I'm someone who is trying to help Adam at the moment. Someone also trying to stop Ricky from bringing any more harm to people. I fear for your friend Tash's life, as I think you do too, isn't that right?'

At which point, Gemma begins to cry. She sobs gently, her head nodding.

'She told me yesterday that she couldn't take any more of Ricky's abuse. She wanted to end it all. I pleaded with her. She wouldn't listen. She went off to Ricky's boat. I haven't seen her since. I suspect the worst.'

She looks at Miss Milner, her eyes brimming.

'Here,' she says, holding out her hand, the USB stick in her open palm. 'Take it. It's what you're after, isn't it?'

Miss Milner reaches for the small device and places it carefully in her handbag's inside pocket before closing the zip.

'Thank you, Gemma. I promise that, whatever happens, I will treat the information on the device with care and sensitivity.'

'Just bring Ricky's house of cards down, will you? And if my cheating husband gets locked up as a result, then you'll only find me cheering.'

Chapter 64

Friday 29ᵗʰ January 2016

London

They gather in one of the small meeting rooms in the Cabinet Office. It is just after seven-thirty in the morning. Sir Philip Angel has brought copies of the morning papers. News about the foreign secretary's secret lovechild is splashed over the headlines of all the tabloids. '*Abandoned*!' is one headline. '*Fit for Office?*' is another. The themes are predictable, the potential damage to the foreign secretary's career ambitions immense. Sir Giles is scanning through the 'exclusive' story written by Michael Myers in the Daily Post.

'This has all the hallmarks of a planned smear campaign against the foreign secretary,' he says once he has finished his skim-read. 'Someone must have tipped off Myers.'

'I think we'd all like to believe it was Jeremy Seymour,' Sir Nigel says. 'Sadly, we'll never be able to prove it. We'd be wasting our time. Michael Myers is not about to reveal his source, never in a million years.'

'Do we think the foreign secretary can recover from this?' Sir Giles asks. 'The Press are having a field day.' The other two turn to Sir Philip Angel to see what he has to say.

'The foreign secretary is being very tight-lipped about it all. She told me last night that she's saying nothing to the press until tomorrow. She wants to give a live interview on the Today programme in the morning.'

'Bloody hell, Philip. That could be political suicide.'

'I know, Nigel, I know. However, as ever, she seems very determined. And I have to say not nearly as flustered about all this as we all feel she has reason to be. She's at her constituency office today and will doubtless get it in the neck from her local party officials. We permanent secretaries can only advise. I did warn her not to go, but she would have none of it.'

'What about damage limitation?'

'What more can be done?' It is Sir Philip speaking once again. 'I briefed Dame Philippa yesterday, and she briefed the PM last night. From rumours reaching me privately, the PM didn't have a very good day yesterday. Did you hear anything, Nigel?'

Sir Nigel shakes his head. 'Not me. What about?'

'I hear your man might also be in a tight spot. The Security Service recorded a private conversation that Russell had with our friend Ricky Al-Shawabi earlier this week. Apparently, it's highly incriminating. Quite probably life-threatening.'

'Bloody hell. How did you hear that? I've not heard a thing.'

'Dame Philippa's private secretary was off sick yesterday. Mine was covering for her in the afternoon.'

'The world's going crazy all of a sudden. If we are not careful, Jeremy Seymour will be our next prime minister after all.'

There is a general shaking of heads from around the table. Eventually, it is Sir Giles who speaks first.

'Unless he can be discredited.'

'That reminds me, Philip. Did you speak to that journalist along the lines we discussed?'

'Yes, I did. He told me privately two days ago that he was on the case and, whilst it's early days, it may yet yield something.'

'I have another idea.' It is Sir Giles again. 'I am going to talk to someone in Thames House. They might be able to find out who Michael

Myers' source is. If they can access Myers' mobile phone records, that might be a useful starting point.'

Chapter 65

Friday 29ᵗʰ January 2016

Iraq

The first vehicle to arrive is indeed an MTVR, a machine gun mounted at the front, above the driver's cab. The second is what is referred to as a Technical: a form of modified four-wheel-drive pick-up with a machine gun at the rear. Adam waits until the first vehicle has come to a stop a few feet from where Ricky's body is lying motionless, the Technical making its final sweeping turn into the empty warehouse. Both vehicles arrive without their headlights on.

Adam has been planning the moves in his head. First, he plans to take out the machine gunners on both vehicles. These are the dangerous ones. As soon as Adam turns on the MRAP's headlights to create the necessary diversion, the shooting can begin. Adam will have the advantage both of surprise and of the dark.

Step one: switch on headlights, two-handed aim, pause and fire. Then swivel, acquire second target, aim, pause and fire.

Two bullets; four seconds; two people dead.

Crouch and run, most likely to the now-familiar oil drums. Another four seconds.

Now step two: stand, two-handed aim at driver one, pause and fire. Then swivel, aim at second driver, pause and fire.

Twelve seconds.

Four bullets.

Four dead and at least four very angry and confused ISIS soldiers now out of their vehicles, scrabbling around in the dark.

The good news is that from the moment Adam flips on the MRAP's headlights, the first four go down almost exactly as he'd planned. The bad news is that Adam thinks there might be five additional, trigger-happy fighters in the warehouse and not four. What's worse is that he's going to be short of a bullet. Always assuming he doesn't waste any.

There is shouting from near one of the MTVRs and a burst of machine-gun fire. In the half-light, Adam can make out two of them. He stands, takes aim and fires two quick shots. Both are on target.

Three remaining. Two bullets left in his gun. Then he hears screaming, and his heart sinks.

'Get off me, let me go, let me go!' It's Emma's voice and it turns Adam's blood to ice. There are two of them, one holding Emma around the neck and the other waving his gun wildly. Without fluster, Adam stands, takes aim and fires.

The one with the gun is now dead.

Two left. One bullet.

'Whoever you are, one of you is going to die. If you come out, she can live. I will count to five.'

Adam desperately searches for the other fighter. He thinks he spots him, stands to take aim, but then drops down again. He had been mistaken. He runs in a crouch to a different location.

'Five.'

He needs to create a distraction.

'Four.'

His back is against the oil drum.

'Three.'

He needs to time this perfectly.

'This is your very last chance. Two.'

At which point, Adam pushes over the oil drum and it lands on the floor with an almighty clatter.

'One.'

Adam is now standing. Taking a deep breath, using a two-handed grip, he locks on to the target and fires his last remaining bullet.

Chapter 66

Friday 29ᵗʰ January 2016

London

Maclean and Beaumont have been watching the arrival of the two Iraqi vehicles in real-time.

'More ex-US military equipment?' Maclean says, pointing to the first vehicle. 'That's an MTVR, isn't it?'

'Looks like it to me. The other's a Technical.'

'At least that one's not American then.'

'Most likely a Japanese four-by-four adaptation. We'll get value for money from our Hellfire missile tonight. Too bad about the two NCA casualties.'

'Sometimes, life's about making tough choices. Okay, let's give 13 Squadron the green light. It's over to them to fire at will. I want that warehouse destroyed as quickly as possible.'

Wing Commander Mike Sutcliffe, former Harrier pilot and now based at 13 Squadron just outside Lincoln, has been at the controls of this particular UAV flight for the last three hours. It is the early hours of a cold wintry morning at RAF Waddington, but for him and his two colleagues on this sortie, night-time operations are what this job is all about. The only time zone he is currently concerned about is over four thousand kilometres away in a south-western corner of Iraq.

Moments earlier, he had received instructions from RAF Command in High Wycombe to deploy his Hellfire missile on the warehouse currently under surveillance. The MQ-9's advanced target acquisition software has already uploaded the firing solution to the Hellfire missile's guidance system. All that remains is for Sutcliffe to choose what he believes is the right moment, lift the toggle switch cover and press the button.

He looks across at his camera operator and she gives him a shrug: now is as good a time as any. Sutcliffe confirms the target, lifts the metal safety cover and firmly depresses the firing button.

Chapter 67

Friday 29th January 2016

Iraq

It is a difficult shot. Adam is usually proficient with handguns. However, this shot is exceptionally tricky. He has little choice but to take the risk. It doesn't make it easier. The bullet blows the Iraqi's head clean away, missing Emma's body by millimetres. Before she can scream, Adam is by her side and dragging her to the nearby Jeep.

'Quiet as you can, close your eyes, come on, you can do it,' he says, coaxing her into the Jeep.

Fight or flight? Unarmed and against an armed and angry terrorist, Adam prefers his chances outside in the open. He leaps into the Jeep, hits the ignition and floors the accelerator.

Chapter 68

Friday 29ᵗʰ January 2016

London

In the war room, the tension is electric. Everyone's eyes are glued to the screens. It is like watching a silent movie. *Now you see the factory; now you see the factory; now you see the factory. Then, kaboom! It's gone.* Weirdly, there is no sound. It is like watching a real-time silent movie. All that can be seen for a few seconds is billowing smoke and dust.

Eventually, the smoke clears, the dust settles, and it is evident that the strike has been on target, the mission a complete success. What had been a disused factory-cum-warehouse is no more. The building has been flattened.

They might almost have missed it had not Sarah's eagle eye been on the lookout. It is a vehicle of some description, on its side some several metres from the destruction zone. The infrared cameras pick out the heat signatures of two bodies on the ground close by.

'Are they moving?'

'Can't see it at the moment.'

'The blast most likely killed them. That's a pity. They so nearly got away. Listen up everybody. Good job this evening. Mission accomplished. Thanks to everyone for staying up late. Time to head home and get some sleep.' Maclean looks at Beaumont and winks. 'Well, at least that's what I'm going to do, I don't know about anyone else.'

Chapter 69

Friday 29th January 2016

Iraq

There is no sound. Everything is covered in dust and sand. It's in her eyes, her nose and her mouth. She feels little of anything. Movement requires effort, and energy feels drastically in short supply. First, she checks her fingers and thumbs, then each arm. These she can all move. She even has feeling in them. Her legs feel heavy. She moves a hand to her face to brush away the sand and filth from her eyes and mouth. She blinks a few times and looks around. Everything looks and feels alien. She is alive. For the moment at least. However, there is no sound.

How long she is like this, she doesn't know. The next thing she sees is Adam. He is on his hands and knees, looking as bad as she feels. He is inching his way towards her; his lips are moving but she can hear nothing. In time she feels him doing something to her legs. He seems to be scraping. Then she understands. Her feet are trapped by debris and he is trying to pull them clear. It takes time but eventually, she can move her legs. Adam's lips are moving once again. She can still hear nothing.

Time passes. The feeble winter sun is weak and the temperature cold. She must have slept because when she next opens her eyes, three elderly men are standing beside where she and Adam are lying. Local tribesmen, most likely from a nearby settlement. They have brought water in skin flasks and pour dribbles of fluid over her lips and into her mouth. She sips at this gratefully and tries to sit up, two men helping her eventually to her feet. At first, she struggles, feeling dizzy. Finally, she is able to stand unaided. Nothing feels broken and for the first time, she can hear faint sounds – the sounds of voices. Adam is, by this stage, also awake and they have helped him to his feet, too. When she and Adam both see each other, they grin broadly, joyous to be alive.

Her hearing returns gradually. Two more locals arrive, younger men this time. A decision seems to have been made: their immediate priority is to get the Jeep, currently lying on its side, back onto its wheels. All five of them set to it. After several abortive attempts, they succeed, the vehicle landing heavily on its wheels. Satisfied that all looks reasonably well, Adam climbs in and presses the ignition. Nothing happens. He tries again, still nothing. One of the men comes to his assistance, pulling the bonnet catch and lifting the hood. One of the younger men fiddles around for several minutes before emerging with a smile, one thumb raised. Adam tries the ignition once more and this time the engine fires. It splutters at first, then starts ticking over nicely.

'Come on, Emms, let's get going,' he says, his voice faint and sounding odd, as if she has thick cotton wool stuffed in each ear. She climbs in beside him and they wave a brief thank you and goodbye to their Iraqi friends and get on their way. As they pass what had been the factory, all that remains now is a massive crater.

'What was it, Adam?'

'Drone strike.'

'Are you sure?'

'Positive. They must have been following us the whole time. We are lucky to be alive.'

'Where to now? Back to Saudi?'

'You've got to be joking! There's no way they would let us across the border. We have no visa. Just look at us. No, our best bet is to drive to Baghdad and catch a plane.'

'Baghdad?! Are you mental?'

'It's not as daft as it sounds. We have loads of cash. Plus, there are now several flights a day to places like Qatar and Dubai. Trust me. It'll be a piece of cake.'

'After all we've just been through, I sincerely hope you're right!'

Chapter 70

Friday 29th January 2016

London

It is one of those 'we're all friends really' sort of gatherings. Akin to a Boxing Day lunch with all the family unavoidably present, including those relations no one likes speaking that much to anymore. The venue might have been awkward had it not been that both sets of offices were only a few hundred metres apart. That, plus the fact that it's Friday afternoon, the implication being that once the meeting is over, everyone can make their excuses and head home early for the weekend.

Citadel Place wins the location battle. Sir Desmond Wheatley doesn't like visitors inside MI6's building at the best of times. Certainly, anyone who might ordinarily be labelled a policeman in his books counted as a visitor. Thus it was that the NCA plays host, the three visitors from Vauxhall Cross braving the late January elements to arrive in the Citadel Place reception at three o'clock sharp. Sir Desmond Wheatley, Annie Maclean and Rory Beaumont are shown into the ground floor lift and whisked in the stainless steel and glass cage to a meeting suite on the fourth floor. On hand to greet them personally is Malcolm Scott. Today it is sombre smiles, hands clasped warmly on each other's shoulders, a subdued, if not full family, welcome. In the meeting room, bounding to her feet on hearing their arrival, is Caroline Wicks. Also in the receiving line is Rollo Campion, good on welcoming handshakes and known to Rory Beaumont from a previous life. At the end of the line is Margaret Milner. She is the last to be introduced and easy to write off as being the least important, had Sir Desmond and his team not been fully briefed in advance. As it was, they happened to know very much all about her.

'Please help yourself to tea and coffee,' Scott booms with more authority than he usually musters. 'We're just waiting for one more person.'

As he says this, there is a knock on the door and his secretary appears with their last guest.

'Speaking of whom, here she is. You all know Dame Philippa Mayhew, the Cabinet secretary, I presume? Perhaps not Rollo? Nor Margaret? Let me introduce you both.'

Once everyone is seated, the meeting gets underway, Scott's secretary joining the party to take notes and write up the minutes later.

'Philippa, you wanted to say a few words first.'

'Yes, thank you, Malcolm. What I would like to call the Ricky Al-Shawabi affair has been a matter of both triumph and disaster. It is our civil service and our elected politicians both at their very best and very worst. Over the coming days, we may risk several details about Ricky and his business affairs getting into the public domain. Be under no illusion: this is no longer about political point-scoring. The nature of these revelations could, as I am sure you are all very well aware, have huge repercussions all over the world.'

There is sage and sombre nodding from around the table.

'Why don't we start with you, Sir Desmond? I understand Operation Contango, as it has been called, came to its natural conclusion early this morning. Perhaps you and your team could give a brief update?'

First up to give an overview is Sir Desmond. Then he hands over to Annie Maclean and Rory Beaumont, who provide a more detailed account. Each describes the events that led to the Hellfire missile strike on a small, abandoned factory site somewhere in south-western Iraq.

'Intelligence estimates suggest that Ricky had approximately three hundred million US dollars in cash waiting to be handed over to the ISIS rebels. The money had been shipped from Latin America on a Saudi owned but Cayman-registered Boeing aircraft. Ricky had brokered the deal and certain radical Saudis had bankrolled the operation. We have reason to believe that not only was Ricky amongst those killed but also,' Rory says, looking directly at Miss Milner, 'your two assets as well. We're very sorry.'

There is widespread, rueful shaking of heads from all family members, particularly from the NCA home team, who look aggrieved at the news.

Malcolm Scott then picks up the reins. It had, he says wistfully, been no one's intention, to run two parallel operations against Ricky. Some painful lessons had been learned. He is in mid-flow when there is a quiet knocking on the door and a young woman enters the room. She sheepishly scans those sitting around the table, spots Miss Milner and catches her eye, beckoning her to step outside. Miss Milner gathers her handbag, nods a brief apology to Rollo Campion, and slips out quietly. When she returns, a few minutes later, Scott has handed over to Rollo who is explaining the practical implications of the home secretary's desire to achieve tangible results on tackling corruption and money laundering. It had been his and his team's genuine regret that due to a number of operational issues, two lives had indeed been lost. Despite their attempts to obtain hard evidence against Ricky, it had regrettably come to nothing. He tries glancing at Margaret Milner but finds her busy cleaning one of the lenses of her reading glasses with a soft cloth.

Caroline Wicks is suddenly on the offensive. 'Was it really necessary to launch that missile when you knew that two of our operatives were caught up in the middle of it all?'

Wicks is spitting venom, angry at the confirmation that two of her team have been killed. She is much more direct in venting her anger than either Scott or Campion. 'Why couldn't you have waited? Seen where the money was being taken and fired the damn thing later?'

Annie Maclean places her hand on Rory Beaumont's arm to indicate that she will answer this one.

'Caroline, we had no option. If we hadn't pressed the button, the Americans had two FA-18C aircraft waiting on the runway at Al Udeid airbase in Qatar ready to bomb the hell out of the place.'

'I still don't see why you couldn't have waited.'

'Because -,' Maclean says acerbically, '- in the real world, sometimes matters are taken out of our hands. It was no longer our sole decision.'

'As I said at the beginning,' Philippa Mayhew says, attempting to calm the recriminatory mood in the room, 'aspects of this operation were a matter of both triumph and disaster.'

'Excuse me, Dame Philippa. Might I be permitted to add something?' Margaret Milner's lens cloth is now back in her handbag, her spectacles once more hanging around her neck on a small, thin gold chain.

'Of course. What is it?'

'I apologise for not being better organised for this meeting, but I have just returned, less than half an hour ago, from a flying visit to Nice. I can understand why some of you may feel that some of the outcomes have been, to use your words, Dame Philippa, a disaster. I have some good news. I had to step out just now because I was wanted on the telephone. It appears that neither Fiona Morris nor Adam Fraser was killed by the Hellfire missile earlier today. They managed to escape. A couple of hours ago, they flew out of Baghdad and have just landed in Dubai. I can also report that the other operative who nearly died had his punctured lung repaired by an excellent Monaco surgeon late last night. I was with him this morning. He is going to make a full recovery.'

'That's tremendous news,' booms Sir Desmond. 'Annie, how does this gel with your intelligence?'

'Actually, yes. We had noticed two bodies and a Jeep had been thrown clear by the blast created by the missile strike. We assumed, I regret to say, that both were dead. I am delighted to have been proved wrong.'

'Quite,' Miss Milner says, her cue to resume speaking. 'One other thing, if I may? While I was in Monaco, I decided to see whether I could find the information that our man, Adam Fraser, had been trying to help us track down. In particular, I knew that there existed an electronic copy of Ricky's secret files purporting to show a complete record of all his most sensitive transactions over the years. The good news, ladies and gentlemen,' she says, reaching into the zipped inner pocket of her handbag, 'is that I have that information with me here.'

She smiles broadly at Dame Philippa as she places the small USB stick triumphantly on the table in front of her.

'Perhaps, in time, we might even be able to look back at the Ricky Al-Shawabi affair and conclude that, against the odds, our operation had been something of a moderate success after all.'

Chapter 71

Saturday 30ᵗʰ January 2016

London

'Silence, please. Cue in five, four, three, two, one . .'

'You're listening to Today and the time is just after eight-thirty. In the last twenty-four hours, there has been nothing short of a media frenzy surrounding one of the most senior members of Justin Ingleby's Cabinet. The foreign secretary, Geraldine Macauley, is one of the main contenders hotly tipped to succeed the prime minister when, as already announced, he steps down from office later this year. The media interest concerns allegations made in a national newspaper that the foreign secretary had a child out of wedlock over thirty years ago. The same paper also alleges that the Foreign Secretary gave this child up for adoption, causing several commentators to criticise her for abandoning a child in favour of her political career. I am joined this morning by the foreign secretary herself to present her side of the story. Good morning, Foreign Secretary.'

'Good morning, James.'

'Let's get straight to the point. Did you or did you not have a child out of wedlock and, if so, did you also give that same child up for adoption?'

'Yes, James, I did. I can't deny what happened.'

'Now that it's all out in the open, are you going to resign?'

'Resign? No, of course not. I would rather this had all not been made public, but that's my personal view. Now that it has, I suggest that there are much more important things for us all to be worried about. We need to move on, James.'

'And that's it? Don't you have regrets about what you did? Can you understand why the public seem so angered by what it is you now have confirmed that you did?'

'Of course I have regrets. Almost every day, I think about what I did. But let me tell you why I wanted to come on air this morning. We have a fabulous press in this country. There is no state interference or censorship, and by and large, the reporters who go about their business do their job honestly and, in the main, fairly. But when the media get it wrong, they get it wrong big time and the innocent party is made to look guilty before he or she has ever been given the right to set the record straight.'

'So, let this be the opportunity for you to set the record straight, then.'

'Thank you. I want you to imagine that you are a woman who is, in every other aspect of her life, perfectly normal, healthy and happily married but for one tiny issue. You are unable to have children. Your twin sister, on the other hand, so similar to you in so many ways, is also happily married, but she, the lucky lady, has two wonderful children of her own. How do you feel?'

'Pretty gutted, I'd imagine.'

'That is precisely how you feel. You try everything in the book to get pregnant: you try IVF, expensive treatments, the works. You spend thousands of pounds of your own money in an attempt to have just one child. When this still produces no results, you feel defeated, let down, sad and depressed. Then one day, your twin sister and her husband come to stay for the weekend and suggest a solution. She is prepared to be a surrogate mother for you. Her husband agrees, your husband agrees and a short while later, your sister is impregnated with your husband's sperm in a professional clinic. Nine months later, a baby girl is born. Your sister is the natural mother. Your husband is named, correctly, on the birth certificate as the father. Within six months of birth, a court grants a Parental Order so that the baby becomes formally adopted as your and your husband's child. That, James, is the story of my poor sister and I, together with our respective husbands. I didn't abandon my child. I had a surrogate baby on my sister's behalf. I was delighted to help her and her husband. We did this willingly, and we did this lovingly. As the birth mother, I naturally had some reservations. However, seeing the joy and happiness that I was able to give to my sister and her husband, it made both myself and my husband feel immensely proud.'

'That certainly puts a very different complexion on the matter. You must have been very angry when you read what had been written these last twenty-four hours?'

'Not angry, just sad. Sad for my sister and her husband and sad in particular for her daughter. If my darling husband were still alive, he would have been mortified. If journalists could sometimes work harder at getting the facts right rather than always assuming the worst, we'd all be much better for it.'

'Looking back on all that you did, how do you feel about it all, with the benefit of hindsight?'

'To tell you the truth, James, as I have already said, I feel unbelievably proud. To have helped one's family in a way such as this was a real honour and privilege. I am not, I certainly believe, the cold, heartless and callous person the media have been suggesting I am these last twenty-four hours. I hope, now that your listeners know the truth, they will understand what I did. Perhaps they might even feel inspired to do the same if the situation ever arose. As you know, James, and I'm sure you'd agree, for those of us who want and are able to have children, being a parent is a wonderful and fabulous gift.'

'It certainly is. Foreign Secretary, Geraldine Macauley, thank you very much for your time this morning.'

Chapter 72

Saturday 30th January 2016

Norfolk, England

'Philippa, Dominic. This is a surprise! What brings you both out to Norfolk on a Saturday morning?'

'Why, you do, of course, Jeremy! We knew you were doing a charity fun run this morning. Now that it's over, we'd like to have a private chat about something, if that's all right?'

They are standing outside the small cottage on the family estate that his brother, Thomas, allows Jeremy to use whenever he's in the constituency.

'Sure,' Seymour says, wiping his face with a towel draped around his neck. It had been a five-mile run, and he'd run it in just under forty-five minutes.

'Why don't you come in? My wife's out shopping. Do you want some coffee?' Dominic Hall shakes his head.

'Nor for me either, thanks. How much money did you raise?' Dame Philippa asks.

'I have pledges worth just over three thousand pounds.'

'That's very good. Where would you like us?'

'Let's go in here,' Seymour says, pointing to a small room he sometimes uses as a study.

'So, what's this all about?'

Dominic Hall does the talking. Dame Philippa opens a leather-bound notebook and prepares to take notes.

'The Sunday Journal seems to have taken a bit of a shine to you at the moment, Jeremy. In particular, they are keen to know both why and how it is that with only an MP's salary, you seem able to pay a lady called Hilary Nesbitt five hundred pounds each and every month. And have been for quite some time now. We wondered what you had to say about that?'

'I think it's none of their business. Or yours for that matter. Who told you this anyway? Was it Hilary?'

'No, Jeremy and the source is hardly relevant.'

'What's this got to do with you, bringing you out here on a Saturday morning? I would have thought you'd have better things to be doing than poking your nose into meaningless gossip like that.'

Dominic looks at Dame Philippa and then removes a smartphone from his jacket pocket.

'We'd like you to listen to something. It won't take a moment.'

He finds the audio file he is looking for and hits the 'play' button.

'Len, how long have you known Jeremy Seymour?'

'For as long as I can remember. Us Nesbitts have worked for the Seymours for years.'

'Has Jeremy Seymour ever asked you to do any special favours for him?'

'I dunno. I suppose he might have done. Come to think of it, yes. Only from time to time that is, but yes, on the odd occasion he has.'

'Does the name Murphy O'Connor mean anything to you?'

There is a pause.

'I might have heard of him.'

There's another long pause.

'Oh, all right then. Yes, I admit it, I know the man.'

'Do you know what Murphy does?'

'He's a private detective. My father used him once.'

'Did Jeremy Seymour ask you to contact Murphy for him?'

There is now an even longer pause.

'You wouldn't be asking me all this if you didn't know. Yes, of course he did. He gave me a package to give to him.'

'What was in the package?'

'I never looked. I promise. I presumed it was money.'

'When was the last time you saw Murphy?'

This time he hesitates a bit longer.

'Come on, Len. It's a simple question. When was the last time you saw Murphy?'

'Thursday this week. I had to give him more money.'

'Why?'

'Because Mister Jeremy asked me to. It was some kind of success fee. I had to raid my bottom drawer, it was so much cash.'

'How much?'

'Ten grand. Mister Jeremy told me on the phone that he'd pay me back this weekend. That's all. I promise.'

Hall presses the stop button and looks at Seymour, who now his head held in his hands.

'Would you like to listen to a conversation that was had with this man Murphy yesterday as well, Jeremy?'

Jeremy shakes his head.

'Here's what going to happen. You are going to write to the prime minister over the weekend and you are going to resign. It doesn't matter what you tell him in the letter. He'll know the reasons and you'll know the reasons. If you don't then the Sunday Journal will go ahead with their story about you and Hilary Nesbitt, the PM will fire you on Monday and the news about you hiring a private detective to try and tarnish the good name of one of your Cabinet colleagues will be leaked to the press. You've fucked up, Jeremy, and that's the long and short of it. I trust that's made everything clear?'

Chapter 73

Monday 1ˢᵗ February 2016
London

It is an unusual request, and one that not even Adam is sure will be granted. He makes it during their extensive debrief on Sunday with a cast that includes increasingly senior dignitaries who keep arriving unannounced to listen to their story. They include people from MI6, MI5 and the NCA. Extras include a few American actors and one or two from other parts who get no introduction: all they do is sit at the back, listen and observe. The conversations are always had with Emma in the room with him and Miss Bateson as his minder. Adam is fully aware that these are both stage names, but in his mind, they are forevermore permanent: the names Morris and Milner may as well no longer exist.

Impossible, is their initial response.

So, he makes the request again. He has information that Ricky has told him in private. It is for the prime minister's ears only. No, Adam is not going to say what it is. It is for Ingleby's ears alone.

It is an intrigue that they can't quite leave alone. An itch they try not to scratch but fail. 'Not possible', they keep saying, but then doubts start to creep in. What if it is important? At one stage during the afternoon, Dame Philippa Mayhew is consulted. She has had a busy weekend, by all accounts. She initially says no. By six o'clock on Sunday night, having spoken to the Prime Minister, she relents. Adam can have fifteen minutes on Monday morning at a quarter past eleven precisely.

Adam arrives five minutes early and is shown to a waiting room. By twenty-five minutes past eleven, he is beginning to wonder whether the meeting will happen after all. Finally, a messenger arrives to escort him to the library. He is shown where to sit and is busy drinking in the unfamiliar surroundings when the door bursts open and in steps Justin Ingleby. He is in his shirtsleeves, rushing from one meeting to another.

'Adam,' he says, closing the door and coming forward to shake hands. 'Good to meet you. Sorry I'm running late. I've had a bit of a crisis that I've been forced to deal with. Please sit down,' he says, moving to the opposite side of the large rectangular table.

'I gather you've been doing brave things in Iraq. Finally saw Ricky Al-Shawabi off to his grave as well. It was too bad. Ricky always was a wild one. Hugely unpredictable, at times a likeable rogue, but still a rogue. I guess he finally got what he deserved.'

'Most people do,' Adam says, his arms resting on the table, hands clasped in front of him.

'I gather you have a message for me from Ricky.' He laughs, pulling a face at the same time. 'From the grave, as it were. It had better be important.'

'Do you remember a young woman at Cambridge, name of Rachel Fraser? She was a historian at St Catherine's College.'

Ingleby pulls another face, making theatre of what he thinks is a frivolous question.

'Can't say I do. There were quite a lot of women in those days.' He laughs in a laddish way. 'Is she your mother?'

'Ricky used to hold parties. Wild parties. Lots of women, drugs and stuff. You were part of his inner circle in those days, weren't you?'

Ingleby shrugs somewhat sheepishly but says nothing.

'He used to call you Jingo.'

'Look, Adam, I'm a busy man. Could we just get to the point, or I'll have to leave? I'm sorry.'

'Ricky liked to play it rough with his women. He liked to tie them up and do all sorts of dreadful and depraved things with them. He got a taste for it at university; he carried on doing it throughout his life. He always liked another man to help him, a second as it were. It was a male dominance sort of thing, I guess. You were part of his trusted inner group, weren't you? One evening – I'm guessing by the timing of events that it must have been November in your final year – there was a party. Lots of people. Lots of alcohol. For those in the know, lots of drugs. One woman in particular. She would have been innocent, rather meek, rather too easily persuadable. Her name was Rachel Fraser. You and Ricky took her by surprise, blindfolded her, it was all part of what she thought was a game but turned out to be worse. Back in your set in John's, Ricky drugged her, or at least he thought he had, but she never swallowed whatever it was she was meant to take. You then both tied her up. She was blindfolded, and then she was raped and abused.'

He looks across the table. Ingleby appears frozen stiff, his expression completely vacant.

'You were careless. The blindfold you had put on this woman was not secure. In the heat of the moment, Ricky calls out a name. '*Your turn, Jingo*' is what my mother remembers, her senses acutely heightened by the blindfold. Then she sees a strange birthmark on her attacker's forearm.'

Ingleby still hasn't moved.

'Rachel Fraser became pregnant that night. She was too ashamed to tell her parents, too ashamed to tell anyone. In those days, rape victims were usually the guilty ones. As a result, she dropped out of university and struggled to bring up her only son as a single mother. Rachel, my mother, never told me any of this until last year when she was terminally ill with cancer.'

For a bit of theatre, Adam now removes his jacket and rolls up his left sleeve to above the elbow.

'I, too, have a strange birthmark.'

A peculiar, brown-coloured marking is visible on his forearm.

'My mother said that she believed it was in the same place as yours. Having replayed the terrible events of that night in her mind so many times over the years, she might have got her lefts and rights confused. In Iraq, I tricked Ricky into believing that I was his son and not yours. But I don't think that is the case, do you? My mother asked me on her deathbed to see that justice was done. So here I am, avenging on her behalf, facing my father across the table for the first time, laying bare his shame and embarrassment. Not wasting your time now am I, Jingo?'

Time stands still. Nothing is said. Like Ricky before the Hellfire missile struck, Ingleby's face has developed involuntary twitches. It looks as if he is trying to speak but no words come out.

'When I was with Ricky at the end, I asked him one final question. He confirmed that it was you with him that night. He said that you and he had become something of a double act at Cambridge. He and his good friend, Jingo, he told me. Latterly you found yourself a girl who later became your wife and Ricky had to move on.'

More silence. Adam can hear a clock ticking in the room somewhere.

'I don't know what to say. There is nothing I can say.'

Ingleby unbuttons the cuff on his left sleeve and rolls up his shirt to the elbow. It is the same birthmark, in an almost identical place to Adam's.

'Both my children have the same mark, in the same place. Weird, isn't it?' He puts his head in his hands. 'Oh my God, what have I done?'

'I want you to resign. This week, as soon as possible. I want you to think about what's the right way for you to atone for what you did, and then let's have another conversation. If you do that, this will remain our little secret. I happen to believe, from a distance at least, that Ricky was likely to have been the truly evil one. I suspect you found yourself caught up in Ricky's almost unstoppable energy and power, unable to get off the train until it was too late.'

'I felt so happy on Friday when I learnt that Ricky had died.'

Ingleby says this more to himself than to Adam.

'Ricky always held this power over me. He simply knew too much about me and my past. When I heard that he'd been killed, I felt as if I'd been given a whole new lease of life. He was a very controlling person, Adam. He kept a lot of filthy secrets on some very influential people, including some in my own Cabinet.' He stands up, the meeting at a close.

'I will do as you ask. The timing is probably right for several reasons. I had wanted to see the referendum through, but now I'm no longer convinced.'

Adam stands, the two men now only a few feet apart.

'I'm not often lost for words. I find it difficult to say anything that might redeem my past actions. Other than how sorry I am. Both to your mother, Rachel. And now to you, my son. Please,' he says, stepping forward to embrace Adam in a hug, 'if we can find a way that makes you one day able to forgive me, that would be so very good.'

Epilogue

A week is, they say, a long time in politics.

On the morning of Tuesday February 2nd, in front of live television cameras positioned on the tarmac in Downing Street, the UK prime minister announced that he was resigning with immediate effect. He wanted his successor to have a clear run at leading the country through the forthcoming referendum on Britain's membership of the European Union. He had agreed with the party chairman, Robin Pemberley, and the chairman of the influential 1922 back-bench committee that a formal process to appoint a successor would begin immediately. Markets initially reacted badly to the news but later recovered when it became clear that Geraldine Macauley, the foreign secretary, was the clear front runner. Two other candidates had also put their hats in the ring. MPs in the party now had two days to cast their votes.

By Thursday lunchtime of that same week, the ballot closed. Geraldine Macauley was confirmed as the overall favourite by a clear majority of two hundred and forty-five votes. That afternoon Ingleby went to Buckingham Palace to tender his resignation. Two hours later, Geraldine Macauley was summoned to the Palace, where Her Majesty invited her to form a new government.

One of Macauley's first acts was to replace the home secretary, Jeremy Seymour, and the chancellor of the exchequer, Stephen Russell. Both were told, privately and in no uncertain terms, that they no longer had any place in Macauley's government and that they were each expected to resign as MPs within the next three months.

In the middle of all of this, it was announced that following a successful joint operation between the Security Services, the National Crime Agency and the Monaco police, a significant battle had been fought and won against corruption and money laundering. The person at the centre of these allegations, Ricky Al-Shawabi, was reported to have died whilst trying to flee authorities in a joint operation in the Middle East. Al-Shawabi, a one-time close personal friend of the outgoing prime minister, Justin Ingleby, was alleged to have been at the centre of a massive web of corruption and money laundering that involved many high-profile politicians and senior officials around the world. Documentary evidence was obtained by the British that was believed to expose hundreds of people who had been secretly dealing with Al-Shawabi to evade taxes and hide money from the authorities.

Within the confines of Vauxhall Cross, Annie Maclean had been instructed by her director-general to track down one Adam Fraser with a view to a possible recruitment. Maclean was not finding this an easy task. Since Adam had returned from Iraq with his girlfriend Fiona Morris, neither had been seen nor did anyone appear to know their whereabouts.

Meanwhile, lawyers acting for the estate of Ricky Al-Shawabi in Geneva confirmed that they were in receipt of properly executed contracts transferring ownership of two tanker-loads of light Arabian crude oil, currently at anchor in the Straits of Malacca, to an oil trader based in Monaco by the name of Aldo Bernadi. They also confirmed that they were holding ten per cent of the accrued profit on the trade, amounting to just over four million US Dollars, for the benefit of an unnamed third party.

Early afternoon sun streams through the windows of the restaurant at the top of Col de Loze. It is now early February. The sun, already higher in the sky, casts warm shadows during the busy lunch service. The rays are strong enough to provide a suntan; even so, most customers at this fashionable restaurant still choose to eat inside. The temperature is a warm seven degrees in the sun. Centigrade.

Two customers are oblivious to the world around them. They are nestled in a cosy corner, having both eaten a hearty lunch of lamb cutlets, grilled on the restaurant's charcoal fire. On the table is a near-empty bottle: one of the most expensive wines the restaurant has to offer. Neither seems to have been concerned about the price.

'How's the knee?'

'Never been better.'

'Fancy a game of chess?'

'Actually,' she says, 'since we've already eaten, I have a better idea. You're a good skier?' She raises one eyebrow – the implied form of question yielding a non-committal shrug from her companion. 'Let's forget chess. It's a glorious day, the slopes are empty, and I feel the need to ski.'

'Tell you what,' he replies. 'I have an even better idea. Why not let's ski back to the chalet and spend the afternoon in bed?'

----- The End -----

THE LATEST THRILLER BY THE SAME AUTHOR

Visit: www.davidnrobinson.com

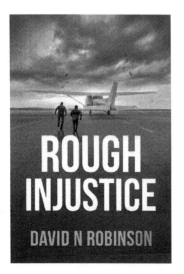

FOR A MAN LIKE RICKY BAXTER, FORGIVENESS DOESN'T COME EASILY

Ostensibly just this disabled guy running a simple charity in a London backwater, anyone underestimating Ricky soon discovers their mistake. He's a man driven to right some of the wrongs of the world – a man who simply doesn't care who gets hurt along the way.

Or so he likes to believe.

When an abused pole dancer comes to him for help, he has little idea of the murky depths of modern-day slavery that he's about to get dragged into. Too late he finds himself up against violent gangs smuggling migrants across Europe, people who'd go to any extremes to exploit their human cargo for profit. People who make Ricky question himself. Has he really got what it takes to stop these people? Or will he find himself losing the moral high ground, drawn into acting more like the gang leaders themselves and, in the process, sinking to their level?

Acknowledgements

I need to put on record my thanks to my wife, Ginny, for putting up with a husband who plots at strange times of the day and night – and for the time she spends tirelessly reading and re-reading different versions of this manuscript, telling me what works and what doesn't. A special thank you also to Nick and his brother Sam, both busy young men but always keen to give different – but helpful – perspectives on their father's writing attempts!

I am grateful to everyone who supports my new career by buying my books and spreading the word about my writing to their friends, families, book groups and colleagues. I am especially grateful to those who take time to post me reviews and give feedback.

Author's Note

As a self-published author, I have, in the past, tried all sorts of different methods to get my books in front of readers yet to discover me. I've tried Facebook and Twitter, I've tried free books to build mailing lists and spent money on book sites like Bookbub and Goodreads. I've even used paid advertising on both Amazon and Facebook as well. All these have helped, but the returns on investment are meagre.

The funny thing is that whilst many successful self-published authors tell new authors like me that I must build a mailing list of my most loyal fans, I've learnt over time that most readers rarely want to be bombarded, week after week, by yet more emails from an author they have only read a few times? I don't think so.

So, these days I rely on people like you who read my books to do three things:

i) if you could leave an honest review on the Amazon page you bought or downloaded this book from, that would be the **very** best help you could give;

ii) two, if you enjoyed the book, perhaps you might tell a few friends and family members about it? and

iii) finally, maybe I might even be able to tempt you to try a few more of the books that I have written?

Thank you for taking the time to read The Reluctant Trader. I sincerely hope you enjoyed it.

In case you're wondering, I do offer a free book on my website, **www.davidnrobinson.com** – but you no longer need to subscribe to a mailing list to download it!

David N Robinson

For many years before COVID 19, I was a business leader: always out and about meeting people, travelling the world regularly. Endless plane and train journeys provided ample time for reflection. In between work, I would read books and plan for a different life.

These days, I am happy to be grounded, living my new life as an independent author. Working from home and living the dream. Writing thrillers, the sort of books I always hankered after on yet another long-haul flight. Fast-paced, contemporary page-turners – with plenty of twists and action along the way. Books about topical subjects that I love researching.

Most of the time, when I'm not researching a new book, my wife and I live in England, close to the fabulous city of Cambridge. The walks are fantastic, the bike rides not too challenging and the streets full of interesting and inspiring people.

Visit **www.davidnrobinson.com** to learn more about my writing.

Printed in Great Britain
by Amazon